NIGHT W... WINTER NIGHT...

A wild dog bayed somewhere out in the gloom. She tried to scream, but her throat was raw with shrieking; only a dry croak would come out.
"Help me, help me, help me…"

—from "THE STAR BEAST"

ABOUT POUL ANDERSON...

Born in 1926 to Scandinavian parents living in Bristol, PA., Poul Anderson was the recipient of numerous accolades throughout his lifetime including seven Hugo and three Nebula awards. It's interesting to note that Anderson received his B. A. in physics with honors, but upon graduating went directly into the field of free-lance writing, never putting his degree to practical use. He continued writing up until his death in 2001, all the while collecting distinction for his timeless allegory, even posthumously. Poul Anderson was easily one of the greatest science fiction writers of all time. We present some of his earliest works in this collection.

TABLE OF CONTENTS

MASTERS OF SCIENCE FICTION

Volume 9

POUL ANDERSON:
"THE STAR BEAST"
and other tales

ARMCHAIR FICTION
PO Box 4369, Medford, Oregon 97504

The original text of these stories first appeared in
*Imagination, Super Science Stories, Planet Stories, Science
Fiction Adventures, Future,* and *Science Fiction Stories.*

*For more information about Armchair Books and products, visit our
website at...*

www.armchairfiction.com

Or email us at...

armchairfiction@yahoo.com

The Star Beast

The ancient enemy whose body served Harol's immortal brain in its ultimate flight was a fraud—a replica shaped by the miracle science of the last men. The real destroyer came striding terribly down from the stars—the forgotten beast-in-man, bred out of helpless Earth for a thousand years!

CHAPTER ONE
Therapy for Paradise

THE REBIRTH technician thought he had heard everything in the course of some three centuries. But he was astonished now.

"My dear fellow—" he said. "Did you say a tiger—"

"That's right," said Harol. "You can do it, can't you?"

"Well—I suppose so. I'd have to study the problem first, of course. Nobody has ever wanted a rebirth that far from human. But offhand I'd say it was possible." The technician's eyes lit with a gleam, which had not been there for many decades. "It would at least be—*interesting.*"

"I think you already have a record of a tiger," said Harol.

"Oh, we must have. We have records of every animal still extant when the technique was invented, and I'm sure there must still have been a few tigers around then. But it's a problem of modification. A human mind just can't exist in a nervous system that different. We'd have to change the record enough—larger brain with more convolutions, of course, and so on... Even then it'd be far from perfect, but your basic mentality should be stable for a year or two, barring accidents. That's all the time you'd want anyway, isn't it?"

"I suppose so," said Harol.

"Rebirth in animal forms is getting fashionable these days," admitted the technician. "But so far they've only wanted

5

animals with easily modified systems. Anthropoid apes, now—
you don't even have to change a chimpanzee's brain at all for it
to hold a stable human mentality for years. Elephants are good
too. But—a tiger—" He shook his head. "I suppose it can be
done, after a fashion. But why not a gorilla?"

"I want a carnivore," said Harol.

"Your phychiatrist, I suppose—" hinted the technician.

Harol nodded curtly. The technician sighed and gave up the
hope of juicy confessions. A worker at Rebirth Station heard a
lot of strange stories, but this fellow wasn't giving. Oh, well, the
mere fact of his demand would furnish gossip for days.

"When can it be ready?" asked Harol.

The technician scratched his head thoughtfully. "It'll take a
while," he said. "We have to get the record scanned, you know,
and work out a basic neural pattern that'll hold the human mind.
It's more than a simple memory-superimposition. The genes
control an organism all through its lifespan, dictating, within the
limits of environment, even the time and speed of aging. You
can't have an animal with an ontogeny entirely opposed to its
basic phylogeny—it wouldn't be viable. So we'll have to modify
the very molecules of the cells, as well as the gross anatomy of
the nervous system."

"In short," smiled Harol, "this intelligent tiger will breed
true."

"If it found a similar tigress," answered the technician. "Not
a real one—there aren't any left, and besides, the heredity would
be too different. But maybe you want a female body for
someone?"

"No. I only want a body for myself." Briefly, Harol thought
of Avi and tried to imagine her incarnated in the supple, deadly
grace of the huge cat. But no, she wasn't the type. And solitude
was part of the therapy anyway.

"Once we have the modified record, of course, there's
nothing to superimposing your memory patterns on it," said the
technician. "That'll be just the usual process, like any human
rebirth. But to make up that record—well, I can put the special

scanning and computing units over at Research on the problem. Nobody's working there. Say a week. Will that do?"

"Fine," said Harol. "I'll be back in a week."

He turned with a brief good-by and went down the long slideway toward the nearest transmitter. It was almost deserted now save for the unhuman forms of mobile robots gliding on their errands. The faint, deep hum of activity, which filled Rebirth Station was almost entirely that of machines, of electronic flows whispering through vacuum, the silent celebration of artificial intellects so far surpassing those of their human creators that men could no longer follow their thoughts. A human brain simply couldn't operate with that many simultaneous factors.

The machines were the latter-day oracles. And the life-giving gods. *We're parasites on our machines,* thought Harol. *We're little fleas hopping around on the giants we created, once. There are no real human scientists any more. How can there be, when the electronic brains and the great machines, which are their bodies, can do it all so much quicker and better—can do things we would never even have dreamed of, things of which man's highest geniuses have only the faintest glimmer of an understanding? That has paralyzed us, that and the rebirth immortality. Now there's nothing left but a life of idleness and a round of pleasure—and how much fun is anything after centuries?*

It was no wonder that animal rebirth was all the rage. It offered some prospect of novelty—for a while.

He passed a mirror and paused to look at himself. There was nothing unusual about him; he had the tall body and handsome features that were uniform today. There was a little gray at his temples and he was getting a bit bald on top, though this body was only thirty-five. But then it always had aged early. In the old days he'd hardly have reached a hundred.

I am—let me see—four hundred and sixty-three years old. At least, my memory is—and what am I, the essential I, but a memory track?

Unlike most of the people in the building, he wore clothes, a light tunic and cloak. He was a little sensitive about the flabbiness of his body. He really should keep himself in better shape. But what was the point of it, really, when his twenty-year-old record was so superb a specimen?

He reached the transmitter booth and hesitated a moment, wondering where to go. He could go home—have to get his affairs in order before undertaking the tiger phase—or he could drop in on Avi or— His mind wandered away until he came to himself with an angry start. After four and a half centuries, it was getting hard to cooordinate all his memories; he was becoming increasingly absent-minded. Have to get the psychostaff at Rebirth to go over his record one of these generations, and eliminate some of that useless clutter from his synapses.

He decided to visit Avi. As he spoke her name to the transmitter and waited for it to hunt through the electronic files at Central for her current residence, the thought came that in all his lifetime he had only twice seen Rebirth Station from the outside. The place was immense; a featureless pile rearing skyward above the almost empty European forests—as impressive a sight, in its way, as Tycho Crater or the rings of Saturn. But when the transmitter sent you directly from booth to booth, inside the buildings, you rarely had occasion to look at their exteriors.

For a moment he toyed with the thought of having himself transmitted to some nearby house just to see the Station. But—oh, well, any time in the next few millennia. The Station would last forever, and so would he.

The transmitter field was generated. At the speed of light, Harold flashed around the world to Avi's dwelling.

THE OCCASION was ceremonial enough for Ramacan to put on his best clothes, a red cloak over his tunic and the many jeweled ornaments prescribed for formal wear. Then he sat down by his transmitter and waited.

The booth stood just inside the colonnaded verandah. From his seat, Ramacan could look through the open doors to the great slopes and peaks of the Caucasus, green now with returning summer save where the everlasting snows flashed under a bright sky. He had lived here for many centuries, contrary to the restlessness of most Earthlings. But he liked the place. It had a quiet immensity; it never changed. Most humans these days sought variety, a feverish quest for the new and untasted, old minds in young bodies trying to recapture a lost freshness. Ramacan was—they called him stodgy, probably. Stable or steady might be closer to the truth. Which made him ideal for his work. Most of what government remained on Earth was left to him.

Felgi was late. Ramacan didn't worry about it; he was never in a hurry himself. But when the Procyonite did arrive, the manner of it brought an amazed oath even from the Earthling.

He didn't come through the transmitter. He came in a boat from his ship, a lean metal shark drifting out of the sky and sighing to the lawn. Ramacan noticed the flat turrets and the ominous muzzles of guns projecting from them. Anachronism—Sol hadn't seen a warship for more centuries than he could remember. But—

Felgi came out of the airlock. He was followed by a squad of armed guards, who ground their blasters and stood to stiff attention. The Procyonite captain walked alone up to the house.

Ramacan had met him before, but he studied the man with a new attention. Like most in his fleet, Felgi was a little undersized by Earthly standards, and the rigidity of his face and posture were almost shocking. His severe, form-fitting black uniform differed little from those of his subordinates except for insignia of rank. His features were gaunt, dark with the protective pigmentation necessary under the terrible blaze of Procyon, and there was something in his eyes that Ramacan had never seen before.

The Procyonites looked human enough. But Ramacan wondered if there was any truth to those rumors, which had been flying about Earth since their arrival that mutation and selection during their long and cruel stay had changed the colonists into something that could never have been at home.

Certainly their social setup and their basic psychology seemed to be—foreign.

Felgi came up the short escalator to the verandah and bowed stiffly. The psychographs had taught him modern Terrestrial, but his voice still held an echo of the harsh colonial tongue and his phrasing was strange: "Greeting to you, Commander."

Ramacan returned the bow, but his was the elaborate sweeping gesture of Earth. "Be welcome, Gen—ah—General Felgi." Then, informally: "Please come in."

"Thank you." The other man walked into the house.

"Your companions—?"

"My *men* will remain outside." Felgi sat down without being invited, a serious breach of etiquette—but after all, the mores of his home were different.

"As you wish." Ramacan dialed for drinks on the room creator.

"No," said Felgi.

"Pardon me?"

"We don't drink at Procyon. I thought you knew that."

"Pardon me. I had forgotten." Regretfully, Ramacan let the wine and glasses return to the matter bank and sat down.

Felgi sat with steely erectness making the efforts of the seat to mold itself to his contours futile. Slowly, Ramacan recognized the emotion that crackled and smoldered behind the dark lean visage.

Anger.

"I trust you are finding your stay on Earth pleasant," he said into the silence.

"Let us not make meaningless words," snapped Felgi. "I am here on business."

"As you wish." Ramacan tried to relax, but he couldn't, his nerves and muscles were suddenly tight.

"As far as I can gather," said Felgi, "you head the government of Sol."

"I suppose you could say that. I have the title of Coordinator. But there isn't much to coordinate these days. Our social system practically runs itself."

"Insofar as you have one. But actually you are completely disorganized. Every individual seems to be sufficient to himself."

"Naturally. When everyone owns a matter creator, which can supply all his ordinary needs, there is bound to be economic and thus a large degree of social independence. We have public services, of course—Rebirth Station, Power Station, Transmitter Central, and a few others. But there aren't many."

"I cannot see why you aren't overwhelmed by crime." The last word was necessarily Procyonian, and Ramacan raised his eyebrows puzzledly. "Antisocial behavior," explained Felgi irritably. "Theft, murder, destruction."

"What possible need has anyone to steal?" asked Ramacan, surprised. "And the present degree of independence virtually eliminates social friction. Actual psychoses have been removed from the neural components of the rebirth records long ago."

"At any rate, I assume you speak for Sol."

"How can I speak for almost a billion different people? I have little authority, you know. So little is needed. However, I'll do all I can if you'll only tell me—"

"The decadence of Sol is incredible," snapped Felgi.

"You may be right." Ramacan's tone was mild, but he bristled under the urbane surface. "I've sometimes thought so myself. However, what has that to do with the present subject of discussion—whatever it may be?"

"You left us in exile," said Felgi, and now the wrath and hate were edging his voice, glittering out of his eyes. "For nine hundred years, Earth lived in luxury while the humans on Procyon fought and suffered and died in the worst kind of hell."

"What reason was there for us to go to Procyon?" asked Ramacan. "After the first few ships had established a colony there—well, we had a whole galaxy before us. When no colonial ships came from your star, I suppose it was assumed the people there had died off. Somebody should perhaps have gone there to check up, but it took twenty years to get there and it was an inhospitable and unrewarding system and there were so many other stars. Then the matter creator came along and Sol no longer had a government to look after such things. Space travel became an individual business, and no individual was interested in Procyon." He shrugged. "I'm sorry."

"You're *sorry?*" Felgi spat the words out. "For nine hundred years our ancestors fought the bitterness of their planets, starved and died in misery, sank back almost to barbarism and had to slug their way every step back upwards, waged the cruelest war of history with the Czernigi—unending centuries of war until one race or the other should be exterminated. We died of old age, generation after generation of us—we wrung our needs out of planets never meant for humans—my ship spent twenty years getting back here, twenty years of short human lives—and you're *sorry?*"

HE SPRANG up and paced the floor, his bitter voice lashing out. "You've had the stars, you've had immortality, you've had everything, which can be made of matter. And we spent twenty years cramped up in metal walls to get here—wondering if perhaps Sol hadn't fallen on evil times and needed our help."

"What would you have us do now?" demanded Ramacan. "All Earth has made you welcome—"

"We're a novelty."

"—all Earth is ready to offer you all it can. What more do you want of us?"

For a moment the rage was still in Felgi's strange eyes. Then it faded, blinked out as if he had drawn a curtain across them, and he stood still and spoke with sudden quietness. "True. I— I should apologize, I suppose. The nervous strain—"

"Don't mention it," said Ramacan. But inwardly he wondered. Just how far could he trust the Procyonites? All those hard centuries of war and intrigue—and then they weren't really human any more, not the way Earth's dwellers were human—but what else could he do? "It's quite all right, I understand."

"Thank you," Felgi sat down again. "May I ask what you offer?"

"Duplicate matter creators, of course. And robots duplicated, to administer the more complex Rebirth techniques. Certain of the processes involved are beyond the understanding of the human mind."

"I'm not sure it would be a good thing for us," said Felgi. "Sol has gotten stagnant. There doesn't seem to have been any significant change in the last half millennium. Why, our spaceship drives are better than yours."

"What do you expect?" shrugged Ramacan. "What possible incentive have we for change? Progress, to use an archaic term, is a means to an end, and we have reached its goal."

"I still don't know—" Felgi rubbed his chin. "I'm not even sure how your duplicators work."

"I can't tell you much about them. But the greatest technical mind on Earth can't tell you everything. As I told you before, the whole thing is just too immense for real knowledge. Only the electronic brains can handle so much at once."

"Maybe you could give me a short resume of it, and tell me just what your setup is. I'm especially interested in the actual means by which it's put to use."

"Well, let me see." Ramacan searched his memory. "The ultrawave was discovered—oh, it must be a good seven or eight hundred years ago now. It carries energy, but it's not electromagnetic. The theory of it, as far as any human can follow it, ties in with wave mechanics.

"The first great application came with the discovery that ultrawaves transmit over distances of many astronomical units, unhindered by intervening matter, and with *no energy loss*. The theory of that has been interpreted as meaning that the wave is, well, I suppose you could say it's 'aware' of the receiver and only goes to it. There must be a receiver as well as a transmitter to generate the wave. Naturally that led to a perfectly efficient power transmitter. Today all the Solar System gets its energy from the Sun—transmitted by the Power Station on the dayside of Mercury. Everything from interplanetary spaceships to televisors and clocks runs from that power source."

"Sounds dangerous to me," said Felgi. "Suppose the station fails?"

"It won't," said Ramacan confidently. "The Station has its own robots, no human technicians at all. Everything is recorded. If anyone part goes wrong, it is automatically dissolved into the nearest matter bank and recreated. There are other safeguards, too. The Station has never given trouble since it was first built."

"I see—" Felgi's tone was thoughtful.

"Soon thereafter," said Ramacan, "it was found that the ultrawave could also transmit matter. Circuits could be built, which would scan any body atom by atom, dissolve it to energy, and transmit this energy on the ultrawave along with the scanning signal. At the receiver, of course, the process is reversed. I'm grossly oversimplifying, naturally. It's not a mere signal that is involved, but a fantastic complex of signals such as only the ultrawave could carry. However, you get the general idea. Just about all transportation today is by this technique. Vehicles for air or space exist only for very special purposes and for pleasure trips."

"You have some kind of controlling center for this too, don't you?"

"Yes. Transmitter Station, on Earth, is in Brazil. It holds all the records of such things as addresses, and it coordinates the millions of units, all over the planet. It's a huge, complicated affair, of course, but perfectly efficient. Since distance no longer means anything, it's most practical to centralize the public-service units.

"Well, from transmission it was but a step to recording the signal and reproducing it out of a bank of any other matter. So—the duplicator. The matter creator. You can imagine what that did to Sol's economy. Today everybody owns one, and if he doesn't have a record of what he wants he can have one duplicated and transmitted from Creator Station's great 'library.' Anything whatsoever in the way of material goods is his for the turning of a dial and the flicking of a switch.

"And this, in turn soon led to the Rebirth technique. It's but an extension of all that has gone before. Your body is recorded at its prime of life, say around twenty years of age. Then you live for as much longer as you care to, say to thirty-five or forty or whenever you begin to get a little old. Then your neural pattern is recorded alone by special scanning units. Memory, as you surely know, is a matter of neural synapses and altered protein molecules, not too difficult to scan and record. This added pattern is superimposed electronically on the record of your twenty-year-old body. Then your own body is used as the matter bank for materializing the pattern in the altered record and—virtually instantaneously—your young body is created—but with all the memories of the old. You're—*immortal.*"

"In a way," said Felgi. "But it still doesn't seem right to me. The ego, the soul, whatever you want to call it—it seems as if you lose that. You create simply a perfect copy."

"When the copy is so perfect it cannot be told from the original," said Ramacan, "then what is the difference? The ego is essentially a matter of continuity. You, your essential self, are a constantly changing pattern of synapses bearing only a temporary relationship to the molecules that happen to carry the pattern at the moment. It is the design, not the structural material that is important. And it is the design that we preserve."

"Do you?" asked Felgi. "I seemed to notice a strange likeness among Earthlings."

"Well, since the records can be altered there was no reason for us to carry around crippled or diseased or deformed bodies," said Ramacan. "Records could be made of perfect specimens and *all* ego-patterns wiped from them; then someone else's neural pattern could be superimposed. Rebirth—in a new body! Naturally, everyone would want to match the prevailing beauty standard, and so a certain uniformity has appeared. A different body would of course lead in time to a different personality, man being a psychosomatic unit. But the continuity, which is the essential attribute of the ego, would still be there."

"Umm—I see. May I ask how old you are?"

"About seven hundred and fifty. I was middle-aged when Rebirth was established, but I had myself put into a young body."

FELGI'S eyes went from Ramacan's smooth, youthful face to his own hands, with the knobby joints and prominent veins of his sixty years. Briefly, the fingers tightened, but his voice remained soft. "Don't you have trouble keeping your memories straight?"

"Yes, but every so often I have some of the useless and repetitious ones taken out of the record, and that helps. The robots know exactly what part of the pattern corresponds to a given memory and can erase it. After, say, another thousand years, I'll probably have big gaps. But they won't be important."

"How about the apparent acceleration of time with age?"

"That was bad after the first couple of centuries, but then it seemed to flatten out, the nervous system adapted to it. I must say, though," admitted Ramacan, "that it as well as lack of incentive is probably responsible for our present static society and general unproductiveness. There's a terrible tendency to procrastination, and a day seems too short a time to get anything done."

"The end of progress, then—of science, or art, of striving, of all which has made man human."

"Not so. We still have our arts and handicrafts and—hobbies, I suppose you could call them. Maybe we don't do so much any more, but—why should we?"

"I'm surprised at finding so much of Earth gone back to wilderness. I should think you'd be badly overcrowded."

"Not so. The creator and the transmitter make it possible for men to live far apart, in physical distance, and still be in as close touch as necessary. Communities are obsolete. As for the population problem, there isn't any. After a few children, not many people want more. It's sort of, well, unfashionable anyway."

"That's right," said Felgi quietly. "I've hardly seen a child on Earth."

"And of course there's a slow drift out to the stars as people seek novelty. You can send your recording in a robot ship, and a journey of centuries becomes nothing. I suppose that's another reason for the tranquility of Earth. The more restless and adventurous elements have moved away."

"Have you any communication with them?"

"None. Not when spaceships can only go at half the speed of light. Once in a while curious wanderers will drop in on us, but it's very rare. They seem to be developing dome strange cultures out in the galaxy."

"Don't you do *any* work on Earth?"

"Oh, some public services must be maintained—psychiatry, human technicians to oversee various stations, and so on. And then there are any number of personal-service enterprises—entertainment, especially, and the creation of intricate handicrafts for the creators to duplicate. But there are enough people willing to work a few hours a month or week, if only to fill in their time or to get the credit-balance, which will enable them to purchase such services for themselves if they desire.

"It's a perfectly stable culture, General Felgi. It's perhaps the only really stable society in all human history."

"I wonder—haven't you any precaution sat all? Any military forces, any defenses against invaders—*anything?*"

"Why in the cosmos should we fear that?" exclaimed Ramacan. "Who would come invading over light-years—at half the speed of light? Or if they did, *why?*"

"Plunder—"

Ramacan laughed. "We could duplicate anything they asked for and give it to them."

"Could you, now?" Suddenly Felgi stood up. "Could you?"

Ramacan rose too, with his nerves and muscles tightening again. There was a hard triumph in the Procyonite's face, vindictive, threatening.

Felgi signaled to his men through the door. They trotted up on the double, and their blasters were raised and something hard and ugly was in their eyes.

"Coordinator Ramacan," said Felgi, "you are under arrest."

"What—what—" The Earthling felt as if someone had struck him a physical blow. He clutched for support. Vaguely he heard the iron tones:

"You've confirmed what I thought. Earth is unarmed, unprepared, helplessly dependent on a few undefended key spots. And I captain a warship of space filled with soldiers.

"We're taking over!"

CHAPTER TWO
"Tiger, Tiger!"

AVI'S current house lay in North America, on the middle Atlantic seaboard. Like most private homes these days, it was small and low ceilinged, with adjustable interior walls and furnishings for easy variegation. She loved flowers, and great brilliant gardens bloomed around her dwelling, down toward the sea and landward to the edge of the immense forest, which had returned with the end of agriculture.

They walked between the shrubs and trees and blossoms, she and Harol. Her unbound hair was long and bright in the sea breeze, her eighteen-year-old form was slim and graceful as a young deer's. Suddenly he hated the thought of leaving her.

"I'll miss you, Harol," she said.

He smiled lopsidedly. "You'll get over that," he said. "There are others. I suppose you'll be looking up some of those spacemen they say arrived from Procyon a few days ago."

"Of course," she said innocently. "I'm surprised you don't stay around and try for some of the women they had along. It would be a change."

"Not much of a change," he answered. "Frankly, I'm at a loss to understand the modern passion for variety. One person seems very much the same as another in that regard."

"It's a matter of companionship," she said. "After not too many years of living with someone, you get to know him too well. You can tell exactly what he's going to do, what he'll say to you; what he'll have for dinner and what sort of show he'll want to go to in the evening. These colonists will be—*new*. They'll have other ways from ours, they'll be able to tell of a new, different planetary system, they'll—" She broke off. "But now so many women will be after the strangers, I doubt if I'll have a chance."

"But if it's conversation you want—oh, well." Harol shrugged. "Anyway, I understand the Procyonites still have family relationships. They'll be quite jealous of their women. And I need this change."

"A carnivore—" Avi laughed, and Harol thought again what music it was. "You have an original mind, at least." Suddenly she was earnest. She held both his hands and looked close into his eyes. "That's always been what I liked about you, Harol. You've always been a thinker and adventurer, you've never let yourself grow mentally lazy like most of us. After we've been apart for a few years, you're always new again, you've gotten out of your rut and done something strange, you've learned something different, you've grown young again. We've always come back to each other, dear, and I've always been glad of it."

"And I," he said quietly. "Though I've regretted the separations, too." He smiled, a wry smile with a tinge of sorrow behind it. "We could have been very happy in the old days, Avi. We would have been married and together for life."

"A few years, and then age and feebleness and death." She shuddered. "Death. Nothingness. Not even the world can exist when one is dead. Not when you've no brain left to know about it. Just—nothing. As if you had never been. Haven't you ever been afraid of the thought?"

"No," he said, and kissed her.

"That's another way you're different," she murmured. "I wonder why you never went out to the stars, Harol. All your children did."

"I asked you to go with me, once."

"Not I. I like it here. Life is fun, Harol. I don't seem to get bored as easily as most people. But that isn't answering my question."

"Yes, it is," he said, and then clamped his mouth shut.

He stood looking at her, wandering if he was the last man on Earth who loved a woman, wondering how she really felt about him. Perhaps, in her way, she loved him—they always came back to each other. But not in the way he cared for her, not so that being apart was a gnawing pain and reunion was— No matter.

"I'll still be around," he said. "I'll be wandering through the woods here. I'll have the Rebirth men transmit me back to your house and then I'll be in the neighborhood."

"My pet tiger," she smiled. "Come around to see me once in a while, Harol. Come with me to some of the parties."

A nice spectacular ornament— "No, thanks. But you can scratch my head and feed me big bloody steaks, and I'll arch my back and purr."

They walked hand in hand toward the beach. "What made you decide to be a tiger?" she asked.

"My psychiatrist recommended an animal rebirth," he replied. "I'm getting terribly neurotic, Avi. I can't sit still five minutes and I get gloomy spells where nothing seems worthwhile any more, life is a dreary farce and—well, it seems to be becoming a rather common disorder these days. Essentially it's boredom. When you have everything without working for it, life can become horribly flat. When you've lived for centuries, tried it all hundreds of times—no change, no real excitement, nothing to call forth all that's in you— Anyway, the doctor suggested I go to the stars. When I refused that, he suggested I change to animal for a while. But I didn't want to be like everyone else. Not an ape or an elephant."

"Same old contrary Harol," she murmured, and kissed him. He responded with unexpected violence.

"A year or two of wild life, in a new and unhuman body, will make all the difference," he said after a while. They lay on the sand, feeling the sunlight wash over them, hearing the lullaby of waves and smelling the clean, harsh tang of sea and salt and many windy kilometers. High overhead a gull circled, white against the blue.

"Won't you change?" she asked.

"Oh, yes. I won't even be able to remember a lot of things I now know. I doubt if even the most intelligent tiger could understand vector analysis. But that won't matter, I'll get it back when they restore my human form. When I feel the personality change has gone as far as is safe, I'll come here and you can send me back to Rebirth. The important thing is the therapy—a change of viewpoint, a new and challenging environment— Avi!" He sat up, on one elbow and looked down at her. "Avi, why don't you come along? Why don't we both become tigers?"

"And have lots of little tigers?" she smiled drowsily. "No, thanks, Harol. Maybe some day, but not now. I'm really not an adventurous person at all." She stretched, and snuggled back against the warm white dune. "I like it the way it is."

And there are those starmen— Sunfire, what's the matter with me? Next thing you know I'll commit an inurbanity against one of her lovers. I need that therapy, all right.

"And then you'll come back and tell me about it," said Avi.

"Maybe not," he teased her. "Maybe I'll find a beautiful tigress somewhere and become so enamored of her I'll never want to change back to human."

"There won't be any tigresses unless you persuade someone else to go along," she answered. "But will you like a human body after having had such a lovely striped skin? Will we poor hairless people still look good to you?"

"Darling," he smiled, "to me you'll always look good enough to eat."

Presently they went back into the house. The seagull still dipped and soared, high in the sky.

THE FOREST was great and green and mysterious, with sunlight dappling the shadows and a riot of ferns and flowers under the huge old trees. There were brooks tinkling their darkling way between cool, mossy banks, fish leaping like silver streaks in the bright shallows, lonely pools where quiet hung like a mantle, open meadows of wind-rippled grass, space and solitude and an unending pulse of life.

Tiger eyes saw less than human; the world seemed dim and flat and colorless until he got used to it. After that he had increasing difficulty remembering what color and perspective were like. And his other senses came alive, he realized what a captive within his own skull he had been—looking out at a world of which he had never been so real a part of as now.

He heard sounds and tones no man had ever perceived, the faint hum and chirr of insects, the rustling of leaves in a light, warm breeze, the vague whisper of an owl's wings, the scurrying of small, frightened creatures through the long grass—it all blended into a rich symphony, the heartbeat and breath of the forest. And his nostrils quivered to the infinite variety of smells, the heady fragrance of crushed grass, the pungency of fungus and decay, the sharp, wild odor of fur, the hot drunkenness of newly spilled blood. And he felt with every hair, his whiskers quivered to the smallest stirrings, he gloried in the deep, strong play of his muscles—he had come alive, he thought; a man was half dead compared to the vitality that throbbed in the tiger.

At night, at night—there was no darkness for him now. Moonlight was a white, cold blaze through which he stole on feathery feet; the blackest gloom was light to him—shadows, wan patches of luminescence, a shifting, sliding fantasy of gray like an old and suddenly remembered dream.

He laired in a cave he found, and his new body had no discomfort from the damp earth. At night he would stalk out, a huge, dim ghost with only the amber gleam of his eyes for light, and the forest would speak to him with sound and scent and feeling, the taste of game on the wind. He was master then, all the woods shivered and huddled away from him. He was death in black and gold.

Once an ancient poem ran through the human part of his mind, he let the words roll like ominous thunder in his brain and tried to speak them aloud. The forest shivered with the tiger's coughing roar,

> *Tiger, tiger, burning bright*
> *In the forest of the night,*
> *What immortal hand or eye*
> *Dared frame thy fearful symmetry?*

And the arrogant feline soul snarled response: *I did!*

Later he tried to recall the poem, but he couldn't.

At first he was not very successful, too much of his human awkwardness clung to him. He snarled his rage and bafflement when rabbits skittered aside, when a deer scented him lurking and bolted. He went to Avi's house and she fed him big chunks of raw meat and laughed and scratched him under the chin. She was delighted with her pet.

Avi, he thought, and remembered that he loved her. But that was with his human body. To the tiger, she had no esthetic or sexual value. But he liked to let her stroke him, he purred like a mighty engine and rubbed against her slim legs. She was still very dear to him, and when he became human again—

But the tiger's instincts fought their way back; the heritage of a million years was not to be denied no matter how much the technicians had tried to alter him. They had accomplished little more than to increase his intelligence, and the tiger nerves and glands were still there.

The night came when he saw a flock of rabbits dancing in the moonlight and pounced on them. One huge, steely-taloned paw swooped down, he felt the ripping flesh and snapping bone and then he was gulping the sweet, hot blood and peeling the meat from the frail ribs. He went wild, he roared and raged all night, shouting his exultance to the pale frosty moon. At dawn he slunk back to his cave, wearied, his human mind a little ashamed of it all. But the next night he was hunting again.

His first deer! He lay patiently on a branch overhanging a trail; only his nervous tail moved while the slow hours dragged by, and he waited. And when the doe passed underneath he was on her like a tawny lightning bolt. A great slapping paw, jaws like shears, a brief, terrible struggle, and she lay dead at his feet. He gorged himself, he ate till he could hardly crawl back to the cave, and then he slept like a drunken man until hunger woke him and he went back to the carcass. A pack of wild dogs were devouring it, he rushed on them and killed one and scattered the rest. Thereafter he continued his feast until only bones were left.

The forest was full of game; it was an easy life for a tiger. But not too easy. He never knew whether he would go back with full or empty belly, and that was part of the pleasure.

They had not removed all the tiger memories; fragments remained to puzzle him; sometimes he woke up whimpering with a dim wonder as to where he was and what had happened. He seemed to remember misty jungle dawns, a broad brown river shining under the sun, another cave and another striped form beside him. As time went on he grew confused, he thought vaguely that he must once have hunted sambar and seen the white rhinoceros go by like a moving mountain in the twilight. It was growing harder to keep things straight.

That was, of course, only to be expected. His feline brain could not possibly hold all the memories and concepts of the human, and with the passage of weeks and months he lost the earlier clarity of recollection. He still identified himself with a certain sound, "Harol," and he remembered other forms and scenes—but more and more dimly, as if they were the fading shards of a dream. And he kept firmly in mind that he had to go back to Avi and let her send—take?—him somewhere else before he forgot who he was.

Well, there was time for that, thought the human component. He wouldn't lose that memory all at once, he'd know well in advance that the superimposed human personality was disintegrating in its strange house and that he ought to get back. Meanwhile he grew more and deeply into the forest life, his horizons narrowed until it seemed the whole of existence.

Now and then he wandered down to the sea and Avi's home, to get a meal and be made much of. But the visits grew more and more infrequent, the open country made him nervous and he couldn't stay indoors after dark.

Tiger, tiger—

And summer wore on.

HE WOKE to a raw wet chill in the cave, rain outside and a mordant wind blowing through dripping dark trees. He shivered and growled, unsheathing his claws, but this was not an enemy he could destroy. The day and the night dragged by in misery.

Tigers had been adaptable beasts in the old days, he recalled; they had ranged as far north as Siberia. But his original had been from the tropics. *Hell!* he cursed, and the thunderous roar rattled through the woods.

But then came crisp, clear days with a wild wind hallooing through a high, pale sky, dead leaves whirling on the gusts and laughing in their thin, dry way. Geese honked in the heavens, southward bound, and the bellowing of stags filled the nights. There was a drunkenness in the air; the tiger rolled in the grass and purred like muted thunder and yowled at the huge orange moon as it rose. His fur thickened, he didn't feel the chill except as a keen tingling in his blood. All his senses were sharpened now, he lived with a knife-edged alertness and learned how to go through the fallen leaves like another shadow.

Indian summer, long lazy days like a resurrected springtime, enormous stars, the crisp smell of rotting vegetation, and his human mind remembered that the leaves were like gold and bronze and flame. He fished in the brooks, scooping up his prey with one hooked sweep; he ranged the woods and roared on the high ridges under the moon.

Then the rains returned, gray and cold and sodden, the world drowned in a wet woe. At night there was frost, numbing his feet and glittering in the starlight, and through the chill silence he could hear the distant beat of the sea. It grew harder to stalk game, he was often hungry. By now he didn't mind that too much, but his reason worried about winter. Maybe he'd better get back.

One night the first snow fell, and in the morning the world was white and still. He plowed through it, growling his anger, and wondered about moving south. But cats aren't given to long journeys. He remembered vaguely that Avi could give him food and shelter.

Avi— For a moment, when he tried to think of her, he thought of a golden, dark-striped body and a harsh feline smell filling the cave above the old wide river. He shook his massive head, angry with himself and the world, and tried to call up her image. The face was dim in his mind, but the scent came back to him, and the low, lovely music of her laughter. He would go to Avi.

He went through the bare forest with the haughty gait of its king, and presently he stood on the beach. The sea was gray and cold and enormous, roaring white-maned on the shore; flying spindrift stung his eyes. He padded along the strand until he saw her house.

It was oddly silent. He went in through the garden. The door stood open, but there was only desertion inside.

Maybe she was away. He curled up on the floor and went to sleep.

He woke much later, hunger gnawing in his guts, and still no one had come. He recalled that she had been wont to go south for the winter. But she wouldn't have forgotten him, she'd have been back from time to time— But the house had little scent of her, she had been away for a long while. And it was disordered. Had she left hastily?

He went over to the creator. He couldn't remember how it worked, but he did recall the process of dialing and switching. He pulled the lever at random with a paw. Nothing happened.

Nothing. The creator was inert.

He roared his disappointment. Slow, puzzled fear came to him. This wasn't as it should be.

But he was hungry. He'd have to try to get his own food, then, and come back later in hopes of finding Avi. He went back into the woods.

Presently he smelled life under the snow. Bear. Previously, he and the bears had been in a state of watchful neutrality. But this one was asleep, unwary, and his belly cried for food. He tore the shelter apart with a few powerful motions and flung himself on the animal.

It is dangerous to wake a hibernating bear. This one came to with a start, his heavy paw lashed out and the tiger sprang back with blood streaming down his muzzle.

Madness came, a berserk rage that sent him leaping forward. The bear snarled and braced himself. They closed, and suddenly the tiger was fighting for his very life.

He never remembered that battle save as a red whirl of shock and fury, tumbling in the snow and spilling blood to steam in the cold air. Strike, bite, rip, thundering blows against his ribs and skull, the taste of blood hot in his mouth and the insanity of death shrieking and gibbering in his head...

In the end, he staggered bloodily and collapsed on the bear's ripped corpse. For a long time he lay there, and the wild dogs hovered near, waiting for him to die.

After a while he stirred weakly and ate of the bear's flesh. But he couldn't leave. His body was one vast pain, his feet wobbled under him, one paw had been crushed by the great jaws. He lay by the dead bear under the tumbled shelter, and snow fell slowly on them.

The battle and the agony and the nearness of death brought his old instincts to the fore. All tiger, he licked his tattered form and gulped hunks of rotting meat as the days went by and waited for a measure of health to return.

In the end, he limped back toward his cave. Dreamlike memories nagged him; there had been a house and someone who was good but—but—

He was cold and lame and hungry. Winter had come.

CHAPTER THREE
Dark Victory

"WE HAVE no further use for you," said Felgi, "but in view of the help you've been, you'll be allowed to live—at least till we get back to Procyon and the Council decides your case. Also, you probably have more valuable information about the Solar System than our other prisoners. They're mostly women."

Ramacan looked at the hard, exultant face and answered dully, "If I'd known what you were planning, I'd never have helped."

"Oh, yes, you would have," snorted Felgi. "I saw your reactions when we showed you some of our means of persuasion. You Earthlings are all alike. You've been hiding from death so long that the backbone has all gone out of you. That alone makes you unfit to hold your planet."

"You have the plans of the duplicators and the transmitters and power-beams—all our technology. I helped you get them from the Stations. What more do you want?"

"Earth."

"But why? With the creators and transmitters, you can make your planets like all the old dreams of paradise. Earth is more congenial, yes, but what does environment matter to you now?"

"Earth is still the true home of man," said Felgi. There was a fanaticism in his eyes such as Ramacan had never seen even in nightmare. "It should belong to the best race of man. Also—well, our culture couldn't stand that technology. Procyonite civilization grew up in adversity, it's been nothing but struggle and hardship, it's became part of our nature now. With the Czernigi destroyed, we *must* find another enemy."

Oh, yes, thought Ramacan. *It's happened before, in Earth's bloody old past. Nations that knew nothing but war and suffering became molded by them, glorified the harsh virtues that had enabled them to survive. A militaristic state can't afford peace and leisure and prosperity; its people might begin to think for themselves. So the government looks for conquest outside the borders— Needful or not, there must be war to maintain the control of the military.*

How human are the Procyonites now! What's twisted them in the centuries of their terrible evolution. They're no longer men, they're fighting robots, beasts of prey, they have to have blood.

"You saw us shell the Stations from space," said Felgi. "Rebirth, Creator, Transmitter—they're radioactive craters now. Not a machine is running on Earth, not a tube is alight—nothing. And with the creators on which their lives depended inert, Earthlings will go back to utter savagery."

"Now what?" asked Ramacan wearily.

"We're standing off Mercury, refueling," said Felgi. "Then it's back to Procyon. We'll use our creator to record most of the crew, they can take turns being briefly recreated during the voyage to maintain the ship and correct the course. We'll be little older when we get home.

"Then, of course, the Council will send out a fleet with recorded crews. They'll take over Sol, eliminate the surviving population, and recolonize Earth. After that—" The mad fires blazed high in his eyes. "The stars! A galactic empire, ultimately."

"Just so you can have war," said Ramacan tonelessly. "Just so you can keep your people stupid slaves."

"That's enough," snapped Felgi. "A decadent culture can't be expected to understand our motives."

Ramacan stood thinking. There would still be humans around when the Procyonites came back. There would be forty years to prepare. Men in spaceships, here and there throughout the System, would come home, would see the ruin of Earth and know who must be guilty. With creators, they could rebuild quickly, they could arm themselves, duplicate vengeance-hungry men by the millions.

Unless Solarian man was so far gone in decay that he was only capable of blind panic. But Ramacan didn't think so. Earth had slipped, but not that far.

Felgi seemed to read his mind. There was cruel satisfaction in his tones: "Earth will have no chance to rearm. We're using the power from Mercury Station to run our own large duplicator, turning rock into osmium fuel for our engines. But when we're finished, we'll blow up the Station, too. Spaceships will drift powerless, the colonists on the planets will die as their environmental regulators stop functioning, no wheel will turn in all the Solar System. That, I should think, will be the final touch."

Indeed, indeed. Without power, without tools, without food or shelter, the final collapse would come. Nothing but a few starveling savages would be left when the Procyonites returned. Ramacan felt an emptiness within himself.

Life had become madness and nightmare. The end...

"You'll stay here till we get around to recording you," said Felgi. He turned on his heel and walked out.

RAMACAN slumped back into a seat. His desperate eyes traveled around and around the bare little cabin that was his prison, around and around like the crazy whirl of his thoughts. He looked at the guard who stood in the doorway, leaning on his blaster, contemptuously bored with the captive. If—if—O almighty gods, if *that* was to inherit green Earth...

What to do, what to do? There must be some answer, some way, no problem was altogether without solution. Or was it? What guarantee did he have of cosmic justice? He buried his face in his hands.

I was a coward, he thought. *I was afraid of pain. So I rationalized, I told myself they probably didn't want much. I used my influence to help them get duplicators and plans. And the others were cowards too, they yielded, they were cravenly eager to help the conquerors—and this is our pay!*

What to do, what to do? If somehow the ship were lost, if it never came back— The Procyonites would wonder. They'd send another ship or two—no more—to investigate. And in forty years Sol could be ready to meet those ships—ready to carry the war to an unprepared enemy—if in the meantime they'd had a chance to rebuild, if Mercury Power Station were spared—

But the ship would blow the Station out of existence, and the ship would return with news of Sol's ruin, and the invaders would come swarming in—would go ravening out through an unsuspecting galaxy like a spreading plague—

How to stop the ship—*now?*

Ramacan grew aware of the thudding of his heart; it seemed to shake his whole body with its violence. And his hands were cold and clumsy, his mouth was parched, he was afraid.

He got up and walked over toward the guard. The Procyonite hefted his blaster, but there was no alertness in him, he had no fear of an unarmed member of the conquered race.

He'll shoot me down, thought Ramacan. *The death I've been running from all my life is on me now. But it's been a long life and a good one, and better to finish it now than drag out a few miserable years as their despised prisoner, and—and—I hate their guts!*

"What do you want?" asked the Procyonite.

"I feel sick," said Ramacan. His voice was almost a whisper in the dryness of his throat. "Let me out."

"Get back."

"It'll be messy. Let me go to the lavatory."

He stumbled, nearly falling. "Go ahead," said the guard curtly. "I'll be along, remember."

Ramacan swayed on his feet as he approached the man. His shaking hands closed on the blaster barrel and yanked the weapon loose. Before the guard could yell, Ramacan drove the butt into his face. A remote corner of his mind was shocked at the savagery that welled up in him when the bones crunched.

The guard toppled. Ramacan eased him to the floor, slugged him again to make sure he would lie quiet, and stripped him of his long outer coat, his boots, and helmet. His hands were really trembling now; he could hardly get the simple garments on.

If he was caught—well, it only made a few minutes' difference. But he was still afraid. Fear screamed inside him.

He forced himself to walk with nightmare slowness down the long corridor. Once he passed another man, but there was no discovery. When he had rounded the corner, he was violently sick.

He went down a ladder to the engine room. Thank the gods he'd been interested enough to inquire about the layout of the ship when they first arrived. The door stood open and he went in.

A couple of engineers were watching the giant creator at work. It pulsed and hummed and throbbed with power, energy from the sun and from dissolving atoms of rocks—atoms recreated as the osmium that would power the ship's engines on the long voyage back. Tons of fuel spilling down into the bins.

Ramacan closed the soundproof door and shot the engineers.

Then he went over to the creator and reset the controls. It began to manufacture plutonium.

He smiled then, with an immense relief, an incredulous realization that he had won. He sat down and cried with sheer joy.

The ship would not get back. Mercury Station would endure. And on that basis, a few determined men in the Solar System could rebuild. There would be horror on Earth, howling chaos, most of its population would plunge into savagery and death. But enough would live, and remain civilized, and get ready for revenge.

Maybe it was for the best, he thought. Maybe Earth really had gone into a twilight of purposeless ease. True it was that there had been none of the old striving and hoping and gallantry, which had made man what he was. No art, no science, no adventure—a smug self-satisfaction, an unreal immortality in a synthetic paradise. Maybe this shock and challenge was what Earth needed, to show the starward way again.

As for him, he had had many centuries of life, and he realized now what a deep inward weariness there had been in him. *Death*, he thought, *death is the longest voyage of all. Without death there is no evolution, no real meaning to life, the ultimate adventure has been snatched away.*

There had been a girl once, he remembered, and she had died before the rebirth machines became available. Odd—after all these centuries he could still remember how her hair had rippled in the wind, one day on a high summery hill. He wondered if he would see her.

He never felt the explosion as the plutonium reached critical mass.

AVI'S feet were bleeding. Her shoes had finally given out, and rocks and twigs tore at her feet. The snow was dappled with blood.

Weariness clawed at her, she couldn't keep going—but she had to, she had to, she was afraid to stop in the wilderness.

She had never been alone in her life. There had always been the televisors and the transmitters, no place on Earth had been more than an instant away. But the world had expanded into immensity, the machines were dead, there was only cold and gloom and empty white distances. The world of warmth and music and laughter and casual enjoyment was as remote and unreal as a dream.

Was it a dream? Had she always stumbled sick and hungry through a nightmare world of leafless trees and drifting snow and wind that sheathed her in cold through the thin rags of her garments? Or was this the dream, a sudden madness of horror and death?

Death—no, no, no, she couldn't die, she was one of the immortals, she mustn't die.

The wind blew and blew.

Night was falling, winter night. A wild dog bayed, somewhere out in the gloom. She tried to scream, but her throat was raw with shrieking; only a dry croak would come out.

Help me, help me, help me.

Maybe she should have stayed with the man. He had devised traps, had caught an occasional rabbit or squirrel and flung her the leavings. But he looked at her so strangely when several days had gone by without a catch. He would have killed her and eaten her; she had to flee.

Run, run, run— She couldn't run, the forest reached on forever, she was caught in cold and night, hunger and death.

What had happened, what had happened, what had become of the world? What would become of her?

She had liked to pretend she was one of the ancient goddesses, creating what she willed out of nothingness, served by a huge and eternal world whose one purpose was to serve her. Where was that world now?

Hunger twisted in her like a knife. She tripped over a snow-buried log and lay there, trying feebly to rise.

We were too soft, too complacent, she thought dimly. *We lost all our powers, we were just little parasites on our machines. Now we're unfit—*

No! I won't have it! I was a goddess once—

Spoiled brat, jeered the demon in her mind. *Baby crying for its mother. You should be old enough to look after yourself—after all these centuries. You shouldn't be running in circles waiting for a help that will never come, you should be helping yourself, making a shelter, finding nuts and roots, building a trap. But you can't. All the self-reliance has withered out of you.*

No—help, help, help—

Something moved in the gloom. She choked a scream. Yellow eyes glowed like twin fires, and the immense form stepped noiselessly forth.

For an instant she gibbered in a madness of fear, and then sudden realization came and left her gaping with unbelief—then instant eager acceptance.

There could only be one tiger in this forest.

"Harol," she whispered, and climbed to her feet. "Harol."

It was all right. The nightmare was over. Harol would look after her. He would hunt for her, protect her, bring her back to the world of machines that *must* still exist. "Harol," she cried. "Harol, my dear—"

The tiger stood motionless; only his twitching tail had life. Briefly, irrelevantly, remembered sounds trickled through his mind: *"Your basic mentality should be stable for a year or two, barring accidents..."* But the noise was meaningless, it slipped through his brain into oblivion.

He was hungry. The crippled paw hadn't healed well, he couldn't catch game.

Hunger, the most elemental need of all, grinding within him, filling his tiger brain and tiger body until nothing else was left.

He stood looking at the thing that didn't run away. He had killed another a while back—he licked his mouth at the thought.

From somewhere long ago he remembered that the thing had once been—she had been—he couldn't remember—

He stalked forward.

"Harol," said Avi. There was fear rising horribly in her voice.

The tiger stopped. He knew that voice. He remembered— he remembered—

He had known her once. There was something about her that held him back.

But he was hungry. And his instincts were clamoring in him.

But if only he could remember, before it was too late—

Time stretched into a horrible eternity while they stood facing each other—the lady and the tiger.

THE END

The Nest

With the Nest and the Rover, Duke Hugo was well set for his
business—which was loot! But he hadn't counted on a mad Cro-
Magnon and a maddened dinosaur, by the name of Iggy!

I'd been out hunting all day, in the reeds and thickets and tall
grass of the bottomlands down by the Styx, and luck had been
bad. The heat and mugginess bothered me worse than it should
have, after all these years in the Nest, and the flies were a small
hell, and there was no game to speak of. We'd killed it all off, I
suppose. Once I did spot the saber-tooth, which had been
hanging around the cattle pens, and shot at him, but he got
away. While chasing him, I went head over heels into a
mudhole and lost my powderhorn and two good flints, besides
ruining my shirt. So I came back toward evening in a devil of a
temper, which is probably what started the trouble.

There was a sort of quiet golden light all over the world as I
rode homeward, filling the air and the wide grasslands and the
forest. Pretty. But I was thinking bitterly about the cave and
The Men and a wet cold wind blowing off the glaciers of home
and roaring in the pines. I wondered why the hell I hadn't had
the brains to stay where I was well off. You got rich working
out of the Nest, if you lived, but was it worth the trouble?

Iggy's feet scrunched on gravel as we came onto the road. A
lot of the boys have kidded me about riding a dinosaur, when a
horse is so much faster and smarter. But what the hell, a young
iguanodon goes quickly enough for me, and the flies don't
bother him. And if the need arises, he's like a small tank—as I
was very shortly going to learn.

I plodded along, swaying in the saddle, ten feet up in the air
on Iggy's shoulders. The fields stretched around me now,
hundreds of acres of wheat and rye and maize, with the orchards
dark against the yellowing sky. The slaves were still at work,

cultivating, and a couple of overseers waved to me from their horses. But I was feeling too grouchy to reply. I sat hunched over pitying myself.

A screen of trees and hedges marked off the fields; beyond, the road went through gardens that blazed with color, all around the Nest. Roses and poppies like fresh blood, white and tiger-tawny lilies, royally purple violets—sure, Duke Hugo was a free-wheeling buzzard, but he did know flowers. Ahead of me, I could see the peaked roofs of the houses, the slave pens beyond them, and the castle black over all. I thought of a hot shower and clicked my tongue at Iggy to make him step faster.

That was where the fight began.

The girl burst out of a clump of cherry trees in blossom, screaming as she saw me. It was a small dry scream, as if she'd already burned out her throat. I only had time to see that she was young and dark and pretty, then she swerved around to dodge me. Her foot slipped and she went down in a heap. I don't know exactly why I grabbed my ax and jumped to the ground. Maybe the long red weals across her naked back had something to do with it.

She tried to scramble up, I put my foot on her back and held her down. As she looked up, I saw big dark eyes, a small curved nose, a wide full mouth, and a hell of a big bruise on one cheek. "What's the hurry, sis?" I asked.

She cried something, I didn't know the language but there was a terrible begging in her voice. A runaway slave—well, let her run. The saber-tooth would be better for her than her owner, judging by those marks. I lifted my foot and bent over and helped the girl rise.

Too late. The man came out through the trees after her. He was a young fellow, short but strongly built, and mad as a Zulu. He wore a gray uniform, a square helmet, and a swastika armband—a Nazi, then—but his only weapons were a broadsword and the long whip in one hand.

The girl screamed once more and took off again. He snarled, and snapped the whip. It was a murderous Boer sjambok; its heavy length coiled around her ankles and she stumbled and fell.

I suppose it was my bad luck that day, which flared up in me. I had no business interfering, but I didn't like Nazis much. I put a hand on his chest and shoved. Down he went.

He scrambled up, bellowing in excellent Norman French. I hefted my ax. "Not so fast, chum," I answered.

"Get out of the way!" He lunged past me toward the girl, who was lying there crying, out of hope, out of tears. I got him by the collar and spun him around, flat on his back.

"I rank thee, friend, in spite of that fancy uniform," I told him. "I rate a flintlock, and thou'st only got that pigsticker. Now behave thyself!"

Sure, I was looking for a fight. It's the best way there is to work off your temper.

"Thou bloody swine—" He got up again, slowly, and his face was strange. It was a look I'd only seen before on children and kings, just about to throw a tantrum. I didn't recognize him, never having had much truck with the Nazis or their friends. Suddenly he lashed out with the whip. It caught me across the chest like a white-hot wire.

That did it. No damned swordsman was going to hit me that way. I didn't even stop to think before my ax bounced off his helmet.

The clang sent him lurching back, but the steel held firm. He screamed, then, and drew his sword and sprang for me. I met the whistling blow in midair. Sparks showered, and our weapons were nearly torn loose.

He growled and tried to thrust, but a broadsword is no good for that. I knocked the blade aside, and my ax whirred down. He was fast, jumped back. I furrowed his shoulder.

"The devil damn thee!" He got two hands on his sword and it flamed against my bare head. I caught the blow on my ax handle, swept it aside, and took one step inward. A sidewise chop, and his head was rolling in the gravel.

Most people think a battleaxe is a clumsy weapon. It isn't. I'll take it for close quarters over any weapon except a .45 or a carbine, which I didn't rate. His pretty sword went spinning as he fell, flashing the sunlight into my eyes like a last thrust.

Breathing hard, I looked around me. I was a little surprised that the girl was still crouched there, but maybe she was too tired and scared to run any more. She was a stranger to me, and I'd have noticed anyone that nice-looking, so I decided she must have been captured just lately. She'd been horribly treated.

"Who art thou, sis?" I asked, trying to be gentle. I asked it in French, English, Latin, Greek, and whatever other languages I had a smattering of—even tried the language of The Men, just for the heel of it. Her eyes were wide and blank, without understanding.

"Well—" I scratched my head, not knowing exactly what to do next. It was decided for me. I heard a barking curse and the sound of hoofs, and looked up to see a dozen Huns charging.

I've no particular race prejudices, not like some of The Men. I'm about a quarter Neanderthal myself, and proud of it—that's where I get my red hair and strong back. We'll say nothing about the brains. Otherwise, of course, I'm a Man. But where it comes to Huns, well, I just ain't like the greasy little devils. That was beside the point right now, though. They were after my skull. I didn't know what business of theirs the fight was, and didn't stop to think why. No time. Not even time to get mad again. The lead man's lance was almost in my throat.

I skipped aside, chopping low, at the horse's forelegs. The poor beast screamed as it fell. The Hun sprang lightly free, but I'd sheared his arm off, before he hit the ground. The next one had his sword out, hewing at me. I turned the blow and chopped at his waist, but he was wearing chain mail. He grunted and swung once more, raking my cheek. Then they were all about me, cutting loose.

I scrambled toward Iggy, where the big stupid brute stood calmly watching. The Huns yammered and crowded their ponies in close. Reaching up in an overhand sweep, I split one brown monkey-face. A sword from behind struck at my neck. I ducked as it whistled over me, and thought in a queer short flash that this was the end of Trebuen.

"Chinga los heréticos!"

The tall horse had come thundering from the Nest and hit the pack like a cyclone. Don Miguel Pedro Estebán Francisco de Otrillo y Guttierez flashed like a sun in his armor. His lance had already spitted one Hun and his sword sent another toppling. Now he reared the Arab back, and the slamming forefeet made a third man's pony yell and buck. The Huns howled and turned to meet him, giving me a chance to cross steel with one at a time.

Slash and bang! We were fighting merrily when a shot cracked in the air, and another and another. That was the signal of the bosses. We broke off and drew away from each other, still growling. There were five dead on the road, too trampled to be recognized. I drew air into lungs that seemed on fire and looked up to the new rider. She'd come galloping from the Nest, not even stopping to saddle her horse.

"Ah, Señorita Olga!" Don Miguel rose in his stirrups and swept her a bow till the plumes on his helmet brushed his horse's mane. He was always polite to women, even to Captain Olga Borisovna Rakitin, who by his lights was not only a heretic but unmaidenly.

I sort of agreed with him there. She was a big woman, as big as most men, and beautifully formed. The tight gray-green uniform of the Martian Soviet left no doubt of that. Under the peaked, red-starred cap, her face was straight, finely cut, with high cheekbones and big gray eyes, and it was a sin the way she cropped her bronze-colored hair. But she was a human icicle; or maybe a chilled-steel punching ram would be better.

She holstered her pistol with a clank and looked us over with eyes like the wind off a glacier. "What is the meaning of this brawl?" She had a nice low voice, but spoke French like a clicking trigger.

Don Miguel's bearded hawk face broke into the famous smile that had made him the terror of husbands and fathers from Lagash to London. "Señorita," he said gently, "when I see my good friend Trebuen set on by pagans and in danger of death before his conversion to the true faith is completed, there is only one thing that any hidalgo can do. Surely a lady will understand."

"And why did ye fight?" she went on, looking at me and the Huns.

One of the horsemen pointed to the battered Nazi body. None of them spoke French very well, so they wouldn't talk it at all if they could help it. It was plain I'd killed a particular pal of theirs. Well, any friend of the Huns is an enemy of mine.

"And thou, Trebuen?" she asked. "I've had about enough of thy Stone Age cannibalism. Thou'rt the worst troublemaker in the Nest."

That wasn't true, and she knew it. The Huns and the Nazis were forever brawling, and the Normans were even worse— though as they owned the place, I suppose they had the right. And I resented her crack about my people. The Men aren't cannibals, they're peaceful hunters, minding their own business. I'd never heard about war before being recruited into the Nest. That was when I chanced to meet a mammoth hunting party, guided them, and had one of the Duke's sons take a fancy to me. They could always use tall husky men here.

"I didn't like his face," I snapped. "So I took it off."

"This girl—" She looked at the plump, dark little chick, who had huddled up close to me.

"My property."

"I didn't know even thou went in for slave-beating," she sneered.

THE NEST

"I didn't do that!" I shouted. Don Miguel had noticed the girl by now. He beamed at her, because she was certainly a knockout. Then he swept off his cloak and threw it over her shoulders. She drew it close around her and gave him a funny look, like a kicked dog that somebody finally pets. One, small hand stole toward mine, and I took it.

By this time the cops had arrived, twenty of them marching in double-time from the Nest. The setting sun glared off their helmets, armor, and shields. They broke formation at their leader's command—he was a centurion, I noticed—and closed in around us, their short swords bare and sharp-looking.

"There've been enough brawls here," said Captain Olga. "This calls for an inquiry. Maybe a hanging or two."

"Señorita," said Don Miguel, very, very softly, his black eyes narrowed on her, "the law of the Nest permits gentlemen to duel. Any subsequent quarrel is between the victor and the dead man's friends."

"We'll see what the Duke has to say about it," she snapped, and wheeled her horse around.

"Come on, friend," said the centurion. "Up to the castle."

I shifted my ax. "Are we under arrest?" I asked, putting a bite in the words. Cops have to be kept in their place.

"Er—not exactly, I guess," said the centurion. "But you'd better stay inside the castle walls till the Duke settles your case."

I shrugged. Killing a man here wasn't a crime—there were plenty more where they came from. I might have to pay a fine, and perhaps some wergild to a few Huns and Nazis. That griped me, but I could afford it.

That's what I thought—then.

I clicked my tongue at Iggy, who stooped over so I could scramble aboard. I took the girl in front of me, which made the ride a pleasant one. She was horribly scared, and clung close to me. Iggy rose back up on his hind legs and stalked alongside Don Miguel's horse. The Huns trotted sulkily in the rear, twittering in their own language. The cops enclosed all of us and marched steadily down the road. They weren't really Romans, most of them were barbaric riffraff from Germany and Thrace, but their discipline was beautiful.

Don Miguel looked up at me. "Who is the young woman?" he asked. "Where is she from?"

"I don't know," I said. "Looks Semitic, but that could mean almost anything."

"Well," he said, "we'll take her to the Wisdom and find out."

"Uh—" I stumbled awkwardly. "I don't know how to thank thee for—"

"De nada, amigo." He waved a long, lily-white hand. "It was a pleasure. Quite apart from the fact that I have to save thy heathenish soul before thou departest this world, unworthy apostle though I am, there is this question: Where else in the Nest would I find a man who could keep up with me in a drinking bout?"

"Well, there is that," I agreed.

We entered on the Via Appia. There was pavement within the bounds of the Nest, beautifully laid—but a lot can be done when you have all the slave labor you want. Small houses lay on either side of the broad street, surrounded by gardens and bowers—the homes of the ordinary warriors. Slaves and naked children stopped to gape at us as we went by. We saw a few friends in the streets or in front of their homes: Thorkel the Berserk, all tricked out in Italian silks; the Mongol Belgutai, swapping small talk with Amir Hassan of Baghdad; the old sea dog Sir Henry Martingale, smoking in his garden while his concubines fanned him and played music. They hailed us cheerfully, not knowing what we had coming to us. But then, neither did we.

The cops' footfalls slammed on the pavement, a dull drumbeat between the fantastic houses. There were about a thousand homes in the Nest, each built according to the owner's fancy. A half-timbered Tudor cottage nestled between a French chateau and a swoop-roofed Chinese affair with one of their silly-looking dragons out in front; across from it were a miniature

Moorish palace and one of those adobe huts the Greeks insisted on kenneling in. We turned at the fountain in the Place d'Ètoile—a lovely piece of Renaissance work, though it had gotten somewhat knocked up en route to us—and crossed London Bridge to the Street of St. Mark. The town muezzin was calling Moslems to prayer as we climbed the hill on which the castle stood.

Its gray stone battlements threw a night-like shadow over us. Looking around, I could see the slave pens on the other side of town; overseers were herding the field workers' back, and such of the city's slaves as worked by day were trotting obediently toward the same place. Not many ever tried to get away—there was no place to go, and if a saber-tooth or nimravus didn't get you first, the Normans would hunt you down with dogs. They thought that was rare sport.

We went through the gate into the flagged courtyard, past the guards—those were specially trusted Janissaries, armed with repeater rifles. "Get on down," said the centurion. "I'll take your mounts to the stables."

"Okay," I said, "but if they don't give Iggy enough to drink there, thou'lt hear from me. He needs lots of water."

We stood in the courtyard. A couple of big mastiffs growled at us. There was a small group of Normans breaking up an outdoor poker game as it got too dark to see—some of the Duke's many sons and grandsons. They swaggered past us into the main keep. Most of them were dressed in Renaissance style, though one wore a Chinese mandarin's robe. Some, the older ones, carried pistols as well as swords.

"I suppose we wait here till the Duke summons us. I hope it won't be long—I'm hungry." Don Miguel spoke to the Nubian porter: "If we are called for, we will be in the Wisdom's chamber, or else in the main gaming room."

The girl shuddered as we walked into the keep. Don Miguel laid a brotherly arm not quite about her waist. "There, there," he said. "We shall find out who thou art, and then we will get thee some wine and dress those hurts."

"How about the rest of her?" I asked.

"Oh, there is no hurry about that," he answered.

I felt a tingle of jealousy. Just lately, I'd lost my concubine in a crap game to Ethelwulf the Saxon—I'm not a harem keeper, I believe in one at a time—and had been thinking that this wench would make a nice replacement when she was patched up. But if a man's saved your life—oh, well. She kept looking in my direction anyway.

We went down long, stony corridors, hung with rich tapestries; the electric lights didn't drive away the gloom and chill, somehow. Now and then we'd pass a slave or a warrior, but no one paid any attention to us, in spite of the fact that I was only wearing breeks and that Don Miguel and I were both spattered with red. You got used to almost anything in the Nest.

"I thought the Duke was away this afternoon?" I said.

"He is. Off to survey the Danelaw. I fear me the poor English will be missing more than the Vikings ever took."

"Well," I said, "it's about time for another expedition anyway. The boys are getting restless." As a warrior third class—technically a musketeer—I had my own responsibilities and command. "And there ought to be good pickings in Saxon England; the Romano-Britons certainly had some fine things."

Don Miguel shrugged delicately. "I wish, my friend, thou wouldst not be quite so blunt about it," he said. "At any rate, Duke Hugo and his party should be back in time for dinner. They took the Rover out this morning."

The Normans were often pretty stupid. They could have brought the Rover back within a second of its leaving the Nest, no matter how long they stayed in the Danelaw, but no, they were too superstitious for that, they had to be gone all day. In fact, they'd never done any of the things they could have done with the machine, except just transport themselves and us. Oh, well, it was theirs.

We came to the fork in the hall. One branch of it went off toward the eating and gaming rooms, another to the guarded door beyond, which was the Rover's place. We took the third branch, toward the harem. That was guarded too, of course, by slaves whose size and strength hadn't been hurt much by Hugo's following the quaint custom of his father, Duke Roger of Sicily; but we didn't go that far. The girl shuddered and moaned as we started up a long stair into the north tower.

A fancy bronze door at its top opened into the Wisdom's laboratory. I slammed the rather gruesome knocker down, and pretty soon his dusty voice said to come in.

The lab was a huge room, most of it filled with bookshelves; an arched doorway led into a still bigger library. One end of the lab, though, was given over to grimoires, wands, skulls, a stuffed crocodile, bottles and flasks, an alembic, a spectroscope, and an induction furnace, for the Wisdom dabbled in alchemy. He came toward us, his long black robe sweeping the ground, his hairless head bent forward as he peered near-sightedly at us. "Ah," he murmured. "The Cro-Magnon and the hidalgo. What can I do for you, gentlemen?"

I never knew just where the Wisdom came from. Some said he was Victorian English, some said he was Reformation German, but my private guess is Byzantine Greek. He was here because of his impossibly good memory and scholar's brain. I don't think there ever was a book he couldn't translate or a language he couldn't soon learn, and if you gave him time and references, he'd tell you what you wanted to know about any sector. It saved a lot of firsthand casing of many joints. Then he was our interpreter and teacher of new arrivals. I didn't like him—nobody did—nasty cold-blooded snake—but we could hardly do without that big head of his.

"We got into a fight about this girl," I said. "Where's she from and so on?"

He blinked at her, touched her with long skinny fingers, tilted her head this way and that. She moaned again and shrank close to me. Finally he began to talk to her, trying this language and that. At one, she brightened a little, under the dirt and tears, and began to jabber back.

He nodded, rubbing his hands together with a dry scaly sound. "The daughter of a Babylonian merchant," he said. "Seventeen years old, carefully brought up. Some of our men snatched her during Assurbanipal's sack and brought her here. She resisted the attentions of the 'one in gray' as she calls him— a Nazi?—broke out of his house, and ran in terror. Then you rescued her. That is all."

"The poor child," said Don Miguel. There was a world of pity on his face. "I fear I shall burn in hell a long time for belonging to the Nest."

"What's her name?" I inquired.

"Oh—that." The Wisdom asked her. "Inini. Is that important?"

"Yes," said Don Miguel stiffly. "She is a human soul, not an animal."

"There is a difference?" The Wisdom shrugged. "Was there anything else?"

"No," I said. "No, I guess not. Thanks. Let's go get some chow."

Don Miguel was still biting his lip. He got those guilty spells now and then, though why he should blame himself, I don't know. He'd been in trouble with the Governor of México when he was located by one of our recruiters, and it was as much as his handsome head was worth to go home.

Now I don't mind a good healthy fight at all. When we took Knossos—yes, we were the ones who did that—or helped in any of several times from Brennus to Charles V, or worked in a hundred other wars, it was good honest battle and we earned our loot. You could say that when we lifted that Prussian city just ahead of the Soviet soldiers, we deserved its loot more than they. And my year of hijacking in Prohibition America—the only time I was ever allowed to carry a real firearm—was just clean fun. But in nearly ten years of the Nest and the Rover, I'd seen a lot of other things that turned my guts. Like this.

"Come on, Inini," I said. "Thou'rt among friends now." She managed a small trembling smile.

We were going out when the door opened before us. Captain Olga Rakitin stood there. Her gun came out as she saw us. "There ye are," she said, slowly. Her lips were drawn back, and her face was very white.

"Uh-huh," I answered. "What of it? Been looking for us?"

"Yes. Drop that ax! Drop it or I'll shoot!" Her voice rose high.

"What the holy hell—"

"Thou knowest who thou killed, Trebuen?" she asked shrilly.

"Some damn Nazi," I answered. My spine prickled, looking down the barrel of that gun. It threw explosive shells.

"No. Not a Nazi. Just a young fellow who admired them, liked to strut around in their costume. He didn't rate a gun yet, but his birth—Trebuen that was Reginald du Arronde. A grandson of the Duke."

There was a long thundering silence. Then Inini shrank back with a little scream, not knowing what went on but seeing death here. *"Nombre de Díos,"* muttered Don Miguel. "Judas priest," I said.

It felt like a blow in the belly. Duke Hugo had some first-class torturers.

Olga's voice was still wobbly. I'd never heard it that way before. "Come on," she said. "The others will find out any moment. Thou mightest as well come quietly with me."

I shook myself. My hands were cold and numb, and I had trouble talking. "No," I said. "Nothing doing, iceberg." I took a step toward her.

"Back!" she screamed. "Back or I'll shoot!"

"Go ahead," I answered. "Think I want to be boiled alongside my own stuffed skin?"

I took another step toward her, very slow and easy. The gun shook, *"Gospody!"* she yelled. "I *will* shoot, *me Hercule!*"

I sprang then, hitting her low. The gun went off like thunder and tore a hole in the ceiling. We fell with a crash. She hit me with her free hand, cursing in Russian. I wrenched the gun loose. She tried to knee me as I scrambled away. I got up and stood over her. She glared at me through tangled ruddy hair and spat like a wildcat.

Don Miguel had his sword out, the point just touching the Wisdom's throat. "Make one sound, *señor*," he purred, "and I trust you will be able to find a suitable guide into the lower regions."

The gun felt odd in my hand, lighter than the American rods. Those Martians built them good, though. I went to the door and peered out. A sound of voices came from below.

"They heard," I grunted. "Coming up the stairs. Gives merry hell now."

"Bar the door," snapped Don Miguel. He pricked the Wisdom's neck a little harder. "Dog of a heathen, I want rope. Swiftly!"

There was a tramping and clanking outside. The knocker banged, and fists thumped on the door. "Go away," quavered the Wisdom at Don Miguel's sharp insistence. "I am working. There is nothing here."

"Open up!" roared a voice. "We seek Trebuen and de Otrillo for the Duke's justice!"

The Wisdom was pulling lengths of cord from a chest and knotting them together. From the edge of an eye, I saw Inini creep timidly forth and test the knots. Smart girl. She didn't know the score, but she knew we had to take it on the lam quick.

"Open, I say!" bellowed the man outside. Other voices clamored behind him. "Open or we break in!"

I took my ax up in one hand, held the pistol in the other, and stood waiting. The door shook. I heard the hinge-rivets pulling loose. "Hurry that rope up, hidalgo," I said.

"It's not long enough yet—a frightful jump down to the court yard— More rope, thou devil, or I'll see thy liver!"

The door buckled.

There was a green-gray blur beside me. Olga's fist came down on my arm. I'd forgotten her! She yanked the gun from me and jumped back, gasping. I whirled to face her, and looked down its barrel. Inini screamed; Don Miguel ripped out a cussword that would cost him another year in Purgatory.

I looked at Olga. She was crouched, shaking, a blindness in her eyes. My brain felt cold and clear. I remembered something that had just happened, when I took the gun from her.

"Okay, iceberg, you win," I said. "I hope you enjoy watching us fry. That's your style, isn't it?" I said it in French, and used *vous* though we'd been *tu* before like the other warriors.

The door crashed down. A tall Norman burst in, with a tommy gun in his hands and hell in his face. I saw spears and swords behind him.

Olga gave a queer, strangled little noise and shot the Norman in the belly.

He pitched over, his gun clattering at my feet. No time to pick it up. I jumped across his body and split the skull of the Papuan behind him. As he fell, I smashed down the sword of a Tartar. A Goth stabbed at my back, I brought the ax around backhanded, catching him with the spike.

"Get out!" yelled Olga. "Get out! I'll hold them!" She fired into the mass of the men. I sent another head jumping free, whirled the ax around, and hit a *Pickelhaube*. My blade glanced off, but bit into the Uhlan's shoulder. A Vandal hollered and swung at me. I caught his blade in the notch I have in my haft, twisted it out of his hands, and cut him down.

They backed away then, snarling at us. There'd be men with guns any second. "Go, Trebuen," cried Don Miguel. "Get free!"

No time to argue with his Spanish pride. I had to be first, because only Olga and I really knew how to leap, and she had the gun. The rope was dangling out the window, knotted to a gargoyle. I took it in my hand and slid into the big darkness below. It scorched my palm.

When its end slipped away, I fell free, not knowing how far. I dropped the ax straight down, relaxed cat-fashion, and hit the stone flags hard enough to knock the wind out of me. About fifteen feet of drop . Staggering up, I yelled to the lighted window.

A dark shape showed against the tower wall—I could barely see it. Inini fell into my arms. Real smart girl—she'd snatched up that tommy gun. But it smashed across my mouth.

Olga came down under her own power. We both caught Don Miguel. Ever catch a man in helmet and corselet? I groaned and fumbled around for my ax while Olga shot at the figures peering out the window.

"This way," I said. "To the stables."

We ran around the high keep, toward the rear. The yard wasn't lit, it was all shadows under the stars. But a party of cops was coming around the other side of the donjon. I grabbed the tommy gun from Inini and gave them a burst. Just like hijacking days. A couple of javelins whizzed wickedly near me, then the cops retreated.

To the stables! Their long forms were like hills of night. I opened the door and went in. A slave groom whimpered and shrank into the straw. "Hold the door, Olga," I said.

"Da, kommissar." Was it a chuckle in her voice? No time for laughter. I switched on the lights and went down the rows of stalls. The place smelled nice and clean, hay and horses.

But it was good old Iggy and his rank alligator stink I was after. I found him at the end of the stalls, next to the Duke's armored jeep and his one tank. I wished we could take a machine, but the Duke had the keys. Anyway, a dinosaur can go where a tank can't. I thumped Iggy on his stupid snout till he bent over and I got the special saddle on his back.

Olga's gun was barking at the entrance. I heard other shots, rifles. When they brought up the big .50-caliber machine-guns that was the end of us. Don Miguel had saddled his Arab by the time I was done.

His face was pretty grim. "I fear we are surrounded," he said. "Can we break through?"

"We can try," I said. "Olga and I will lead on Iggy. You take Inini." I wished he could use the tommy gun—it was easy enough, but his stallion would bolt. The brute's eyes were already rolling. Praise be, dinosaurs are too dumb to know fear.

I led Iggy toward the door, where Olga was firing through the crack. "Hop on, icicle," I said.

Her face was a dim shadow and a few soft highlights as she turned to me. "What will we do?" she whispered. "What will we do but die?"

"I don't know. Let's find out." I scrambled into the saddle while she slammed and bolted the door. She jumped up in front of me; the seat was big enough for that, and we crouched there waiting.

The door shook and cracked and went down. "Whoop!" I yelled. "Giddap, boy!"

Iggy straightened, almost taking my head off as he went through the door. Olga had holstered her pistol and grabbed the tommy gun. She sprayed the mob before us. Iggy plowed right through them, trampling any that didn't get out of the way in time. Spears and swords and arrows bit at him, but he didn't mind, and his tall form shielded us.

Across the courtyard! Iggy broke into an earthshaking run as I spurred him with the ax spike. Don Miguel's horse galloped beside us. The moon was just starting to rise, shadows and white light weird between the high walls. A machine-gun opened up, hunting for us with fingers of fire.

They were closing the portcullis as we reached the main gate. Don Miguel darted ahead, the iron teeth clashing behind him. "Hang on!" I yelled. "Hang on! Go it, Iggy!"

The dinosaur grunted as he hit the barrier. The shock damn near threw me loose. I jammed my feet into the stirrups and clutched Olga to me. A ragged piece of iron furrowed my scalp. Then the portcullis tore loose and Iggy walked over it and on down the Street of St. Mark.

"This way!" cried Don Miguel, wheeling about. "Out of the Nest!"

We shook the ground on our way. Turning at Zulu House—Lobengula's exiled warriors still preferred barracks—we came out on Broadway and went down it to the Street of the Fishing Cat. Across Moloch Plaza, through an alley where Iggy scraped the walls, through an orchard that scattered like matchwood, and then we were out and away.

The Oligocene night was warm around us. A wet wind blew from across the great river, smell of reeds and muck and green water, the strong wild perfume of flowers that died with the glaciers. The low moon was orange-colored, huge on the rim of the world. I heard a nimravus screeching out in the dark, and the grunt and splash of some big mammal. Grass whispered around our mounts' legs. Looking behind me, I saw the castle all one blaze of light. It was the only building with electricity—the rest of them huddled in darkness, showing red and yellow fire-gleams. But there were torches bobbing in the streets.

Don Miguel edged closer to me. His face was a blur under the moonlit shimmer of his helmet. "Where do we go now, Trebuen?" he asked.

We had gotten away. Somehow, in some crazy fashion, we'd cut our way out. But before long, the Normans would be after us with dogs. They could trail us anywhere.

Swim the river—with the kind of fish they had there? I'd sooner take a few more Normans to hell with me.

"I think—" Olga's voice was as cool as it had always been. "I think they will not start hunting us before dawn. We are too dangerous in the dark. Perhaps we can put a good distance between in the meantime."

"Not too good," I answered. "The horse is carrying double, and Iggy just won't go very far; he'll lie down and go on strike after a few more miles. But yeah, I do think we have a breather. Let's rest."

We got off, tethered our mounts to a clump of trees, and sat down. The grass was cool and damp, and the earth smelled rich. Inini crept into my arms like a frightened little kid, and I held her close without thinking much about it. Mostly, I was drawing air into my lungs, looking at the stars and the rising moon, and thinking that life was pretty good. I'd be sorry to leave it.

Don Miguel spoke out of the shadow that was his face. "Señorita Olga," he said, "we owe our lives to thy kindness. Thou hast a Christian soul."

"Tchort!" She spoke coldly. I sat watching the moonlight shimmer on her hair. "I've had enough of the Nest, that's all."

I smiled to myself, just a little. I knew better, though maybe she didn't herself.

"How long hast thou been with us, iceberg?" I asked. "Five years, isn't it? Why didst thou enlist?"

She shrugged. "I was in trouble," she said. "I spoke my mind too freely. The Martian government resented it. I stole a spaceship and got to Earth, where I was not especially welcome either. While I was dodging Martian agents, I met one of Hugo's recruiters. What else could I do but join? I didn't like the 22nd Century much anyway."

I could understand that. And it wasn't strange she'd been picked up, out of all the reaches of time. Recruiters visited places where there were pirates and warriors, or else where there was an underworld. Olga would naturally have had something to do with the latter, she'd have had no choice with Soviet assassins after her. And she'd be wanted here for her technical knowledge, which was scarce in the Nest.

"Has the Duke or his men ever explored beyond thy century?" asked Don Miguel idly. A proper caballero wouldn't be thinking of his own coming death, he'd hold polite chitchat going till the end.

"No, I think not," she answered. "They would be afraid that the true owners of the Rover would detect them. It is in the anarchic periods where they can operate safely."

I wondered, not for the first time, what those builders were like, and where they were from. It must have been a pretty gentle, guileless culture, by all accounts. Some twenty historians and sociologists, making the mistake of dropping in on the court of Duke Roger of Sicily. But even though Roger himself had been off in Italy at the time, they might have foreseen that one of his illegitimate sons, young Hugo, would suspect these strangers weren't all they seemed. Just because a man is ignorant of science, he isn't necessarily stupid, but the time travelers overlooked that—which was costly for them when Hugo and some of his bravos grabbed them, tortured the facts out of them, and knocked them off. Of course, once that had happened, anyone could have predicted that those few Normans would take the Rover and go happily off to plunder through all space—on Earth, at least—and all time—short of some era where the Builders could find them; and that they'd slowly build up their forces by recruiting through the ages, until now—

"I wonder if the Builders ever *will* find us," mused Don Miguel.

"Hardly," said Olga. "Or they'd have been here before now. It seems pretty silly to hide out way back in the American Oligocene. But I must say the operations are shrewdly planned. No anachronistic weapons used, no possible historical record of our appearances—oh, yes."

"This era has a good climate, and no humans to give trouble," I said. "That's probably why Hugo picked it."

Inini murmured wearily. Her dark hair flowed softly over my arms as she stirred. Poor kid. Poor scared kid, snatched out of home and time into horror. "Look," I said, "are we just going to sit and take it? Can't we think of a way to hit back where it'll really hurt?"

It was funny how fast we'd all switched loyalties. None of us had ever much liked Duke Hugo or the company he kept, but the bandit's life had been a high and handsome one. In many ways, those had been good years. Only now— It was, somehow, more than the fact Hugo was out to fry our gizzards.

That was just the little nudge, which had overturned some kind of mountain inside us.

Olga spoke like a machine. "We are three—well, four, I suppose—possessed of two working guns, a sword, an ax, a horse, and a dinosaur. Against us are a good thousand fighting men, of whom a hundred or so possess firearms. Perhaps a few of our friends might swing to our side, out of comradeship or to sack the castle, but still the odds are ridiculous." She chuckled, a low pleasant sound in the murmuring night. "And as a Martian, I am Dostoyevskian enough to enjoy the fact a trifle."

Inini whispered something and raised her face. I bent my head and brushed her lips. Poor little slave! I wished she'd been mine from the start—everything would have been so much simpler.

Slaves!

I sat bolt upright, spilling Inini to the grass. By the horns of Pan and the eye of Odin—slaves!

"Five thousand slaves!"

"Eh?" Don Miguel came over to pick up the girl. "Thou'rt most unknightly at times, *amigo*... There, there, my little partridge, all is well, be calm..."

Olga got it right away. I heard her fist slam the ground.

"By Lenin! I think thou'st got it, Trebuen!"

Five thousand slaves, mostly male, penned up in a wire stockade, not very heavily guarded— Swiftly, we settled the plan of action. I showed Inini how to operate the tommy gun; she caught on fast and laughed savagely in the dark. I hoped she wouldn't shoot the wrong people. Then we mounted and trotted back toward the Nest, changing women passengers this time.

The moon had now cleared the eastern forests and was flooding the plain. It was a white, cold, unreal light, dripping from the grass, spattering the trees, gleaming off water and Don Miguel's armor. I swore at it. Damn the moon, anyway! We needed darkness.

We swung far around the Nest, to approach it from the side of the slave pens. Luckily, there was a lot of orchard there. Trees grew fast in the Oligocene, these were tall ones. Twigs and leaves brushed my face, branches creaked and snapped as Iggy went through them, speckles of light broke the thick shadows. I halted on the edge of the shelter and looked across a hundred feet toward the pens. The castle beyond was black against the high stars, most of its lights turned off again. The hunt for us must have died down in the hour or two we'd been gone.

The pens were a long double row of wooden barracks fenced in with charged wire. There was a wooden guard tower, about thirty feet high, on each side, with searchlights and machineguns on top; but there'd only be a few men on each. Olga slid off the horse—her gun would frighten it too much—but Inini stayed with me, sitting in front and cradling her weapon. Nothing moved. It was all black and white and silence there under the moon. I licked my lips; they felt like sandpaper, and my heart was thumping. Two minutes from now we might be so much cold meat.

"Okay, Iggy." I nudged him with my heels, trying to hold my voice hard. "Let's go. *Giddap!*"

He broke into that lumbering run of his. The shock of his footfalls jarred back into me. Someone yelled, far and faint. The searchlights glared out, grabbing after me. I heard the machine-gun begin stuttering, and crouched low behind Iggy's neck. He grunted as the slugs hit him. Then he got mad.

We hit the tower full on, and I nearly pitched out of the saddle. Wood thundered and crashed around me. The machine-gunners screamed and tried to drag their weapon over to the parapet. Iggy heaved against the walls; they buckled, and the lights went out. Then the tower caved in around us. Something hit me, stars exploded, and I hung on in a whirling darkness.

Iggy was trampling the beams underfoot. Wires snapped, and the juice in them blazed and crackled. One of the guards, still on his feet, tried to run for help. Inini cut him down.

The gun on the other side of the stockade began hammering. I shook my head, trying to clear it. "Go get 'em, Iggy! Goddam thee, go get that gunner!" He was too busy stamping on the tower we'd just demolished to notice. His breath was hissing as he wrecked it.

Olga dashed past us on foot, shooting at the other post. She was hard to see in that tricky light. The tracer bullets marked the gun for her. Bullets were sleeting around me now. A few slaves began coming out of the barracks, yelling their panic.

Iggy finally made up his stupid mind that the slugs still hitting him now and then were from the other tall shape. He turned and ran to do battle. Inini fired ahead of us as we charged. Olga had to jump to get out of the way. Iggy started pulling down the tower.

Don Miguel was shouting to the slaves as they boiled out of their houses. "Forward, comrades! On to liberty! Kill your oppressors!" They gaped at his sword. God! Wouldn't they ever catch on?

Men must be pouring from the Nest now. I kicked and cursed, trying to face my idiotic mount around to meet them. The tower began crumpling. It went down in a slow heave of timbers and splinters. Don Miguel was still haranguing the slaves. Trouble was, about the only ones who knew much Norman French had been here so long the spirit was beaten out of them. The newcomers, who might fight, didn't know what he was talking of.

A horn blew from the castle hill. Turning my face from where Iggy stood over the ruins, I saw metal flash in the moonlight. Hoofs rolled their noise through the ground. Cavalry! And if the Duke got his armored vehicles going—

Olga darted almost under Iggy's feet, to where the machine-gun lay on its splintered platform. She heaved it back into position and crouched over it. As the horsemen entered the stockade, she cut loose.

They broke, screaming. Huns and Tartars, mostly, with some mounted Normans and others. Bullets whined from their side, badly aimed in the confusion.

I heard a slow drawl from down under me. Looking, I saw a tall man in the tattered leavings of a gray uniform. "So thet's the idee," he called. "Whah, stranger, you should'a said so the fuhst time."

"Who the hell are you?" I found time to gasp in English.

"Captain Jebel Morrison, late o' the Red Horse Cavalry, Confederate States of America, at yo' suhvice. The buzzahds grabbed me an' mah boys when we was on patrol in Tennessee— All right, y'all!" He turned back to the milling, muttering slaves and shouted: "Kill the Yankees!"

There was a scattering of rebel yells, and some other men came running out toward him. They snatched swords and spears from the riders we'd cut down, let out that blood-freezing screech once more, and trotted toward the entrance of the pen.

"So 'tis smite the Papists, eh?" roared an English voice. "Truly the hand of the Lord is on us!" And a bull-necked Roundhead darted after the Southerners.

"Allah akbar!"—*"Vive la republique!"*—*"Hola, Odin!"*—*"St. George for merrie England!"*—*"Ave, Caesar!"*— The mob spirit caught them, and the huge dark mass of men surged forth toward the Nest. About half the slaves, the rest were still afraid, and they were unarmed and unprotected—but God, how they hated!

Don Miguel galloped forth to put himself at their head. I cursed Iggy and beat him on the snout till he turned around and lumbered after them. Inini laughed shrilly and waved her tommy gun in the air. We broke out of the pen and rolled in one swarm against the enemy.

Somebody reached up to touch my leg. I saw Olga trotting beside me; she'd grabbed one of those Hunnish ponies stampeding around the pen. "I didn't know thou wert a cowboy!" I yelled at her.

"Neither did I!" Her teeth gleamed in the moonlight as she laughed back at me. "But I'd better learn fast!" She snubbed in the pony's neck as it skittered. I suppose her interplanetary flying had trained nerve and muscle—

It must have been bare minutes from the time we first charged the stockade. Only the castle guard had been ready to fight us. But now as we entered the streets, going down long white lanes of moon between the black forms of houses, I saw the bandits rallying. Shots began to crack again. Men crumpled in our ranks. We had to hit them before they got organized.

We went over one thin line of Romans with a rush, grabbing up their weapons. Circling the castle hill, we began mounting it on the side of the broken portcullis. Men were streaming from the houses and dashing toward our host. It was a bad light for shooting guns or arrows, but plenty bright enough for a sword.

Inini and Olga blazed at them as they came up the Street of St. Mark. No one could miss a bunch of men, and both sides were having heavy loss; but individuals, like myself, were hard to hit. I saw the attackers recoil and churn about, waiting for reinforcements. We struggled on up the hill, in the face of gunfire from the castle.

The bandits behind us were piling up now, into a solid wall of armed men across the street. I lifted my voice and bellowed: "Who wants to overthrow the castle?"

They hesitated, swaying back and forth. Suddenly a shout rose. "By Tyr! I do!" A couple of men pitched aside as Thorkel the Berserk darted toward us. Inini fired at him. I slapped her gun aside. "Not him, wench!"

Hoofs clattered on the street. I saw moonlight like water on the lacquered leather breastplates of Belgutai's Mongol troop. *God help us now*, I thought, and then the Mongols crashed into the other bandits. Belgutai had always been a good friend of mine.

Steel hammered on steel as they fought. I knew that a lot of those wolves would switch to our side if they thought we had a fair chance of winning. Hugo had trained them to steal anything that wasn't welded down, and then stuffed his own home with loot—a mistake, that! But we had to take the castle before we could count on turncoats to help us.

We were up under the walls now, out of reach of the tower guns, but our numbers were fearfully reduced. The slaves weren't running forth so fast now, they were beginning to be afraid. I jabbed Iggy with my ax, driving him forward against the gate and its rifle-armed defenders. We hit them like a tornado, and they fled.

I was hardly in the courtyard before a new bellowing lifted. The tank was coming around the keep. It was a light one, 1918 model, but it could easily stop our whole force. For a minute, my world caved in around me.

The tank's machine-guns opened up on Iggy. He'd already been wounded, and this must have hurt. He hissed and charged. I saw what was coming, dropped my ax, and jumped to the ground. Inini followed me. We hit the pavement and rolled over and bounced up again.

Iggy was crawling on top of the tank, trying to rip steel apart. His blood streamed over the metal, he was dying, but the poor brave brute was too dumb to know it. The tank growled, backing up. Iggy slapped his big stiff tail into the treads. The tank choked to a halt. Its cannon burped at us. The shell exploded against the gateway arch. Iggy stamped a foot down on the barrel and it twisted. Someone opened the turret and threw out a grenade. It burst against Iggy's throat. He got his taloned forepaws into the turret and began pulling things into chunks. Even a dying dinosaur is no safe playmate.

There was fighting all around the courtyard. A lot of the men with guns must have been disposed of by now. Those of the slaves who knew how to use firearms were grabbing them out of the hands of bandits who'd been mobbed, and turning them on the Normans. The rest of our boys were seizing axes, spears, swords, and chopping loose. Captain Morrison had somehow—God knows how—managed to hold them more or less together. The Normans and their cohorts charging out of the keep joined forces and hit that little army. It became hand-to-hand, and murder.

I was only hazily aware of all that. Olga came running up to me as I got on my feet. Her pony must have been shot from under her. "What now?" she cried. "What should we do?"

"Get to the Rover," I said. "It's the only way—they're better armed than we, they'll finish us unless—"

Don Miguel was fighting a mounted knight. He cut him down and clattered over to us as we and Inini ran for the keep. "With ye, my friends," he cried gaily. I imagine this work was taking a lot of guilt off his conscience. Maybe that was one reason why some of the other bandits, down in the street, had thrown in with us.

We ran along the hallway. It was empty except for some terrified women. Around a bend of the forbidden corridor was the Rover. I skidded to a halt. Machine-gunners watched over it. "Gimme that!" I snatched the tommy gun from Inini and burst around the corner, firing. The two Mamelukes dropped.

The door was locked. I took my ax this time, and battered at it. Wood splintered before me. I turned at Olga's yell and the bark of her gun. A party of Normans, a good dozen of them, was attacking. I saw Duke Hugo's burly white-haired form in the lead. They must have heard the racket and—

They were on us before we could use our guns to stop them. A sword whistled above my head as I ducked. I reached up and cut at the hands. As the man fell against me, screaming, I flung him into another chainmailed figure. They went down with a clash. Two-handed, I bashed in a skull. Hugo had a revolver almost in my belly. I slewed the ax around and knocked it from him with the flat of the weapon. His sword hissed free before I could brain him. It raked me down the side as I dodged. I smashed at his unhelmeted head, but he turned the blow.

"Haro!" he yelled. Edged metal whined down against my haft. I twisted the ax, forcing his blade aside. My left fist jumped out into his face. He staggered back, and I killed him.

Don Miguel's horse was pulled down and slain, but he was laying merrily around him. We cleared a space between us. Then Olga and Inini could use their guns.

I went back to the door and smashed it in. We broke into the high chamber. The Rover lay there, a tapered hundred-foot cylinder. Inside, I knew, it was mostly empty space, with a few simple dials and studs. I'd watched it being operated.

Don Miguel grabbed my arm as I entered. "We can't leave our comrades out there Trebuen!" he gasped. "As soon as the Normans get organized it will be slaughter."

"I know," I said. "Come on inside, though, all of you."

When I turned a certain dial, the Rover moved. There was no sense of it within us, only a glowing light told us we were on our way through time. A thousand years in the future.

Hugo had never checked his own tomorrows, and wouldn't let anyone else do it. That was understandable, I guess, especially if you were a medieval man. I couldn't resist looking out. The chamber was still there, but it was dark and still, thick with dust, and some animal, which had made its lair here, scrambled away in alarm. The castle was empty. In a million years or so of rain and wind, and finally the glaciers grinding down over it, no trace would be left.

I drew a shuddering sigh into the stillness. But I knew I was going back. We'd left a lot of friends back there in the mess of the Nest. And besides, I'd always had an idea about the Rover. Those Normans had been too superstitious to try it, but it should work. Don Miguel swore, but agreed. And Olga helped me work out the details. Then we took off.

The verniers were marked in strange numerals, but you could read them all right, once you'd figured them out. And the Rover was accurate to a second or less. We jumped back to within one second of our departure time.

The rest of the fight is blurred. I don't *want* to remember the next twenty minutes—or twenty-four hours, depending on how you look at it. We stepped out of the machine. We turned and went quickly from the chamber. As we reached its door, the machine appeared again, next to itself, and three dim figures came out. I looked away from my own face. Soon there was a mob of ourselves there.

We stuck together, running out and firing. Twenty minutes later, each time we finished, we'd dart back to the Rover, jump it into the future, and return within one second and some feet of our last departure point. There were a good three hundred of us, all brought to the same time, approximately. And in a group like that, we had firepower. It was too much for the enemy. Screaming about witchcraft, they finally threw down their weapons and ran. I hate to think about seventy-five of myself acting as targets at the same time, though. It would only have needed one bullet.

But twenty minutes after the last trip, our messed-up time lines straightened out, and the four of us were all there—victors.

I stood on the castle walls, looking over the Nest as sunrise climbed into the sky. Places were burning here and there, and bodies were strewn across the ground. The bandits who'd fought with us or surrendered were holed up in a tower, guarding themselves against the slaves who were running wild as they celebrated their freedom. I only allowed firearms to those people I could trust, so now I was king of the Nest.

Olga came to me where I stood. The damp morning wind ruffled her hair, and her eyes were bright in spite of the weariness in us all. She'd changed her ragged uniform for a Grecian dress, and its white simplicity was beautiful on her.

We stood side by side for awhile, not speaking. Finally I shook my head. "I don't feel too happy about this, iceberg," I said. "In its own way, the Nest was something glorious."

"Was?" she asked softly.

"Sure. We can't start it up again—at least I can't, after this night. I've seen enough bloodshed for the rest of my life. We'll

THE NEST

have to organize things here, and return everyone to whatever time they pick; not all of them will want to go home, I suppose. I don't think I will. Life with The Men would be sort of—limited, after this."

She nodded. "I can do without my own century too," she said. "It could be fun to keep on exploring in time for awhile, till I find some era I really want to settle down in."

I looked at her, and slowly the darkness lifted from me. "Till *we* do," I said.

"We?" She frowned. "Don't get ideas, Sir Caveman." Her lips trembled. "Thou and th-th-thy Babylonian wench..."

"Oh, Inini's a sweet kid," I grinned. "Don Miguel was giving her the old line when I saw them last, and she seemed to enjoy it. But she'd be kind of dull for me."

"Of all the insufferable, conceited—"

"Look," I said patiently, "thou couldst easily have shot me when I first grabbed for thy gun. But underneath, thou didn't want to—be honest, now!—so thou missed. And I don't think thou changed sides a little later because of a sudden attack of conscience, any more than the rest of us, iceberg." I switched into Americanese, with Elizabethan overtones. "C'mere, youse, and let me clutch thee!"

She did.

THE END

Honorable Enemies

Earth was tired, Earthmen weary of the pomp of empire. Yet, survival dictated that the balance of power be maintained. But, how could the necessary diplomacy be carried out when one's rival intriguers could read minds?

CHAPTER ONE

THE DOOR SWUNG OPEN behind him and a voice murmured gently: "Good evening, Captain Flandry."

He spun around, grabbing for his stun pistol in a wild reflex, and found himself looking down the muzzle of a blaster. Slowly, then, he let his hands fall and stood taut, his eyes searching beyond the weapon, and the slender six-fingered hand that held it, to the tall gaunt body and the sardonically smiling face behind.

The face was humanoid—lean, hawk-nosed, golden-skinned, with brilliant amber eyes under feathery blue brows, and a high crest of shining blue feathers rising from the narrow hairless skull. The being was dressed in the simple white tunic of his people, leaving his clawed avian feet bare, but there were insignia of rank bejeweled around his neck and a cloak like a gush of blood from his wide shoulders. A Merseian.

But they'd all been occupied elsewhere—Flandry had seen to that. What had slipped up—?

With an effort, Flandry relaxed and let a wry smile cross his face. Never mind who was to blame; he was trapped in the Merseian chambers and had to think of a way to escape with a whole skin. His mind whirred with thought. Memory came—this was Aycharaych of Chereion, who had come to join the Merseian embassy only a few days before, presumably on some mission corresponding to Flandry's.

"Pardon the intrusion," he said, "it was purely professional. No offense meant."

"And none taken," said Aycharaych politely. He spoke faultless Anglic, only the faintest hint of his race's harsh accent in the syllables. But courtesy between spies was meaningless. It would be too easy to blast down the intruder and later express his immense regret that he had shot down the ace intelligence officer of the Terrestrial Empire under the mistaken impression that it was a burglar.

Somehow, though, Flandry didn't think that the Chereionite would be guilty of such crudeness. His mysterious people were too old, too coldly civilized, and Aycharaych himself had too great a reputation for subtlety. Flandry had heard of him before; he would be planning something worse.

"That is quite correct," nodded Aycharaych. Flandry started—could the being guess his exact thoughts? "But if you will pardon my saying so, you yourself have committed a bit of clumsiness in trying to search our quarters. There are better ways of getting information."

Flandry gauged distances and angles. There was a vase on a table close to hand. If he could grab it up and throw it at Aycharaych's gun hand—

The blaster waved negligently. "I would advise against the attempt," said the Chereionite.

He stood aside. "Good evening, Captain Flandry," he said.

The Terran moved toward the door. He couldn't let himself be thrown out this way, not when his whole mission depended on finding out what the Merseians were up to. If he could make a sudden lunge as he passed close—

He threw himself sideways with a twisting motion that brought him under the blaster muzzle. Hampered by a greater gravity than the folk of his small planet were used to, Ayharaych couldn't dodge quickly enough. But he swung the blaster with a vicious precision across Flandry's jaw. The Terran stumbled, clasping the Chereionite's narrow waist. Aycharaych slugged him at the base of the skull and he fell to the floor.

He lay there a moment, gasping, blood running from his face. Aycharaych's voice jeered at him from a roaring darkness: "Really, Captain Flandry. I had thought better of you. Now please leave."

Sickly, the Terran crawled to his feet and went out the door. Aycharaych stood in the entrance watching him go, a faint smile on his hard, gaunt visage.

FLANDRY WENT DOWN endless corridors of polished stone to the suite given the Terrestrial mission. Most of them were at the feast, the ornate rooms stood almost empty. He threw himself into a chair and signaled his personal slave for a drink. A stiff one.

There was a light step and the suggestive whisper of a long silkite skirt behind him. He looked around and saw Aline Chang-Lei, the Lady Marr of Syrtis, his partner on the mission and one of Sol's loveliest women—as well as one of its top field agents for intelligence.

She was tall and slender, dark of hair and eye, with the high cheekbones and ivory skin, of a mixed heritage such as most Terrans showed these days; her sea-blue gown did little more than emphasize the appropriate features. Flandry liked to look at her, though he was pretty well immune to beautiful women by now.

"What was the trouble?" she asked at once.

"What brings you here?" he responded. "I thought you'd be at the party, helping distract everyone."

"I just wanted to rest for a while," she said. "Official functions at Sol get awfully dull and stuffy, but they go to the other extreme at Betelgeuse. I wanted to hear silence for a while." And then, with grave concern: "But you ran into trouble."

"How the hell it happened, I can't imagine," said Flandry. "Look—we prevailed on the Sartaz to throw a brawl with everybody invited. We made double sure that every Merseian on the planet would be there. They'd trust to their robolocks to keep their quarters safe—they have absolutely no way of knowing that I've found a way to nullify a robolock. So what happens? I no sooner get inside than Aycharaych of Chereion walks in with a blaster in his hot little hand. He anticipates everything I try and finally shows me the door. Finis."

"Aycharaych—I've heard the name somewhere. But it doesn't sound Merseian."

"It isn't. Chereion is an obscure but very old planet in the Merseian Empire. Its people have full citizenship with the dominant race, just as our empire grants Terrestrial citizenship to many non-humans. Aycharaych is one of Merseia's leading intelligence agents. Few people have heard of him, precisely because he is so good. I've never clashed with him before, though."

"I know whom you mean now," she nodded. "If he's as you say, and he's here on Alfzar, it isn't good news."

Flandry shrugged. "We'll just have to take him into account, then. As if this mission weren't tough enough!"

HE GOT UP AND WALKED to the balcony window. The two moons of Alfzar were up, pouring coppery light on the broad reach of the palace gardens. The warm wind blew in with scent of strange flowers that had never bloomed under Sol and they caught the faint sound of the weird, tuneless music, which the monarch of Betelgeuse favored.

For a moment, as he looked at the ruddy moonlight and the thronging stars, Flandry felt a wave of discouragement. The Galaxy was too big. Even the four million stars of the Terrestrial Empire were too many for one man ever to know in a lifetime. And there were the rival imperia out in the darkness of space, Gorrazan and Ythri and Merseia, like a hungry beast of prey—

Too much, too much. The individual counted for too little in the enormous chaos, which was modern civilization. He thought of Aline—it was her business to know who such beings as Aycharaych were, but one human skull couldn't hold a universe; knowledge and power were lacking.

Too many mutually alien races; too many forces clashing in space, and so desperately few who comprehended the situation and tried their feeble best to help—naked hands battering at an avalanche as it ground down on them.

Aline came over and took his arm. Her white lovely face turned up to his, vague in the moonlight, with a look he knew too well. He'd have to avoid her, when or if they got back to Terra; he didn't want to hurt her but neither could he be tied to any single human.

"You're discouraged with one failure?" she asked lightly. "Dominic Flandry, the single-handed conqueror of Scothania, worried by one skinny bird-being?"

"I just don't see how he knew I was going to search his place," muttered Flandry. "I've never been caught that way before, not even when I was the worst cub in the Service. Some of our best men have gone down before Aycharaych. I'm convinced MacMurtrie's disappearance at Polaris was his work. Maybe it's our turn now."

"Oh, come off it," she laughed. "You must have been drinking *sorgan* when they told you about him."

"*Sorgan?*" His brows lifted.

"Ah, now I can tell you something you don't know." She was trying desperately hard to be gay. "Not that it's very important; I only happened to hear of it while talking with one of the Alfzarian narcotics detail. It's just a drug produced on one of the planets here—Cingetor I think—with the curious property of depressing certain brain centers such that the victim loses all critical sense. He has absolute faith in whatever he's told."

"Hmm. Could be useful in our line of work."

"Not very. Hypnoprobes are better for interrogation, and there are more reliable ways of producing fanatics. The drug has an antidote, which also confers permanent immunity. So it's not much use, really, and the Sartaz has suppressed its manufacture."

"I should think our Intelligence would like to keep a little on hand, just in case," he said thoughtfully. "And of course certain nobles in all the empires, ours included, would find it handy for purposes of seduction."

"What *are* you thinking of?" she teased him.

"Nothing; I don't need it," he said smugly.

The digression had shaken him out of his dark mood. "Come on," he said. "Let's go join the party."

She went along at his side. There was a speculative look about her.

CHAPTER TWO

USUALLY THE GIANT stars have many planets, and Betelgeuse, with forty-seven, is no exception. Of these, six have intelligent native races, and the combined resources of the whole system are considerable, even in a civilization used to thinking in terms of thousands of stars.

When the first Terrestrial explorers arrived, almost a thousand years previously, they found that the people of Alfzar had already mastered interplanetary travel and were in the process of conquering the other worlds—a process speeded up by their rapid adoption of the more advanced human technology. However, they had not attempted to establish an empire on the scale of Sol or Merseia, contenting themselves with maintaining hegemony over enough neighbor suns to protect themselves. There had been clashes with the expanding powers around them, but generations of wily Sartazes had found it profitable to play their potential enemies off against each other; and the great states had, in turn, found it expedient to maintain Betelgeuse as a buffer against their rivals and against the peripheral barbarians.

But the gathering tension between Terra and Merseia had raised Betelgeuse to a position of critical importance. Lying squarely between the two great empires, she was in a position with her powerful fleet to command the most direct route between them and if allied with either one, to strike at the heart of the other. If Merseia could get the alliance, it would very probably be the last preparation she considered necessary for war with Terra. If Terra could get it, Merseia would suddenly be in a deteriorated position and would almost have to make concessions.

So both empires had missions on Alfzar trying to persuade the Sartaz of the rightness of their respective causes and the immense profits to be had by joining. Pressure was being applied wherever possible; officials were lavishly bribed; spies were swarming through the system getting whatever information they could and—of course—being immediately disowned by their governments if they were caught.

It was normal diplomatic procedure, but its critical importance had made the Service send two of its best agents, Flandry and Aline, to Betelgeuse to do what they could in persuading the Sartaz, finding out his weaknesses, and throwing as many monkey wrenches as possible into the Merseian activities. Aline was especially useful in working on the many humans who had settled in the system long before and become citizens of the kingdom—quite a few of them held important positions in the government and the military. Flandry—

And now, it seemed, Merseia had called in *her* top spy, and the subtle, polite, and utterly deadly battle was on.

THE SARTAZ GAVE A hunting party for his distinguished guests. It pleased his sardonic temperament to bring enemies together under conditions where they had to be friendly to each other. Most of the Merseians must have been pleased, too; hunting was their favorite sport. The more citified Terrestrials were not at all happy about it, but they could hardly refuse.

Flandry was especially disgruntled at the prospect. He had never cared for physical exertion, though he kept his wiry body in trim as a matter of necessity. And he had too much else to do.

Too many things were going disastrously wrong. The network of agents, both Imperial and bribed Betelgeusean—who ultimately were under his command—were finding the going suddenly rugged. One after another, they disappeared; they walked into Merseian or Betelgeusean traps; they found their best approaches blocked by unexpected watchfulness. Flandry couldn't locate the source of the difficulty, but since it had begun with Aycharaych's arrival, he could guess. The Chereionite was too damned smart to be true. Sunblaze, it just wasn't possible that anyone could have known about those Jurovian projects, or that Yamatsu's hiding place should have been discovered, or— And now this damned hunting party! Flandry groaned.

His slave roused him in the dawn. Mist, tinged with blood by the red sun, drifted through the high windows of his suite. Someone was blowing a horn somewhere, a wild call in the vague mysterious light, and he heard the growl of engines warming up.

"Sometimes," he muttered sourly, "I feel like going to the Emperor and telling him where to put our beloved Empire."

Breakfast made the universe slightly more tolerable. Flandry dressed with his usual finicky care; an ornate suit of skin-tight green and a golden cloak with hood and goggles, hung a needle gun and dueling sword at his waist, and let the slave trim his reddish-brown mustache to the micrometric precision he demanded. Then he went down long flights of marble stairs, past royal guards in helmet and corselet, to the courtyard.

The hunting party was gathering. The Sartaz himself was present, a typical Alfzarian humanoid—short, stocky, hairless, blue-skinned, with huge yellow eyes in the round, blunt-faced head. There were other nobles of Alfzar and its fellow planets, more guardsmen, a riot of color in the brightening dawn. There were the other members of the regular Terrestrial embassy and the special mission, a harried and unhappy-looking crew. And there were the Merseians.

Flandry gave them all formal greetings—after all, Terra and Merseia were nominally at peace, however many men were being shot and cities burning on the marches. His gray eyes looked sleepy and indifferent, but they missed no detail of the enemy's appearance.

The Merseian nobles glanced at him with the thinly covered contempt they had for all humans. They were mammals, but with more traces of reptilian ancestry in them than Terrans showed. A huge-thewed two meters they stood, with a spiny ridge running from forehead to the end of the long, thick tail, which they could use to such terrible effect in hand-to-hand battle. Their hairless skins were pale green, faintly scaled, but their massive faces were practically human. Arrogant black eyes under heavy brow ridges met Flandry's gaze with a challenge.

I can understand that they despise us, he thought. Their civilization is young and vigorous, its energies turned ruthlessly outward; Terra is old, satiated—decadent. Our whole policy is directed toward maintaining the Galactic status quo, not because we love peace but because we're comfortable the way things are. We stand in the way of Merseia's dream of an all-embracing Galactic Empire. We're the first ones they have to smash.

I wonder—historically, they may be on the right side. But Terra has seen too much bloodshed in her history, has too wise and weary a view of life. We've given up seeking perfection and glory; we've learned that they're chimerical—but that knowledge is a kind of death within us.

Still—I certainly don't want to see planets aflame and humans enslaved and an alien culture taking up the future. Terra is willing to compromise; but the only compromise Merseia will ever make is with overwhelming force. Which is why I'm here.

THERE WAS A STIR IN the streaming red mist, and Aycharaych's tall form was beside him. The Chereionite's lean face smiled amiably at him. "Good morning, Captain Flandry," he said.

"Oh—good morning," said Flandry, starting. The avian unnerved him. For the first time, he had met his professional superior, and he didn't like it.

But he couldn't help liking Aycharaych personally. As they stood waiting, they fell to talking of Polaris and its strange worlds, from which the conversation drifted to the comparative "anthropology" of intelligent primitives throughout the Galaxy. Aycharaych had a vast fund of knowledge and a wry humor matching Flandry's. When the horn blew for assembly, they exchanged the regretful glance of brave enemies. *It's too bad we have to be on opposite sides. If things had been different—*

But they weren't.

The hunters strapped themselves into their tiny one-man airjets. There was a needle-beam projector in the nose of each one, not too much armament when you hunted the Borthudian dragons. Flandry thought that the Sartaz would be more than pleased if the game disposed of one or more of his guests.

The squadron lifted into the sky and streaked northward for the mountains. Fields and forests lay in dissolving fog below them, and the enormous red disc of Betelgeuse was rising into a purplish sky. Despite himself, Flandry enjoyed the reckless speed and the roar of cloven air around him. It was godlike, this rushing over the world to fight the monsters at its edge.

In a couple of hours, they raised the Borthudian mountains, gaunt windy peaks rearing into the upper sky, the snow on their flanks like blood in the ominous light. Signals began coming over the radio; scouts had spotted dragons here and there, and jet after jet broke away to pursue them. Presently Flandry found himself alone with one other vessel.

As they hummed over fanged crags and swooping canyons, he saw two shadows rise from the ground and his belly muscles tightened. Dragons!

The monsters were a good ten meters of scaled, snake-like length, with jaws and talons to rend steel. Huge leathery wings bore them aloft, riding the wind with lordly arrogance as they hunted the great beasts that terrorized villagers but were their prey.

Flandry kicked over his jet and swooped for one of them. It grew monstrously in his sights; he caught the red glare of its eyes as it banked to meet him. No running away here; the dragons had never learned to be afraid. It rose against him.

He squeezed his trigger and a thin sword of energy leaped out to burn past the creature's scales into its belly. The dragon held to its collision course. Flandry rolled out of its way; the mighty wings clashed meters from him.

He had not allowed for the tail. It swung savagely, and the blow shivered the teeth in his skull. The airjet reeled and went into a spin. The dragon stooped down on it, and the terrible claws ripped through the thin hull.

WILDLY, FLANDRY slammed over his controls, tearing himself loose. He barrel-rolled, metal screaming as he swung about to meet the charge. His needle beam lashed into the open jaws and the dragon stumbled in mid-flight. Flandry pulled away and shot again, flaying one of the wings.

He could hear the dragon's scream. It rushed straight at him, swinging with fantastic speed and precision as he sought to dodge. The jaws snapped together and a section of hull skin was torn from the framework. Wind came in to sear the man with numbing cold.

Recklessly, he dove to meet the plunging monster, his beam before him like a lance. The dragon recoiled. With a savage grin, Flandry pursued, slashing and tearing.

The torn airjet handled clumsily. In mid-flight, it lurched and the dragon was out of his sights. Its wings buffeted him and he went spinning aside with the dragon after him.

The damned thing was forcing him toward the cragged mountainside. Its peaks reached hungrily after him, and the wind seemed to be a demon harrying him closer to disaster. He swung desperately, aware with sudden grimness that it had become a struggle for life with the odds on the dragon's side.

If this was the end, to be shattered against a mountain and eaten by his own quarry— He fought for control.

The dragon was almost on him rushing down like a thunderbolt. It could survive a collision, but the jet would be knocked to earth. Flandry fired again, struggling to pull free. The dragon swerved and came on in the very teeth of his beam.

Suddenly it reeled and fell aside. The other jet was on it from behind, searing it with deadly precision. Flandry thought briefly that the remaining dragon must be dead or escaped and now its hunter had come to his aid—all the gods bless him, whoever he was!

Even as he watched, the dragon fell to earth, writhing and snapping as it died. It crashed onto a ledge and lay still.

Flandry brought his jet to a landing nearby. He was shaking with reaction, but his chief emotion was a sudden overwhelming sadness. There went another brave creature down into darkness, wiped out by a senseless history that seemed only to have the objective of destroying. He raised a hand in salute as he grounded.

The other jet had already landed a few meters off. As Flandry opened his cockpit canopy, its pilot stepped out.

Aycharaych.

The man's reaction was almost instantaneous. Gratitude and honor had no part in the grim code of the Service—here was his greatest enemy, all unsuspecting, and it would be the simplest thing in the world to shoot him down. Aycharaych of Chereion, lost in a hunt for dangerous game, too bad—and remorse could come later, when there was time—

His needle pistol was halfway from the holster when Aycharaych's weapon was drawn. Through the booming wind, he heard the alien's quiet voice: "No."

He raised his own hands, and his smile was bitter. "Go ahead," he invited. "You've got the drop on me."

"Not at all," said Aycharaych. "Believe me, Captain Flandry, I will never kill you except in self-defense. But since I will always be forewarned of your plans, you may as well abandon them."

The man nodded, too weary to feel the shock of the tremendous revelation which was here. "Thanks," he said. "For saving my life, that is."

"You're too useful to die," replied Aycharaych candidly; "but I'm glad of it."

They took the dragon's head and flew slowly back toward the palace. Flandry's mind whirled with a gathering dismay.

There was only one way in which Aycharaych could have known of the murder plan, when it had sprung into instantaneous being. And that same fact explained how he knew of every activity and scheme the Terrestrials tried, and how he could frustrate everyone of them while his own work went on unhampered.

Aycharaych could read minds.

CHAPTER THREE

ALINE'S FACE was white and tense in the red light that streamed into the room. "No," she whispered.

"Yes," said Flandry grimly. "It's the only answer."

"But telepathy—everyone knows its limitations—"

Flandry nodded. "The mental patterns of different races are so alien that a telepath who can sense them has to learn a different 'language' for every species—in fact, for every individual among non-telepathic peoples, whose minds, lacking mutual contact, develop purely personal thought-types. Even then it's irregular and unreliable. I've never let myself be studied by any telepath not on our side, so I'd always considered myself safe.

"But Chereion is a very old planet. Its people have the reputation among the more superstitious Merseians of being sorcerers. Actually, of course, it's simply that they've discovered certain things about the nervous system, which nobody else suspects yet. Somehow, Aycharaych must be able to detect some underlying resonance-pattern common to all intelligent beings.

"I'm sure he can only read surface thoughts, those in the immediate consciousness. Otherwise he'd have found out so much from all the Terrans with whom he must have had contact that Merseia would be ruling Sol by now. But that's bad enough!"

Aline said drearily, "No wonder he spared your life; you've become the most valuable man on his side."

"And not a thing I can do about it," said Flandry dully. "He sees me every day. I don't know what the range of his mind is—probably only a few meters; it's known that all mental pulses are weak and fade rapidly with distance. But in any case, every time he meets me he skims my mind, reads all my plans—I just can't help thinking about them all the time—and takes action to forestall them."

"We'll have to get the Imperial scientists to work on a thought screen."

"Of course. But that doesn't help us now."

"Couldn't you just avoid him, stay in your rooms—"

"Sure. And become a complete cipher. I have to get around, see my agents and the rulers of Betelgeuse, learn facts and keep my network operating. And very single thing I learn is just so much work done for Aycharaych—with no effort on his part." Flandry puffed a cigarette into lighting and blew nervous clouds of smoke. "What to do, what to do?"

"Whatever we do," said Aline, "it has to be done fast. The Sartaz is getting more and more cool toward our people. While we blunder and fail, Aycharaych is working—bribing, blackmailing, influencing one key official after another. We'll wake up some fine morning to find ourselves under arrest and Betelgeuse the loyal ally of Merseia."

"Fine prospect," said Flandry bitterly.

THE WANING RED sunlight streamed through his windows, throwing pools of dried blood on the floor. The palace was quiet, the nobles resting after the hunt, the servants scurrying about preparing the night's feast. Flandry looked around at the weird decorations, at the unearthly light and the distorted landscape beyond the windows. Strange world under a strange sun, and himself the virtual prisoner of its alien and increasingly hostile people. He had a sudden wild feeling of being trapped.

"I suppose I should be spinning some elaborate counterplot," he said hopelessly. "And then, of course, I'll have to go down to the banquet and let Aycharaych read every detail of it—every little thing I know, laid open to his eyes because I just can't suppress my own thoughts—"

Aline's eyes widened, and her slim hand tightened over his. "What is it?" he asked. "What's your idea?"

"Oh—nothing, Dominic, nothing." She smiled wearily. "I have some direct contact with Sol and—"

"You never told me that."

"No reason for you to know it. I was just wondering if I should report this new trouble or not. Galaxy knows how those muddleheaded bureaucrats back home will react to the news. Probably yank us back and cashier us for incompetence."

She leaned closer and her words came low and urgent, "Go find Aycharaych, Dominic. Talk to him, keep him busy, don't let him come near me to interfere. He'll know what you're doing, naturally, but he won't be able to do much about it if you're as clever a talker as they say. Make some excuse for me tonight, too, so I don't have to attend the banquet—tell them I'm sick or something. Keep *him* away from me."

"Sure," he said with a little of his old spirit. "But whatever you're hatching in that lovely head, be quick about it. He'll get at you mighty soon, you know."

He got up and left. She watched him go and there was a dawning smile on her lips.

FLANDRY WAS MORE than a little drunk when the party ended. Wine flowed freely at a Betelgeusean banquet, together with music, good, and dancing girls of every race present. He had enjoyed himself—in spite of every thing—most of all, he admitted, he'd enjoyed talking to Aycharaych. The being was a genius of the first order in almost every field, and it had been pleasant to forget the dreadfully imminent catastrophe for a while.

He entered his chambers. Aline stood by a little table, and the muted light streamed off her unbound hair and the shimmering robe she wore. Impulsively, he kissed her.

"Goodnight, honey," he said. "It was nice of you to wait for me."

She didn't leave for her own quarters. Instead, she held out one of the ornate goblets on the table. "Have a nightcap, Dominic," she invited.

"No, thanks. I've had entirely too many."

"For me." She smiled irresistibly. He clinked glasses with her and let the dark wine go down his throat.

It had a peculiar taste, and suddenly he felt dizzy, the room wavered and tilted under him. He sat down on his bed until it had passed, but there was an—oddness—in his head that wouldn't go away.

"Potent stuff," he muttered.

"We don't have the easiest job in the world," said Aline softly. "We deserve a little relaxation." She sat down beside him. "Just tonight, that's all we have. Tomorrow is another day, and a worse day."

He would never have agreed before, his nature was too cool and self-contained, but now it was all at once utterly reasonable. He nodded.

"And you love me, you know," said Aline.

And he did.

Much later, she leaned close against him in the dark, her hair brushing his cheek, and whispered urgently: "Listen, Dominic, I have to tell you this regardless of the consequences; you have to be prepared for it."

He stiffened with a return of the old tension. Her voice went on, a muted whisper in the night: "I've called Sol on the secret beam and gotten in touch with Fenross. He has brains, and he saw at once what must be done. It's a poor way, but the only way.

"The fleet is already bound for Betelgeuse. The Merseians think most of our strength is concentrated near Llynathawr, but that's just a brilliant piece of deception—Fenross' work. Actually, the main body is quite near, and they've got a new energy screen that'll let them slip past the Betelgeusean cordon without being detected. The night after tomorrow, a strong squadron will land in Gunazar Valley, in the Borthudians, and establish a beachhead. A detachment will immediately move to occupy the capital and capture the Sartaz and his court."

Flandry lay rigid with the shock of it. "But this means war," he gasped. "Merseia will strike at once, and we'll have to fight Betelgeuse, too."

"I know. But the Imperium has decided we'll have a better chance this way. Otherwise, it looks as if Betelgeuse will go to the enemy by default.

"It's up to us to keep the Sartaz and his court from suspecting the truth till too late. We have to keep them here at the palace. The capture of the leaders of an absolute monarchy is always a disastrous blow—Fenross and Walton think Betelgeuse will surrender before Merseia can get here.

"By hook or crook, Dominic, you've got to keep them unaware. That's your job; at the same time, keep on distracting Aycharaych, keep him off my neck."

She yawned and kissed him. "Better go to sleep now," she said. "We've got a tough couple of days ahead of us."

He couldn't sleep. He got up when she was breathing quietly and walked over to the balcony. The knowledge was staggering. That the Empire, the bungling decadent Empire, could pull such a stroke and hope to get away with it!

Something stirred in the garden below. The moonlight was like clotted blood on the figure that paced between two Merseian bodyguards. Aycharaych!

Flandry stiffened in dismay. The Chereionite looked up and he saw the wise smile on the telepath's face. *He knew.*

IN THE FOLLOWING TWO days, Flandry worked as he had rarely worked before. There wasn't much physical labor involved, but he had to maintain a web of complications such that the Sartaz would have no chance for a private audience with Merseian and would not leave the capital on one of his capricious journeys. There was also the matter of informing such Betelgeusean traitors as were on his side to be ready, and—

It was nerve-shattering. To make matters worse, something was wrong with him; clear thought was an effort; he had a new and disastrous tendency to take everything at face value. What had happened to him?

Aycharaych excused himself on the morning after Aline's revelation and disappeared. He was out arranging something hellish for the Terrans when they arrived, and there was nothing Flandry could do about it. But at least it left him and Aline free to carry on their own work.

He knew the Merseian fleet could not get near Betelgeuse before the Terrans landed. It is simply not possible to conceal the approximate whereabouts of a large fighting force from the enemy. How it had been managed for Terra, Flandry couldn't imagine. He supposed that it would not be too large a task force that was to occupy Alfzar—but that made its mission all the more precarious.

The tension gathered, hour by slow hour. Aline went her own way, conferring with General Bronson—the human-Betelgeusean officer whom she had made her personal property. Perhaps he could disorganize the native fleet at the moment when Terra struck. The Merseian nobles plainly knew what Aycharaych had found out; they looked at the humans with frank hatred, but they made no overt attempt to warn the Sartaz.

Maybe they didn't think they could work through the wall of suborned and confused officials whom Flandry had built around him—more likely, Aycharaych had suggested a better plan for them. There was none of the sense of defeat in them, which slowly gathered in the human.

It was like being caught in spider webs, fighting clinging gray stuff that blinded and choked and couldn't be pulled away. Flandry grew haggard, he shook with nervousness, and the two days dragged on.

He looked up Gunazar Valley in the atlas. It was uninhabited and desolate, the home of winds and the lair of dragons, a good place for a secret landing—only how secret was a landing that Aycharaych knew all about and was obviously ready to meet?

"There isn't much chance, Aline," he said to her. "Not a prayer, really."

"We'll just have to keep going." She was more buoyant than he, seemed almost cheerful as time stumbled past. She stroked his hair tenderly. "Poor Dominic, it isn't easy for you—"

The huge sun sank below the horizon—the second day, and tonight was the hour of decision. Flandry came into the great conference hall to find it almost empty.

"Where are the Merseians, your majesty?" he asked the Sartaz.

"They all went off on a special mission," snapped the ruler. He was plainly ill pleased with the intriguing around him, of which he would be well aware.

A special mission—O almighty gods!

Aline and Bronson came in and gave the monarch formal greeting. "With your permission, your majesty," said the general, "I would like to show you something of great importance in about two hours."

"Yes, yes," mumbled the Sartaz and stalked out.

Flandry sat down and rested his head on one hand, Aline touched his shoulder gently. "Tired, Dominic?" she asked.

"Yeah," he said. "I feel rotten. Just can't think these days."

She signaled to a slave, who brought a beaker forward. "This will help," she said. He noticed sudden tears in her eyes. What was the matter?

He drank it down without thought. It caught at him, he choked and grabbed the chair arms for support. "What the devil—" he gasped.

It spread through him with a sudden coolness that ran along his nerves toward his brain. It was like the hand that Aline had laid on his head, calming, soothing—

Clearing!

Suddenly he sprang to his feet. The whole preposterous thing stood forth in its raw grotesquerie—tissue of falsehoods, monstrosity of illogic!

The Fleet *couldn't* have moved a whole task force this close without the Merseian intelligence knowing of it. There *couldn't* be a new energy screen that he hadn't heard of. Fenross would never try so fantastic a scheme as the occupation of Betelgeuse before all hope was gone.

He didn't love Aline. She was brave and lovely, but he didn't love her.

But he *had.* Three minutes ago, he had been desperately in love with her.

He looked at her through blurring eyes as the enormous truth grew on him. She nodded, gravely, not seeming to care that tears were running down her cheeks. Her lips whispered a word that he could barely catch.

"Goodbye. Goodbye, my dearest."

CHAPTER FOUR

THEY HAD set up a giant televisor screen in the conference hall, with a row of seats for the great of Alfzar. Bronson had also taken the precaution of lining the walls with royal guardsmen whom he could trust—long rows of flashing steel and impassive blue faces, silent and moveless as the great pillars holding up the soaring roof.

The general paced nervously up and down before the screen, looking at his watch unnecessarily often. Sweat glistened on his forehead. Flandry sat relaxed; only one who knew him well could have read the tension that was like a coiled spring in him. Only Aline seemed remote from the scene, too wrapped in her own thoughts to care what went on.

"If this doesn't work, you know we'll probably be hanged," said Bronson.

"It ought to," answered Flandry tonelessly. "If it doesn't, I won't give much of a damn whether we hang or not."

He was prevaricating there; Flandry was uncommonly fond of living, for all the wistful half-dreams that sometimes rose to torment him.

A trumpet shrilled, high brassy music between the walls and up to the ringing rafters. They rose and stood at attention as the Sartaz and his court swept in.

His yellow eyes were suspicious as they raked the three humans.

"You said that there was to be a showing of an important matter," he declared flatly. "I hope that is correct."

"It is, your majesty," said Flandry easily. He was back in his element, the fencing with words, the casting of nets to entrap minds. "It is a matter of such immense importance that it should have been revealed to you weeks ago. Unfortunately, circumstances did not permit that—as the court shall presently see—so that your majesty's loyal general was forced to act on his own discretion with what help we of Terra could give him. But if our work has gone well, the moment of revelation should also be that of salvation."

"It had better be," said the Sartaz ominously. "I warn you— all of you—that I am sick of the spying and corruption the empires have brought with them. It is about time to cut the evil growth from Betelgeuse."

"Terra has never wished Betelgeuse anything but good, your majesty," said Flandry, "and as it happens, we can now offer proof of that. If—"

Another trumpet cut off his voice, and the warder's shout rang and boomed down the hall: "Your majesty, the Ambassador of the Empire of Merseia asks audience."

The huge green form of Lord Korvash of Merseia filled the doorway with a flare of gold and jewelry. And beside him—Aycharaych.

Flandry was briefly rigid with shock. If his brilliant and deadly opponent came into the game now, the whole plan might crash to ruin. It was a daring, precarious structure, which Aline had built; the faintest breath of argument could dissolve it—and then the lightnings would strike!

It was not permitted to bear firearms within the palace, but the dueling sword was a part of full dress. Flandry drew his with a hiss of metal and shouted aloud: "Seize those beings! They mean to kill the Sartaz!"

Aycharaych's golden eyes widened as he saw what was in Flandry's mind. He opened his mouth to denounce the Terran—and leaped back just in time to avoid the man's murderous thrust.

His own rapier sprang into his hand. In a *whirr* of steel, the two spies met.

Korvash the Merseian drew his own great blade in sheer reflex. "Strike him down!" yelled Aline. Before the amazed Sartaz could act, she had pulled the stun pistol he carried from the holster and sent the Merseian toppling to the floor.

She bent over him, deftly removing a tiny needle gun from her bodice and palming it on the, ambassador. "Look, your majesty," she said breathlessly, "he had a deadly weapon. We knew the Merseians planned no good, but we never thought they would dare—"

The Sartaz's gaze was shrewd on her. "Maybe we'd better wait to hear his side of it," he murmured.

Since Korvash would be in no position to explain his side for a good hour, Aline considered it a victory.

But Flandry—her eyes grew wide and she drew a hissing gasp as she saw him fighting Aycharaych. It was the swiftest, most vicious duel she had ever seen, leaping figures and blades that were a blur of speed, back and forth along the hall in a clamor of steel and blood.

"Stop them!" she cried, and raised the stunner.

The Sartaz laid a hand on hers and took the weapon away. "No," he said. "Let them have it out. I haven't seen such a show in years."

"Dominic—" she whispered.

FLANDRY HAD ALWAYS thought himself a peerless fencer, but Aycharaych was his match. The Chereionite was hampered by gravity, but he had a speed and precision that no human could ever meet, his thin blade whistled in and out, around and under the man's guard to rake face and hands and breast, and he was smiling—smiling.

His telepathy did him little or no good. Fencing is a matter of conditioned reflex—at such speeds, there isn't time for conscious thought. But perhaps it gave him an extra edge, just compensating for the handicap of weight.

Leaping, slashing, thrusting, parrying, clang and clash of cold steel, no time to feel the biting edge or the growing weariness— dance of death while the court stood by and cheered.

Flandry's own blade was finding its mark; blood ran down Aycharaych's gaunt cheeks and his tunic was slashed to red ribbons. The Terran's plan was simple and the only one possible for him. Aycharaych would tire sooner, his reactions would slow—the thing to do was to stay alive that long.

He let the Chereionite drive him backward down the length of the hall, leap by leap, whirling around with sword shrieking in hand. Thrust, parry, riposte, recovery—*whirr, clang!* The rattle of steel filled the hall and the Sartaz watched with hungry eyes.

The end came as he was wondering if he would ever live to see Betelgeuse rise again. Aycharaych lunged and his blade pierced Flandry's left shoulder. Before he could disengage it, the man had knocked the weapon spinning from his hand and had his own point against the throat of the Chereionite.

The hall rang with the savage cheering of Betelgeuse's masters. "Disarm them!" shouted the Sartaz.

Flandry drew a sobbing breath. "Your majesty," he gasped, "let me guard this fellow while General Bronson goes on with our show."

The Sartaz nodded. It fitted his sense of things.

Flandry thought with a hard glee; *Aycharaych, if you open your mouth, so help me, I'll run you through.*

The Chereionite shrugged, but his smile was bitter.

"Dominic, Dominic!" cried Aline, between laughter and tears.

General Bronson turned to her. He was shaken by the near ruin. "Can you talk to them?" he whispered. "I'm no good at it."

Aline nodded and stood boldly forth. "Your majesty and nobles of the court," she said, "we shall now prove the statements we made about the treachery of Merseia.

"We of Terra found out that the Merseians were planning to seize Alfzar and hold it and yourselves until their own fleet could arrive to complete the occupation. To that end they are assembling this very night in Gunazar Valley of the Borthudian range. A flying squad will attack and capture the place—"

She waited until the uproar had subsided. "We could not tell your majesty or any of the highest in the court," she resumed coolly, "for the Merseian spies were everywhere and we had reason to believe that one of them could read your minds. If they had known anyone knew of their plans, they would have acted at once. Instead we contacted General Bronson, who was not high enough to merit their attention, but who did have enough power to act as the situation required.

"We planted a trap for the enemy. For one thing, we mounted telescopic telecameras in the valley. With your permission, I will now show what is going on there this instant."

SHE TURNED A SWITCH and the scene came to life— naked crags and cliffs reaching up toward the red moons, and a stir of activity in the shadows. Armored forms were moving about, setting up atomic guns, warming the engines of spaceships—and they were Merseians.

The Sartaz snarled. Someone asked, "How do we know this is not a falsified transmission?"

"You will be able to see their remains for yourself," said Aline. "Our plan was very simple. We planted atomic land mines in the ground. They are radio controlled." She held up a small switch-box wired to the televisor, and her smile was grim. "This is the control. Perhaps your majesty would like to press the button?"

"Give it to me," said the Sartaz thickly. He thumbed the switch.

A blue-white glare of hell-flame lit the screen. They had a vision of the ground fountaining upward, the cliffs toppling down, a cloud of radioactive dust boiling up toward the moons, and then the screen went dark.

"The cameras have been destroyed," said Aline quietly. "Now, your majesty, I suggest that you send scouts there immediately. They will find enough remains to verify what the televisor has shown. I would further suggest that a power, which maintains armed forces within your own territory, is *not* a friendly one."

KORVASH AND Aycharaych were to be deported with whatever other Merseians were left in the system—once Betelgeuse had broken diplomatic relations with their state and begun negotiating an alliance with Terra. The evening before they left, Flandry gave a small party for them in his apartment. Only he and Aline were there to meet them when they entered.

"Congratulations," said Aycharaych wryly. "The Sartaz was so furious he wouldn't even listen to our protestations. I can't blame him—you certainly put us in a bad light."

"No worse than your own," grunted Korvash angrily. "Hell take you for a lying hypocrite, Flandry. You know that Terra has her own forces and agents in the Betelgeusean System, hidden on wild moons and asteroids. It's part of the game."

"Of course I know it," smiled the Terran. "But does the Sartaz? However, it's as you say—the game, the great game. You don't hate the one who beats you in chess. Why then hate us for winning this round?"

"Oh, I don't," said Aycharaych. "There will be other rounds."

"You've lost much less than we would have," said Flandry. "This alliance has strengthened Terra enough for her to halt your designs, at least temporarily. But we aren't going to use that strength to launch a war against you, though I admit that we should. The Empire wants only to keep the peace."

"Because it doesn't dare fight a war," snapped Korvash.

They didn't answer. Perhaps they were thinking of the cities that would not be bombed and the young men that would not have to go out to be killed. Perhaps they were simply enjoying a victory.

Flandry poured wine. "To our future amiable enmity," he toasted.

"I still don't see how you did it," said Korvash.

"Aline did it," said Flandry. "Tell them, Aline."

She shook her head. She had withdrawn into a quietness that was foreign to her. "Go ahead, Dominic," she murmured. "It was really your show."

"Well," said Flandry, not loath to expound, "when we realized that Aycharaych could read our minds, it looked pretty hopeless. How can you possibly lie to a telepath? Aline found the answer—by getting information, which just isn't true.

"There's a drug in this system called *sorgan,* which has the property of making its user believe anything he's told. Aline fed me some without my knowledge and then told me that fantastic lie about Terra coming in to occupy Alfzar. And, of course, I accepted it as absolute truth. Which you, Aycharaych, read in my mind."

"I was puzzled," admitted the Chereionite. "It just didn't look reasonable to me; but as you said, there didn't seem to be any way to lie to a telepath."

"Aline's main worry was then to keep out of mind-reading range," said Flandry. "You helped us there by going off to prepare a warm reception for the Terrans. You gathered all your forces in the valley, ready to blast our ships out of the sky."

"Why didn't you go to the Sartaz with what you knew—or thought you knew?" asked Korvash accusingly.

Aycharaych shrugged. "I knew Captain Flandry would be doing his best to prevent me from doing that and to discredit any information I could get that high," he said. "You yourself agreed that our best opportunity lay in repulsing the initial attack ourselves. That would gain us far more favor with the Sartaz; moreover, since there would have been overt acts on both sides, war between Betelgeuse and Terra would then have been inevitable—whereas if the Sartaz had learned in time of the impending assault, he might have tried to negotiate."

"I suppose so," said Korvash glumly.

"Aline, of course, prevailed on Bronson to mine the valley," said Flandry. "The rest you know. When you yourselves showed up—"

"To tell the Sartaz, now that it was too late," said Aycharaych.

"—we were afraid that the ensuing argument would damage our own show. So we used violence to shut you up until it had been played out." Flandry spread his hands in a gesture of finality. "And that, gentlemen, is that."

"There will be other tomorrows," said Aycharaych gently. "But I am glad we can meet in peace tonight."

The party lasted well on toward dawn. When the aliens left, with many slightly tipsy expressions of good will and respect, Aycharaych took Aline's hand in his own bony fingers. His strange golden eyes searched hers, even as she knew his mind was looking into the depths of her own.

"Goodbye, my dear," he said, too softly for the others to hear. "As long as there are women like you, I think Terra will endure."

She watched his tall form go down the corridor and her vision blurred a little. It was strange to think that her enemy knew what the man beside her did not.

THE END

Lord of A Thousand Suns

A Man without a World, this 1,000,000-year-old Daryesh! Once Lord of a Thousand Suns, now condemned to rove the spaceways in alien form, searching for love, for life, for the great lost Vwyrdda.

"YES, YOU'LL FIND ALMOST anything man has ever imagined, somewhere out in the Galaxy," I said. "There are so damned many millions of planets, and such a fantastic variety of surface conditions and of life evolving to meet them, and of intelligence and civilization appearing in that life. Why, I've been on worlds with fire-breathing dragons, and on worlds where dwarfs fought things that could pass for the goblins our mothers used to scare us with and on a planet where a race of witches lived—telepathic pseudohypnosis, you know—oh, I'll bet there's not a tall story or fairy tale ever told, which doesn't have some kind of counterpart somewhere in the universe."

Laird nodded. "Uh-huh," he answered, in that oddly slow and soft voice of his. "I once let a genie out of a bottle."

"Eh? What happened?"

"It killed me."

I opened my mouth to laugh, and then took a second glance at him and shut it again. He was just too dead-pan serious about it. Not poker-faced, the way a good actor can be when he's slipping over a tall one—no, there was a sudden misery behind his eyes, and somehow it was mixed with the damnedest cold humor.

I didn't know Laird very well. Nobody did. He was out most of the time on Galactic Survey, prowling a thousand eldritch planets never meant for human eyes. He came back to the Solar System more rarely and for briefer visits than anyone else in his job, and had less to say about what he had found.

A huge man, six-and-a-half feet tall, with dark aquiline features and curiously brilliant greenish-grey eyes, middle-aged now though it didn't show except at the temples. He was courteous enough to everyone, but short-spoken and slow to laugh. Old friends, who had known him thirty years before when he was the gayest and most reckless officer in the Solar Navy, thought something during the Revolt had changed him more than any psychologist would admit was possible. But he had never said anything about it, merely resigning his commission after the war and going into Survey.

We were sitting alone in a corner of the lounge. The Lunar branch of the Explorers' Club maintains its building outside the main dome of Selene Center, and we were sitting beside one of the great windows, drinking Centaurian sidecars and swapping the inevitable shop-talk. Even Laird indulged in that, though I suspected more because of the information he could get than for any desire of companionship.

Behind us, the long quiet room was almost empty. Before us, the window opened on the raw magnificence of moonscape, a sweep of crags and cliffs down the crater wall to the riven black plains, washed in the eerie blue of Earth's light. Space blazed above us, utter black and a million sparks of frozen flame.

"Come again?" I said.

HE LAUGHED, without much humor. "I might as well tell you," he said. "You won't believe it, and even if you did it'd make no difference. Sometimes I tell the story—alcohol makes me feel like it—I start remembering old times…"

He settled farther back in his chair. "Maybe it wasn't a real genie," he went on. "More of a ghost, perhaps. That was a haunted planet. They were great a million years before man existed on Earth. They spanned the stars and they knew things the present civilization hasn't even guessed at. And then they died. Their own weapons swept them away in one burst of fire, and only broken ruins were left—ruins and desert, and the ghost who lay waiting in that bottle."

I signaled for another round of drinks, wondering what he meant, wondering just how sane that big man with the worn, rocky face was. Still—you never know. I've seen things out beyond that veil of stars, which your maddest dreams never hinted at. I've seen men carried home mumbling and empty-eyed, the hollow cold of space filling their brains where something had broken the thin taut wall of their reason. They say spacemen are a credulous breed. Before Heaven, they have to be!

"You don't mean New Egypt?" I asked.

"Stupid name. Just because there are remnants of a great dead culture, they have to name it after an insignificant valley of ephemeral peasants. I tell you, the men of Vwyrdda were like gods, and when they were destroyed whole suns were darkened by the forces they used. Why, they killed off Earth's dinosaurs in a day, millions of years ago, and only used one ship to do it."

"How in hell do you know that? I didn't think the archeologists had deciphered their records."

"They haven't. All our archeologists will ever know is that the Vwyrddans were a race of remarkably humanoid appearance, with a highly advanced interstellar culture wiped out about a million Earth-years ago. Matter of fact, I don't really know that they did it to Earth, but I do know that they had a regular policy of exterminating the great reptiles of terrestroid planets with an eye to later colonization, and I know that they got this far, so I suppose our planet got the treatment too." Laird accepted his fresh drink and raised the glass to me. "Thanks. But now do be a good fellow and let me ramble on in my own way.

"It was—let me see—thirty-three years ago now, when I was a bright young lieutenant with bright young ideas. The Revolt was in full swing then, and the Janyards held all that region of space, out Sagittari way you know. Things looked bad for Sol then—I don't think it's ever been appreciated how close we were to defeat. They were poised to drive right through our lines with their battle-fleets, slash past our frontiers, and hit Earth itself with the rain of hell that had already sterilized a score of planets. We were fighting on the defensive, spread over several million cubic light-years, spread horribly thin. Oh, bad!

"Vwyrdda—New Egypt—had been discovered and some excavation done shortly before the war began. We knew about as much then as we do now. Especially, we knew that the so-called Valley of the Gods held more relics than any other spot on the surface. I'd been quite interested in the work, visited the planet myself, even worked with the crew that found and restored that gravitomagnetic generator—the one that taught us half of what we know now about g-m fields.

"It was my young and fanciful notion that there might be more to be found, somewhere in that labyrinth—and from study of the reports I even thought I knew about what and where it would be. One of the weapons that had novaed suns, a million years ago—

"The planet was far behind the Janyard lines, but militarily valueless. They wouldn't garrison it, and I was sure that such semi-barbarians wouldn't have my idea, especially with victory so close. A one-man sneakboat could get in readily enough—it just isn't possible to blockade a region of space; too damned inhumanly big. We had nothing to lose but me, and maybe a lot to gain, so in I went.

"I made the planet without trouble and landed in the Valley of the Gods and began work. And that's where the fun started."

Laird laughed again, with no more mirth than before.

THERE WAS A MOON hanging low over the hills, a great scarred shield thrice the size of Earth's, and its chill white radiance filled the Valley with colorless light and long shadows. Overhead flamed the incredible sky of the Sagittarian regions, thousands upon thousands of great blazing suns swarming in strings and clusters and constellations strange to human eyes, blinking and glittering in the thin cold air. It was so bright that Laird could see the fine patterns of his skin, loops and whorls on the numbed fingers that groped against the pyramid. He shivered in the wind that streamed past him, blowing dust devils with a dry whisper, searching under his clothes to sheathe his flesh in cold. His breath was ghostly white before him, the bitter air felt liquid when he breathed.

Around him loomed the fragments of what must have been a city, now reduced to a few columns and crumbling walls held up by the lava that had flowed. The stones reared high in the unreal moonlight, seeming almost to move as the shadows and the drifting sand passed them. Ghost city. Ghost planet. He was the last life that stirred on its bleak surface.

But somewhere above that surface—

What was it, that descending hum high in the sky, sweeping closer out of stars and moon and wind? Minutes ago the needle on his gravitomagnetic detector had wavered down in the depths of the pyramid. He had hurried up and now stood looking and listening and feeling his heart turn stiff.

No, no, no—not a Janyard ship, not now—it was the end of everything if they came.

Laird cursed with a hopeless fury. The wind caught his mouthings and blew them away with the scudding sand, buried them under the everlasting silence of the valley.

His eyes traveled to his sneakboat. It was invisible against the great pyramid—he'd taken that much precaution, shoveling a low grave of sand over it—but, if they used metal detectors that was valueless. He was fast, yes, but almost unarmed, they could easily follow his trail down into the labyrinth and locate the vault.

Lord if he had led them here—if his planning and striving had only resulted in giving the enemy the weapon that would destroy Earth—

His hand closed about the butt of his blaster. Silly weapon, stupid pop-gun—what could he do?

Decision came. With a curse, he whirled and ran back into the pyramid.

His flash lit the endless downward passages with a dim bobbing radiance, and the shadows swept above and behind and marched beside, the shadows of a million years closing in to smother him. His boots slammed against the stone floor, *thud-thud-thud*—the echoes caught the rhythm and rolled it boomingly ahead of him. A primitive terror rose to drown his dismay; he was going down into the grave of a thousand millennia, the grave of the gods, and it took all the nerve he had to keep running and never look back. He didn't dare look back.

Down and down and down, past this winding tunnel, along this ramp, through this passageway into the guts of the planet. A man could get lost here. A man could wander in the cold and the dark and the echoes till he died. It had taken him weeks to find his way into the great vault; and only the clues given by Murchison's reports had made it possible at all. Now—

HE BURST INTO a narrow antechamber. The door he had blasted open leaned drunkenly against a well of night. It was fifty feet high that door. He fled past it like an ant and came into the pyramid storehouse.

His flash gleamed off metal, glass, substances he could not identify that had lain sealed against a million years till he came to wake the machines. What they were, he did not know. He had energized some of the units, and they had hummed and flickered, but he had not dared experiment. His idea had been to rig an antigrav unit, which would enable him to haul the entire mass of it up to his boat. Once he was home, the scientists could take over. But now—

He skinned his teeth in a wolfish grin and switched on the big lamp he had installed. White light flooded the tomb, shining darkly back from the monstrous bulks of things he could not use, the wisdom and techniques of a race, which had spanned the stars and moved planets and endured for fifty million years. Maybe he could puzzle out the use of something before the enemy came. Maybe he could wipe them out in one demoniac sweep—just like a stereofilm hero, jeered his mind—or maybe he could simply destroy it all, keep it from Janyard hands.

He should have provided against this. He should have rigged a bomb, to blow the whole pyramid to hell—

With an effort, he stopped the frantic racing of his mind and looked around. There were paintings on the walls, dim with age but still legible, pictographs, meant perhaps for the one who finally found this treasure. The men of New Egypt were shown, hardly distinguishable from humans—dark of skin and hair, keen of feature, tall and stately and robed in living light. He had paid special attention to one representation. It showed a series of actions, like an old time comic strip—a man taking up a glassy object, fitting it over his head, throwing a small switch. He had been tempted to try it, but—gods, what would it do?

He found the helmet and slipped it gingerly over his skull. It might be some kind of last-ditch chance for him. The thing was cold and smooth and hard, it settled on his head with a slow massiveness that was strangely—*living*. He shuddered and turned back to the machines.

This thing now with the long coil-wrapped barrel—an energy projector of some sort? How did you activate it? Hellfire, which was the muzzle end?

He heard the faint banging of feet winding closer down the endless passageways. Gods, his mind groaned. They didn't waste any time, did they?

But they hadn't needed t...a metal detector would have located his boat, told them that he was in this pyramid rather than one of the dozen others scattered through the valley. And energy tracers would spot him down here...

He doused the light and crouched in darkness behind one of the machines. The blaster was heavy in his hand.

A voice hailed him from outside the door. "It's useless, Solman. Come out of there!"

He bit back a reply and lay waiting.

A woman's voice took up the refrain. It was a good voice, he thought irrelevantly, low and well modulated, but it had an iron ring to it. They were hard, these Janyards, even their women led troops and piloted ships and killed men.

"You may as well surrender, Solman. All you have done has been to accomplish our work for us. We suspected such an attempt might be made. Lacking the archeological records, we couldn't hope for much success ourselves, but since my force was stationed near this sun I had a boat lie in an orbit around the planet with detectors wide open. We trailed you down, and let you work, and now we are here to get what you have found."

"Go back," he bluffed desperately. "I planted a bomb. Go back or I'll set it off."

The laugh was hard with scorn. "Do you think we wouldn't know it if you had? You haven't even a spacesuit on. Come out with your hands up or we'll flood the vault with gas."

Laird's teeth flashed in a snarling grin. "All right," he shouted, only half-aware of what he was saying. "All right, you asked for it!"

He threw the switch on his helmet.

IT WAS LIKE a burst of fire in his brain, a soundless roar of splintering darkness. He screamed half crazy with the fury that poured into him, feeling the hideous thrumming along every nerve and sinew, feeling his muscles cave in and his body hit the floor. The shadows close in, roaring and rolling, night and death, and the wreck of the universe, and high above it all he heard—laughter.

He lay sprawled behind the machine, twitching and whimpering. They had heard him, out in the tunnels, and with slow caution they entered and stood over him and watched his spasms jerk toward stillness.

They were tall and well-formed, the Janyard rebels—Earth had sent her best out to colonize the Sagittarian worlds, three hundred years ago. But the long cruel struggle, conquering and building and adapting to planets that never were and never could be Earth, had changed them, hardened their metal and froze something in their souls.

Ostensibly it was a quarrel over tariff and trade rights, which had led to their revolt against the Empire; actually, it was a new culture yelling to life, a thing born of fire and loneliness and the great empty reaches between the stars, the savage rebellion of a mutant child. They stood impassively watching the body until it lay quiet. Then one of them stooped over and removed the shining glassy helmet.

"He must have taken it for something he could use against us," said the Janyard, turning the helmet in his hands, "but it wasn't adapted to his sort of life. The old dwellers here looked human, but I don't think it went any deeper than their skins."

The woman commander looked down with a certain pity. "He was a brave man," she said.

"Wait—he's still alive, ma'am—he's sitting up—"

Daryesh forced the shaking body to hands and knees. He felt its sickness, wretched and cold in throat and nerves and muscles, and he felt the roiling of fear and urgency in the brain. These were enemies. There was death for a world and a civilization here. Most of all, he felt the horrible numbness of the nervous system, deaf and dumb and blind, cut off in its house of bone and peering out through five weak senses...

Vwyrdda, Vwyrdda, he was a prisoner in a brain without a telepathy transceiver lobe. He was a ghost reincarnated in a thing that was half a corpse!

Strong arms helped him to his feet. "That was a foolish thing to try," said the woman's cool voice.

Daryesh felt strength flowing back as the nervous and muscular and endocrine systems found a new balance, as his mind took over and fought down the gibbering madness, which had been Laird. He drew a shuddering breath. Air in his nostrils after—how long? How long had he been dead?

His eyes focused on the woman. She was tall and handsome. Ruddy hair spilled from under a peaked cap, wide-set blue eyes regarded him frankly out of a face sculptured in clean lines and strong curves and fresh young coloring. For a moment he thought of Ilorna, and the old sickness rose—then he throttled it and looked again at the woman and smiled.

It was an insolent grin, and she stiffened angrily. "Who are you, Solman?" she asked.

The meaning was clear enough to Daryesh, who had his—host's—memory patterns and linguistic habits as well as those of Vwyrdda. He replied steadily, "Lieutenant John Laird of the Imperial Solar Navy, at your service. And your name?"

"You are exceeding yourself," she replied with frost in her voice. "But since I will wish to question you at length…I am Captain Joana Rostov of the Janyard Fleet. Conduct yourself accordingly."

Daryesh looked around him. This wasn't good. He hadn't the chance now to search Laird's memories in detail, but it was clear enough that this was a force of enemies. The rights and wrongs of a quarrel ages after the death of all that had been Vwyrdda meant nothing to him, but he had to learn more of the situation, and be free to act as he chose. Especially since Laird would presently be reviving and start to resist.

The familiar sight of the machines was at once steadying and unnerving. There were powers here, which could smash planets. It looked barbaric, this successor culture, and in any event the decision as to the use of this leashed hell had to be his. His head lifted in unconscious arrogance. *His!* For he was the last man of Vwyrdda, and they had wrought the machines, and the heritage was his.

He had to escape.

JOANA ROSTOV was looking at him with an odd blend of hard suspicion and half-frightened puzzlement. "There's something wrong about you, Lieutenant," she said. "You don't behave like a man whose project has just gone to smash. What was that helmet for?"

Daryesh shrugged. "Part of a control device," he said easily. "In my excitement I failed to adjust it properly. No matter. There are plenty of other machines here."

"What use to you?"

"Oh—all sorts of uses. For instance, that one over there is a nucleonic disintegrator, and this is a shield projector, and..."

"You're lying. You can't know more about this than we do."

"Shall I prove it?"

"Certainly not. Come back from there!"

Coldly, Daryesh estimated distances. He had all the superb psychosomatic coordination of his race, the training evolved through millions of years, but the sub-cellular components would be lacking in this body. Still—he had to take the chance.

He launched himself against the Janyard who stood beside him. One hand chopped into the man's larynx, the other grabbed him by the tunic and threw him into the man beyond. In the same movement, Daryesh stepped over the falling bodies, picked up the machine rifle, which one had dropped, and slammed over the switch of the magnetic shield projector with its long barrel.

Guns blazed in the dimness. Bullets exploded into molten spray as they hit that fantastic magnetic field. Daryesh, behind it raced through the door and out the tunnel.

They'd be after him in seconds, but this was a strong long-legged body and he was getting the feel of it. He ran easily, breathing in coordination with every movement, conserving his strength. He couldn't master control of the involuntary functions yet, the nervous system was too different, but he could last for a long while at this pace.

He ducked into a remembered side passage. A rifle spewed a rain of slugs after him as someone came through the magnetic field. He chuckled in the dark. Unless they had mapped every labyrinthine twist and turn of the tunnels, or had life-energy detectors, they'd never dare trail him. They'd get lost and wander in here till they starved.

Still, that woman had a brain. She'd guess he was making for the surface and the boats, and try to cut him off. It would be a near thing. He settled down to running.

It was long and black and hollow here, cold with age. The air was dry and dusty, little moisture could be left on Vwyrdda. How long has it been? How long has it been?

JOHN Laird stirred back toward consciousness, stunned neurons lapsing into familiar pathways of synapse, the pattern, which was personality, fighting to restore itself. Daryesh stumbled as the groping mind flashed a random command to his muscles, cursed, and willed the other self back to blankness. Hold on, Daryesh, hold on, a few minutes only—

He burst out of a small side entrance and stood in the tumbled desolation of the valley. The keen tenuous air raked his sobbing lungs as he looked wildly around at sand and stone and the alien stars. New constellations—Gods, it had been a long time! The moon was larger than he remembered, flooding the dead landscape with a frosty arrogance. It must have spiraled close in all these uncounted ages.

The boat! Hellblaze, where was the boat?

He saw the Janyard ship not far away, a long lean torpedo resting on the dunes, but it would be guarded—no use trying to steal it. Where was this Laird's vessel, then?

Tumbling through a confusion of alien memories, he recalled burying it on the west side...No, it wasn't he who had done that but Laird. Damnation, he had to work fast. He plunged around the monstrous eroded shape of the pyramid, found the long mound, saw the moon gleam where the wind had blown sand off the metal. What a clumsy pup this Laird was.

He shoveled the sand away from the airlock, scooping with his hands, the breath raw in throat and lungs. Any second now they'd be on him, any instant, and now that they really believed he understood the machines—

The lock shone dully before him, cold under his hands. He spun the outer dog, swearing with a frantic emotion foreign to old Vwyrdda, but that was the habit of his host, untrained psychosomatically, unevolved— There they came!

Scooping up the stolen rifle, Daryesh fired a chattering burst at the group that swarmed around the edge of the pyramid. They tumbled like jointed dolls, screaming in the death-white moonlight. Bullets howled around him and ricocheted off the boat hull.

He got the lock open as they retreated for another charge. For an instant his teeth flashed under the moon, the cold grin of Daryesh the warrior who had ruled a thousand suns in his day and led the fleets of Vwyrdda.

"Farewell, my lovelies," he murmured and the remembered syllables of the old planet were soft on his tongue.

Slamming the lock behind him, he ran to the control room, letting John Laird's almost unconscious habits carry him along. He got off to a clumsy start—but then he was climbing for the sky, free and away—

A fist slammed into his back, tossed him in his pilot chair to the screaming roar of sundered metal. Gods, O gods, the Janyards had fired a heavy ship's gun, they'd scored a direct hit on his engines and the boat was whistling groundward again.

Grimly, he estimated that the initial impetus had given him a good trajectory—that he'd come down in the hills about a hundred miles north of the valley. But then he'd have to run for it, they'd be after him like beasts of prey in their ship—and John Laird would not be denied, muscles were twitching and sinews tightening and throat mumbling insanity as the resurgent personality fought to regain itself. That was one battle he'd have to have out soon!

Well—mentally, Daryesh shrugged. At worst, he could surrender to the Janyards, make common cause with them. It really didn't matter who won this idiotic little war. He had other things to do.

NIGHTMARE. John Laird crouched in a wind-worn cave and looked out over hills lit by icy moonlight. Through a stranger's eyes, he saw the Janyard ship landing near the down-glided wreck of his boat, saw the glitter of steel as they poured out and started hunting. Hunting *him*.

Or was it him any longer, was he more than a prisoner in his own skull? He thought back to memories that were not his, memories of himself thinking thoughts that were not his own, himself escaping from the enemy while he, Laird, whirled in a black abyss of half-conscious madness. Beyond that, he recalled his own life, and he recalled another life, which had endured a thousand years before it died. He looked out on the wilderness of rock and sand and blowing dust, and remembered it as it had been, green and fair, and remembered that he was Daryesh of Tollogh, who had ruled over whole planetary systems in the Empire of Vwyrdda. And at the same time he was John Laird of Earth, and two streams of thought flowed through the brain, listening to each other, shouting at each other in the darkness of his skull.

A million years! Horror and loneliness and a wrenching sorrow were in the mind of Daryesh as he looked upon the ruin of Vwyrdda. A million years ago!

Who are you? cried Laird. What have you done to me? And even as he asked, memories, which were his own now rose to answer him.

It had been the Erai who rebelled, the Erai whose fathers came from Vwyrdda the fair but who had been strangely altered by centuries of environment. They had revolted against the static rule of the Immortals, and in a century of warfare they had overrun half the Empire and rallied its populations under them. And the Immortals had unleashed their most terrible powers, the sun-smashing ultimate weapons, which had lain forbidden in the vault of Vwyrdda for ten million years. Only the Erai had known about it. And they had had the weapons too.

In the end, Vwyrdda went under, her fleets broken and her armies reeling in retreat over ten thousand scorched planets. The triumphant Erai had roared in to make an end of the mother world, and nothing in all the mighty Imperial arsenals could stop them now.

LORD OF A THOUSAND SUNS

Theirs was an unstable culture, it could not endure as that of Vwyrdda had. In ten thousand years or so, they would be gone, and the Galaxy would not have even a memory of that which had been. Which was small help to us, thought Laird grimly, and realized with an icy shock that it had been the thought of Daryesh.

The Vwyrddan's mental tone rose, suddenly, almost conversational, and Laird realized what an immensity of trained effort it must have taken to overcome that loneliness of a million years. "See here, Laird, we are apparently doomed to occupy the same body till one of us gets rid of the other, and it is a body that the Janyards seem to want. Rather than fight each other, which would leave the body helpless, we'd better cooperate."

"But—Lord, man! What do you think I am? Do you think I want a vampire like you up there in my brain?"

The answer was fierce and cold. "What of me, Laird? I, who was Daryesh of Tollogh, lord of a thousand suns and lover of Ilorna the Fair, immortalized noble of the greatest empire the universe has ever seen—I am now trapped in the half-evolved body of a hunted alien, a million years after the death of all which mattered. Better be glad I'm here, Laird. I can handle those weapons, you know."

The eyes looked out over the bleak windy hillscape, and the double mind watched distance-dwarfed forms clambering in the rocks, searching for a trail. "A hell of a lot of good that does us now," said Laird. "Besides, I can hear you thinking, you know, and I can remember your own past thoughts. Sol or Janya, it's the same to you. How do I know you'll play ball with me?"

The answer was instant, but dark with an unpleasant laughter. "Why—read my mind, Laird. It's your mind too, isn't it?" Then, more soberly: "Apparently history is repeating itself in the revolt of the barbarians against the mother planet, though on a smaller scale and with a less developed science. I do not expect the result to be any happier for civilization than before. So perhaps I may take a more effective hand than I did before."

It was ghostly, lying here in the wind-grieved remnants of a world, watching the hunters move through a bitter haze of moonlight, and having thoughts, which were not one's own, thoughts over which there was no control. Laird clenched his fists, fighting for stability.

"That's better," said Daryesh's sardonic mind. "But relax. Breathe slowly and deeply, concentrate only on the breathing for a while—and then search my mind, which is also yours."

"Shut up! Shut up!"

"I am afraid that is impossible. We're in the same brain, you know, and we'll have to get used to each other's streams of consciousness. Relax, man, lie still, think over the thing that has happened to you and know it for the wonder it is."

Man, they say, is a time-binding animal. But only the mighty will and yearning of Vwyrdda had ever leaped across the borders of death itself, waited a million years that that which was a world might not die out of all history.

What is the personality? It is not a thing, discrete and material, it is a pattern and a process. The body starts with a certain genetic inheritance and meets all the manifold complexities of environment. The whole organism is a set of reactions between the two. The primarily mental component, sometimes called the ego, is not separable from the body but can in some ways be studied apart.

The scientists had found a way to save something of that which was Daryesh. While the enemy was blazing and thundering at the gates of Vwyrdda, while all the planet waited for the last battle and the ultimate night, quiet men in laboratories had perfected the molecular scanner so that the pattern of synapses, which made up all memory, habit, reflex, instinct, the continuity of the ego, could be recorded upon the electronic structure of certain crystals. They took the pattern of Daryesh and of none other, for only he of the remaining Immortals was willing. Who else would want a pattern to be repeated, ages after he himself was dead, ages after all the world and all history and meaning were lost? But Daryesh had always been reckless, and Ilorna was dead, and he didn't care much for what happened.

Ilorna, Ilorna! Laird saw the unforgotten image rise in his memory, golden-eyed and laughing, the long dark hair flowing around the lovely suppleness of her. He remembered the sound of her voice and the sweetness of her lips, and he loved her. A million years, and she was dust blowing on the night wind, and he loved her with that part of him, which was Daryesh and with more than a little of John Laird...O Ilorna...

And Daryesh the man had gone to die with his planet, but the crystal pattern, which reproduced the ego of Daryesh, lay in the vault they had made, surrounded by all the mightiest works of Vwyrdda. Sooner or later, sometime in the infinite future of the universe someone would come; someone or something would put the helmet on his head and activate it. And the pattern would be reproduced on the neurons, the mind of Daryesh would live again, and he would speak for dead Vwyrdda and seek to renew the tradition of fifty million years. It would be the will of Vwyrdda, reaching across time— But Vwyrdda is *dead*, thought Laird frantically. Vwyrdda is gone— this is a new history—you've got no business telling us what to do!

The reply was cold with arrogance. "I shall do as I see fit. Meanwhile, I advise that you lie passive and do not attempt to interfere with me."

"Cram it, Daryesh!" Laird's mouth drew back in a snarl. "I won't be dictated to by anyone, let alone a ghost."

Persuasively, the answer came, "At the moment, neither of us has much choice. We are hunted, and if they have energy trackers—yes, I see they do—they'll find us by this body's thermal radiation alone. Best we surrender peaceably. Once aboard the ship, loaded with all the might of Vwyrdda, our chance should come."

Laird lay quietly, watching the hunters move closer, and the sense of defeat came down on him like a falling world. What else could he do? What other chance was there?

"All right," he said at last, audibly. "All right. But I'll be watching your every thought, understand? I don't think you can stop me from committing suicide if I must."

"I think I can. But opposing signals to the body may only neutralize each other, leave it helplessly fighting itself. Relax, Laird, lie back and let me handle this. I am Daryesh the warrior, and I have come through harder battles than this."

They rose and began walking down the hillside with arms lifted. Daryesh's thought ran on, "Besides—that's a nice-looking wench in command. It could be interesting!"

His laughter rang out under the moon, and it was not the laughter of a human being.

"I CAN'T understand you, John Laird," said Joana.

"Sometimes," replied Daryesh lightly, "I don't understand myself very well—or you, my dear."

She stiffened a little. "That will do, Lieutenant. Remember your position here."

"Oh, the devil with our ranks and countries. Let's be live entities for a change."

Her glance was quizzical. "That's an odd way for a Solman to phrase it."

Mentally, Daryesh swore. Damn this body, anyway! The strength, the fineness of coordination and perception, half the senses he had known, were missing from it. The gross brain structure couldn't hold the reasoning powers he had once had. His thinking was dull and sluggish. He made blunders the old Daryesh would never have committed. And this young woman was quick to see them, and he was a prisoner of John Laird's deadly enemies, and the mind of Laird himself was tangled in thought and will and memory, ready to fight him if he gave the least sign of—

The Solarian's ego chuckled nastily. Easy, Daryesh, easy.

Shut up, his mind snapped back, and he knew drearily that his own trained nervous system would not have been guilty, of such a childishly emotional response.

"I may as well tell you the truth, Captain Rostov," he said aloud. "I am not Laird at all. Not any more."

She made no response, merely drooped the lids over her eyes and leaned back in her chair. He noticed abstractedly how long her lashes were—or was that Laird's appreciative mind, unhindered by too much remembrance of Ilorna?

They sat alone, the two of them, in her small cabin aboard the Janyard cruiser. A guard stood outside the door, but it was closed. From time to time they would hear a dull thump or clang as the heavy machines of Vwyrdda were dragged aboard—otherwise they might have been the last two alive on the scarred old planet.

The room was austerely furnished, but there were touches of the feminine here and there—curtains, a small pot of flowers, a formal dress hung in a half-open closet. And the woman who sat across the desk from him was very beautiful, with the loosened ruddy hair streaming to her shoulders and the brilliant eyes never wavering from his. But one slender hand rested on a pistol.

She had told him frankly, "I want to talk privately with you. There is something I don't understand...but I'll be ready to shoot at the first suspicion of a false move. And even if you should somehow overpower me, I'd be no good as a hostage. We're Janyards here, and the ship is more than the life of any one of us."

Now she waited for him to go on talking.

He took a cigarette from the box on her desk—Laird's habits again—and lit it and took a slow drag of smoke into his lungs. *All right, Daryesh, go ahead. I suppose your idea is the best, if anything can be made to work at all. But I'm listening, remember.*

"I am all that is left of this planet," he said tonelessly. "This is the ego of Daryesh of Tollogh, Immortal of Vwyrdda, and in one sense I died a million years ago."

She remained quiet, but he saw how her hands clenched and he heard the sharp small hiss of breath sucked between the teeth.

Briefly, then, he explained how his mental pattern had been preserved, and how it had entered the brain of John Laird.

"You don't expect me to believe that story," she said contemptuously.

"Do you have a lie detector aboard?"

"I have one in this cabin, and I can operate it myself." She got up and fetched the machine from a cabinet. He watched her, noticing the grace of her movements. You died long ago, Ilorna—you died and the universe will never know another like you. But I go on, and she reminds me somehow of you.

IT WAS a small black thing that hummed and glowed on the desk between them. He put the metal tap on his head, and took the knobs in his hands, and waited while she adjusted the controls. From Laird's memories, he recalled the principle of the thing, the measurement of activity in separate brain centers, the precise detection of the slight extra energy needed in the higher cerebral cortex to invent a falsehood.

"I have to calibrate," she said. "Make up something I know to be a lie."

"New Egypt has rings," he smiled, "which are made of Limburger cheese. However, the main body of the planet is a delicious Camembert—"

"That will do. Now repeat your previous statements."

Relax, Laird, damn it—blank yourself! I can't control this thing with you interfering.

He told his story again in a firm voice, and meanwhile he was working within the brain of Laird, getting the feel of it, applying the lessons of nerve control, which had been part of his Vwyrddan education. It should certainly be possible to fool a simple electronic gadget, to heighten activity in all centers to such an extent that the added effort of his creative cells could not be spotted.

He went on without hesitation, wondering if the flickering needles would betray him and if her gun would spit death into his heart in the next moment. "Naturally, Laird's personality was completely lost, its fixed patterns obliterated by the superimposition of my own. I have his memories, but otherwise I am Daryesh of Vwyrdda, at your service."

She bit her lip. "What service? You shot four of my men."

"Consider my situation, woman. I came into instantaneous existence. I remember sitting in the laboratory under the scanner, a slight dizziness, and then immediately I was in an alien body. Its nervous system was stunned by the shock of my entry, I couldn't think clearly. All I had to go on was Laird's remembered conviction that these were deadly foes surrounding me, murderous creatures bent on killing me and wiping out my planet. I acted half instinctively. Also, I wanted, in my own personality, to be a free agent, to get away and think this out for myself. So I did. I regret the death of your men, but I think they will be amply compensated for."

"Hmm—you surrendered when we all but had you anyway."

"Yes, of course, but I had about decided to do so in all-events." Her eyes never lifted from the dials that wavered life or death. "I was, after all, in your territory, with little or no hope of getting clear, and you were the winning side of this war, which meant nothing to me emotionally. Insofar as I have any convictions in this matter, it is that the human race will best be served by a Janyard victory. History has shown that when the frontier cultures—which the old empire calls barbaric but which are actually new and better adapted civilizations—when they win out over the older and more conservative nations, the result is a synthesis and a period of unusual achievement."

He saw her visibly relaxing, and inwardly he smiled. It was so easy, so easy. They were such children in this later age. All he had to do was hand her a smooth lie, which fitted in with the propaganda that had been her mental environment from birth, and she could not seriously think of him as an enemy.

The blue gaze lifted to his, and the lips were parted. "You will help us?" she whispered.

Daryesh nodded. "I know the principles and construction and use of those engines, and in truth there is in them the force that molds planets. Your scientists would never work out the half of all that there is to be found. I will show you the proper operation of them all." He shrugged. "Naturally, I will expect commensurate rewards. But even altruistically speaking, this is the best thing I can do. Those energies should remain under the direction of one who understands them, and not be misused in ignorance. That could lead to unimaginable catastrophes."

Suddenly she picked up her gun and shoved it back into its holster. She stood up, smiling, and held out her hand.

He shook it vigorously, and then bent over and kissed it. When he looked up, she stood uncertain, half afraid and half glad.

It's not fair! protested Laird. The poor girl has never known anything of this sort. She's never heard of coquetry. To her love isn't a game, it's something mysterious and earnest and decent—

I told you to shut up, answered Daryesh coldly. Look, man, even if we do have an official safe-conduct, this is still a ship full of watchful hostility. We have to consolidate our position by every means at hand. Now relax and enjoy this.

HE WALKED around the desk and took her hands again. "You know," he said, and the crooked smile on his mouth reminded him that this was more than half a truth, "you make me think of the woman I loved, a million years ago on Vwyrdda."

She shrank back a little. "I can't get over it," she whispered. "You—you're old, and you don't belong to this cycle of time at all, and what you must think and know makes me feel like a child—Daryesh, it frightens me."

"Don't let it, Joana," he said gently. "My mind is young, and very lonely." He put a wistfulness in his voice. "Joana, I need someone to talk to. You can't imagine what it is to wake up a million years after all your world is dead, more alone than—oh, let me come in once in a while and talk to you, as one friend to another. Let's forget time and death and loneliness, I need someone like you."

She lowered her eyes, and said with a stubborn honesty, "I think that would be good too, Daryesh. A ship's captain doesn't have friends, you know. They put me in this service because I had the aptitude, and that's really all I've ever had. Oh, comets!" She forced a laugh. "To space with all that self-pity. Certainly you may come in whenever you like. I hope it'll be often."

They talked for quite a while longer, and when he kissed her goodnight it was the most natural thing in the universe. He walked to his bunk—transferred from the brig to a tiny unused compartment—with his mind in pleasant haze.

Lying in the dark, he began the silent argument with Laird anew. "Now what?" demanded the Solarian.

"We play it slow and easy," said Daryesh patiently—as if the fool couldn't read it directly in their common brain. "We watch our chance, but don't act for a while yet. Under the pretext of rigging the energy projectors for action, we'll arrange a setup, which can destroy the ship at the flick of a switch. They won't know it. They haven't an inkling about subspatial flows. Then, when an opportunity to escape offers itself, we throw that switch and get away and try to return to Sol. With my knowledge of Vwyrddan science, we can turn the tide of the war. It's risky—sure—but it's the only chance I see. And for Heaven's sake let me handle matters. You're supposed to be dead."

"And what happens when we finally settle this business? How can I get rid of you?"

"Frankly, I don't see any way to do it. Our patterns have become too entangled. The scanners necessarily work on the whole nervous system. We'll just have to learn to live together." Persuasively: "It will be to your own advantage. Think, man! We can do as we choose with Sol. With the Galaxy. And I'll set up a life-tank and make us a new body to which we'll transfer the pattern, a body with all the intelligence and abilities of a Vwyrddan, and I'll immortalize it. Man, you'll never die!"

It wasn't too happy a prospect, thought Laird skeptically. His own chances of dominating that combination were small. In time, his own personality might be completely absorbed by Daryesh's greater one.

Of course—a psychiatrist—narcosis, hypnosis—

"No, you don't," said Daryesh grimly. "I'm just as fond of my own individuality as you are."

The mouth, which was theirs, twisted wryly in the dark. "Guess we'll just have to learn to love each other," thought Laird.

The body dropped into slumber. Presently Laird's cells were asleep, his personality faded into a shadowland of dreams. Daryesh remained awake a while longer. Sleep—waste of time—the Immortals had never been plagued by fatigue—

He chuckled to himself. What a web of lies and counterlies he had woven. If Joana and Laird both knew—

THE MIND is an intricate thing. It can conceal facts from itself, make itself forget that which is painful to remember, persuade its own higher components of whatever the subconscious deems right. Rationalization, schizophrenia, autohypnosis, they are but pale indications of the self-deception, which the brain practices. And the training of the Immortals included full neural coordination; they could consciously utilize the powers latent in themselves. They could by an act of conscious will stop the heart, or block off pain, or split their own personalities.

Daryesh had known his ego would be fighting whatever host it found, and he had made preparations before he was scanned. Only a part of his mind was in full contact with Laird's. Another section, split off from the main stream of consciousness by deliberate and controlled schizophrenia, was thinking its own thoughts and making its own plans. Self-hypnotized, he automatically reunited his ego at such times as Laird was not aware, otherwise there was only subconscious contact. In effect a private compartment of his mind, inaccessible to the Solarian, was making its own plans.

That destructive switch would have to be installed to satisfy Laird's waking personality, he thought. But it would never be thrown. For he had been telling Joana that much of the truth—his own advantage lay with the Janyards, and he meant to see them through to final victory.

It would be simple enough to get rid of Laird temporarily. Persuade him that for some reason it was advisable to get dead drunk. Daryesh's more controlled ego would remain conscious after Laird's had passed out. Then he could make all arrangements with Joana, who by that time should be ready to do whatever he wanted.

Psychiatry—yes, Laird's brief idea had been the right one. The methods of treating schizophrenia could, with some modifications, be applied to suppressing Daryesh's extra personality. He'd blank out that Solarian...permanently.

And after that would come his undying new body, and centuries and millennia in which he could do what he wanted with this young civilization.

The demon exorcising the man— He grinned drowsily. Presently he slept.

THE SHIP drove through a night of stars and distance. Time was meaningless, was the position of the hands on a clock, was the succession of sleeps and meals, was the slow shift in the constellations as they gulped the light-years.

On and on, the mighty drone of the second-order drive filling their bones and their days, the round of work and food and sleep and Joana. Laird wondered if it would ever end. He wondered if he might not be the Flying Dutchman, outward bound for eternity, locked in his own skull with the thing that had possessed him. At such times the only comfort was in Joana's arms. He drew of the wild young strength of her, and he and Daryesh were one. But afterward—

We're going to join the Grand Fleet. You heard her, Daryesh. She's making a triumphal pilgrimage to the gathered power of Janya, bringing the invincible weapons of Vwyrdda to her admiral.

Why not? She's young and ambitious. she wants glory as much as you do. What of it?

We have to escape before she gets there. We have to steal a lifeboat and destroy this ship and all in it soon.

All in it? Joana Rostov, too?

Damn it, we'll kidnap her or something. You know I'm in love with the girl, you devil. But it's a matter of all Earth. This one cruiser has enough stuff in it now to wreck a planet. I have parents, brothers, friends—a civilization. We've got to act!

All right, all right, Laird. But take it easy. We have to get the energy devices installed first. We'll have to give them enough of a demonstration to allay their suspicions. Joana's the only one aboard here who trusts us. None of her officers do.

The body and the double mind labored as the slow days passed, directing Janyard technicians who could not understand what it was they built. Laird, drawing on Daryesh's memories, knew what giant slept in those coils and tubes and invisible energy-fields. Here were forces to trigger the great creative powers of the universe and turn them to destruction—distorted space-time, atoms dissolving into pure energy, vibrations to upset the stability of force fields, which maintained order in the cosmos. Laird remembered the ruin of Vwyrdda, and shuddered.

They got a projector mounted and operating, and Daryesh suggested that the cruiser halt somewhere that he could prove his words. They picked a barren planet in an uninhabited system and lay in an orbit fifty thousand miles out. In an hour Daryesh had turned the facing hemisphere into a sea of lava.

"If the dis-fields were going," he said absent-mindedly, "I'd pull the planet into chunks for you."

Laird saw the pale taut faces around him. Sweat was shining on foreheads, and a couple of men looked sick. Joana forgot her position enough to come shivering into his arms.

But the visage she lifted in a minute was exultant and eager, with the thoughtless cruelty of a swooping hawk. "There's an end of Earth, gentlemen!"

"Nothing they have can stop us," murmured her exec dazedly. "Why, this one ship, protected by one of those spacewarp screens you spoke of, sir—this one little ship could sail in and lay the Solar System waste."

DARYESH NODDED. It was entirely possible. Not much energy was required, since the generators of Vwyrdda served only as catalysts releasing fantastically greater forces. And Sol had none of the defensive science, which had enabled his world to hold out for a while. Yes, it could be done.

He stiffened with the sudden furious thought of Laird: *That's it, Daryesh! That's the answer.*

The thought-stream was his own too, flowing through the same brain, and indeed it was simple. They could have the whole ship armed and armored beyond the touch of Janya. And since none of the technicians aboard understood the machines, and since they were now wholly trusted, they could install robot controls without anyone's knowing.

Then—the massed Grand Fleet of Janya—a flick of the main switch—man-killing energies would flood the cruiser's interior, and only corpses would remain aboard. Dead men and the robots that would open fire on the Fleet. This one ship could ruin all the barbarian hopes in a few bursts of incredible flame. And the robots could then be set to destroy her as well, lest by some chance the remaining Janyards manage to board her.

And we—we can escape in the initial confusion, Daryesh. We can give orders to the robot to spare the captain's gig, and we can get Joana aboard and head for Sol! There'll be no one left to pursue!

Slowly, the Vwyrddan's thought made reply: A good plan. Yes, a bold stroke. We'll do it!

"What's the matter, Daryesh?" Joana's voice was suddenly anxious. "You look—"

"Just thinking, that's all. Never think, Captain Rostov. Bad for the brain."

Later, as he kissed her, Laird felt ill at the thought of the treachery he planned. Her friends, her world, her cause—wiped out in a single shattering blow, and he would have struck it. He wondered if she would speak to him ever again, once it was over.

Daryesh, the heartless devil, seemed only to find a sardonic amusement in the situation.

And later, when Laird slept, Daryesh thought that the young man's scheme was good. Certainly he'd fall in with it. It would keep Laird busy till they were at the Grand Fleet rendezvous. And after that it would be too late. The Janyard victory would be sealed. All he, Daryesh, had to do when the time came was keep away from that master switch. If Laird tried to reach it their opposed wills would only result in nullity—which was victory for Janya.

He liked this new civilization. It had a freshness, a vigor and hopefulness, which he could not find in Laird's memories of Earth. It had a tough-minded purposefulness that would get it far. And being young and fluid, it would be amenable to such pressures of psychology and force as he chose to apply.

Vwyrdda, his mind whispered. Vwyrdda, we'll make them over in your image. You'll live again!

GRAND FLEET! A million capital ships and their auxiliaries lay marshaled at a dim red dwarf of a sun, massed together and spinning in the same mighty orbit. Against the incandescent whiteness of stars and the blackness of the old deeps, armored flanks gleamed like flame as far as eyes could see, rank after rank, tier upon tier of titanic sharks swimming through space—guns and armor and torpedoes and bombs and men to smash a planet and end a civilization. The sight was too big, imagination could not make the leap, and the human mind had only a dazed impression of vastness beyond vision.

This was the great spearhead of Janya, a shining lance poised to drive through Sol's thin defense lines and roar out of the sky to rain hell on the seat of empire. They can't really be human any more, thought Laird sickly. Space and strangeness have changed them too much. No human being could think of destroying Man's home. Then, fiercely: All right Daryesh. This is our chance!

Not yet, Laird. Wait a while. Wait till we have a legitimate excuse for leaving the ship.

Well—come up to the control room with me. I want to stay near that switch. Lord, Lord, everything that is Man and me depends on us now!

Daryesh agreed with a certain reluctance that faintly puzzled the part of his mind open to Laird. The other half, crouched deep in his subconscious, knew the reason: It was waiting the posthypnotic signal, the key event, which would trigger its emergence into the higher brain-centers.

The ship bore a tangled and unfinished look. All its conventional armament had been ripped out and the machines of Vwyrdda installed in its place. A robot brain, half-alive in its complexity, was gunner and pilot and ruling intelligence of the vessel now, and only the double mind of one man knew what orders had really been given it. *When the main switch is thrown, you will flood the ship with ten units of disrupting radiation. Then, when the captain's gig is well away, you will destroy this fleet, sparing only that one boat. When no more ships in operative condition are in range, you will activate the disintegrators and dissolve this whole vessel and all its contents to basic energy.*

With a certain morbid fascination, Laird looked at that switch. An ordinary double-throw knife type—Lord of space, could it be possible, was it logical that all history should depend on the angle it made with the control panel? He pulled his eyes away, stared out at the swarming ships and the greater host of the stars, lit a cigarette with shaking hands, paced and sweated and waited.

Joana came to him, a couple of crewmen marching solemnly behind. Her eyes shone and her cheeks were flushed and the turret light was like molten copper in her hair. No woman, thought Laird, had ever been so lovely, and he was going to destroy that to which she had given her life.

"Daryesh." Laughter danced in her voice. "Daryesh, the high admiral wants to see us in his flagship. He'll probably ask for a demonstration and then I think the fleet will start for Sol at once with us in the van. Daryesh—oh, Daryesh, the war is almost over!"

Now! blazed the thought of Laird, and his hand reached for the main switch. Now—easily, causally, with a remark about letting the generators warm up--and then go with her, overpower those guardsmen in their surprise and head for home!

And Daryesh's mind reunited itself at that signal, and the hand froze...

No!

What? But—

The memory of the suppressed half of Daryesh's mind was open to Laird, and the triumph of the whole of it, and Laird knew that his defeat was here.

SO SIMPLE, so cruelly simple—Daryesh could stop him, lock the body in a conflict of wills, and that would be enough. For while Laird slept, while Daryesh's own major ego was unconscious, the trained subconscious of the Vwyrddan had taken over. It had written, in its self-created somnambulism, a letter to Joana explaining the whole truth, and had put it where it would easily be found once they started looking through his effects in search of an explanation for his paralysis.

And the letter directed, among other things, that Daryesh's body should be kept under restraint until certain specified methods known to Vwyrddan psychiatry—drugs, electric waves, hypnosis—had been applied to eradicate the Laird half of his mind.

Janyard victory was near.

"Daryesh!" Joana's voice seemed to come from immensely far away; her face swam in a haze and a roar of fainting consciousness. "Daryesh, what's the matter? Oh, my dear, what's wrong?"

Grimly, the Vwyrddan thought: Give up, Laird. Surrender to me, and you can keep your ego. I'll destroy that letter. See, my whole mind is open to you now—you can see that I mean it honestly this time. I'd rather avoid treatment if possible, and I do owe you something. But surrender now, or be wiped out of your own brain.

Defeat and ruin—and nothing but slow distorting death as reward for resistance. Laird's will caved in, his mind too chaotic for clear thought. Only one dull impulse came: I give up. You win, Daryesh.

The collapsed body picked itself off the floor. Joana was bending anxiously over him. "Oh, what is it, what's wrong?"

Daryesh collected himself and smiled shakily. "Excitement will do this to me, now and then. I haven't fully mastered this alien nervous system yet. I'm all right now. Let's go."

Laird's hand reached out and pulled the switch over.

Daryesh shouted, an animal roar from the throat, and tried to recover it, and the body toppled again in a stasis of locked wills.

It was like a deliverance from hell, and still it was but the inevitable logic of events, as Laird's own self reunited. Half of him still shaking with defeat, half realizing its own victory, he thought savagely:

None of them noticed me do that. They were paying too much attention to my face. Or if they did, we've proved to them before that it's only a harmless regulating switch. And—the lethal radiations are already flooding us. If you don't cooperate now, Daryesh, I'll hold us here till we're both dead!

So simple, so simple. Because, sharing Daryesh's memory, Laird had shared his knowledge of self-deception techniques.

He had anticipated, with the buried half of his mind that the Vwyrddan might pull some such trick, and had installed a posthypnotic command of his own. In a situation like this, when everything looked hopeless, his conscious mind was to surrender, and then his subconscious would order that the switch be thrown.

Cooperate, Daryesh!   You're as fond of living as I. Cooperate, and let's get the hell out of here!

Grudgingly, wrly: Y ou win, Laird.

The body rose again, and leaned on Joana's arm, and made its slow way toward the boat blisters. The undetectable rays of death poured through them, piling up their cumulative effects. In three minutes, a nervous system would be ruined.

Too slow, too slow. "Come on, Joana. Run!"

"Why—" She stopped, and a hard suspicion came into the faces of the two men behind her. "Daryesh—what do you mean? What's come over you?"

"Ma'am..." One of the crewmen stepped forward. "Ma'am, I wonder...I saw him pull down the main switch. And now he's in a hurry to leave the ship. And none of us really know how all that machinery ticks."

Laird pulled the gun out of Joana's holster and shot him. The other gasped, reaching for his own side arm, and Laird's weapon blazed again.

His fist leaped out, striking Joana on the angle of the jaw, and she sagged. He caught her up and started to run.

A pair of crewmen stood in the corridor leading to the boats. "What's the matter, sir?" one asked.

"Collapsed—radiation from the machines—got to get her to a hospital ship," gasped Daryesh.

They stood aside, wonderingly, and he spun the dogs of the blister valve and stepped into the gig. "Shall we come, sir?" asked one of the men.

"No." Laird felt a little dizzy. The radiation was streaming through him, and death was coming with giant strides. "No—"

He smashed a fist into the insistent face, slammed the valve back, and vaulted to the pilot's chair.

The engines hummed, warming up. Fists and feet battered on the valve. The sickness made him retch.

O Joana, if this kills you—

He threw the main-drive switch. Acceleration jammed him back as the gig leaped free.

Staring out the ports, he saw fire blossom in space as the great guns of Vwyrdda opened up.

MY GLASS was empty. I signaled for a refill and sat wondering just how much of the yarn one could believe.

"I've read the histories," I said slowly. "I do know that some mysterious catastrophe annihilated the massed fleet of Janya and turned the balance of the war. Sol speared in and won inside of a year. And you mean that you did it?"

"In a way. Or Daryesh did. We were acting as one personality, you know. He was a thoroughgoing realist, and the moment he saw his defeat he switched wholeheartedly to the other side."

"But—Lord, man! Why've we never heard anything about this? You mean you never told anyone, never rebuilt any of those machines, never did anything?"

Laird's dark, worn face twisted in a bleak smile. "Certainly. This civilization isn't ready for such things. Even Vwyrdda wasn't, and it'll take us millions of years to reach their stage. Besides, it was part of the bargain."

"Bargain?"

"Just as certainly, Daryesh and I still had to live together, you know. Life under suspicion of mutual trickery, never trusting your own brain, would have been intolerable. We reached an agreement during that long voyage back to Sol, and used Vwyrddan methods of autohypnosis to assure that it could not be broken."

He looked somberly out at the lunar night. "That's why I said the genie in the bottle killed me. Inevitably, the two personalities merged, became one. And that one was, of course, mostly Daryesh, with overtones of Laird.

"Oh, it isn't so horrible. We retain the memories of our separate existences, and the continuity, which is the most basic attribute of the ego. In fact, Laird's life was so limited, so blind to all the possibilities and wonder of the universe, that I don't regret him very often. Once in a while I still get nostalgic moments and have to talk to a human. But I always pick one who won't know whether or not to believe me, and won't be able to do much of anything about it if he should."

"And why did you go into Survey?" I asked, very softly.

"I want to get a good look at the universe before the change. Daryesh wants to orient himself, gather enough data for a sound basis of decision. When we—I—switch over to the new immortal body, there'll be work to do, a galaxy to remake in a newer and better pattern by Vwyrddan standards somnambulism. It'll take millennia, but we've got all time before us. Or I do—what do I mean, anyway?" He ran a hand through his gray-streaked hair.

"But Laird's part of the bargain was that there should be as nearly normal a human life as possible until this body gets inconveniently old. So—" He shrugged. "So that's how it worked out."

We sat for a while longer, saying little, and then he got up. "Excuse me," he said. "There's my wife. Thanks for the talk."

I saw him walk over to greet a tall, handsome red-haired woman. His voice drifted back: "Hello, Joana—"

They walked out of the room together in perfectly ordinary and human fashion.

I wonder what history has in store for us.

THE END

The Long Return

They were an odd pair, Thornton, the idealist philosopher, and Moss
Henry, ship's captain and fighting man. Yet, they both hated war—
each in his own way—both dreaded the seemingly inevitable conflict
between Earth and Venus. Then the Ancient Race, the long-forgotten
Martians, returned from the stars and Thornton found that his pacifism
had doomed both planets to certain destruction...

CHAPTER ONE

THE MATE, Eisenberg, was on the bridge and saw it first.
His voice came over the intercom and rattled against Captain
Henry's sleep-walled consciousness: "Spaceship detected.
Better come up and have a look, sir."

"Eh—oh—" With an effort, Moss Henry pulled himself out
of warmth and darkness. He blinked, focusing his eyes on the
dim, crowded cubbyhole, which passed for his cabin.
"Spaceship—oh, yes. Yeah. I'll be right up."

Momentarily, unbuckling from the stanchions that held him
in place against weightlessness, he thought wryly that the use of
such terms as "up" and "down" was sheer anachronism. But no
matter. There was more urgent business at hand. Another ship,
out here in the utter desolation of trans-Neptunian space,
meant—well—

He weighed the possibilities with a sudden cold realization
that his life might depend on a correct assessment. Neptune
itself was a quarter way further on its orbit, so this would not be
some supply ship for Triton Colony. In fact, it was highly
unlikely to be any Terrestrial craft. There was no reason for
merchant vessels to come out here, and with all hell ready to
explode in the inner System no navy units would be in outer
space. A few would be guarding Neptune, but the Fleet as a
whole would be patrolling around Earth.

That meant—another archeological ship? No, that was definitely out. They were sweeping certain well-defined regions of space, and the nearest one to the *Bolivar* was a good many megamiles off.

So the strange craft was most likely Venusian. Which meant—

"Battle stations!" His voice sounded hollow in the little cabin, but it went roaring over the intercom; he could almost feel the sudden tensing of every man aboard, of the whole ship. "Strange vessel detected. All hands to battle stations!"

There might not be a fight, he thought, scrambling into the worn dungarees, which were his closet approximation to a uniform. Every Terrestrial-Venusian encounter did not lead to a skirmish. Sometimes they passed each other in a sullen silence. But too often there would be another "incident," followed by diplomatic protests from either government, inflammatory speeches at home, and the racking up of tension another notch toward the breaking point. Or there might simply be a brief notice in the official journals of one planet or the other that such-and-such a ship was overdue, search parties had found no trace—they rarely did, in the vastness of space—and the ship must be presumed lost. *Next of kin have been notified.*

THE *BOLIVAR* was only a small merchant ship, and more than a little obsolete. But she carried guns and space torpedoes, as all ships did these days, and there were a dozen men to man them. For a moment the thought crossed Henry's mind that the ship could easily get by with a crew of three or four, if it weren't for that possibility of attack. And what the hell was the sense of all this squabbling with Venus? What did it mean for either side but death and ruination and needless expense?

He pulled himself out of the cabin by the handholds and gave a shove that sent him rapidly down the corridor toward the bridge. As he came to the companionway, he collided violently with Thornton.

"Hell," snarled Captain Henry. "Get out o' the way!"

Bradley Thornton stiffened. The archeologist was tall and lean and gray, with long, thin-chiseled features burned dark by years under the acrid sun of Mars. Henry knew vaguely that he came of one of Earth's old and wealthy families. Insofar as Earth had an aristocracy these days, Thornton belonged to it. Which hadn't improved relations between the two men; Henry had begun as a Negro stevedore in the Terraport slums.

"Captain," said Thornton coldly, "I represent the Terrestrial Archeological Institute, which hired this ship with the understanding that I retain the final authority."

"You moron, this is an emergency! If that's a Venusian ship—"

"Then you may have the command." The way he said it, Thornton relegated Venusian ships to the category of work suitable for the lower classes. "But—I don't think it is, Captain Henry."

"What—"

"We'll see." Thornton led the way "up" the companionway.

They came onto the bridge, and the tremendous blazing dark of space swam before their eyes. Eisenberg looked up from the oscilloscope of the detector. His voice held puzzlement and a dim fear, as if the cold outside had reached through and touched his heart. "She—its coming in almighty fast, sir," he said. "And—not in the ecliptic plane. From about forty degrees north of it—"

Henry heard Thornton draw a sudden gasping breath, and saw the archeologist's eyes light with a sudden incredulous triumph. For an instant the captain hung wondering in midair. He had never seen such a light in a man's face before.

But there was work to do, no time to lose; he shoved his stocky form over to the instrument board and glared at the dials.

The signal on the oscilloscope wavered before his eyes, dancing, blurred by cosmic interference. But no doubt of it, the radar was reporting a considerable metallic mass approaching from—well, approaching the sun from somewhere else. Somewhere out of the ecliptic plane—

He looked up at Thornton, and realization came slowly to him. But he should have known it, he should have known it. He said quietly: "You knew this was coming."

"Yes—yes—but I didn't dare hope *our* ship would be the one to— Quick, man, quick! Intercept it!"

Automatically, Henry's attention shifted back to the instruments. The continuously recording tape of the detector held already enough data to work out the thing's orbit with fair accuracy. The radar time-signal gave the component of the stranger's velocity in this direction, and from the rate of angular shift it was easy to calculate the orthogonal component. Then if you assumed that the course was a straight line—which would, out here so far from the sun, be very nearly true—you could plot a trajectory for yourself, which would intersect that of the other craft and match velocities— Henry's fingers danced over the computer keys. Almost absently, he spoke into the intercom: "Stand by to accelerate."

There was no word between him and Thornton until the *Bolivar* was leaping forward at a gravity and a half. Then Henry sat back and got out a stubby pipe. "We'll make contact in about ten hours," he said. "Assuming, of course, that they don't take evasive action. And now, Doctor Thornton, would you mind telling me what in the hell this is all about?"

THORNTON smiled wryly. "To tell the truth," he said, "I'm not too sure myself. But—well—maybe I'd better lead up to it gradually. Because this is perhaps the greatest moment in the history of the Solar System."

"I should think the first visit from outside would be." Henry's voice fell as low as Thornton's in the awe of that instant. His eyes dropped from the bitter white blaze of stars spilling across the sky, down to the wavering, pulsing signal on the oscilloscope. For a moment, it seemed to be tracing cabalistic signs, hieroglyphs of some unknown unhuman language whispered across the universe. Outside, outside, the terror of utter emptiness and strangeness, twenty-odd trillion miles of cold and dark and vacuum to the next nearest sun—fear clutched at him and his big work-scarred hands gripped futilely against the arms of his chair.

And he was here on the very borders of that infinity, with Sol no more than the brightest of that arrogant host of stars, too remote from the next nearest humanity—a feeble radio voice—cut off, alone against the universe, sweeping to a rendezvous with the unknown powers of Outside.

Well—he gathered himself, raised a wall of solid practicality between himself and the blind terror of infinity, and let the muscles loosen in his arms and belly and heavy shoulders. His broad blunt face turned to challenge Thornton's gray eyes, and his voice lashed savagely at the almost religious ecstasy in the other man. That was no mood in which to face the cosmos—damn it—that thing out there was from far away but it wasn't from beyond death, a man could handle it.

"Obviously," he said, "the Institute was expecting this ship. Has been expecting it for years, in fact, and hiring merchant craft to patrol outer space to meet it when it came. But the government don't know about it—I checked on that when you approached me with your contract, and they said as far as they knew you were only after relics of the old Martian space traffic. Which didn't make too much sense to me, but it seemed an easy way to make money. But—you must've had powerful backing, to hire that many ships and men. Somebody big was behind you. And what I want to know now is—who?"

"The Institute is an old and well established organization, with adequate resources," said Thornton coldly. "I don't mind adding that certain of its members are wealthy and subscribed large amounts of money for this project. But I am not required to say more."

"Oh, yes, you are; I'm captain here—"

"Your contract—"

"I know space law as well as you do, Dr. Thornton. Maybe a little better." Henry grinned mirthlessly, a white gleam of teeth in the darkness of his features. "I had quite a few contacts with it, while I was fighting up through the ranks. And in an emergency, the captain is captain; contracts don't count."

SEEING the archeologist's hostile stiffening, he went on rapidly, "I am not unreasonable, Dr. Thornton. I'm glad to cooperate with any legitimate and sane undertaking. But I must know what it is first."

"I did not intend to conceal it from you," said Thornton. It was plain he would much have preferred to sit in rapt contemplation of this great moment. "The Institute, through its researches on Mars, has come into the possession of certain knowledge so important that the future of the Solar System may depend on it—knowledge far too great to be trusted to the militaristic morons who run the government of Earth. Accordingly, we have chosen to act privately, meet this ship as individuals rather than regulation-bound representatives of officialdom, and base future action on the result of that meeting. To put it briefly—"

The meteor alarm buzzed. After a second, the buzz changed to the high-pitched whine, which meant that the object detected was probably a ship.

Thornton's voice trailed off into blankness. Henry leaned forward over the instruments, reading, computing. There was silence on the bridge, a taut quivering silence in which the noise of engines and air circulators were meaningless vacuum behind that drumhead skin of quiet. Outside, the Milky Way gleamed frostily around the arc of the heavens.

When Henry looked up, his face was as if cast in dark iron, and his voice was cold and colorless: "Another ship, on an accelerated path, which should intersect ours about the same time as we meet the outsider. Only—this one's moving in the ecliptic plane too, from Sunward. Did you have anyone set to meet us, Thornton?"

"No," whispered the archeologist. "No one."

"It's Solar, all right," nodded Henry grimly, "and I'm pretty damn sure that if it isn't one of yours it won't be Terrestrial at all.

"Which means—Venusian!"

CHAPTER TWO

WHEN THE frantic scurrying and preparing were over and the *Bolivar* was crouched into alertness, a bleak waiting for the slow hours to end and the inevitable meeting to take place, Henry found himself alone on the bridge with Thornton. There was little for anyone to do while the many miles were devoured. Eisenberg had gone down to the engine room to make certain preparations with Olsen, and only the captain and the passenger sat looking out at the stars now.

"Oh, luck, luck, luck." A tormented bitterness rode Thornton's voice. His eyes were desperate. "That this should happen, in the greatest moment of history—that man's last chance for sanity should be lost by blind accident—"

"I wonder just how accidental," murmured Henry, studying the flickering oscillograph. "A Venusian wouldn't just happen by; space is too big. I have a hunch that he was waiting, too."

"He couldn't have been! No one, no one in the Solar System knew this except for a select group within the Institute and a few other scientists whom we could trust."

"Well—you still haven't told me what this mysterious 'it' is, Thornton," said Henry. "I'm waiting."

"I—well—" The archeologist fumbled with a cigarette, groping for words. "It's a very long story. It goes back ten thousand years, really, to the last dying Martians. But it was Blakiston who found the record, ten years ago. Have you ever been on Mars, Captain Henry?" At the spaceman's disgusted scowl, he added hastily, "Of course you have. But I don't mean Aresport or Drygulch or any of the other new colonies, Terrestrial or Venusian. They aren't Mars. The planet—its soul is out in the deserts, in the ruins and the graves and the inscriptions. Have you ever visited them?"

"A little."

Henry remembered those trips, over the rusty desolation of a dead world, to the huge silence of those incredible works. Some said that the golden age of Mars had been a hundred thousand years ago. For a thousand centuries, those lovely fluted columns had stood under the dark greenish sky; f or a thousand centuries wind and sand and the slow rusting out of the planet's heart had eaten at them, and still they seemed almost alive. He remembered the vivid murals, the vaulted temple choked with blowing sand, the exquisite fragment of a golden brooch worn thin as paper by erosion...and now there were only the desert and the tumbled ruins and the strange light-boned skeletons...yes, he remembered.

"The last Martians must have died ten thousand years or so ago," said Thornton. "It was too much for them. For millennia they had been fighting a losing way with the drying and cooling of their world, the exhaustion of the soil, the attenuation of the atmosphere, the whole despair and hopelessness of it. Their once-mighty civilization was crumbled to savagery, only a few refuges remained for the ancient learning... But, to the end, they had a few spaceships. They must have visited Neolithic Earth and Venus, seen how unexpectedly rapid progress was. You do know that there was a great burst of inventiveness on both planets about that time, such fundamental inventions as the ship and the wheel being produced—"

"I know it now," said Henry.

"The Martians guessed that perhaps these seemingly inferior life-forms were actually their betters in inherent skill. After all, the Martian race was not technologically inclined. Their science was so great, greater even than ours today, simply because their culture was so enormously older. Anyway, those last Martian visitors must have foreseen that Earth and Venus would be traveling between the planets, perhaps even before the—the event that is now on us. So—they left word for us.

"You know of the New Karnak Stones?"

"Umm—yeah, a little. Found about fifty years ago, weren't they? Held the key to the Martian written language—"

"That's right. A key obviously designed for alien philologists. It started with a purely ideographic script, which can be deciphered. Then it gave the equivalents in the regular Martian alphabet. It took years of work, on the part of LeClerc and others, but the riddle was finally solved. Today, those who care to learn can read the old Martian writings. In fact, thanks to the alphabet's being phonetic, they can speak the language."

"So—?"

"It was an immense help to archeology, of course, and until Blakiston's find ten years ago it was thought that the Martians had left that key simply as an altruistic gesture, or perhaps to save the memory of their race from total oblivion. But then, in the ruins of one of those last civilized communities, he found the inscription, which revealed their true purpose."

HENRY remained silent. The ship whispered around them, driving through a night of bitter stars.

"It was an appeal," said Thornton softly. "I won't quote the whole of it—it was very long—but it said in part: *We have seen the races of the inner planets rising more swiftly than we ever thought possible, and have stood dumb before their supreme skill in mastering the world about them. They have done in centuries what took the folk of Mars thousands of years. Yet they are young, these races, young; they will grasp the powers of gods with the hands of children, and we have stood appalled before their utter savagery and heedlessness. They are hard and cruel and reckless. They have it in them to conquer the stars—but will they ever conquer themselves?*

"*Yet there are wise ones among them, beings with the slow deep patience of the thinker, dreamers who know that murder breeds its like and that in the end only the mind and the soul can bring peace to the body. Only that breed will have the patience to learn our language, so foreign to them. Only these few will be able to read this last message. And—we pray that they will have the sense to keep the secret, to use it as they see fit—for only they know what is for the best.*

"Into your hands, stranger from a strange world, we give the Future."

Henry said nothing. He fiddled with his pipe, embarrassed by the emotion that quivered in Thornton's voice.

The archeologist looked at him for a long moment. Then he sighed, wearily, and said: "The inscription told the story of what had happened some five thousand years earlier. At that time, Martian civilization was declining, but still not too far from its peak. They knew what was coming. They could see the slow planetary death awaiting them. There was no other planet in the Solar System to which they could hope to move, and lacking as I said the essentially dynamic attitude of Earthly technology, they did not have much hope of saving the home world. But they had to save the race.

"You can guess what happened. They built three giant spaceships, the greatest ships that history had ever seen, and they loaded them with colonists and supplies, and sent them blindly out among the stars to look for a new planet."

HENRY NODDED, slowly, slowly. He had been expecting the revelation. He looked down to the signal pulsing on the oscilloscope, and out to the swarming blazing stars, and sought one mote of thin light among them. "The Martians are coming back."

"Aye," Thornton nodded. "The colonists were to go out in these mighty ships, traveling very nearly at the speed of light, and look for a world like Mars, but one younger, more habitable. They would never come back. It would not be practicable to ferry immigrants from Sol—besides, all the energies of the race would be needed for the gigantic attempt, which *might* after all succeed, to rebuild at home. But this fragment of the species would certainly be saved.

"And it was agreed that they would send an expedition, which was to arrive at a certain time, some fifteen thousand Terrestrial years after the emigrants had departed."

Henry whistled. "Fifteen thousand years! That's a hell of a long time."

"Yes. But after all, it would take them an enormous time to find a world. It had to be definitely safe, definitely habitable. And, Martian morality being as high as it was, there could be no indigenous race, which would have to be ousted. Once such a planet had been found and settled, it would take time for the colony to become established, time for its population to grow so far that there was no doubt of the species having survived beyond all chance of random extinction. And then there would be the trip back itself, which might take centuries of time as measured outside the ship.

"And, too, the Martians had a different attitude toward time from ours. Their civilization was already at least half a million years old, and it was more stable than ours; it lacked our frantic desire and need for change. Progress was slow, very slow... In fact, the Martian mentality is so alien to ours that even I, who have spent my life studying it, know only how far I am from understanding.

"In any case, the Martians were to return at about this time. To return to their old home, their own people—or to the graves of their race. To return with all the powers of a science already beyond ours, a science that has since had fifteen thousand years to grow. But—those Martians will not be expecting to find Earth and Venus ruling the Solar System. They'll look for us still to be savages. As we are, Captain Henry, as we are—but mechanized savages, immensely dangerous barbarians.

"And how the Martians will react—now—only God knows."

"And you didn't tell anyone?" Henry's eyes were incredulous, searching Thornton's in bafflement, fear, and a dawning rage. "You kept it secret?"

"As the Martians asked," said Thornton quietly; "it was their last appeal, and we have heeded it.

"Just suppose they were to be met by the fleet of battleships Earth would send out if its government knew. They would be frightened, suspicious, ready to fight or flee. Then some pompous red-necked admiral would tell them that Mars was now a colony of Earth, in spite of claims by those damned Venusians, and that the ruins of the Sun Pyramid had been leveled to build a rocket port. He would welcome them to the Solar System they once ruled, and would ask them please to come aboard so a Terrestrial prize crew could take their ship to Luna Base. He would demand from them all their knowledge, to be used in murdering Venusians, and would threaten them with prison or hypnoquizzing when they refused. He would speak of human destiny among the stars, an Empire of Sol including, perhaps, the Martians' new planet—

"The militarists would degrade this discovery as they have perverted the atom and the spaceship and the electronic brain. Or else—they would fail; they would provoke the Martians into unleashing all their fantastic arsenal on us—or simply into leaving the System, leaving us to our one little sun and the darkness of our own ignorance and cruelty.

"No, Henry—we decided long ago that the Martians must be met by that breed of men to whom they had appealed, by scientists and philosophers, by men who believe that violence is not an answer to anything. Men who could explain to them how the situation was, appeal to them for help—get their knowledge and wisdom and power to end this miserable struggle with Venus in a peace just to both planets. It is the only way."

Henry stirred restlessly. His wide mouth curled. "So—you're a pacifist," he said slowly.

"Yes. And I am proud of it."

"It's your right to be, I suppose; but I've known too many men and Venusians who needed killing."

"The sort of attitude I would have expected from you."

"Anyway," said Henry bitterly, "your wonderful scientific cleverness hasn't had much more result than throwing us against a probably more powerful Venusian ship, which now has a chance to take over both us and the Martians. I can see the Venusian fleet over our cities now. Tell me, Dr. Pacifist

Thornton, is a Venusian navy man less militaristic than your red-necked Earthling? Or maybe you've never seen a Venusian torture ceremony?"

CHAPTER THREE

THE SHIP was visible to the naked eye now, frighteningly visible against the cloudy glory of the Milky Way, and radio beams were hunting up and down the spectrum in frantic search of a voice.

A voice, a face, a flicker of recognition out of the dark and silence of fifteen thousand years—but the ship was silent. The Martians were silent.

Henry's eyes roved from the ship to his instruments and back again, prowling a path of numbed fascination. Ye gods, it must be huge! A five-mile cylinder, a mile in diameter, sheening faint gold in the dim bitter light of stars and nebulae and the far tiny sun, wrapped in some inexplicable halo of vague blue shimmer, it held otherness in its every line and curve and sweep of incredible mass. A tingle of fear shivered along his spine, he felt a crawling germ of panic in the face of the utterly unknown stir within him and throttled it fiercely.

Thornton gave him a cold look. "You're afraid," he said.

"I—don't entirely like it," admitted Henry slowly. "The powers they may have—"

"You're afraid. You're afraid of the new and strange and wonderful. You're attributing our own childish murderousness to them, and so you fear them. When you could meet them as a friend!"

"I wonder... But one thing's for damn sure, we aren't going to meet that Venusian as any friend. It'll be here inside half an hour, and there isn't much we can do about it." The *Bolivar* shuddered in another rocket blast, groaning with the strain of matching velocity to the Martian. The two vessels sped on parallel Sunward tracks, a hundred miles apart and the *Bolivar's* radio beams flickered and questioned and waited for a reply out of humming silence.

"Strange—" Henry looked at his instruments, got out his slide rule and nodded at the answer. "That thing has a fantastic mass. But—for its size, fantastically low. Damn it. Unless my gravito-meter and slip stick are both liars, that big hull must be over ninety percent empty!"

"Perhaps—" Thornton's guess was not completed. There was a buzz from the ship's main televisor—a call on the standard FM band. For a moment the two men were galvanized with an incredible hope, but it faded as Henry shook his head and opened the receiving channel.

"Could only be the Venusian," he said.

THE SCREEN flickered to life with a face that bore out his statement. For a moment Thornton's attention was held by the gaudy uniform covering the big green-skinned body; the elaborate dazzle of gold and jewelry; even the anachronism of a long, curved sword. He remembered that the Venusians had been behind Earth, technologically and socially, when the first visits were made. They had caught up in scientific achievement with an almost frightening speed, driven perhaps by some desire to prove their own superiority to the strangers from beyond the sky; but their society was still almost feudal, dominated by the great aristocratic families and a tradition regulating even the smallest details of life.

But there was nothing stupid or ignorant about the lean hairless features and the arrogant dark eyes that looked into theirs. Save for the bony crest on the bald skull, and the green skin and lack of external ears, it could have been the face of some Terrestrial leader, shrewd and strong and ruthless.

He spoke in the near-perfect English, which was required knowledge for all Venusian officers: "Imperial Zamandarian cruiser *Xiucuayotl*, Commander Uincozuma speaking, calling Terrestrial spaceship *Bolivar.*"

"Terrestrial spaceship *Bolivar,* Captain Henry speaking," replied the man automatically, and then in sudden realization: "You—know what ship this is?"

"Of course." The Venusian's face split in a steely smile. "The intelligence services of Zamandar are not staffed by utter fools, Captain Henry. When we learned that an ostensibly private organization was maintaining a costly patrol in outer space, it was only natural to assume that those ships would bear watching."

"But—" Thornton came forth into the scanner area. "But—a private archeological research project—"

"Surely your government did not expect anyone on Zamandar to believe such a feeble story," said Uincozuma contemptuously.

Henry smiled thinly at Thornton. "You'll never change his conviction," he said. "A planet where everything is controlled by a ruling class, among which intrigue is the normal order of things, would never take a statement such as that at face value. So it seems that regardless of your desire to meet—them—unofficially, we'll still have to represent all Earth."

"And now—" Uincozuma leaned forward until his stiff countenance seemed to project from the screen, his strong presence to fill the bridge—"now, Captain Henry and gentlemen, what is the identity of that ship? Where is it from? How did you know when it was due—or even that it was coming at all?"

"Our secret—" began Thornton.

"Nonsense!" The metal voice shivered in the telescreen with its violence. "You are a merchant ship, feebly armed at best and manned by civilians. This is a cruiser of the Imperial navy. Conduct yourselves accordingly.

"If necessary, I will not hesitate to blow you out of the sky and deal directly with the stranger. But—"

The screen flickered and buzzed with interference. The excited voice of the *Bolivar's* radioman came over the intercom: "Sir, there's another signal. The strange ship is calling us—"

"At last," Thornton gasped the words, and Henry saw the hope in his eyes. Perhaps even now—

Uincozuma smiled, grimly. "This should be an interesting conversation," he said. "You might as well arrange for a three-way hookup, Captain Henry. I'll be listening anyway."

Thornton laughed, shakily. "Go ahead," he challenged, "and may you get joy of it."

Henry brought the auxiliary telescreen around in such a manner that it scanned the *Bolivar's* bridge, including the main screen with Uincozuma's face. His hand shook a little as he turned it on. After fifteen thousand years—

THE FACE grew into the screen, and he knew that it was Martian. It was the face that had looked out of the old murals in New Thebes one unforgotten day when he had been there. Henry remembered the faint chill he had felt then, as he comprehended the age of that painted face, for fifty thousand years the painter had been dust and still those strange golden eyes had looked out over the iron deserts and watched a planet die. And now, before him, it was the same undying countenance, beautiful and ageless and unhuman, and its blind stare had become fierce and alive, and it spoke to him.

It was an avian face, with a long curved beak reaching out from the narrow skull, a long slim neck down to the half manlike body, which sat wrapped in a red cloak. A smooth white coat of feathers covered the Martian, flaring into a shining blue crest on his head—the whole being, face and body, had a stark simplicity, which was somehow utterly awesome and beautiful. It was the eyes that held his most, the great golden eyes with fire smoldering and swirling behind them, he could not meet that terrible gaze for long at a time.

He thought, briefly, of the unbelievable ages of civilization behind that being, of a journey across a waste of light-years to find an empty planet and back to find the homeland of powers and wisdom beyond his guessing—and it seemed only right that this one who faced him should be thus. He imagined, vaguely, that a god might look something like that.

Uincozuma's amazed oaths faded into silence, and the Venusian regained the aristocrat's iron self-possession. Glancing at him, Henry could almost see the brain whirring at top speed behind that impassive visage. The nobles of Zamandas could be disturbingly keen—and Uincozuma commanded an armed cruiser.

His attention turned back to Thornton. The archeologist was crouched before the screen, tensed to the breaking point, and a devouring ecstasy lit his whole being. This was the culmination of ten years' work and waiting and hope; he faced the stranger from the stars and it was now he who might carry destiny. It was almost a religious feeling, and Henry scowled. His own hard practicality was returning to the spaceman; mysticism was no attitude just now.

The Martian spoke, a rippling, clicking flow of syllables, like a brook running over stones, with here and there a guttural singing or a high thin whistle, the language of birds. Thornton nodded. "It's the old language," he said. "The crew of this ship learned it, as a tongue they would have in common with Mars— or more likely the colonists never abandoned it. It's a perfect language in its way—"

He answered the Martian, slowly shaping his tongue and throat to sounds never meant for human utterance. Briefly the Martian started obviously amazed, and then lapsed into his statuesque immobility, the quiet of an eagle on its perch.

Henry could not even distinguish many of the sounds, but he could guess at what was said, *Welcome, welcome back to the Solar System.*

You are not—of our race.

No, we are of the inner planets, we are younger than you. Your own world died long ago, long ago, your people are dust on the lonely desert wind, you have had your long journey across space for nothing—but welcome, welcome home!

"Henry. Captain Henry."

THE SPACEMAN turned at the voice, to meet Uincozuma's bleak gaze. "There is no longer any need for you to attempt concealment," said the Venusian matter of factly. "It is perfectly obvious what happened. The dying Martians sent out a few colonists to some other star. Their descendants were to return at a certain time, and your archeological society found the records telling of that return. So you kept it secret, meaning to deal with the Martians for the benefit of Earth. But I am here now; I can deal too."

"Without speaking their language?" jeered Henry.

"There are other ways. Let the Martians but come to Venus, and we have our own scientists who can talk to them."

"But not out here."

"No. However—the Martians will most certainly try to communicate with me, somehow, as well as with you. After all—your race is just as foreign to them as mine. If everything else fails—I still command a starship!"

Henry looked out the port. The *Xiucuayotl* was visible to the naked eye now, a thin metal sliver splashing bright flames of rocket jets across the sky. He had seen the sleek deadly vessels of her class at close range, he knew how hopelessly more powerful she was than the *Bolivar*. If Uincozuma could deal directly with the Martians, even if the Martian ship stayed neutral in any battle, the Earthlings might as well not be here.

If on the other hand the Martians could be persuaded to side with the *Bolivar*, their own immense powers— But did they have any? That monster craft didn't look like a warship— anyway, according to Thornton they hadn't come expecting to find the younger races advanced beyond a barbaric state. Even if the *Xiucuayotl* had to fight the Martian vessel, she might still be the winner. Uincozuma might still take his prize and his captives back to Venus.

And the Martian technology—oh, what must they not know! Even back in that age when they were still in the System, they had known things at which modern science could only offer conjectures. The records told of disintegrant beams, control of gravity, chain reactions, which could wrap a whole planet in flame. Not enough apparatus had survived to teach latter-day science much—and if now that power were thrown into the balance—

CHAPTER FOUR

THORNTON turned back to face Henry and the image of Uincozuma. "He wants to talk to all three of us," said the archeologist. "He wants me to interpret. I'll do it, of course—whatever is said." His eyes challenged both the captains."

"Good," said the Venusian. "Bid him welcome in the name of Imperial Zamandar—"

"I took that for granted," said Thornton dryly.

"—and ask him who he is and what his errand, that we may best assist him," finished Uincozuma smoothly.

"He has already told me. As nearly as I can render the names, he is Herakon, *phryon*—that's only approximately equivalent to 'captain'—of the ship *Delphis* from the planet Kiarios. And, of course, he is here with his fellows on the long-planned visit to the Solar System. They are peaceful scientists and 'other citizens'—whatever that phrase means—who desired only to make contact with their fellow Martians or, since these are no longer living, to visit their graves and get some relics for the new world." Thornton frowned a little. "By all we know of Mars from the records, the race has always had an extremely devout regard for the past and its physical remains. They may not like the fact that we—Earth and Venus—have left the ruins unrestored, and removed much of the old works and even bones to our museums, and built blatant new structures allover the old deserts."

"How could two young races be expected—dead aliens—" Henry caught his temper. This was no time to jet off; now, if ever, the desperate need was for cool and careful and hard-boiled thinking. With the Martians, of Lord knew what powers and intentions, and the Venusians, whose strength and purpose were all too plain, catastrophe loomed for all Earth unless—

Thornton gave him a cold look. "I daresay the Martians will allow for the immaturity of our races," he said. "But sometimes it is necessary to punish children."

"Damn it, man, it isn't right to try and look at your own race from outside that way. It's Earth—mankind—"

"The usual slogans by which the militarists gain the witless allegiance of fools. I did not choose my race, Captain Henry, but I did choose my allegiance—to the ideals of peace and sanity. If, as I think, the Martians are closer than Earth or Venus to those ideals, then the Martians are my People."

Henry half opened his mouth, and snapped it shut again. You couldn't argue with a fanatic, and they needed Thornton. As long as he was the only one who could talk to the Martians, they needed him.

The archeologist was conversing with Herakon again. Henry turned away from the flow of unhuman syllables with something of a shudder. It was almost with a feeling of relief that he faced Uincozuma's cold strength and the understandable problem that the Venusian represented. "What're we to do?" he asked.

THERE WAS a certain sympathy, but no comfort, in the steely reply: "Whatever circumstances dictate. In a way, it simplifies matters that your archeologist is on the Martian side—assuming that they want him. Otherwise, the best thing might have been for me to destroy your ship and try to get the Martians to accompany me—they would understand some sort of sign language or picture writing, I suppose. But as it is—we shall see."

"We both represent Sol in a way, Uincozuma. Couldn't we make some kind of working truce to deal with these strangers? They aren't really Solarian any longer. Their real interests lie in whatever new system they inhabit."

"Earth and Venus can only agree against Kiarios if it proves equally hostile to both. But if there is any faintest chance that the Martians—Kiarians, if you like—can be persuaded to help either of our planets—if only to the extent of giving us any of their scientific knowledge—then, of course, it is my duty to see that Venus gets that help. If the Martians want to help you, I shall have to destroy you and try to destroy or capture them—at the very least, destroy you and run Sunward till I can get in radio range and call the Imperial fleet to my aid. If on the other hand the Martians choose to help me—why, then I must capture or destroy you anyway, to keep you from carrying the news back to Earth." There was no personal hostility in the cool statement, but neither was there any pity. Mercy was no consideration whatever with the Venusian aristocracy.

Henry turned to Thornton. "You see," he began angrily, *"that's* the sort of thing the 'red-necked admirals' you despise are protecting us against. If it weren't for our 'militaristic morons,' Earthlings would have been serfs to Venusian overlords twenty years ago. If you can wrap yourself in your own smug virtuousness and let that sort of thing happen to men and women and children who never gave anyone any offense—"

"How about Venusian males and females and young?" snapped the scientist. "They weren't hurting anyone either, but they've died in the 'border incidents;' they don't want to knuckle under to *our* military commanders and plantation owners any more than we want— Oh, shut up, anyway." He turned back to Herakon. The Martian sat wrapped in his cloak of silence, watching them. Henry thought of old, vaguely remembered myths, Osiris weighing the hearts of the dead in the Hall of Judgement. And what was the Martian thinking now behind those eyes of molten gold?

He grew aware that Herakon was talking again and that Thornton was translating into English, almost unconsciously, as an aid in guiding his own mind through the intricacies of the ancient language. He listened, and Uincozuma listened, and save for that lilting, fluting flow of unhuman words and the low-voiced, stumbling human tongue, there was silence on the bridge, the silence of space.

"—far and far they went, ever seeking, and suns bloomed out of the great dark and faded behind them, and never was there the world they sought. Many and strange were the planets they left behind them, much did they see and learn in those centuries, but home became a myth to them, a hopeless racial dream. A few, a very few planets they found, which were as their longings, but these all bore intelligent life of their own, and our ancestors would no more than we displace the rightful owners of a land were that the Lost Country itself."

"And you *never* fought a war?" asked Uincozuma softly. Thornton scowled, but put the question into Martian. The great beaked head nodded, slowly.

"Twice have we fought, in all the long time since Mars was young. Once on our way between the stars, we found a system wherein were three races, and one of these was utterly evil. It was a race of carnivores, which had murder in their hearts as an instinct; they had fought each other in devastating wars, driven by what seemed a need of combat, until they reached the other planets. Then they forgot their quarrels in the rush on their defenseless neighbors. One race they had enslaved, when our ancestors arrived, and the other they had condemned to death because it would not yield; only a few gallant remnants of it fought on. Our ancestors recoiled in horror, but they had a plain duty. The surgeon does not hesitate to destroy a billion lives of disease germs to save the life of one intelligent being. They used their knowledge and the world-smashing power of their ships to help the two attacked races, and they wiped out every last one of the enemy species before leaving that system. It was a hard and cruel thing to do, but the universe is a cleaner place for it.

"Then once again we fought, some centuries after the landing on Kiarios, when the natives of another star came conquering. These were not so evil as the earlier aggressors, but they were dangerous and they wrought great damage ere we mobilized our powers. Here again we resolved on extermination, simply as a safeguard for the future." The metallic yellow eyes blazed with cold pride. "No race has a right to pick a fight, but it has a right to guard itself against potential wars' by the most appropriate means. Kiarios sent a fleet to the enemy's home planet and unleashed the atomic fire. That world will still be a white blaze a hundred thousand years from today. It will be a beacon warning the war-makers in the cosmos to let Kiarios be!"

THE MARTIAN made an imperious gesture with one claw-like hand, and a blank stillness descended. Henry fought for control. Fear, it was fear that crawled along his spine and shrieked in his brain, a fear less of personal death than of the extinction of all which had made him, the death of Earth and mankind. Earth, Earth, the blue skies and the rolling hills and the broad wild seas—was Earth to stand in one lurid blaze because the Martians decided that Earthlings were evil?

We are, in a way. Both we and Venus have sinned beyond redemption by Martian standards in our silly, bloody wars, in our childish grasping for political and economic power, in the—simply in the potential menace to Kiarios which we represent. The Martians are not aggressive like us, but they are utterly ruthless. To safeguard themselves, or even to vindicate an abstract moral principle, they would not hesitate to blow up the Sun.

Herakon was speaking again in answer to some question of Thornton's: "Aye, we found our world at last, and it was worth every second of the bitter, weary centuries, it was like Mars come young again, green and fair and alive, with seas that sparkled in the sun and mountains that reached for the sky. And no strangers walked over the wide windy plains or flew through the fair skies, it was a lonely world—it was our own. We had come home.

"So we landed on Kiarios, strange planet of a strange sun five hundred light-years from Sol, and the wanderers—or their children or grandchildren—felt it was more their home than the barren deserts of Mars had ever been. And that was more than thirteen thousand years ago, and they have been there ever since.

"It was hard at first, bitterly hard. Our species is not by nature given to pioneering, physical or technological; only in art and philosophy do we feel free to make the great bold advances, which are the justification of intelligence. But we have, at least, the will and the strength to survive.

"And over the centuries we built out culture anew, and slowly we even learned what our ancestors had not known, and we perfected ourselves and our achievements. Today we hold the system of Kiarios in a perfectly balanced civilization. Nothing can ever go wrong internally; we can endure forever, and in our own way we are happy."

(Thornton raised a puzzled face. "I can't quite translate that," he whispered. "That phrase—well, it doesn't really mean 'happy' or 'contented' or 'successful' or any other state that might make sense to an Earthling or a Venusian. It means the Martian equivalent, but that is something unimaginable to us, a state which is, in its own way, dynamic—but wait." He turned back to the speaking Martian.)

HERAKON continued. "But there was an ancient promise made, and it had to be fulfilled. The completion of our task required a full cycle, a return to the descendants of our ancestors—or their graves. A young race, which has not that feeling of kinship with an immense and overwhelmingly great past, cannot realize what a basic need that is. And so this ship came back; for five hundred years it traveled at nearly the speed of light, and it will be five hundred years again in getting back. We will only have lived a hundred years inside the ship, because of the relativistic time-shift, but even that is long, long—and a thousand years will have gone by when we return..." For an instant, Henry caught the note of utter longing in the Martian's voice, and he knew that he himself would never have had the courage to attempt that dreadful journey. "Even for a race as long-lived as ours, a hundred years is long, and a thousand years longer. We can never really return. The civilization of Kiarios will still be there, unchanged, but all that we knew, all our friends and kin and *etai* ("I can't translate that," said Thornton) will be in the tombs, and we will live alone." The head lifted again, the eyes blazed with the old iron pride that had carried the race across space and time and conquered a planet's death to do it. "But the blood of Mars will live! The *race* will have been to its ancestors and returned with their strength."

"Your ancestors are gone," said Thornton quietly. "The old cities are crumbled in ruin, and your kin of Mars is dust on a lonely wind."

"So we feared, so we feared. We had hoped— But no matter." Again the undying will, which had defied time and space and death, which had vanquished worlds and crossed the stars. "If Mars is indeed dead, if only the wind stirs between the hollow bones of the old ones, then still we have not come in vain. We *know*. We will bring back the knowledge of what happened to Kiarios, and our race will again have the past that it must have for its sanity. And on old Mars we will raise a cenotaph, and some day others will come to restore her."

"I wonder what the colonial commissions of our respective planets will think of *that*," muttered Henry in an aside to Uincozuma.

The Venusian grinned. "Unless the Martians will sign a thousand forms in triplicate, they won't like it," he said. Then suddenly, almost wistfully: "Damn it, Earthling, I like you; we're two sane men against a thing from outside older than all our races' memories. It's too bad I have to destroy you."

"Or I you," said Henry and added bleakly: "Or the Martians both of us."

CHAPTER FIVE

THORNTON was talking to the Martian again, rapidly, and Henry saw the beaked face suddenly alive with an expression of—horror, disgust, almost hatred. Then steely control clamped down once more, it was again the face of an impersonal judging god, but for that instant Henry knew he had looked on death.

Uincozuma must have caught that fleeting glimpse. He leaned forward in the screen and said suddenly, softly and hurriedly: "That thing may be dangerous to both of us, Captain Henry."

"It may indeed." Glancing out, the Earthling saw the Venusian cruiser against the Milky Way. It was near, quite near, its shark form lay across the sky in deadly menace. It dwarfed the *Bolivar*. But its mass was insignificant beside the looming bulk of the *Delphis,* even though—even though the Martian vessel was strangely empty—

"The Martians are unpredictable," said Uincozuma. "They may decide to sterilize our respective planets as a precautionary measure, or simply because our races don't fit their moral standards. At the very least, they may sneak undetected out of the Solar System—but that would mean destroying the *Xiucuayotl* and the *Bolivar* lest we carry word of their visit back to our planets."

"I don't like it," admitted Henry. He cast an uneasy glance over at Thornton and Herakon. The Martian was speaking now, slowly and weightily, and there was a tightening in the archeologist's gaunt face, which showed that even his pacifistic fanaticism was being shaken.

"You have guns, of course?" Uincozuma's urgent voice came harshly in his ears. "Stand by to turn them on the Martian, if the need arises. I'll go after those tubes or whatever they are at the stern—must be part of her drive, we may be able to disable her. Between us, we might be able to stand off, or capture her."

"And then have you open up on us, so that only Venus will know?" bristled Henry. "Nothin' doing, Commander; it's Earth that comes first with me."

"I admire your patriotism," said Uincozlma, "but it may cost your planet its life unless we can stop—"

Thornton turned and interrupted them; his face was very white. "The Martians don't—they don't like the idea of races as young and uncivilized as ours possessing space travel," he said tensely. "They say our technical abilities, far superior even to their own, outstrip our social culture so greatly that we're a danger to the universe and to ourselves—"

Henry could not resist a barbed answer to the aristocrat who had snubbed him during the many months: "Isn't that what you've been saying all along?"

"Yes, but—I never thought—the Martians are outsiders! Herakon says they think we shouldn't have the science we do. He says we may even find a way to travel faster than light, which the Martians know is theoretically possible but which they've never managed to put into practice—and then the whole Galaxy is in danger from us!"

"And what they think *should* be, has a nasty habit of coming to pass," murmured Uincozuma. "What do they propose to do now?"

"Their ship still represents a greater power than all the combined might of Earth and Venus." Thornton's voice was thick now, and he was shivering violently. "They're going to go on into the inner system and see for themselves. If matters are as I've described—and they are—I told the truth; I thought they'd understand—I thought their old wisdom would bring peace to us—"

"You're a romantic," said Uincozuma, with a sardonic humor that somehow increased Henry's reluctant liking for him. That the Venusian could smile, however wryly, in this moment— "You thought because the Martians weren't actively aggressive that they were a race of gods or saints. They aren't; in some ways, they're crueler than we. They're certainly just as selfish in protecting themselves, or just as unreasonable when their morals have been offended." His voice rapped out: "What will they do?"

"They'll force us, Earth and Venus, to blow up all our machines, burn all our books, go back to barbarism—or else they'll rain fire from the sky till we do it anyway."

"We—shall—see!" The Venusian's eyes narrowed. Suddenly he was snapping orders in his guttural native tongue.

"They're going to attack the *Delphis*," choked Thornton. "Oh, no—"

"Why not?" asked Henry grimly. "More power to them." But he made no move toward his own intercom.

"But aren't you—won't you help—"

"No, you fool! Let the Venusians exhaust themselves against the Martians; we may find our own chance somewhere in the scramble to come out on top of both the others."

"You incredible scoundrel—" Thornton took a step forward, the breath rattling in his throat. "The Venusians are our allies, fighting for Sol against this—invader—and you stand coldly by and let them die for—Earth—" He balled his fists.

HENRY STOPPED the clumsy lunge with contemptuous ease. His big hands seized Thornton's skinny wrists and pulled the taller man around with brutal force. "Shut up and behave yourself," growled the captain. "You've made enough trouble already with your damned self-righteousness; you're no better than the Martians. I'm for Earth first and last and forever, because it's *my* planet, *my* home, *my* wife and kids there—and to hell with the rest of the universe."

"That's the sort of narrowness which has ruined— Oh, God!" Thornton's voice was almost a scream.

Henry saw the *Xiucayotl* sweep in for the attack. He saw fire streak from her sides, a hailing hell of shells and torpedoes and blistering atomic-nitrogen flames, radioactive gas and saw nuclear energy, a ship-ruining barrage that would have left any Solarian craft in molten wreckage. And he saw the bombardment strike the dim blue haze around the *Delphis* and explode in a blue-white ravenousness of incandescent power.

Sight came back as the dazzle swirled raggedly away from his eyes. The *Delphis* loomed enormously, untouched, scatheless. Henry heard a voice choking, and was vaguely aware that it was his own: "They have the energy screen. Our own physicists think it may be possible, a screen of pure energy, impenetrable to matter—and the Martians have it; they've had it for a hundred thousand years—"

Herakon spoke, harshly and curtly, and Thornton's frightened eyes went to Uincozuma's taut face. "Having showed you—their defensive strength—" he mumbled, "they'll now show you—as little—of their offensive power—"

The Venusian snarled something inarticulate. It was terrible to see the high pride of invincibility crumbling in him.

And from the *Delphis* sprang a long finger of light, pure white light like a living sunbeam, and almost caressingly it felt out along the *Xiucuayotl.* Where it touched, steel puffed into vapor and open wounds gaped in the armored hull. There was no puff of air from those bulkheaded compartments; the air must have exploded outward at velocities too great for visibility, and every being in those sections must be dead, cooked in his spacesuit—

Invincible, impregnable, with a hundred thousand years of science behind her, the *Delphis* could sail through space and not all the weapons that Earth and Venus together could hurl at her would change that inexorable course. She could hover beyond a planet's atmosphere, and that beam of living energy could slash across continents and explode cities into white-hot gas, and civilization would crash to nothing.

But damn it, damn it, the ship was only one vessel, it was one hollow vessel, all but empty—it wasn't *reasonable* that—

UINCOZUMA'S haggard eyes sought Henry's. The Venusian was trembling with rage and grief and the dawn of fear. He said, very slowly and bitterly: "We had best start to bargain with them, Captain Henry."

"Yes—no—wait—" The Earthling's gaze swung back to meet the bright gold of Herakon's. There was something funny about that Martian, he wasn't the judging god any longer, however hard he tried to be; he was just a shade too tense and eager himself. Could it be—

A hollow ship five hundred light-years from home, facing two alien races of incredible technical skill, races, which might have done almost anything in the long time since they had been left behind— *How would you feel, Moss Henry? How'd you like to be up against that?*

Wait—wait! No, by Heaven! Could it be—COULD IT BE—

His hands were shaking so badly that he could hardly grasp pencil and paper. He had to figure now; he had to think as coolly and clearly as man had ever thought before—and that under the lash of time, with a finger of pure energy waiting to reach out and touch him— *Stall them off! Stall them both!*

"Thornton," he said, "ask the Martians if all their weapons are energy weapons?"

"Why—well—all right." The archeologist turned back to the stranger. He had the look of an utterly beaten man. Presently he looked around again.

"Herakon says yes, as far as this ship is concerned. After all, The *Delphis* did not come expecting to fight anybody. He sees no harm in admitting that all the defensive and offensive strength of this vessel comes from the main drive-converters. And he adds that they have many forms of energy weapons other than what they have just shown us."

"I don't doubt it." *Damn it, what are those Einstein formulas now? Ah, yes—but my math is pretty rusty—* "Okay—Uincozuma!"

"Yes?" It was a dull tone; the Venusian hadn't admitted defeat yet, but he saw no hope of victory.

"Run for Venus. Highest acceleration your ship and crew can stand."

"Run? But why—"

"Carry word back, if nothing else. Not that the Martians won't let you, in the present situation, but—well—get out of range of their energy beam. Now! You'll still be in radio range. Quick!"

"Well—" Uincozuma smiled bitterly. "I suppose it's best. It will save one Imperial ship, to smash itself later against that screen. But you—?"

"I'll come as soon as I can. Having a little engine trouble right now. I don't think that beam is effective at more than fifty thousand miles. If you can get that far, you'll be safe."

"But Venus won't—"

"Get *going!*"

Uincozuma nodded, wearily. In his own indecision, the effect of a lifetime of naval discipline was to make him obey an authoritative voice. He gave his orders, and in moments the *Xiucuayotl* was splashing the void with rocket fire.

Henry worked on, unobtrusively computing. *Damn that integration! The mass-velocity formula—* "Herakon wants to know why the Venusian is fleeing," said Thornton.

Uincozuma bristled in the screen. Henry smiled humorlessly. "Oh, tell him it's to get word to his home planet as quickly as possible; he shouldn't care."

"He doesn't. The *Delphis* will be starting to accelerate for the inner planets soon. He wants you to give him figures for computing an orbit to Mars."

HENRY FROWNED. "I will, in a minute." He finished his calculation, and nodded. It worked. Yes, it worked. But he felt no special triumph, the hardest, most desperate gamble was just starting.

"Thornton," he said suddenly, *"sprechen Sie Deutsch?"*

"Eh?" The archeologist blinked, wondering if the madness of crumbling dreams had not also fallen on the captain. "Do I—do I speak German? No—but you—"

"You didn't think a dumb space-hound would know any foreign language? I know a few. I learned German to read Goethe in the original. But no matter—I'll have to take a longer chance—*Habla usted espanol?"*

"Si, naturalmente. Pero—por que—?"

"It gives us a secret language," said Henry in Spanish, "unless Uincozuma knows it too, which is possible but doubtful." He glanced at the screen, but the Venusian was too busy with commands to pay them any attention. "The Latin units of the

Terrestrial fleet usually use English except aboard their own craft.

"Now listen—I'm about to pull the most colossal bluff in all history. If it works, we might still have a chance to salvage something—we may even end up a little better off than we were. If it doesn't—the *Bolivar* is finished, but Earth is in no worse fix. Not that it could be." Henry smiled thinly. "But you've got to be my interpreter with Herakon. No matter what I say, you've got to look unsurprised and render it exactly into Martian. Got it?"

"I—yes." Thornton nodded, something of his self-possession returning to him. *He isn't a bad fellow,* thought Henry. *He's just been living too long in his own ideal dreamworld.*

"Okay. Now—Uincozuma." The Venusian's image was getting a little fainter and blurrier on the screen with distance, but it was still clear enough. "Are you out of energy beam range?"

The voice was tight with the strain of brutal accelerations: "Not quite, I think. But I should soon be."

"Now look, Uincozuma. That Martian ship is powerful enough to destroy our combined fleets and lay waste our home planets—*and it intends to,* for its own safety and its people's. We may be able to bargain. The Martians aren't devils; they'll agree to any proposal, which looks reasonable to them. But it must guarantee them absolute safety from us."

"To be sure. Have you any suggestion?"

"I have a vague sort of idea kicking around in my head, but we'll have to bluff and bargain. In the end, of course, we'll have to yield to whatever they say; theirs is the final word. But I just might be able to trick them into thinking we're more powerful than we really are."

"How?"

"I'd rather not say, just now. It's too nebulous in my own head. I just want you to back me up in whatever I may do or say. Don't look surprised, whatever it is."

159

Uincozuma sat pondering while the seconds fled by, and with each instant his dwindling ship was farther away, safer from destruction. At last he nodded. "Why not? I'll do it, Captain Henry; somehow, I trust you."

"Good!" Henry grinned; almost wolfishly, as he faced back to Thornton and said in Spanish: "I wonder what our dear green friend will say when he finds how we're going to use his trust?"

"You mean you'd betray him—for Earth's advantage—"

"I told you I'm first and foremost an Earthman. But now to the Martians. Tell Herakon that I've guessed his secret. Tell him that the *Xiucuayotl* is safe from him now, bearing word of his fatal weakness back to Earth and Venus."

"*What?*"

"You heard me. Quick, now! And for the love of mercy, don't look so astonished. Act natural!"

THORNTON looked shakily toward the screen and rattled forth a string of harsh sounds. Henry reflected irrelevantly on how peculiarly expressive the Martian language was. It had sung and wept with joy and sorrow, now it snarled with menace—it might not be a bad common tongue for all the planets. Someday.

Herakon was shaken. For a moment his hands lifted like eagle talons. Henry quivered in expectation of the flame that would devour him— With a supreme effort, the Martian mastered himself. When he spoke, through Thornton, it was coldly and calmly.

"He asks—"

"In Spanish, man, in Spanish!"

"He asks what you are talking about; he says you must be mad."

"Then ask him if the relativistic equations are mad? Tell him I know he's been bluffing us. He ran his ship up to a speed that brought his own time rate up to ten times that of the outside universe. But by Einstein's formulas, the ship's mass must have increased in the same proportion. That mass—his kinetic energy—could only have come from fuel carried along. An immense amount of fuel, especially if you allow for his having to decelerate, too, and for his power requirements en route. When he started, over ninety percent of his ship's total mass must have been fuel.

"But his ship is almost empty now. That means he must have used up almost all his fuel getting here. He can't leave the Solar System till he gets more. He must be running on his last reserves of energy—and all his weapons, with their fantastic power needs, have to run off that store too.

"He *can't* stand off Earth and Venus; he's been bluffing. He can, at best, destroy a large percentage of an attacking fleet—but in the end his screens must go, down, his projectors must go dark, and he will lie helpless before us.

"And Uincozuma is now out of range of his weapons, bearing the word of his weakness back to the united inner planets!"

Thornton spoke, the words stumbling over themselves in their haste, and for an instant Henry looked on utter despair waging a devil's war with a blind destroying fury in the Martian's eyes. Herakon snapped one grim command, and the awful flames leaped out—out, out, after the *Xiucuayotl* at the speed of light—but even their raging fury was swallowed by the sheer distance.

Uincozuma's hard face smiled bleakly in the telescreen. "Our ship's getting hot," he said. "But it's not worse than the refrigerating units can handle. What did you say to him, Henry?"

"I think I got him a little peeved," grinned the Earthling tightly. "But he'll cool off. Just tell Thornton to tell Herakon that you're one hundred percent with us. Tell the Martian to start talking turkey—fast."

"Consider it said," nodded Uincozuma, and Thornton conveyed the word. The searching energy beams died.

"It's no good trying to destroy the *Bolivar*," said Henry to Herakon, via the Spanish language. "You can do it, of course, but you can't fight the Solar System. However, Earth and Venus aren't the mindlessly destructive barbarians you think. We're perfectly willing to bargain. It would be the greatest loss we have ever sustained, if you destroyed yourselves and your knowledge. Not that it would do any good. Sooner or later, we'd come looking for you, probably in faster-than light ships. Best you make a friendly agreement now, between mutually respectful equals.

HERAKON spoke, slowly, and there was defeat and despair in his tones. Thornton rendered it into Spanish: "You will never be satisfied, I see, until you have our scientific knowledge, which your own perverted ingenuity will quickly apply far more effectively than we ever could. But how can children grasp such powers without ruining themselves and the rest of the Galaxy? But you give us fuel to go, lest you learn too much for your own good. Or best we smash everything in our ship, and kill ourselves as you suggest. It will be for your own race's good, too."

"Knowledge is never evil," said Henry, "but sometimes it needs control. I admit that there are factions on Earth and Venus who should not be allowed to get possession of these new powers. But that can be arranged.

"Suppose, for instance, that Earth and Venus set up a council with control over the new powers, a council empowered and enjoined to keep peace in the Solar System. It would keep that peace, since nothing could stand up against its weapons; therefore it could as well be given control of all military forces, and would be. If it were set up democratically, giving each planet a chance to attain its ends peacefully, war would become obsolete. And if Mars—Kiarios—sent representatives with an equal voice on the council, you would, in fact, benefit since you would be in on the scientific advances that will be made with the old Martian knowledge as a basis and your own interests would be safeguarded.

"And there need never be war."

Herakon sat quietly, digesting it, his strange golden eyes lost in thought. And Thornton looked with suddenly shining eyes on Henry and gasped: "You. You, the narrow patriot, are the one who thought how to get peace—"

"I'm still a provincial," said Henry tiredly. "I'll always put myself, my wife, and my little Harvey with the bandy legs' first. But—well, I have enough common sense to know that war is not the beat solution for anyone concerned."

Uincozuma spoke, slowly and suspiciously: "What are you two talking in that language for? What are you plotting?"

"Plots," grinned Henry. "And what are you going to do about it?"

"Nothing—now. But if you've betrayed Zamandar—"

Herakon spoke, gravely, and Thornton listened long before he said to Henry: "Briefly, he agrees to the proposal. He says it involves a certain risk, but that the gains for Kiarios and all other worlds are great enough to outweigh that. He'll go through with it. And—he compliments us. He says perhaps he misjudged our races."

"Well, tell him that there are elements on both planets who'll oppose the solution. Tell him he'll have to continue his bluff that we'll have to spread an official story of the Martians forcing us, for our own good, to make this treaty. Once his ship is refueled and really invincible, we can let out the truth; in the meantime the concept of the Martains as the all-powerful altruists will be useful."

"Won't others guess the secret as you did?"

"They may. But there isn't too much danger. Your despised 'militarists' aren't as bloodthirsty as you think. I believe it'll work."

HENRY turned to Uincozuma. "Herakon has agreed to a compromise," he said. "He'll let our civilizations live. But he'll need adequate guarantees against any danger we carry; that means a control council for the new powers, with the Martians having an equal voice with Earth and Venus. It means—the end of war, Uincozuma."

"Well—" The aristocrat looked, briefly, glum. Henry thought wryly that he was out of a job now. "Well—I suppose we have very little choice. I'll carry his word to my planet."

"Good. I'll go to Earth. And we'll all meet the *Delphis* again, somewhere off Mars."

Henry bent over his controls, preparing to accelerate Sunward. He felt no great elation. He was too exhausted emotionally, for that. But there was a quiet satisfaction within him.

He wondered if perhaps Venus and Kiarios had not felt the same way as he, had not looked for a peaceful solution, which would guarantee their own safety. Mutual fear—that was the great destroyer. Races might wipe each other out, because they feared. They might all be equally glad of this enforced peace and cooperation—even though the force was the most shadowy structure of bluff and trickery. Once the council was set up, peace would be stable, but right now—

Uincozuma's image was fading on the screen as his hurtling ship went out of radio range. The Venusian smiled at the Earthling, the smile of one warrior for another, and said in perfect Mexican Spanish: *"Adios, capitan, Hasta la vista!"*

Ye gods—Uincozuma knew!

But—wait! If he meant to betray the secret, he wouldn't have bothered to conceal his knowledge of Spanish; he'd been safely out of harm's way before the bargaining started. But he'd had to pretend not to know—or Henry, paralyzed by the old terrible fear of treachery and death, would not have driven his bargain with the Martians, would have sought some other solution, which would not have been as satisfactory to Venus as to Earth.

Uincozuma's on my side. He's a good fellow, that Venusian. And it's good to know his race can want peace as much as mine.

Looking over toward the other screen, Henry caught Herakon's eye. And for one fleeting instant, he could have sworn that it closed in a friendly wink, and that a chuckle vibrated in the long throat.

Ye gods—did he guess too? Did we all know? Were we all pretending to be fooled—for the sake of peace?

Suddenly Henry was laughing. He didn't stop laughing for a long time.

THE END

Earthman, Beware!

"Come and get me!" he thundered into the empty vastness of space, this tiny, earthbound creature who dared to challenge the dread, immortal race that had tamed the stars...and he cowered in fear as the answer echoed back.

CHAPTER ONE

AS HE neared the cabin; he grew aware that someone was waiting for him.

He paused for a moment, scowling, and sent his perceptions ahead to analyze that flash of knowledge. Something in his brain thrilled to the presence of metal, and there were subtler overtones of the organic—oil and rubber and plastic—he dismissed it as an ordinary small helicopter and concentrated on the faint, maddeningly elusive fragments of thought, nervous energy, life-flows between cells and molecules. There was only one person, and the sketchy outline of his data fitted only a single possibility.

Margaret.

For another instant he stood quietly, and his primary emotion was sadness. He felt annoyance, perhaps a subtle dismay that his hiding place had finally been located, but mostly it was pity that held him. Poor Peggy. Poor kid.

Well--he'd have to have it out. He straightened his slim shoulders and resumed his walk.

The Alaskan forest was quiet around him. A faint evening breeze rustled the dark pines and drifted past his cheeks, a cool lonesome presence in the stillness. Somewhere birds were twittering as they settled toward rest, and the mosquitoes raised a high, thin buzz as they whirled outside the charmed circle of the odorless repellent he had devised.

Otherwise, there was only the low scrunch of his footsteps on the ancient floor of needles. After two years of silence, the vibrations of human presence were like a great shout along his nerves.

When he came out into the little meadow, the sun was going down behind the northern hills. Long aureate rays slanted across the grass, touching the huddled shack with a wizard glow and sending enormous shadows before them. The helicopter was a metallic dazzle against the darkling forest, and he was quite close before his blinded eyes could discern the woman.

She stood in front of the door, waiting, and the sunset turned her hair to ruddy gold. She wore the red sweater and the navy-blue skirt she had worn when they had last been together, and her slim hands were crossed before her. So she had waited for him many times when he came out of the laboratory, quiet as an obedient child. She had never turned her pert vivacity on him, not after noticing how it streamed off his uncomprehending mind like rain off one of the big pines.

He smiled lopsidedly. "Hullo, Peggy," he said, feeling the blind inadequacy of words. But what could he say to her?

"Joel…" she whispered.

He saw her start and felt the shock along her nerves. His smile grew more crooked, and he nodded. "Yeah," he said. "I've been bald as an egg all my life. Out here, alone, I had no reason to use a wig."

Her wide hazel eyes searched him. He wore backwoodsman's clothes, plaid shirt and stained jeans and heavy shoes, and he carried a fishing rod and tackle box and a string of perch. But he had not changed at all. The small slender body, the fine-boned ageless features, the luminous dark eyes under the high forehead, they were all the same. Time had laid no finger on him.

Even the very baldness seemed a completion, letting the strong classic arch of his skull stand forth, stripping away another of the layers of ordinariness with which he had covered himself.

He saw that she had grown thin, and it was suddenly too great an effort to smile. "How did you find me, Peggy?" he asked quietly.

From her first word, his mind leaped ahead to the answer, but he let her say it out. "After you'd been gone six months with no word, we—all your friends, insofar as you ever had any—grew worried. We thought maybe something had happened to you in the interior of China. So we started investigating, with the help of the Chinese government, and soon learned you'd never gone there at all. It had just been a red herring that story about investigating Chinese archeological sites, a blind to gain time while you— disappeared. I just kept on hunting, even after everyone else had given up, and finally Alaska occurred to me. In Nome I picked up rumors of an odd and unfriendly squatter out in the bush. So, I came here."

"Couldn't you just have let me stay vanished?" he asked wearily.

"No." Her voice was trembling with her lips. "Not till I knew for sure, Joel. Not till I knew you were safe and— and—"

He kissed her, tasting salt on her mouth, catching the faint fragrance of her hair. The broken waves of her thoughts and emotions washed over him, swirling through his brain in a tide of loneliness and desolation.

SUDDENLY he knew exactly what was going to happen, what he would have to tell her and the responses she would make—almost to the word, he foresaw it, and the futility of it was like a leaden weight on his mind. But he had to go through with it, every wrenching syllable must come out. Humans were that way, groping through a darkness of solitude, calling to each other across abysses and never, never understanding.

"It was sweet of you," he said awkwardly. "You shouldn't have, Peggy, but it was…" His voice trailed off and his prevision failed. There were no words, which were not banal and meaningless.

"I couldn't help it," she whispered. "You know I love you."

"Look, Peggy," he said. "This can't go on. We'll have to have it out now. If I tell you who I am, and why I ran away—" He tried to force cheerfulness. "But never have an emotional scene on an empty stomach. Come on in and I'll fry up these fish."

"I will," she said with something of her old spirit. "I'm a better cook than you."

It would hurt her, but: "I'm afraid you couldn't use my equipment, Peggy."

He signaled to the door, and it opened for him. As she preceded him inside, he saw that her face and hands were red with mosquito bites. She must have been waiting a long time for him to come home.

"Too bad you came today," he said desperately. "I'm usually working in here. I just happened to take today off."

She didn't answer. Her eyes were traveling around the cabin, trying to find the immense order that she knew must underlie its chaos of material.

He had put logs and shingles on the outside to disguise it as an ordinary shack. Within, it might have been his Cambridge laboratory, and she recognized some of the equipment. He had filled a plane with it before leaving. Other things she did not remember, the work of his hands through two lonely years, jungles of wiring and tubing and meters and less understandable apparatus. Only a little of it had the crude, unfinished look of experimental setups. He had been working on some enormous project of his own, and it must be near its end now.

But after that—?

The gray cat, which had been his only real companion, even back in Cambridge, rubbed against her legs with a mew that might be recognition. *A friendlier welcome than* he *gave me,* she thought bitterly, and then, seeing his grave eyes on her, flushed. It was unjust. She had hunted him out of his self-chosen solitude, and he had been more than decent about it.

Decent—but not human. No unattached human male could have been chased across the world by an attractive woman without feeling more than the quiet regret and pity he showed.

Or did he feel something else? She would never know. No one would ever know all that went on within that beautiful skull. The rest of humanity had too little in common with Joel Weatherfield.

"The *rest* of humanity?" he asked softly.

She started. That old mind-reading trick of his had been enough to alienate most people. You never knew when he would spring it on you, how much of it was guesswork based on a transcendent logic and how much was—was—

He nodded. "I'm partly telepathic," he said, "and I can fill in the gaps for myself—like Poe's Dupin, only better and easier. There are other things involved too—but never mind that for now. Later."

He threw the fish into a cabinet and adjusted several dials on its face. "Supper coming up," he said.

"So now you've invented the robot chef," she said.

"Saves me work."

"You could make another million dollars or so if you marketed it."

"Why? I have more money right now than any reasonable being needs."

"You'd save people a lot of time, you know."

He shrugged.

She looked into a smaller room where he must live. It was sparsely furnished, a cot and a desk and some shelves holding his enormous microprinted library. In one corner stood the multitone instrument with which he composed the music that no one had ever liked—or understood. But he had always found the music of man shallow and pointless. And the art of man and the literature of man and all the works' and live's of man.

"How's Langtree coming with his new encephalograph?" he asked, though he could guess the answer. "You were going to assist him on it, I recall."

"I don't know." She wondered if her voice reflected her own weariness. "I've been spending all my time looking, Joel."

He grimaced with pain and turned to the automatic cook. A door opened in it and it slid out a tray with two dishes. He put them on a table and gestured to chairs. "Fall to Peggy."

In spite of herself, the machine fascinated her. "You must have an induction unit to cook that fast," she murmured, "and I suppose your potatoes and greens are stored right inside it. But the mechanical parts—" She shook her head in baffled wonderment, knowing that a blueprint would have revealed some utterly simple arrangement involving only ingenuity.

Dewed cans of beer came out of another cabinet. He grinned and lifted his. "Man's greatest achievement. Skoal."

She hadn't realized she was so hungry. He ate more slowly, watching her, thinking of the incongruity of Dr. Margaret Logan, of M.I.T. wolfing fish and beer in a backwoods Alaskan cabin.

Maybe he should have gone to Mars or some outer-planet satellite. But no, that would have involved leaving a much clearer trail for anyone to follow—you couldn't take off in a spaceship as casually as you could dash over to China. If he had to be found out, he would rather that she did it. For later on she'd keep his secret with the stubborn loyalty he had come to know.

She had always been good to have around, ever since he met her when he was helping M.IT. on their latest cybernetics work. Twenty-four year old Ph.D's with brilliant records were rare enough—when they were also good-looking young women, they became unique. Langtree had been quite hopelessly in love with her, of course. But she had taken on a double program of work, helping Weatherfield at his private laboratories in addition to her usual duties—and she planned to end the latter when her contract expired. She'd been more than useful to him, and he had not been blind to her looks, but it was the same admiration that he had for landscapes and thoroughbred cats and open space. And she had been one of the few humans with whom he could talk at all.

Had been. He exhausted her possibilities, in a year, as he drained most people in a month. He had known how she would react to any situation, what she would say to any remark of his, he knew her feelings, with a sensitive perception beyond her own knowledge. And the loneliness had returned.

But he hadn't anticipated her finding him, he thought wryly. After planning his flight he had not cared—or dared—to follow out all its logical consequences. Well, he was certainly paying for it now, and so was she.

HE HAD cleared the table and put out coffee and cigarettes before they began to talk. Darkness veiled the windows, but his fluorotubes came on automatically. She heard the far faint baying of a wolf out in the night, and thought that the forest was less alien to her than this room of machines and the man who sat looking at her with that too brilliant gaze.

He had settled himself in an easy chair and the gray cat had jumped up into his lap and lay purring as his thin fingers stroked its fur. She came over and sat on the stool at his feet, laying one hand on his knee. It was useless to suppress impulses when he knew them before she did.

Joel sighed. "Peggy," he said slowly, "you're making a hell of a mistake."

She thought briefly, how banal his words were, and then remembered that he had always been awkward in speech. It was as if he didn't feel the ordinary human nuances and had to find his way through society by mechanical rote.

He nodded. "That's right," he said.

"But what's the matter with you?" she protested desperately. "I know they all used to call you 'cold fish' and 'brain-heavy' and 'animated vacuum tube,' but it isn't so. I know you feel more than any of us do, only—only—"

"Only not the same way," he finished gently.

"Oh, you always were a strange sort," she said dully. "The boy wonder, weren't you? Obscure farm kid who entered Harvard at thirteen and graduated with every honor they could give at fifteen. Inventor of the ion-jet space drive, the controlled-disintegration iron process, the cure for the common cold, the crystalline-structure determination of geological age, and only Heaven and the patent office know how much else. Nobel prize winner in physics for your relativistic wave mechanics. Pioneer in a whole new branch of mathematical series theory. Brilliant writer on archeology, economics, ecology and semantics. Founder of whole new schools in painting and poetry. What's your I.Q., Joel?"

"How should I know? Above 200 or so, I.Q. in the ordinary sense becomes meaningless. I was pretty foolish, Peggy. Most of my published work was done at an early age, out of a childish desire for praise and recognition. Afterward, I couldn't just stop—conditions wouldn't allow it. And, of course, I had to do something with my time."

"Then at thirty, you pack up and disappear. *Why?*"

"I'd hoped they'd think I was dead," he murmured. "I had a beautiful faked crash in the Gobi, but I guess nobody ever found it. Because poor loyal fools like you just didn't believe I could die. It never occurred to you to look for my remains." His hand passed over her hair, and she sighed and rested her head against his knee. "I should have foreseen that."

"Why in hell I should have fallen in love with a goof like you, I'll never know," she said at last. "Most women ran in fright. Even your money couldn't get them close." She answered her own question with the precision of long thought. "But it was sheer quality, I suppose. After you, everyone else became so trite and insipid." She raised her eyes to him, and there was sudden terrified understanding in them. "And is that why you never married?" she whispered.

He nodded compassionately. Then, slowly, he added, "Also, I'm not too interested in sex yet. I'm still in early adolescence, you know."

"No, I don't know." She didn't move, but he felt her stiffen against him.

"I'm not human," said Joel Weatherfield quietly.

"A mutant? No, you couldn't be." He could feel the tensing of her, the sudden rush of wild thought and wordless nerve current, pulse of blood as the endocrines sought balance on a high taut level of danger. It was the old instinctive dread of the dark and the unknown and the hungry presences beyond a dim circle of firelights—she held herself moveless, but she was an animal bristling in panic.

Calmness came, after a while during which he simply sat stroking her hair. She looked up at him again, forcing herself to meet his eyes.

He smiled as well as he could and said, "No, Peggy, all this could never happen in one mutation. I was found in a field of grain one summer morning thirty years ago. A...woman ...who must have been my mother, was lying beside me. They told me later she was of my physical type, and that and the curious iridescent garments she wore made them think she was some circus freak. But she was dead, burned and torn by energies against which she had shielded me with her body. There were only a few crystalline fragments lying around. The people disposed of that and buried her.

"The Weatherfields were an elderly local couple, childless and kindly. I was only a baby, naturally, and they took me in. I grew quite slowly physically, but of course mentally it was another story. They came to be very proud of me in spite of my odd appearance. I soon devised the perfect toupee to cover my hairlessness, and with that and ordinary clothes I've always been able to pass for human. But you may remember I've never let any human see me without shirt and pants on.

"Naturally, I quickly decided where the truth must lie. Somewhere there must be a race, humanoid but well ahead of man in evolution, which can travel between the stars. Somehow my mother and I had been cast away on this desert planet, and in the vastness of the universe any searchers that there may be have never found us."

He fell back into silence. Presently Margaret whispered, "How—human—are you, Joel?"

"Not very," he said with a flash of the old candid smile she remembered. How often had she seen him look up from some piece of work, which was going particularly well, and give her just that look! "Here, I'll show you."

He whistled, and the cat jumped from his lap. Another whistle, and the animal was across the room pawing at a switch. Several large plates were released, which the cat carried back in its mouth.

Margaret drew a shaky breath. "I never yet heard of anyone training a cat to run errands."

"This is a rather special cat," he replied absently, and leaned forward to show her the plates. "These are X-rays of myself. You know my technique for photographing different layers of tissue? I developed that just to study myself. I also confess to exhuming my mother's bones, but they proved to be simply a female version of my own. However, a variation of the crystalline structure method did show that she was at least five hundred years old."

"*Five hundred years!*"

He nodded. "That's one of several reasons why I'm sure I'm a very young member of my race. Incidentally, her bones showed no sign of age, she corresponded about to a human twenty-five. I don't know whether the natural life span of the race is that great or whether they have some way of arresting senility, but I do know I can expect at least half a millennium of life on Earth. And Earth seems to have a higher gravity than our home world; it's not a very healthy spot for me."

She was too dazed to do more than nod. His finger traced over the X-ray plates. "The skeletal differences aren't too great, but look here and here—the foot, the spine—the skull bones are especially peculiar— Then the internal organs. You can see for yourself that no human being ever had—"

"A double heart?" she asked dully.

"Sort of. It's a single organ, but with more functions than the human heart. Never mind that, it's the neural structure that's most important. Here are several of the brain, taken at different depths and angles."

She fought down a gasp. Her work on encephalography had required a good knowledge of the brain's anatomy. *No human being carries this in his head.*

It wasn't too much bigger than the human. Better organization, she thought; Joel' s people would never go insane. There were analogues, a highly convoluted cortex, a medulla, the rest of it. But there were other sections and growths, which had no correspondent in any human.

"What are *they?*" she asked.

"I'm not very sure," he replied slowly, a little distastefully. "This one here is what I might call the telepathy center. It's sensitive to neural currents in other organisms. By comparing human reactions and words with the emanations I can detect, I've picked up a very limited degree of telepathy. I can emit, too, but since no human can detect it I've had little use for that power. Then this seems to be for voluntary control of ordinarily involuntary functions—pain blocs, endocrine regulation, and so on—but I've never learned to use it very effectively and I don't dare experiment much on myself. There are other centers—most of them, I don't even know what they're for."

His smile was weary. "You've heard of feral children—the occasional human children who're raised by animals? They never learn to speak, or to exercise any of their specifically human abilities, till they're captured and taught by men. In fact, they're hardly human at all.

"I'm a feral child, Peggy."

She began to cry, deep racking sobs that shook her like a giant's hand. He held her until it passed and she sat again at his knee with the slow tears going down her cheeks. Her voice was a shuddering whisper:

"Oh, my dear, my dear, how lonely you must have been…"

CHAPTER TWO
Forgetfulness

LONELY? No human being would ever know how lonely.

It hadn't been too bad at first. As a child, he had been too preoccupied and delighted with his expanding intellectual horizons to care that the other children bored him—and they, in their turn, heartily disliked Joel for his strangeness and the aloofness they called "snooty." His foster parents had soon learned that normal standards just didn't apply to him, they kept him out of school and bought him the books and equipment he wanted. They'd been able to afford that: at the age of six he had patented, in old Weatherfield's name, improvements on farm machinery that made the family more than well-to-do. He'd always been a "good boy," as far as he was able. They'd had no cause to regret adopting him, but it had been pathetically like the hen who has hatched ducklings and watches them swim away from her.

The years at Harvard had been sheer heaven, an orgy of learning, of conversations and friendship with the great who came to see an equal in the solemn child. He had had no normal social life then either, but he hadn't missed it, the undergraduates were dull and a little frightening. He'd soon learned how to avoid most publicity—after all, infant geniuses weren't altogether unknown. His only real trouble had been with a psychiatrist who wanted him to be more "normal." He grinned as he remembered the rather fiendish ways in which he had frightened the man into leaving him entirely alone.

But toward the end, he had found limitations in the life. It seemed utterly pointless to sit through lectures on the obvious and to turn in assignments of problems, which had been done a thousand times before. And he was beginning to find the professors a little tedious, more and more he was able to anticipate their answers to his questions and remarks, and those answers were becoming ever more trite.

He had long been aware of what his true nature must be, though he had had the sense not to pass the information on. Now the dream began to grow in him: To find his people!

What was the use of everything he did, when their children must be playing with the same forces as toys, when his greatest discoveries would be as old in their culture as fire in man's? What pride did he have in his achievements, when none of the witless animals who saw them could say, "Well done!" as it should be said? What comradeship could he ever know with blind and stupid creatures who soon became as predictable as his machines? *With whom could he think?*

He flung himself savagely into work, with the simple goal of making money. It hadn't been hard. In five years he was a multimillionaire, with agents to relieve him of all the worry and responsibility, with freedom to do as he chose. To work for escape.

How weary, flat, stale and unprofitable seem to me all the uses of this world!

But not of every world! Somewhere, somewhere out among the grand host of the stars...

THE long night wore on.

"Why did you come here?" asked Margaret. Her voice was quiet now, muted with hopelessness.

"I wanted secrecy. And human society was getting to be more than I could stand."

She winced, then: "Have you found a way to build a faster-than-light spaceship?"

"No. Nothing I've ever discovered indicates any way of getting around Einstein's limitation. There must be a way, but I just can't find it. Not too surprising, really. Our feral child would probably never be able to duplicate ocean-going ships."

"But how do you ever hope to get out of the Solar System, then?"

"I thought of a robot-manned spaceship going from star to star, with myself in suspended animation." He spoke of it as casually as a man might describe some scheme for repairing a leaky faucet. "But it was utterly impractical. My people can't live anywhere near, or we'd have had more indication of them than one shipwreck. They may not live in this galaxy at all. I'll save that idea for a last resort."

"But you and your mother must have been in some kind of ship. Wasn't anything ever found?"

"Just those few glassy fragments I mentioned. It makes me wonder if my people use spaceships at all. Maybe they have some sort of matter transmitter. No, my main hope is some kind of distress signal that will attract help."

"But if they live so many light-years away—"

"I've discovered a strange sort of—well, you might call it radiation, though it has no relation to the electromagnetic spectrum. Energy fields vibrating a certain way produce detectable effects in a similar setup well removed from the first. It's roughly analogous to the old spark-gap radio transmitters. The important thing is that these effects are transmitted with no measurable time lag or diminution with distance."

She would have been aflame with wonder in earlier times. Now she simply nodded. "I see. It's a sort of ultrawave. But if there are no time or distance effects, how can it be traced? It'd be completely non-directional, unless you could beam it."

"I can't—yet. But I've recorded a pattern of pulses, which are to correspond to the arrangement of stars in this part of the galaxy. Each pulse stands for a star, its intensity for the absolute brightness, and its time separation from the other pulses for the distance from the other stars."

"But that's a one-dimensional representation, and space is three dimensional."

"I know. It's not as simple as I said. The problem of such representation was an interesting problem in applied topology—took me a good week to solve. You might be interested in the mathematics. I've got my notes here somewhere— But anyway, my people, when they detect those pulses, should easily be able to deduce what I'm trying to say. I've put Sol at the head of each series of pulses, so they'll even know what particular star it is that I'm at. Anyway, there can only be one or a few configurations exactly like this in the universe, so I've given them a fix. I've set up an apparatus to broadcast my call automatically. Now I can only wait."

"How long have you waited?"

He scowled. "A good year now—and no sign. I'm setting worried. Maybe I should try something else."

"Maybe they don't use your ultrawave at all. It might be obsolete in their culture."

He nodded. "It could well be. But what else is there?"

She was silent.

Presently Joel stirred and sighed, "That's the story, Peggy."

She nodded mutely.

"Don't feel sorry for me," he said. "I'm doing all right. My research here is interesting, I like the country, I'm happier than I've been for a long time."

"That's not saying much, I'm afraid," she answered.

"No, but— Look, Peggy, you know what I am now. A monster. More alien to you than an ape. It shouldn't be hard to forget me."

"Harder than you think, Joel. I love you. I'll always love you."

"But—Peggy, it's ridiculous. Just suppose that I did come live with you. There could never be children...but I suppose that doesn't matter too much. We'd have nothing in common, though. Not a thing. We couldn't talk, we couldn't share any of the million little things that make a marriage, we could hardly even work together. I can't live in human society any more, you'd soon lose all your friends, you'd become as lonely as I. And in the end you'd grow old, your powers would fade and die, and I'd still be approaching my maturity. Peggy, neither of us could stand it."

"I know."

"Langtree is a fine man. It'd be easy to love him. You've no right to withhold a heredity as magnificent as yours from your race."

"You may be right."

He put a hand under her chin and tilted her face up to his. "I have some powers over the mind," he said slowly. "With your cooperation, I could adjust your feelings about this."

She tensed back from him, her eyes wide and frightened. "No—"

"Don't be a fool. It would only be doing now what time will do anyway." His smile was tired, crooked. "I'm really a remarkably easy person to forget, Peggy."

His will was too strong. It radiated from him, in the lambent eyes and the delicately carved features that were almost human, it pulsed in great drowsy waves from his telepathic brain and seemed almost to flow through the thin hands. Useless to resist, futile to deny—give up, give up and sleep, she was so tired.

She nodded, finally. Joel smiled the old smile she knew so well. He began to talk.

She never remembered the rest of the night, save as a blur of half awareness, a soft voice that whispered in her head, a face dimly seen through wavering mists. Once, she recalled, there was a machine that clicked and hummed, and little lights flashing and spinning in darkness. Her memory was stirred, roiled like a quiet pool, things she had forgotten through most of her life floated to the surface. It seemed as if her mother was beside her.

In the vague foggy dawn, he let her go. There was a deep unhuman calm in her, she looked at him with something of a sleepwalker's empty stare and her voice was flat. It would pass, she would soon become normal again, but Joel Weatherfield would be a memory with little emotional color, a ghost somewhere in the back of her mind.

A ghost. He felt utterly tired, drained of strength and will. He didn't belong here, he was a shadow that should have been flitting between the stars, the sunlight of Earth erased him.

"Good-by, Peggy," he said. "Keep my secret. Don't let anyone know where I am. And good luck go with you all your days."

"Joel—" She paused on the doorstep, a puzzled frown crossing her features. "Joel, if you can think at me that way, can't your people do the same?"

"Of course. What of it?" For the first time, he didn't know what was coming, he had changed her too much for prediction.

"Just that—why should they bother with gadgets like your ultrawave for talking to each other? They should he able to think between the stars."

He blinked. It had occurred to him, but he had not thought much beyond it, he had been too preoccupied with his work.

"Good-by, Joel." She turned and walked away through the dripping gray fog. An early sunbeam struck through a chance rift and glanced off her hair. He stood in the doorway until she was gone.

HE SLEPT through most of the day. Awakening, he began to think over what had been said.

By all that was holy, Peggy was right! He had immersed himself too deeply in the purely technical problems of the ultrawave, and since then in mathematical research, which passed the time of waiting, to stand off and consider the basic logic of the situation. But this—it made sense.

He had only the vaguest notion of the inherent powers of his own mind. Physical science had offered too easy an outlet for him. Nor could he, unaided, hope to get far in such studies. A human feral child might have the heredity of a mathematical genius, but unless he was found and taught by his own kind he would never comprehend the elements of arithmetic—or of speech or sociability or any of the activities, which set man off from the other animal. There was just too long a heritage of pre-human and early human development for one man alone to recapitulate in a lifetime, when his environment held no indication of the particular road his ancestors had taken.

But those idle nerves and brain centers must be for something. He suspected that they were means of direct control over the most basic forces in the universe. Telepathy, telekinesis, precognition—what godlike heritage had been denied him?

At any rate, it did seem that his race had gone beyond the need of physical mechanisms. With complete understanding of the structure of the space-time-energy continuum, with control by direct will of its underlying processes, they would project themselves or their thoughts from star to star, create what they needed by sheer thought—and pay no attention to the gibberings of lesser races.

Fantastic, dizzying prospect! He stood breathless before the great shining vision that opened to his eyes.

He shook himself back to reality. The immediate problem was getting in touch with his race. That meant a study of the telepathic energies he had hitherto almost ignored.

He plunged into a fever of work. Time became meaningless, a succession of days and nights, waning light and drifting snow and the slow return of spring. He had never had much except his work to live for, now it devoured the last of his thoughts. Even during the periods of rest and exercise he forced himself to take, his mind was still at the problem, gnawing at it like a dog with a bone. And slowly, slowly, knowledge grew.

TELEPATHY was not directly related to the brain pulses measured by encephalography. Those were feeble, short-range by-products of neuronic activity. Telepathy, properly controlled, leaped over any intervening space with an arrogant ignoring of time. It was, he decided, another part of what he had labeled the ultrawave spectrum, which was related to gravitation as an effect of the geometry of space-time. But, while gravitational effects were produced by the presence of matter, ultrawave effects came into being when certain energy fields vibrated. However they did not appear unless there was a properly tuned receiver somewhere. They seemed somehow "aware" of a listener even before they came into existence. That suggested fascinating speculations about the nature of time, but he turned away from it. His people would know more about it than he could ever find out alone.

But the concept of waves was hardly applicable to something that traveled with an "infinite velocity"—a poor term semantically, but convenient. He could assign an ultrawave a frequency that of the generating energy fields, but then the wavelength would be infinite. Better to think of it in terms of tensors, and drop all pictorial analogies.

His nervous system did not itself contain the ultra-energies. Those were omnipresent, inherent in the very structure of the cosmos. But his telepathy centers, properly trained, were somehow coupled to that great underlying flow, they could impose the desired vibrations on it. Similarly, he supposed, his other centers could control those forces to create or destroy or move matter, to cross space, to scan the past and future probability-worlds, to...

He couldn't do it himself. He just couldn't find out enough in even his lifetime. Were he literally immortal, he might still never learn what he had to know; his mind had been trained into human thought patterns, and this was something that lay beyond man's power of comprehension.

But all I need is to send one clear call...

He struggled with it. Through the endless winter nights he sat in the cabin and fought to master his brain. How did you send a shout to the stars?

Tell me, feral child, how do you solve a partial differential equation?

Perhaps some of the answer lay in his own mind. The brain has two types of memory, the "permanent" and the "circulating," and apparently the former kind is never lost. It recedes into the subconscious, but it is still there, and it can be brought out again. As a child, a baby, he would have observed things, remembered sights of apparatus and feelings of vibration, which his more mature mind could now analyze.

He practiced autohypnosis, using a machine he devised to help him, and the memories came back, memories of warmth and light and great pulsing forces. Yes—yes, there was an engine of some sort, he could see it thrumming and flickering before him. It took a while before he could translate the infant's alien impressions into his present sensory evaluations, but when that job was done he had a clear picture of— something.

That helped, just a little. It suggested certain types of hookup, empirical patterns, which had not occurred to him before. And now slowly, slowly, he began to make progress.

An ultrawave demands a receiver for its very existence. So he could not flash a thought to any of his people unless one of them happened to be listening on that particular "wave"— its pattern of frequency; modulation; and other physical characteristics. And his untrained mind simply did not send on that "band." He couldn't do it, he couldn't imagine the waveform of his race's normal thought. He was faced with a problem similar to that of a man in a foreign country who must invent its language for himself before he can communicate—without even being allowed to listen to it, and knowing only that its phonetic, grammatical, and semantic values are entirely different from those of his native speech.

Insoluble? No, maybe not. His mind lacked the power to send a call out through the stars, lacked the ability to make itself intelligible. But a machine has no such limitations.

He could modify his ultrawave; it already had the power, and he could give it the coherence. For he could insert a random factor in it, a device encephalography that would vary the basic wave-form in every conceivable permutation of characteristics, running through millions or billions of tries in a second—and the random wave could be modulated too, his own thoughts could be superimposed. Whenever the machine found resonance with anything that could receive— anything, literally, for millions of light-years—an ultrawave would he generated and the random element cut off. Joel could stay on that band then, examining it at his leisure.

Sooner or later, one of the bands he hit would be that of his race. And he would know it.

CHAPTER THREE
Contact!

THE device, when he finished, was crude and ugly, a great ungainly thing of tangled wires and gleaming tubes and swirling cosmic energies. One lead from it connected to a metal band around his own head, imposing his basic ultrawave pattern on the random factor and feeding back whatever was received into his brain. He lay on his bunk, with a control panel beside him, and started the machine working.

Vague mutterings, sliding shadows, strangeness rising out of the roiled depths of his mind... He grinned thinly, battling down the cold apprehension, which rose in his abused nerves, and began experimenting with the machine. He wasn't too sure of all its characteristics himself, and it would take a while too, before he had full control of his thought-pattern.

Silence, darkness, and now and then a glimpse, a brief blinding instant when the random gropings struck some basic resonance and a wave sprang into being and talked to his brain. Once he looked through Margaret's eyes, across a table to Langtree's face. There was candlelight, he remembered afterward, and a small string orchestra was playing in the background. Once he saw the ragged outlines of a city men had never built, rising up toward a cloudy sky while a strangely slow and heavy sea lapped against its walls.

Once, too, he did catch a thought flashing between the stars. But it was no thought of his kind, it was a great white blaze like a sun exploding in his head, and cold, cold. He screamed aloud, and for a week afterward dared not resume his experiments.

In the springtime dusk he found his answer.

The first time the shock was so great that he lost contact again. He lay shaking, forcing calm on himself, trying to reproduce the exact pattern his own brain, as well as the machine, had been sending. Easy, easy— The baby's mind had been drifting in a mist of dreams, *thus…*

The baby. For his groping, uncontrollable brain could not resonate with any of the superbly trained adult minds of his people.

But a baby has no spoken language. Its mind slides amorphously from one pattern to another, there are no habits as yet to fix it, and one tongue is as good as any other. By the laws of randomness, Joel had struck the pattern, which an infant of his race happened to be giving out at the moment.

He found it again, and the tingling warmth of contact flowed into him, deliciously, marvelously, a river in a dusty desert, a sun warming the chill of the solipsistic loneliness in which humans wandered from their births to the end of their brief meaningless lives. He fitted his mind to the baby's, let the two streams of consciousness flow into one, a river running toward the mighty sea of the race.

The feral child crept out of the forest. Wolves howled at his back, the hairy four-footed brothers of cave, and chase and darkness, but he heard them not. He bent over the baby's cradle, the tangled hair falling past his gaunt witless face, and looked with a dim stirring of awe and wonder. The baby spread its hand, a little soft starfish, and his own gnarled fingers stole toward it, trembling at the knowledge that this was a paw like his own.

Now he had only to wait until some adult looked into the child's mind. It shouldn't be long, and meanwhile he rested in the timeless drowsy peace of the very young.

Somewhere in the outer cosmos, perhaps on a planet swinging about a sun no one of Earth would ever see, the baby rested in a cradle of warm, pulsing forces. He did not have a room around him, there was a shadowiness, which no human could ever quite comprehend, lit by flashes of the energy that created the stars.

The baby sensed the nearing of something that meant warmth and softness, sweetness in his mouth and murmuring in his mind. He cooed with delight, reaching his hands out into the shaking twilight of the room. His mother's mind ran ahead of her, folding about the little one.

A scream!

Frantically, Joel reached for her mind, flashing and flashing the pattern of location-pulses through the baby's brain into hers. He lost her, his mind fell sickeningly in on itself—no, no, someone else was reaching for him now, analyzing the pattern of the machine and his own wild oscillations and fitting smoothly into them.

A deep, strong voice in his brain, somehow unmistakably male—Joel relaxed, letting the other mind control his, simply emitting his signals.

It would take—them—a little while to analyze the meaning of his call. Joel lay in a half conscious state, aware of one small part of the being's mind maintaining a thread of contact with him while the rest reached out, summoning others across the universe, calling for help and information.

So he had won. Joel thought of Earth, dreamily and somehow wistfully. Odd that in this moment of triumph his mind should dwell on the little things he was leaving behind—an Arizona sunset, a nightingale under the moon. Peggy's flushed face bent over an instrument beside his. Beer and music and windy pines.

But O my people! Never more to be lonely...

Decision. A sensation of falling, rushing down a vortex of stars toward Sol—approach!

The being would have to locate him on Earth. Joel tried to picture a map, though the thought-patterns that corresponded in his brain to a particular visualization would not make sense to the other. But in some obscure way, it might help.

Maybe it did. Suddenly the telepathic band snapped, but there was a rush of other impulses, life forces like flame, the nearness of a god. Joel stumbled gasping to his feet and flung open the door.

THE moon was rising above the dark hills, a hazy light over trees and patches of snow and the wet ground. The air was chill and damp, sharp in his lungs.

The being who stood there, outlined in the radiance of his garments, was taller than Joel, an adult. His grave eyes were too brilliant to meet, it was as if the life within him were incandescent. And when the full force of his mind reached out, flowing over and into Joel, running along every nerve and cell of him...

He cried out with the pain of it and fell to his hands and knees. The intolerable force lightened, faded to a thrumming in his brain that shook every fiber of it. He was being studied, analyzed, no tiniest part of him was hidden from those terrible eyes and from the logic that recreated more of him than he knew himself. His own distorted telepathic language was at once intelligible to the watcher, and he croaked his appeal.

The answer held pity, but it was as remote and inexorable as the thunders on Olympus.

Child, it is too late. Your mother must have been caught in a—?— energy vortex and caused to—?—on Earth, and now you have been raised by the animals.

Think, child. Think of the feral children of this native race. When they were restored to their own kind, did they become human? No, it was too late. The basic personality traits are determined in the first years of childhood, and their specifically human attributes, unused, had atrophied.

It is too late, too late. Your mind has become too fixed in rigid and limited patterns. Your body has made a different adjustment from that which is necessary to sense and control the forces we use. You even need a machine to speak.

You no longer belong to our race.

Joel lay huddled on the ground, shaking, not thinking or daring to think.

The thunders rolled through his head:

We cannot have you interfering with the proper mental training of our children. And since you can never rejoin our kind, but must make the best adaptation you can to the race you live with, the kindest as well as the wisest thing for us to do is to make certain changes. Your memory and that of others, your body, the work you are doing and have done—

There were others filling the night, the gods come to Earth, shining and terrible beings who lifted each fragment of experience he had ever had out of him and made their judgments on it. Darkness closed over him, and he fell endlessly into oblivion.

HE AWOKE, in his bed, wondering why he should be so tired.

Well, the cosmic-ray research had been a hard and lonely grind. Thank heaven and his lucky stars it was over! He'd take a well-earned vacation at home now. It'd be good to see his friends again—and Peggy.

Dr. Joel Weatherfield, eminent young physicist, rose cheerfully and began making ready to go home.

THE END

Terminal Quest

An orphan of the eons was he, the last of a hated race...needing only death to make him immortal!

THE sun woke him. He stirred uneasily, feeling the long shafts of light slant over the land. The muted gossip of birds became a rush of noise and a small wind blew till the leaves chattered at him. Wake up, wake up, wake up, Rugo, there is a new day on the hills and you can't lie sleeping, wake up!

The light reached under his eyelids, roiling the darkness of dreams. He mumbled and curled into a tighter knot, drawing sleep back around him like a cloak, sinking toward the dark and the unknowingness with his mother's face before him.

She laughed down the long ways of night, calling and calling, and he tried to follow her, but the sun wouldn't let him.

Mother, he whimpered. *Mother, please come back, mother.*

She had gone and left him, once very long ago. He had been little then and the cave had been big and gloomy and cold, and there were flutterings and watchings in the shadows of it and he had been frightened. She had said she was going after food, and had kissed him and gone off down the steep moonlit valley. And there she must have met the Strangers, because she never came back. And he had cried for a long time and called her name, but she didn't return.

That had been so long ago that he couldn't number the years. But now that he was getting old, she must have remembered him and been sorry she left, for lately she often came back at night.

The dew was cold on his skin. He felt the stiffness in him, the ache of muscle and bone and dulling nerve, and forced himself to move. If he stirred all at once, stretching himself and not letting his throat rasp with the pain of it, he could work the damp and the cold and the earth out, he could open his eyes and look at the new day.

It was going to be hot. Rugo's vision wasn't so good any more, the sun was only a blur of fire low on the shadowy horizon, and the mist that streamed through the dales turned it ruddy. But he knew that before midday it would be hot.

He got up, slowly climbing to all four feet, pulling himself erect with the help of a low branch. Hunger was a dull ache in him. He looked emptily around at the thicket, a copse of scrub halfway up the hillside. There were the bushes and the trees, a hard summer green that would be like metal later in the day. There were the dead leaves rustling soggily underfoot, still wet with the dew that steamed away in white vapors. There were birds piping up the sun, but nowhere food, nowhere anything to eat.

Mother, you said you would bring back something to eat.

He shook his big scaly head, clearing out the fog of dreams. Today he would have to go down into the valley. He had eaten the last berries on the hillside, he had waited here for days with weakness creeping from his belly through his bones, and now he would have to go down to the Strangers.

He went slowly out of the thicket and started down the hillside. The grass rustled under his feet, the earth quivered a little beneath his great weight. The hill slanted up to the sky and down to the misty dales, and he was alone with the morning.

Only grass and the small flowers grew here. Once the hills had been tall with forest; he recalled cool shadowy depths and the windy roar of the treetops, small suns spattered on the ground and the drunken sweetness of resin smell in summer and the blaze of broken light from a million winter crystals. But the Strangers had cut down the woods and now there were only rotting stumps and his blurred remembering. His alone, for the men who had hewed down the forest were dead and their sons never knew—and when he was gone, who would care? Who would be left to care?

He came to a brook that rushed down the hillside, rising from a spring higher up and flowing to join the Thunder River. The water was cold and clean and he drank heavily, slopping it into him with both hand's and wriggling his tail with the refreshment of it. This much remained to him, at least, though the source was dwindling now that the watershed was gone. But he would be dead before the brook was dry, so it didn't matter too much.

He waded over it. The cold water set his lame foot to tingling and needling. Beyond it he found the old logging trail and went down that. He walked slowly, not being eager to do that which he must, and tried to make a plan.

The Strangers had given him food now and then, out of charity or in return for work. Once he had labored almost a year for a man, who had given him a place to sleep and as much as he wanted to eat—a good man to work for, not full of the hurry, which seemed to be in his race, with a quiet voice and gentle eyes. But then the man had taken a woman, and she was afraid of Rugo, so he had had to leave.

A couple of times, too, men from Earth itself had come to talk to him. They had asked him many questions about his people. How had they lived, what was their word for this and that, did he remember any of their dances or music? But he couldn't tell them much, for his folk had been hunted before he was born, he had seen a flying-thing spear his father with flame and later his mother had gone to look for food and not come back. The men from Earth had, in fact, told him more than he could give them, told him about cities and books and gods, which his people had had, and if he had wanted to learn these things from the Strangers they could have told him more. They, too, had paid him something, and he had eaten well for a while.

I am old now, thought Rugo, *and not very strong. I never was strong, beside the powers they have. One of us could drive fifty of them before him—but one of them, seated at the wheel of a thing of metal and fire, could reap a thousand of us. And I frighten their women and children and animals. So it will be hard to find work, and I may have to beg a little bread for no more return than going away. And the grain that they will feed me grew in the soil of this world; it is strong with the bones of my father and fat with the flesh of my mother. But one must eat.*

WHEN he came down into the valley, the mists had lifted in ragged streamers and already he could feel the heat of the sun. The trail led onto a road, and he turned north toward the human settlements. Nobody was in sight yet, and it was quiet. His footfalls rang loud on the pavement, it was hard under his soles and the impact of walking jarred up into his legs like small sharp needles. He looked around him, trying to ignore the hurting.

They had cut down the trees and harrowed the land and sowed grain of Earth, until now the valley lay open to the sky. The brassy sun of summer and the mordant winds of winter rode over the deep glens he remembered, and the only trees were in neat orchards bearing alien fruit. It was as if these Strangers were afraid of the dark, as if they were so frightened by shadows and half-lights and rustling unseen distances that they had to clear it all away, one sweep of fire and thunder and then the bright inflexible steel of their world rising above the dusty plains.

Only fear could make beings so vicious, even as fear had driven Rugo's folk to rush, huge and scaled and black, out of the mountains, to smash houses and burn grain fields and wreck machines, even as fear had brought an answer from the

Strangers, which heaped stinking bodies in the tumbled ruins of the cities he had never seen. Only the Strangers were more powerful, and their fears had won.

He heard the machine coming behind him, roaring and pounding down the road with a whistle of cloven air flapping in its wake, and remembered in a sudden gulping that it was forbidden to walk in the middle of the road. He scrambled to one side, but it was the wrong one, the side they drove on, and the truck screamed around him on smoking tires and ground to a halt on the shoulder.

A Stranger climbed out, and he was almost dancing with fury. His curses poured forth so fast that Rugo couldn't follow them. He caught a few words: "Damned weird thing...Coulda killed me...Oughta be shot...Have the law on yuh..."

Rugo stood watching. He had twice the height of the skinny pink shape that jittered and railed before him, and some four times the bulk, and though he was old, one sweep of his hand would stave in the skull and spatter the brains on the hot hard concrete. Only all the power of the Strangers was behind the creature, fire and ruin and flying steel, and he was the last of his folk and sometimes his mother came at night to see him. So he stood quietly, hoping the man would get tired and go away.

A booted foot slammed against his shin, and he cried out with the pain of it and lifted one arm the way he had done as a child when the bombs were falling and metal rained around him.

The man sprang back. "Don't yuh try it," he said quickly. "Don't do nothing. They'll hunt yuh down if yuh touch me."

"Go," said Rugo, twisting his tongue and throat to the foreign syllables, which he knew better than the dimly recalled language of his people. "Please go."

"Yuh're on'y here while yuh behave yuhrself. Keep yuhr place, see. Nasty devil! Watch yuhrself." The man got back into the truck and started it. The spinning tires threw gravel back at Rugo.

He stood watching the machine, his hands hanging empty at his sides, until it was beyond his aging sight. Then he started walking again, careful to stay on the correct edge of the road.

Presently a farm appeared over a ridge. It lay a little way in from the highway, a neat white house sitting primly among trees with its big outbuildings clustered behind it and the broad yellowing grain fields beyond. The sun was well into the sky now, mist and dew had burned away, the wind had fallen asleep. It was still and hot. Rugo's feet throbbed with the hardness of the road.

He stood at the entrance, wondering if he should go in or not. It was a rich place, they'd have machines and no use for his labor. When he passed by here before, the man had told him shortly to be on his way. But they could perhaps spare a piece of bread and a jug of water, just to be rid of him or maybe to keep him alive. He knew he was one of the neighborhood sights, the last native. Visitors often climbed up his hill to see him and toss a few coins at his feet and take pictures while he gathered them.

He puzzled out the name on the mailbox. *Elias Whately.* He'd try his luck with Elias Whately.

As he came up the driveway a dog bounded forth and started barking, high shrill notes that hurt his ears. The animal danced around and snapped with a rage that was half panic. None of the beasts from Earth could stand the sight and smell of him; they knew he was not of their world and a primitive terror rose in them. He remembered the pain when teeth nipped his rheumatic legs. Once he had killed a dog that bit him, a single unthinking swipe of his tail, and the owner had fired a shotgun at him. His scales had turned most of the charge, but some was still lodged deep in his flesh and bit him again when the days were cold.

"Please," he said to the dog. His bass rumbled in the warm still air and the barking grew more frantic. "Please, I will not harm, please do not bite."

"*O-oh!*"

The woman in the front yard let out a little scream and ran before him, up the steps and through the door to slam it in his face. Rugo sighed, feeling suddenly tired. She was afraid. They were all afraid. They had called his folk trolls, which were something evil in their old myths. He remembered that his grandfather, before he died in a shelterless winter, had called them torrogs, which he said were pale bony things that ate the dead, and Rugo smiled with a wryness that was sour in his mouth.

But little use in trying here. He turned to go.

"You!"

He turned back to face the tall man who stood in the door. The man held a rifle, and his long face was clamped tight. Behind him peeked a redheaded boy, maybe thirteen years old, a cub with the same narrow eyes as his father.

"What's the idea of coming in here?" asked the man. His voice was like the grating of iron.

"Please, sir," said Rugo. "I am hungry. I thought if I could do some work, or if you had any scraps—"

"So, now it's begging, eh?" demanded Whately. "Don't you know that's against the law? You could be put in jail. By heaven, you ought to be! Public nuisance, that's all you are."

"I only wanted work," said Rugo.

"So, you come in and frighten my wife? You know there's nothing here for a savage to do. Can you run a tractor? Can you repair a generator? Can you even eat without slobbering it on the ground?" Whately spat. "You're a squatter on somebody else's land, and you know it. If I owned that property you'd be out on your worthless butt so fast you wouldn't know which end was up.

"Be glad you're alive. When I think of what you murdering slimy monsters did—Forty years! Forty years, crammed in stinking spaceships, cutting themselves off from Earth and all the human race, dying without seeing ground, fighting every foot of all the light-years, to get to Tau Ceti—and then you said the Earthmen couldn't stay! Then you came and burned their homes and butchered women and children. The planet's well rid of you, all the scum of you, and it's a wonder somebody doesn't take a gun and clear off the last of the garbage." He half lifted his weapon.

It was no use explaining, thought Rugo. Maybe there really had been a misunderstanding, as his grandfather had claimed, maybe the old counselors had thought the first explorers were only asking if more like them could come and had not expected settlers when they gave permission—or maybe, realizing that the Strangers would be too strong, they had decided to break their word and fight to hold their planet.

But what use now? The Strangers had won the war, with guns and bombs and a plague virus that went like a scythe through the natives; they had hunted the few immunes down like animals, and now he was the last of his kind in all the world and it was too late to explain.

"Sic 'im, Shep!" cried the boy. "Sic 'im! Go get 'im!"

The dog barked in closer, rushing and retreating, trying to work its cowardice into rage.

"Shut up, Sam," said Whately to his son. Then to Rugo, "*Get.*"

"I will leave," said Rugo. He tried to stop the trembling that shuddered in him, the nerve-wrenching fear of what the gun could spit. He was not afraid to die, he thought sickly, he would welcome the darkness when it came—but his life was so deep-seated, he would live and live and live while the slugs tore into him. He might take hours to die.

"I will be on my way, sir," he said.

"No, you won't," snapped Whately. "I won't have you going down to the village and scaring little kids there. Back where you came from."

"But, sir—please—"

"Get!" The gun pointed at him, he looked down the muzzle and turned and went out the gate. Whately waved him to the left, back down the road.

The dog charged in and sank its teeth in an ankle where the scales had fallen away. He screamed with the pain of it and began to run, slowly and heavily, weaving in his course. The boy Sam laughed and followed him.

"Nyaah, nyaah, nyaah, ugly ol' troll, crawl back down in yuhr dirty ol' hole!"

AFTER a while there were other children, come from the neighboring farms in that timeless blur of running and raw lungs and thudding heart and howling, thundering noise. They followed him, and their dogs barked, and the flung stones rattled off his sides with little swords where they struck.

"Nyaah, nyaah, nyaah, ugly ol' troll, crawl back down in yuhr dirty ol' hole!"

"Please," he whispered. "Please."

When he came to the old trail he hardly saw it. The road danced in a blinding glimmer of heat and dust, the world was tipping and whirling about him, and the clamor in his ears drowned out their shrilling. They danced around him, sure of their immunity, sure of the pain and the weakness and the loneliness that whimpered in his throat, and the dogs yammered and rushed in and nipped his tail and his swollen legs.

Presently he couldn't go on. The hillside was too steep, there was no will left to drive his muscles. He sat down, pulling in knees and tail, hiding his head in his arms, hardly aware in the hot, roaring, whirling blindness that they stoned him and pummeled him and screamed at him.

Night and rain and the west wind crying in high trees, a cool wet softness of grass and the wavering little fire, the grave eyes of my father and the dear lost face of my mother— Out of the night and the rainy wind and the forest they hewed down, out of the years and the blurring memories and the shadowland of dreams, come to me, mother, come to me and take me in your arms and carry me home.

After a while they grew tired of it and went away, some turning back and some wandering higher up into the hills after berries. Rugo sat unmoving, buried in himself, letting a measure of strength and the awareness of his pain seep back.

He burned and pulsed, jagged bolts shot through his nerves, his throat was too dry for swallowing and the hunger was like a wild animal deep in his belly. And overhead the sun swam in a haze of heat, pouring it down over him, filling the air with an incandescence of arid light.

After still a longer time, he opened his eyes. The lids felt raw and sandy, vision wavered as if the heat-shimmer had entered his brain. There was a man who stood watching him.

Rugo shrank back, lifting a hand before his face. But the man stood quietly, puffing away on a battered old pipe. He was shabbily dressed and there was a rolled bundle on his shoulders.

"Had a pretty rough session there, didn't you, old-timer?" he asked. His voice was soft. "Here." He bent a lanky frame over the crouching native. "Here, you need a drink."

Rugo lifted the canteen to his lips and gulped till it was empty. The man looked him over. "You're not too banged up," he decided. "Just cuts and abrasions; you trolls always were a tough breed. I'll give you some aneurine, though."

He fished a tube of yellow salve out of one pocket and smeared it on the wounds. The hurt eased, faded to a warm tingle, and Rugo sighed.

"You are very kind, sir," he said unsurely.

"Nah. I wanted to see you anyway. How you feel now? Better?"

Rugo nodded, slowly, trying to stop the shivers, which still ran in him. "I am well, sir," he said.

"Don't 'sir' me. Too many people'd laugh themselves sick to hear it. What was your trouble, anyway?"

"I—I wanted food, sir—pardon me. I w-wanted food. But they—he—told me to go back. Then the dogs came, and the young ones—"

"Kids can be pretty gruesome little monsters at times, all right. Can you walk, old fella? I'd like to find some shade."

Rugo pulled himself to his feet. It was easier than he had thought it would be. "Please, if you will be so kind, I know a place with trees—"

The man swore, softly and imaginatively. "So, that's what they've done. Not content with blotting out a whole race, they have to take the guts from the last one left. Look, you, I'm Manuel Jones, and you'll speak to me as one free bum to another or not at all. Now let's find your trees."

They went up the trail without speaking much, though the man whistled a dirty song to himself, and crossed the brook and came to the thicket. When Rugo lay down in the light-speckled shade it was as if he had been born again. He sighed and let his body relax, flowing into the ground, drawing of its old strength.

The human started a fire and opened some cans in his pack and threw their contents into a small kettle. Rugo watched hungrily, hoping he would give him a little, ashamed and angry with himself for the way his stomach rumbled. Manuel Jones squatted under a tree, shoved his hat off his forehead, and got his pipe going afresh.

Blue eyes in a weather-beaten face watched Rugo with steadiness and no hate nor fear. "I've been looking forward to seeing you," he said. "I wanted to meet the last member of a race, which could build the Temple of Otheii."

"What is that?" asked Rugo.

"You don't *know?*"

"No, sir—I mean, pardon me, no, Mr. Jones—"

"Manuel. And don't you forget it."

"No. I was born while the Strangers were hunting the last of us—Manuel. We were always fleeing. I was only a few years old when my mother was killed. I met the last other Gunnur—member of my race—when I was only about twenty. That was almost two hundred years ago. Since then I have been the last."

"God," whispered Manuel. "God, what a race of free-wheeling devils we are."

"You were stronger," said Rugo. "And anyway it is very long ago now. Those who did it are dead. Some humans have been good to me. One of them saved my life; he got the others to let me live. And some of the rest have been kind."

"Funny sort of kindness, I'd say," Manuel shrugged. "But as you put it, Rugo, it's too late now."

He drew heavily on his pipe. "Still, you had a great civilization. It wasn't technically minded like ours, it wasn't human or fully understandable to humans, but it had its own greatness. Oh, it was a bloody crime to slaughter you, and we'll have to answer for it some day."

"I am old," said Rugo. "I am too old to hate."

"But not too old to be lonesome, eh?" Manuel's smile was lopsided. He fell into silence, puffing blue clouds into the blaze of air.

Presently he went on, thoughtfully, "Of course, one can understand the humans. They were the poor and the disinherited of our land-hungry Earth, they came forty years over empty space with all their hopes, giving their lives to the ships so their children might land—and then your council forbade it. They *couldn't* return, and man never was too nice about his methods when need drove him. They were lonely and scared, and your hulking horrible appearance made it worse. So, they fought. But they needn't have been so thorough about it. That was sheer hellishness."

"It does not matter," said Rugo. "It was long ago."

They sat for a while in silence, huddled under the shade against the white flame of sunlight, until the food was ready.

"Ah." Manuel reached gratefully for his eating utensils. "It's not too good, beans and stuff, and I haven't an extra plate. Mind just reaching into the kettle?"

"I—I— It is not needful," mumbled Rugo, suddenly shy again.

"The devil it isn't. Help yourself, old-timer, plenty for all."

The smell of food filled Rugo's nostrils, he could feel his mouth going wet and his stomach screaming at him. And the Stranger really seemed to mean it. Slowly, he dipped his hands into the vessel and brought them out full and ate with the ungraceful manners of his people.

AFTERWARD they lay back, stretching and sighing and letting the faint breeze blow over them. There hadn't been much for one of Rugo's size, but he had emptied the kettle and was more full than he had been for longer than he could well recall.

" I am afraid this meal used all your supplies," he said clumsily.

"No matter," yawned Manuel. "I was damn sick of beans anyway. Meant to lift a chicken tonight."

"You are not from these parts," said Rugo. There was a thawing within him. Here was someone who seemed to expect nothing more than friendship. You could lie in the shade beside him and watch a lone shred of cloud drift over the hot blue sky and let every nerve and muscle go easy. You felt the fullness of your stomach, and you lolled on the grass, and idle words went from one to another, and that was all there was and it was enough.

"You are not a plain tramp," he added thoughtfully.

"Maybe not," said Manuel. "I taught school a good many years ago, in Cetusport. Got into a bit of trouble and had to hit the road and liked it well enough not to settle down anywhere since. Hobo, hunter, traveler to any place that sounds interesting—it's a big world and there's enough in it for a lifetime. I want to get to know this New Terra planet, Rugo. Not that I mean to write a book or any such nonsense. I just want to know it."

He sat up on one elbow. "That's why I came to see you," he said. "You're part of the old world, the last part of it except for empty ruins and a few torn pages in museums. But I have a notion that your race will always haunt us that no matter how long man is here something of you will enter into him." There was a half-mystical look on his lean face. He was not the dusty tramp now but something else, which Rugo could not recognize.

"The planet was yours before we came," he said, "and it shaped you and you shaped it; and now the landscape, which was yours will become part of us, and it'll change us in its own slow and subtle ways. I think that whenever a man camps out alone on New Terra, in the big hills where you hear the night talking up in the trees, I think he'll always remember something. There'll always be a shadow just beyond his fire, a voice in the wind and in the rivers, something in the soil that will enter the bread he eats and the water he drinks, and that will be the lost race, which was yours."

"It may be so," said Rugo unsurely. "But we are all gone now. Nothing of ours is left."

"Some day," said Manuel, "the last man is going to face your loneliness. We won't last forever either. Sooner or later age or enemies or our own stupidity or the darkening of the universe will come for us. I hope that the last man can endure life as bravely as you did."

"I was not brave," said Ruga. "I was often afraid. They hurt me, sometimes, and I ran."

"Brave in the way that counts," said Manuel.

They talked for a while longer and then the human rose. "I've got to go, Rugo," he said. "If I'm going to stay here for a while, I'll have to go down to the village and get a job of some sort. May I come up again tomorrow and see you?"

Rugo got up with him and wrapped the dignity of a host about his nakedness. "I would be honored," he said gravely.

He stood watching the man go until he was lost to sight down the curve of the trail. Then he sighed a little. Manuel was good, yes, he was the first one in a hundred years who had not hated or feared him, or been overly polite and apologetic, but had simply traded words as one free being to another.

What had he said? "One free bum to another." Yes, Manuel was a good bum.

He would bring food tomorrow, Rugo knew, and this time there would be more said, the comradeship would be wholly easy and the eyes wholly frank. It pained him that he could offer nothing in return.

But wait, maybe he could. The farther hills were thick with berries, some must still be there even this late in the season. Birds and animals and humans couldn't have taken them all, and he knew how to look. Yes, he could bring back a great many berries that would go well with a meal.

It was a long trip, and his sinews protested at the thought. He grunted and set out, slowly. The sun was wheeling horizonward, but it would be a few hours yet till dark.

He went over the crest of the hill and down the other side. It was hot and quiet, the air shimmered around him, leaves hung limp on the few remaining trees. The summer-dried grass rustled harshly under his feet, rocks rolled aside and skittered down the long slope with a faint click. Beyond, the range stretched into a blue haze of distance. It was lonely up here, but he was used to that and liked it.

Berries—yes, a lot of them clustered around Thunder Falls, where there was always coolness and damp. To be sure, the other pickers knew that as well as he, but they didn't know all the little spots, the slanting rocks and the wet crannies and the sheltering overgrowths of brush. He could bring home enough for a good meal.

He wound down the hillside and up the next. More trees grew here. He was glad of the shade and moved a little faster. Maybe he should pull out of this district altogether. Maybe he would do better in a less thickly settled region, where there might be more people like Manuel. He needed humans, he was too old now to live off the country, but they might be easier to get along with on the frontier.

They weren't such a bad race, the Stranger's. They had made war with all the fury that was in them, had wiped out a threat with unnecessary savagery; they still fought and cheated and oppressed each other; they were silly and cruel and they cut down the forests and dug up the earth and turned the rivers dry. But among them were a few like Manuel, and he wondered if his own people had boasted more of that sort than the Strangers did.

Presently he came out on the slope of the highest hill in the region and started climbing it toward Thunder Falls. He could hear the distant roaring of a cataract, half lost in the pounding of his own blood as he fought his aging body slowly up the rocky slant, and in the dance of sunlight he stopped to breathe and tell himself that not far ahead were shadow and mist and a coolness of rushing waters. And when he was ready to come back, the night would be there to walk home with him.

The shouting falls drowned out the voices of the children, nor had he looked for them since he knew they were forbidden to visit this danger spot without adults along. When he topped the stony ridge and stood looking down into the gorge, he saw them just below and his heart stumbled in sickness.

The whole troop was there, with red-haired Sam Whately leading them in a berry hunt up and down the cragged rocks and along the pebbled beach. Rugo stood on the bluff above them, peering down through the fine cold spray and trying to tell his panting body to turn and run before they saw him. Then it was too late; they had spotted his dark form and were crowding closer, scrambling up the bluff with a wicked rain of laughter.

"Looka that." He heard Sam's voice faintly through the roar and crash of the falls. "Looky who's here. Ol' Blackie."

A stone cracked against his ribs. He half turned to go, knowing dully that he could not outrun them. Then he remembered that he had come to gather berries for Manuel Jones, who had called him brave, and a thought came.

He called out in a bass that trembled through the rocks. "Do not do that!"

"Yaah, listen what he says, ha-ha-ha!"

"Leave me alone," cried Rugo, "or I will tell your parents that you were here."

They stopped then, almost up to him, and for a moment only the yapping dogs spoke. Then Sam sneered at him. "Aw, who'd lissen to yuh, ol' troll?"

"I think they will believe me," said Rugo. "But if you do not believe it, try and find out."

They hovered for a moment, unsure, staring at each other. Then Sam said, "Okay, ol' tattletale, okay. But you let us be, see?"

"I will do that," said Rugo, and the hard held breath puffed out of him in a great sigh. He realized how painfully his heart had been fluttering, and weakness was watery in his legs.

THEY went sullenly back to their berry gathering, and Rugo scrambled down the bluff and took the opposite direction.

They called off the dogs too, and soon he was out of sight of them.

The gorge walls rose high and steep on either side of the falls. Here the river ran fast, green and boiling white, cold and loud as it sprang over the edge in a veil of rainbowed mist. Its noise filled the air, rang between the crags and hooted in the water hollowed caves. The vibrations of the toppling stream shivered unceasingly through the ground. It was cool and wet here, and there was always a wind blowing down the length of the ravine. The fall wasn't high, only about twenty feet, but the river thundered down it with brawling violence and below the cataract it was deep and fast and full of rocks and whirlpools.

Plants were scattered between the stones, small bushes and a few slender trees. Rugo found some big tsugi leaves and twisted them together into a good-sized bag as his mother had taught him, and started hunting. The berries grew on low, round-leafed bushes that clustered under rocks and taller plants, wherever they could find shelter, and it was something of an art to locate them easily. Rugo had had many decades of practice.

It was peaceful work. He felt his heart and lungs slowing, content and restfulness stole over him. So had he gone with his mother, often and often in the time that was clearer to him than all the blurred years between, and it was as if she walked beside him now and showed him where to look and smiled when he turned over a bush and found the little blue spheres. He was gathering food for his friend, and that was good.

After some time, he grew aware that a couple of the children had left the main group and were following him, a small boy and girl tagging at a discreet distance and saying nothing. He turned and stared at them, wondering if they meant to attack him after all, and they looked shyly away.

"You sure find a lot of them, Mister Troll," said the boy at last, timidly.

"They grow here," grunted Ruga with unease.

"I'm sorry they was so mean to you," said the girl. "Me and Tommy wasn't there or we wouldn't of let them."

Rugo couldn't remember if they had been with the pack that morning or not. It didn't matter. They were only being friendly in the hope he would show them where to find the berries.

Still, no few of the Stranger cubs had liked him in the past, those who were too old to be frightened into screaming fits by his appearance and too young to be drilled into prejudice, and he had been fond of them in turn. And whatever the reason of these two, they were speaking nicely.

"My dad said the other day he thought he could get you to do some work for him," said the boy. "He'd pay you good."

"Who is your father?" asked Rugo uncertainly.

"He's Mr. Jim Stackman."

Yes, Stackman had never been anything but pleasant, in the somewhat strained and awkward manner of humans. They felt guilty for what their grandparents had done, as if that could change matters. But it was something. Most humans were pretty decent; their main fault was the way they stood by when others of their race did evil, stood by and said nothing and felt embarrassed.

"Mr. Whately won't let me go down there," said Rugo.

"Oh, *him*," said the boy with elaborate scorn. "My dad'll take care of old Sourpuss Whately."

"I don't like Sam Whately neither," said the girl. "He's mean, like his old man."

"Why do you do as he says, then?" asked Rugo.

The boy looked uncomfortable. "He's bigger'n the rest of us," he muttered.

Yes, that was the way of humans, and it wasn't really their fault that the Manuel Joneses were so few among them. They suffered more for it than anyone else, probably.

"Here is a nice berry bush," said Rugo. "You can pick it if you want to."

He sat down on a mossy bank, watching them eat, thinking that maybe things had changed today. Maybe he wouldn't need to move away after all.

The girl came and sat down beside him. "Can you tell me a story, Mister Troll?" she asked.

"Hmm?" Rugo was startled out of his reverie.

"My daddy says an old-timer like you must know lots of things," she said.

Why, yes, thought Rugo, he did know a good deal, but it wasn't the sort of tale you could give children. They didn't know hunger and loneliness and shuddering winter cold, weakness and pain and the slow grinding out of hope, and he didn't want them ever to know it. But, well, he could remember a few things besides. His father had told him stories of what had once been, and—

Your race will always haunt us, no matter how long man is here something of you will enter into him... There'll always be a shadow just beyond the fire, a voice in the wind and in the rivers, something in the soil that will enter the bread he eats and the water he drinks, and that will be the lost race, which was yours.

"Why, yes," he said slowly. "I think so."

The boy came and sat beside the girl, and they watched him with large eyes. He leaned back against the bank and fumbled around in his mind.

"A LONG time ago," he said, "before people had come to New Terra, there were trolls like me living here. We built houses and farms, and we had our songs and our stories just like you do. So I can tell you a little bit about that, and maybe some day when you are grown up and have children of your own you can tell them."

"Sure," said the boy.

"Well," said Rugo, "there was once a troll king named Utorri who lived in the Western Dales, not far from the sea. He lived in a big castle with towers reaching up so they nearly scraped the stars, and the wind was always blowing around the towers and ringing the bells. Even when the trolls were asleep they could hear the shivering of the bells. And it was a rich castle, whose doors always stood open to any wayfarers, and each night there was a feast where all the great trolls met and music sounded and the heroes told of their wanderings—"

"Hey, look!"

The children's heads turned, and Rugo's annoyed glance followed theirs. The sun was low now, its rays were long and slanting and touched the hair of Sam Whately with fire where he stood. He had climbed up on the highest crag above the falls and balanced swaying on the narrow perch, laughing. The laughter drifted down through the boom of waters, faint and clear in the evening.

"Gee, he shouldn't," said the little girl.

"I'm the king of the mountain!"

"Young fool," grumbled Rugo.

"I'm the king of the mountain!"

"Sam, come down—" The child's voice was almost lost in thunder.

He laughed again and crouched, feeling with his hands along the rough stone for a way back. Rugo stiffened, remembering how slippery the rocks were and how the river hungered.

The boy started down, and lost his hold and toppled.

Rugo had a glimpse of the redhead as it rose over the foaming green. Then it was gone, snuffed like a torch as the river sucked it under.

Rugo started to his feet, yelling, remembering that even now he had the strength of many humans and that a man had called him brave. Some dim corner of his mind told him to wait, to stop and think, and he ran to the shore with the frantic knowledge that if he did consider the matter wisely he would never go in.

The water was cold around him, it sank fangs of cold into his body and he cried out with the pain.

Sam's head appeared briefly at the foot of the cataract, whirling downstream. Rugo's feet lost bottom and he struck out, feeling the current grab him and yank him from shore.

Swimming, whipping downstream, he shook the water from his eyes and gasped and looked wildly around. Yes, there came Sam, a little above him, swimming with mindless reflex.

The slight body crashed against his shoulder. Almost, the river had its way, then he got a clutch on the arm and his legs and tail and free hand were working.

They whirled on down the stream and he was deaf and blind and the strength was spilling from him like blood from an open wound.

There was a rock ahead. Dimly he saw it through the cruel blaze of sunlight, a broad flat stone rearing above a foam of water. He flailed, striving for it, sobbing the wind into his empty lungs, and they hit with a shock that exploded in his bones.

Wildly he grabbed at the smooth surface, groping for a handhold. One arm lifted Sam Whately's feebly stirring body out, fairly tossed it on top of the rock, and then the river had him again.

The boy hadn't breathed too much water thought Rugo in his darkening brain. He could lie there till a flying-thing from the village picked him up. *Only—why did I save him? Why did I save him? He stoned me, and now I'll never be able to give Manuel those berries. I'll never finish the story of King Utorri and his heroes.*

The water was cool and green around him as he sank. He wondered if his mother would come for him.

A few miles farther down, the river flows broad and quiet between gentle banks. Trees grow there, and the last sunlight streams through their leaves to glisten on the surface. This is down in the valley, where the homes of man are built.

THE END

World of the Mad

Langdon had found immortality on the planet Tanith. Naturally he wanted his wife to share it—if he could prevent her from going insane first...

HE walked slowly through the curling purple mists, feeling the ground roll and quiver under his feet, hearing the deep voiced rumble of shifting strata far underground. There were voices in the fog, singing in high unhuman tones, and no man had ever learned what it was that sang—for could the wind utter sounds so elfishly sweet, almost words that haunted you with half understanding of something you had forgotten and needed desperately to remember?

A face floated through the swirling mist. It was not human, but it was very beautiful, and it was blind. He looked away as it mouthed voiceless murmurs at him.

Somewhere a crystal tree was chiming, a delicate pizzicato of glass-like leaves vibrating against each other. The man listened to it and to the low muttering of the earth, for those at least were real and he was not at all sure whether the other things were there or not.

Even after two hundred years, he wasn't sure.

He went on through the mist. Flowers grew up around him, great fragile laceries of shining crystalline petals that budded and bloomed and died even as he walked by. Some of them reached hungrily for him, but he sidestepped their groping mouths with the unthinking ease of long habit.

Compasses didn't work on Tanith, and only a few men could even operate a radio direction finder, but Langdon knew his way and walked steadily ahead. His sense of direction kept rotating crazily; it insisted he was going the wrong way, no, now the house lay over to the right—no, now the left, and a few paces straight up… But by now he had compensated for that; he didn't need eyes or kinesthetic sense to find his way home.

There was a new singing in the violet air. Langdon checked his stride with a sudden eerie prickling along his spine. The mist eddied about him, thick and blinding, but now the city was growing out of it; he saw the towers and streets and thronging airways come raggedly into being.

Suddenly he stood in the middle of the city. It was complete this time, not the few fragmentary glimpses he ordinarily had. The mist flowed through the ghostly spires and pylons but somehow he could see anyway, the city lay for kilometers around.

IT was not a human city. It lay under three hurtling moons, lit only by their brilliant silver. But it lived, it pulsed with life about him; the shining dwellers soared past and seemed to leave a trail of little sparks luminous against the night. They were not men, the old folk of Tanith, but they were beautiful.

There was no sound. Langdon stood in a well of silence while the city lay around him, and he thought that perhaps he was the ghost, alone and excommunicated on a world, which lay beyond even the dreams of man.

But that was nonsense, he thought, angry with himself. It was simply that temporal mirages transmitted only light, not sound. He was here, now, alive, and the city was dust these many million years.

Two dwellers flew past him; male and female with arms linked, laughing soundlessly into each other's golden eyes. The male's great glowing wings brushed through Langdon's body. He stood briefly in a shower of whirling light-motes— and they didn't heed him, they didn't know he was there.

They were only for each other, those two, and he was a ghost out of an unreal and unthinkably remote future.

The mirage faded. Slowly, in bits and patches, it dissolved back into the purple fog. He was alone again.

He shivered and hastened his steps homeward.

The mist began to break, raggedly as he came out of the forest. He went by a lake of life with only a passing glance at the strangeness of the new shapes that seethed and bubbled, rose out of its slime and took shifting form and sank back into chemical disintegration. There was always something new, grotesque and horrible and sometimes eerily lovely, to be seen at such a place, but spontaneous generation was an old story to Langdon by now. And Eileen was waiting.

He came out on the brow of a steep hill that slanted down into the little cup-like valley where he had his dwelling. The hills were blue around it, blue with grass that tomorrow might be gold or green or gray, and the sky was currently blood-red. A grove of feather-like trees hid the house, swaying where there was no wind and murmuring to each other in their own language, and a few winged things hovered darkly overhead. For a moment Langdon paused there, savoring the richness of it. This was his home.

His land. Back on Terra they had forgotten the fullness that came with belonging to the earth, but the men who colonized among the stars remembered. Looking back, Langdon thought that the real instability and alienness was in the Solar System. Men had no roots there, and it was a secret woe in them and made them feverish and restless, eager to taste from all cups but shuddering away from draining any one.

On Tanith, thought Langdon with a quiet sort of exultation, a man drank his cup to the bottom, and there were many cups—or, if only one, it was never the same and could never be emptied.

For a man on Tanith did not grow old.

SUDDENLY he stiffened, and a psyche-feeder swooped low to absorb his furiously radiated nervous energy. The reaction of it eddied in his mind as a chilling fear. Angrily, without having to think about it, he drove the creature off with a jaggedly pulsed mental vibration and remained standing and listening.

Someone had screamed.

It came again, distorted by the wavering air, hardly recognizable to one who had not had time to adjust to Tanith, and it was Eileen's voice. "Joe, Joe, Joe—help—"

He ran, scrambling down the unstable hillside with his mist-wet cloak flapping behind him. A sword-plant slashed at him with its steely leaves. He swerved and went on down into the valley, running, leaping, a bounding black shadow against the burning sky.

Static electricity discharged in crackling blue sheets as he tore through the grove, hissing against his insulating clothes and stinging his face and hands. Something floated through the dark air, long and supple and dripping slime, grimacing at him with its horrible wet mouth. Another illusion or mirage, he thought somewhere in the back of his mind. They no longer bothered him—in fact, he'd have missed them if they never showed up again—but—Eileen—

The cottage nestled under the tall whispering trees, a peak-roofed stone building in the ancient style that Langdon had thought most appropriate to the enchanted planet. There was little of Terra about it after its century and a half of existence; it was covered with fire-vines over which danced the seeming of little flames; luminous flying creatures nestled against the doorway, and he had never found the cause of the dim sweet singing he could always hear around it.

The door stood ajar, and Eileen was sobbing inside. Langdon came in and found her huddled on a couch before the fireplace, trembling so that it seemed her body must be shaken apart, and crying, crying.

He sat down and put his arms about her and let her cry herself out.

Then he remained for a while stroking her hair and saying nothing.

She bit her lip to keep it steady. Her voice was like a small child's, high and toneless and frightened. "It bit," she said.

"It was an illusion," he murmured.

"No. It bit at me. And its eyes were dead. It came out of the floor there, and it was all in rags."

"You had an illusion frighten you," he said. "A psyche-feeder flying nearby caught your increased nervous output, drew on it, and that of course frightened you still more...they're easy to drive away, Eileen. They don't like certain pulse patterns—you just think at them the way I showed you—"

"It was real," she insisted, quietly, with something of a child's puzzlement that anything should have wanted to hurt her. "It was black, but there were grays and browns and red too, and it was ragged."

HE went over to the cupboard and got out a darkly glowing bottle and poured two full glasses. "This'll help," he said, trying hard to smile at her. *"Prosit."*

"I shouldn't," said Eileen, still shakily but with some return of saneness. "Junior—"

"Junior won't take harm from a glass of wine," said Langdon. He sat down beside her again and they clinked goblets and drank. The fire wavered ruddily before them, filling the room with warm restless light and with dancing shadows from which Eileen looked away.

"I'll get an electronic range installed soon," said Langdon, trying to fill the silence with trivia. "It can't be convenient for you cooking on an ancient-style stove."

"I thought they didn't work on Tanith—electronics, I mean," she answered with the same effort of ordinariness.

"Not at first, with the different laws prevailing here. In the first few decades, we were forced back to the old chemical techniques like fires. That's one reason so few colonists ever came, or stayed long if they did come. But bit by bit, little by little, we're learning the scientific laws and applying them. They've had all the standard household equipment available here for a century, I guess, but by that time I'd already built this place and liked my own things, fires and stoves and all the rest, too well to change. But now that I've got a wife to do my housekeeping, I ought to provide her with conveniences. In fact, I should have done so right away."

"It isn't that, Joe," she said. "I'd have squawked long ago if those little things made any difference. I like handling things myself rather than turning them over to some robot. It's fun to cook and get wood, but Joe, it's no fun when a thing rises out of the steam and screams at you. It's no fun when electric sparks jump over the house and all of a sudden there's only fear, the whole place is choked with fear—" She shuddered closer against him.

"This planet is haunted," she whispered.

"The laws of nature are a little different," he answered as calmly as he could. "But they are still laws. Tanith seems like a chaos, governed by living spirits and most of them malignant, only because you don't see the regularity. Its pattern is too different from what you're used to. Terra herself must have seemed that way to primitive man, before he discovered order in nature.

"Our scientists here are slowly finding out the answers. Talk to old Chang sometime, he can tell you more about it than I. But I can see the order now, a little of it, and it's a richer and deeper thing than the rest of the universe.

"And you live forever." He gripped her shoulders and looked into her wide eyes. He had to expel the demons of terror from her. A woman five months pregnant couldn't go on this way. He was suddenly shocked by how thin she had grown, and she never stopped shivering under his hands.

"You won't grow old," he said slowly. "We'll be together forever, Eileen. And our children won't die either."

She looked away from him, and sudden bitterness twisted her mouth. "I wonder," she said thinly, "whether immortality is worth having—on this planet."

Suddenly she stiffened, and her lips opened to scream again. Langdon forgot the hurt of her words and looked wildly about the room. But there was only the furniture and the firelight and the weaving shadows. Inside the blood-red windows, the room was sane and real and human.

Eileen shrank against him. "It's over there," she gasped. "Over there in that corner, creeping closer—"

Langdon's face grew bleak, and there was a desolation rising in him. Illusions of one sort or another were part of daily life on Tanith, but they had reality in that they were produced by physical processes and more than one person could perceive them. But hallucinations were another story.

He thought back over two hundred years to the first attempts to colonize. Of an initial three hundred or so, over two-thirds had left within the first three years. And many of them had been insane when the ships took them home.

Men came to Tanith and stayed if they could endure it. But if they couldn't, and tried to stay anyway, they soon fled from the unendurable madness of its reality to a safer and more orderly madness of their own.

From what he had heard, few of them were cured again, even back on Terra.

"I'VE got to see Chang," he said.

The colonists on Tanith tended to live well apart from each other, and unless they owned the new televisors designed especially for the planet their only contact was physical. Once a month or so he would go to the planet's one town for supplies and a mild spree, and somewhat oftener he would spend a while at another house or have guests himself. But most of the time he had been alone.

And as a man grew older, without loss of physical and mental faculties, he found more and more within himself, an unfolding inward richness, which none of the short-lived would ever appreciate or even comprehend. He had less need of other men to prop him up. Or perhaps it was simply that the wisdom, the fullness, which came with immortality, made a little of the other colonists' company go a long ways.

There was no denying it, Eileen's twenty-three years of life could not compare with Langdon's two hundred or more. She was like a child, thoughtless, mentally and physically timid, ignorant, essentially shallow.

But I love her. And I can afford to wait. In fifty or a hundred years she'll begin to grow up. In two hundred or so we'll begin to understand each other. As our ages increase, the absolute difference between them will become proportionately insignificant.

An immortal learns patience. I can wait—and meanwhile I love her very dearly.

"What do you have to see him about?" asked Eileen.

"Us," he answered bluntly. "Our situation. It isn't good."

"No," she whispered.

"Can't you learn that there's nothing to fear on Tanith?" he asked. "Death itself, the greatest dread of all, is gone. We've eliminated all actually dangerous life in the neighborhood of our settlements. There are things that can be annoying—the sword-plants, the psyche-feeders, the static discharges—but it's no trick to learn how to avoid them. Nothing here can hurt you, Eileen."

"I know," she said hopelessly.

"But I'm still afraid. Day and night, I'm afraid. There are worse things than death, Joe."

"But afraid of *what?*"

"I don't know. Fear itself, maybe. How do I know something won't suddenly be deadly? But I'm not afraid of death. Even with the baby, I wouldn't be afraid of wild beasts or plague or—anything that I could understand." She shook her shining head, slowly. "That's just it, Joe. I don't understand this planet. Nobody does. You don't...you admit it yourself."

"Someday I'll know it."

"When? A thousand years from now? A thousand years of horror...Joe, some of those things are so hideous I think I'll go mad when they appear."

"A deep-sea fish on Terra is hideous."

"Not this way. These things aren't right. They can't exist, but still there they are, and I can't forget them, and I never know when they'll appear next or what they'll be this time—" She checked herself, gulping.

"This is a very beautiful world," he said stubbornly. "The colors, the forms, the sounds—"

"None of them are right. Grass may look just as well when it's red or blue or yellow—but it shouldn't be all of them at different times. The sky is wrong, the trees are wrong. Those hideous lakes of life and the things in them, obscene—those voices singing out in the mists, nobody knows what they are—those images of things a hundred million years dead—and the faces, and the whisperings, and there's always something watching and waiting and moving just a little outside the corner of your eye... Oh, Joe, Joe, this planet is haunted!"

SHE sobbed in his arms with a rising note of hysteria that she couldn't quite suppress. He looked grimly over her shoulder. A swirling, chiming mist of color formed on one corner of the room, amorphous stirrings within it, a sudden shining birth that laughed and jeered and slipped out through the wall.

He remembered that he had been frightened and repelled when he first came here. But not to this degree, and he soon got over it. Now, even while Eileen wept, he admired the shifting pulse of colors and his heart quickened to the elfin bells. Terran music sounded wrong to him after two hundred years of the sounds of Tanith.

He thought that all those voices and whisperings and singings, sliding up and down an inhuman scale, and the dreams and the visions had a pattern, an overall immensity, which some day he would grasp. And that would be a moment of revelation, he would see and know the wholeness of Tanith and there would be meaning in it. Not the chaotic jumble of random events, which made up the rest of the universe—death-doomed universe tumbling blindly toward a wreck of level entropy and ashen suns—but a glimpse of that ultimate purposefulness, which some men called God.

Briefly, a temporal mirage showed beyond the window, a fragmentary glimpse of a tower reaching for the sky. And it was no work of man, nor could it ever be, but it was of a heartbreaking loveliness.

He wondered about the ancient natives. Had they simply become extinct, reached a point of declining evolutionary efficiency such as seemed fated for all species and gone into limbo some millions of years previously? Or had they, perhaps, finally seen the allness of the world and gone—

elsewhere? Privately, Langdon rather thought it was the latter. *World without end—*

But Eileen was crying in his arms.

He kissed her, and tasted salt on her lips that trembled under his, poor kid, poor kid, and with a baby on the way…

SOMETHING of the magic of their first days together came back to him. It was a disappointment in love, which had sent him to Tanith in the first place, and for all his time here he had lived without that sort of affection. The women of the town served the casual needs of sex, which seemed to become less and less frequently manifest as his own undying personality grew in fullness and self-sufficiency, and that was all.

Still, a single man was incomplete. And a year ago, one of the few colony ships landed, and Eileen had been aboard, and a forgotten springtime stirred within him.

Now…well…

She released herself, smiling with unsteady lips. "I'll be all right now, dear," she said. "Let's go."

I have to talk this matter over privately with Chang. His wife can take care of Eileen. Certainly I can't leave her here alone.

But sooner or later he would have to. It wasn't only that he had to go out and oversee some of the fields, on which grew the native plants whose secretions, needed by Terran chemistry, gave them their livelihood. Solitude and long walks through the misty forests and over the whispering hills had become virtual necessities to him. He had to get away and think, the mighty thoughts of an immortal, which no Terran could ever comprehend in his pathetic lifetime were being gestated in his brain. Slowly, piece by piece, the coherent philosophy, which is necessary for sanity was coalescing within him, and he was gathering into himself the essence of Tanith. Someday, perhaps a thousand years hence, he would know what it was that haunted him now.

He could not suppress a feeling of annoyance, however. Eileen had had over a year to adjust now and she was getting worse instead of better. A brief sojourn in utter alienness might be merely pleasing and interesting, but over a longer time one either got used to it or— She'd have to learn, have to accept the sanity of Tanith and know it for a deeper and more real one than the sanity of Terra.

Others had done it, why couldn't she?

CHANG Simon and his wife lived several hundred kilometers away, an hour's flight by airjet. Their spacious house lay amid lawns and trees sloping down to a broad river; it held a serenity and graciousness, which Terra had forgotten. Langdon was always glad to be there, and even Eileen seemed to be soothed. She had screamed once on the flight over, when the sky had suddenly seethed with hell-blue flame, and she was still trembling when they arrived. Their hostess took her off for one of those mysterious private conferences between women, which no merely male creature will ever understand, and Langdon and Chang sat out on the veranda and talked.

The Chinese had been in his fifties when he came, one of the first load of colonists, and Tanith could not restore lost youth. But a healthy middle age had its own advantages, it conferred a peace and depth of mind more rapidly than an endlessly young body would permit. In the Solar System, Chang had been a synthesist, taking all knowledge and its correlation as his field of work, and he had come to Tanith in some of Langdon's mood of abandonment—futile to attempt the knowing and understanding of all things, when life had flickered out in a hundred years. But as an immortal synthesist...

The two men sat in the long twilight, saying little at first. It was good just to sit, thought Langdon, to let a glass of wine and a cigar relax tensed muscles while the dusk deepened toward night. At such times he felt more than ever drawn into the secret whole that was Tanith—almost, it seemed, he was on the verge of that revelation, of seeing the manifold aspects of reality gather themselves into one overwhelming entity of which he would be an integral part. The philosophers and mystics of Terra had sought such identification, and the scientists were still striving to build a unified picture of the cosmic whole. Here, in this environment and with all the ages before him, a man had a chance to reach that ancient goal, intellectual understanding and emotional integration—someday, someday.

The twilight was deep and blue and full of flitting ghostly lights. The feathery trees murmured to each other in a language of their own, and down under the long slope of dew-shining grass the river gleamed with shifting phosphorescence. Something was singing in the night, an eerie wavering scale that woke faint longings and dreads in men and set them straining after something they had once known and forgotten.

OVERHEAD the million thronging stars of Galactic center winked, and blazed through the flickering aurora. One of the moons rose, trailing golden light through the sky. A wind blew through drifting clouds, and it seemed as if the wind had language too and spoke to the men, if they could but understand it.

Chang said at last, slowly and heavily: "I don't know how she got past the psychologists on Terra."

"Eileen?" asked Langdon unnecessarily.

"Of course." The older man was a shadow in the dusk, but the red tip of his cigar waxed and waned as he drew on it for comfort. "Somebody blundered. Or—wait—perhaps it was only that, while she was fundamentally stable, the otherness of Tanith touched some deep-seated psychological flaw in her, something that would never appear under any other environment."

"I don't quite know the system," said Langdon. "What do they do back at Sol?"

"The first attempts at colonization showed that only the most stable personalities could adapt to—or even survive—the apparent instability of this planet. There aren't many who want to come here at all, of course, but our planetary government maintains a psychological staff in the more important worlds of the Galaxy to check those who do apply. They're supposed to weed out all who couldn't take the strangeness, and so far it's been very successful. Eileen is the first failure I know of."

Something cold seemed to close around Langdon. And then, he realized wryly, he was skirting the main issue—afraid to face it.

"I wonder if we really have the right to keep secret the fact that there is no death here," he said.

"It was a hard decision to make," answered Chang, "but leaving the morals of it aside, it was the only practicable way. Suppose it were generally known that this one place, in all the known universe, has no age. Imagine all who would want to come here! The planet couldn't hold a fraction of them. Even as it is, we have to space births very carefully lest in a few centuries we crowd ourselves off the world. Furthermore, the unstable social environment produced by such an influx of colonists, most of whom couldn't stand the place anyway, would delay, perhaps ruin, the research by which we hope to find out why life does not grow old here. When we have that answer, and can apply it outside this region of space, all the Galaxy will have immortality. But until then, we must wait." He shrugged, a dim movement in the shining night. "And immortals know how to wait."

"So instead, we simply accept colonists who agree to stay here for life—and then once they get here they're told how long that life will be."

"YES. Actually, the miracle is that the first colonists stayed at all, after most had fled or gone insane. After all, it was ten or twenty years before we even suspected the truth. A world as alien as this was settled only because planets habitable to man and without aborigines are hard to find. Since then, many more such worlds—normal ones—have been discovered, and few people care to risk madness by coming here. Tanith is an obscure dominion of the Galactic Union, having a certain scientific interest because of its unique natural laws—but not too great even there, when science has so many other things to investigate just now. And we're quite content to remain in the shadow."

"Of course." Langdon looked up to the swarming stars. A sheet of blue auroral flame covered them for a moment.

He asked presently: "How much further have our scientists gotten in explaining the phenomenon?"

"We've come quite a ways, but progress has been mostly in highly technical fields of mathematical physics. You'll have to take a decade or two off soon, Joseph, and learn that subject. Briefly, we do know that this is a region of warped space, similar to those in the neighborhood of massive bodies but of a different character. As you know, natural constants are different in such regions from free space, phenomena such as gravitation and the bending of light appear. This is another sort of geometric distortion, but basically the same. It produces differences in—well, in optics, in thermodynamics, in psi functions, in almost everything. The very laws of probabilities are different here. As a result, the curious phenomena we know appear. Many of them, of course, are simply illusions produced by complex refractions of light and sound waves; others are very real. The time axis itself is subject to certain transformations, which produce the temporal mirages. And so it goes."

"Yes, yes, I know all that. But what causes the warp itself?"

"We're not sure yet, but we think it's an effect of our being near the Galactic center of mass, together with—no, it would take me a week to write out the equations, let alone explain them."

There was a comfort in impersonal discourse, but it was a retreat from more immediate problems. Langdon fairly rapped out the question: "How close are you to understanding why we are immortal?"

"Not at all close in detail," said Chang. "We think that it's due to the difference in thermodynamic properties of matter I mentioned just now, producing a balance of colloidal entropy. Well, elsewhere life is metastable and can only endure so long. Here it is the natural tendency of things, so much so indeed that life is generated spontaneously from the proper chemical mixtures such as occur in many of the lakes and pools hereabouts. In our own bodies, there is none of that tendency toward chemical and colloidal degradation, which I think lies at the root of aging and death.

"But that's just my guess, you know, and biological phenomena are so extraordinarily complex that it will probably take us centuries to work it out. After all, we haven't even settled all the laws of Tanith's physics yet."

"Several centuries... And there is no other planet where this might also happen?"

"NONE have been found, and on the basis of our theory I'm inclined to believe that Tanith is unique in the Galaxy—

perhaps in the universe." Langdon was aware of Chang's speculative gaze on him. "And if there were others, they'd be just as foreign to Terra."

"I see—" Langdon looked away, down to the streaming silver gleam of the river. There was a ring of little lights dancing on the lawn; he could hear the tinkle of elfland bells and he thought he could see glowing wings and lithe light forms that were not human—but very lovely.

"You were thinking of moving away?" asked the synthesist at last.

"Yes. I hated the thought, but Eileen—well—you saw her. And you remember those first colonists."

"I do. She is exhibiting all their symptoms. She can't stand the unpredictability of her environment, and she can't adjust her scale of values enough to see the beauty in what to her is wrong and horrible." In the vague golden light, Langdon thought he glimpsed a grim smile on the other man's face. "Perhaps she is right, Joseph. Perhaps it takes someone not quite sane by the rest of the Galaxy's standards to adjust to Tanith."

"But—can't she see—I've told her—"

"Intellectual understanding of a problem never solves it, though it may help. Eileen takes your word for these being purely natural phenomena. She's not superstitious. It might help if she were. Because explaining the horror doesn't lessen it to her. Man is not a rational animal, Joseph, though he likes to pretend he is."

"Can't she be helped? Psychology?"

"No." The old voice held pity, but it did not waver. "I've studied such cases. If you keep her here much longer, she'll have a miscarriage and go insane. The insanity might be curable, back at Sol, or it might not, but as soon as she returned it would come again. Not that she could ever stand to come back.

"She is inherently unable to adapt herself to an utterly foreign environment. You'll have to send her home, Joseph, soon."

"But...she's my *wife*..."

Chang said nothing. A shining golden head swooped past in the darkness, laughing at them, and the laughter was visible as red pulses in the night.

There came a step on the veranda. Langdon turned and saw Chang's wife coming out with Eileen. The girl walked more steadily now. In the dim radiance from the window, her face was calmer than it had been for some time, and for an instant there was a flood of love and joy and relief within Langdon.

Chang was wrong, Eileen would learn. She was already starting to learn. Tonight was the turning point. Tanith would take her to itself and they would be together forever.

"Eileen," he said, very softly, and got up and walked toward her. "Eileen, darling."

The atmosphere trembled between them. She saw the flesh run from his bones, it was a skull that grinned at her, shining evilly green against the dark, and the sounds that rasped from it were the mouthings of nightmare.

Somewhere, far back in the depths of her mind, a little cool voice told her that there was nothing to be afraid of that it was a brief variation in optical and sonic constants, which would pass away and then Joe would be there. But the voice was drowned in her own screaming, she was screaming for her mother to come and get her, it was a nightmare *and she couldn't wake up*—

Langdon ran toward her, with the rags of flesh hanging from his phosphorescent bones, until Chang grabbed him back with a violence he had never known to be possible in the old man.

THERE was a storm outside; the cottage shook to a fury of wind and was filled with its noise and power. They had a fire going, and its restless glow played over the room and beat against the calm white light of fluorotubes, but it could not drive out the luminousness beyond the window.

"Pull the shades," asked Eileen. "Please, Joe."

He looked away from the window where he stood staring out at the storm. Fire sleeted across the landscape, whirling heatless flames that hissed and crackled around the wind-tossed trees, red and blue and yellow and icy white. The wind roared and boomed, with a hollow voice that seemed to shout words in some unknown tongue, and from behind the curtain of flaming rain there was the crimson glow of an open furnace. As if, thought Langdon, as if the gates of Hell stood open just beyond the hills.

"It won't hurt us," he said. "It's only a matter of phosphorescence and static discharges."

"Please, Joe." Her voice was very small in the racket of wind.

He shrugged, and covered the wild scene. He used to like to go out in fire-storms, he remembered, their blinding berserk fury woke something elemental in him and he would go striding through them like a god shouting back at the wind.

Well, it wouldn't be long now. The *Betelgeuse Queen* was due in a couple of days on the intragalactic orbit that would take her back to Sol. Eileen didn't have long to wait.

He took a moody turn about the room. His wife had been very quiet since her collapse of a week ago. Too quiet. He didn't like it.

She looked wistfully up at his tall form. He thought that she looked pathetically small and alone, curled up—almost crouched—in the big armchair. Like a very beautiful child, too thin and hollow-eyed now but beautiful.

A child.

She has to go. She can't live here. And I—well—if she goes, it will be like a death within me, I love her.

"I remember winter storms on Terra," said Eileen softly. "It would be cold and dark, with a big wind driving snow against the house. We'd come inside, cold but warm underneath with being out in it, and we'd sit in front of a fire and have hot cocoa and cheese sandwiches. If it was around Christmas time, we'd be singing the old songs—"

THE wind yammered, banging on the door. A stealthy shape of light and shadow wavered halfway between existence and nonexistence, over in a corner of the room. Eileen's voice trailed off and her eyes widened and there was a small dry rattle in her throat. She gripped the arms of her chair with an unnatural tension.

Langdon saw it and came over to sit beside her on one arm of the chair. Her hand closed tightly around his and she looked away from the weaving shape in the corner.

"You were always good to me, Joe," she murmured.

"How could I be anything else?" he asked tonelessly. There was a new voice in the storm now, a great belling organ was crying to him to come out. Tanith was dancing in a sleet of fire just beyond the door.

"I'll miss you," she said. "I'll miss you very much."

"Why should you? I'll be along."

"Will you, Joe? I wonder. I can't ask it of you. I can't ask you to trade a thousand years of life, or ten thousand or a million, for the little sixty or seventy you'll have left out there. I can't ask you to leave your world for mine. You'll never be at home on Terra."

He smiled, without much mirth. "It's a trite phrase," he said, "but you know I'd die for you."

"I don't doubt that, Joe. But would you—live for me?"

He kissed her to avoid answering. *I don't know. I honestly don't know.*

It isn't so much a question of losing immortality, though God knows that means a lot. It means more than any mortal will ever know. It's that I'd be losing—Tanith.

He thought of Sol, Sirius, Antares, the great suns and planets of the Galaxy, and could not keep from shuddering. Drabness, deadness, colorlessness, meaninglessness! Life was a brief blind spasm of accident and catastrophe, walled in by its own shortness and the barren environment of a death-doomed cosmos. Too small to achieve any purpose, too limited even to imagine a goal, it flickered and went out into an utter dark.

> *Tomorrow and tomorrow and tomorrow*
> *Creeps in this petty place from day to day*
> *To the last syllable of recorded time,*
> *And all our yesterdays have lighted fools*
> *The way to dusty death*

The storm sang outside, and he heard music and lure and enchantment. It was not a discord, after two centuries he could hear some of the tremendous harmony—after another while, he might begin to understand the song.

If he stayed, if he stayed.

Eileen.

His face twisted. She saw it, and pain bit at her, but there was nothing she could say.

He began pacing, and his mind took up the weary track of the past week. Logic—think it out like a rational being.

EILEEN had to go. But he could stay, and she would understand insofar as any mortal could. Somewhere else, back in the Solar system or on some other of man's many planets, she would find another husband who could give her all his heart. *Which I could never do, because I love Tanith. She would come to think of me as dead, she would hold him dear for the brief span of their lives. She'd be happy. And maybe someday she'd send the child back to me.*

As for himself—well, the initial pain of separation would be hard to take, but he had an immortal's endurance. Sooner or later, the longing would die. And there would be another woman someday on one of the colony ships whom he could love and take to wife forever. He could wait, he had all time before him...

And he would be on Tanith...

And there would be his friends. He thought of the utter loneliness that waited for him in the Galaxy. Two hundred years was a sizeable draft of eternity; he had acquired enough of the immortal's viewpoint and personality to find the short-lived completely alien. He could never know more than the most superficial comradeship with even the oldest of those who were younger than he. He could never be close to his wife; she would occupy only the smallest part of the emptiness within him. Because before she had grown enough to match him, they would both be dead.

We'll die, go down in the futility of the universe, and Tanith will go on. I might have been a god, but I'll go down in dust and nothingness. No one will have gotten any good of me. Unless I stay.

The wind called and called.

Eileen was right. I'm not afraid to die. But I am afraid to live, in the way she must. Horribly afraid.

But I love her.

Fifty years hence there'll be another woman.

But I love Eileen now!

Round and round, a crazy roaring whirlpool swinging and crashing toward madness. His thoughts were running in a meaningless circle, the familiar landmarks flickered by with ghastly speed in that devil's race, the room wavered before him.

He snarled with sudden inarticulate rage and grabbed his insulating cloak and rushed out the door.

EILEEN shrank back in her chair. He was gone. She was alone now and all the powers of Tanith were rising up against her. The wind hooted and whistled, piping down the chimney and skirling under the eaves. The blind lifted to an invisible force and she saw the red flames of Hell blazing outside. The fluoroglobes flickered toward extinction, darkness closed down; but it was full of dancing light and glimmering shapes that gibed and jeered and spun closer to her. The room began to whirl, faster and faster, a tipping tilting saraband on the edge of madness.

All the old forgotten powers of night and dark and Hell were abroad, whirling on the wind and slamming against the door and banging their heels on the roof. They rose out of the floor and seeped from the walls and the air. Fire danced around them, and they neared her, crying something that she knew would drive her mad when she understood it.

Joe, Joe, Joe—Mother—God— Joe was gone out into the storm. Mother was dead these many years, God had forgotten. And the powers closed in laughing at her and mocking and whispering what she could not stand to hear and there and around and around and around and around and around down, down, down, down, down into darkness—

LANGDON did not hear her scream the first time. He stood in the living torrent of light. Fire streamed about him and dripped from his hands; his hair crackled with static electricity and the wind sang to him. It filled him, the song of the wind, the song of Tanith. He was lost in it, whirled up in a great singing joyous laughter. He *knew*—in another moment he would know, he would be part of the allness and have peace within him.

Fire, wind, the slender graceful trees laughing as the flames leaped around them, a great exultant chant from the living forests and the dancing hills, a glimpse of an ancient Tanithian across many million years, flying in the storm with the red and gold and blue and bronze rushing off his wings. Tanith, Tanith, Tanith.

Tanith, I love you, I am part of you. I can never go. This is the thing other men do not know. More than immortality, more than all the mighty dreams you give us, there is yourself. A day on Tanith is more than a lifetime on Terra, but they will never know that because they have never felt it. The strong love of a man for his home—but this is passion, it is the whole of life, and Tanith gives it back. Here, and here alone, is meaning and beauty and an unending splendid horizon. Here alone a man can belong.

See, see that bird with wings like molten silver!

The second scream was wordless and crazy and horrible, but the dying fragment of his own name went through him like a knife. For the barest instant he stood there while the storm roared about him and the fire rushed over the world. Then, quite simply, he ran back into the house.

The blood and pain and screeching horror of the abortion left him physically ill, but he managed to get her to bed and even, after a long while, to sleep. Then he walked over to the window and drew the blind. His shoulders sagged with the defeat and death and ruin that was here...

THE captain of the *Betelgeuse Queen* did not like Tanith and said as much to his mate as they relaxed on the promenade deck.

"The place gives you the blue willies," he declared. "Everything's *wrong* there. Praise the powers it's so backward and obscure we only have to stop there once a year or so."

"The colonists seem to like it," said the mate.

"They would," snorted the captain. "Worst bunch of clannish provincials I ever saw. Why, they hardly ever leave the planet, except maybe for a year or so at a time on essential business, and they won't be friendly with anybody. Takes a crazy man to stand that world in the first place."

He pointed to a tall man who was half leading, half supporting a young woman along the deck. She would have been beautiful had she not been badly underweight. She smiled at the man, but her eyes were haunted, and his answering smile was far away. It went no deeper than his lips.

"That fellow Langdon is the only long-time colonist I ever heard of who left Tanith for good," said the captain. "He must have been there for years. Maybe he was born there, but he's coming back to Sol now. His wife couldn't take the place."

"I think I remember her from a year or so ago," nodded the mate. "Didn't we carry her out with a few other colonists? Pretty as a picture then, and full of life and fun—now look at her. Tanith did that to her."

"Uh-huh," agreed the captain. "I heard a little of the story down by the spaceport. She nearly went crazy—finally had a miscarriage. It was all they could do to save her life and sanity. Only then would that Langdon take her back. He let her go on that way for months." The captain's mouth twisted with contempt. "Holy sunspots, what a cold-blooded devil!"

THE END

Sentiment, Inc.

*The way we feel about another person, or about objects, is often bound
up in associations that have no direct connection with the person or
object at all. Often, what we call a "change of heart" comes about
sheerly from a change in the many associations which make up our
present viewpoint. Now, suppose that these associations could be
altered artificially, at the option of the person who was in charge of the
process...*

CHAPTER ONE

SHE was twenty-two years old, fresh out of college, full of
life and hope, and all set to conquer the world. Colin Fraser
happened to be on vacation on Cape Cod, where she was
playing summer stock, and went to more shows than he had
planned. It wasn't hard to get an introduction, and before
long he and Judy Sanders were seeing a lot of each other.

"Of course," she told him one afternoon on the beach,
"my real name is Harkness."

He raised his arm, letting the sand run through his fingers.
The beach was big and dazzling white around them, the sea
galloped in with a steady roar, and a gull rode the breeze
overhead. "What was wrong with it?" he asked. "For a
professional monicker, I mean."

She laughed and shook the long hair back over her
shoulders. "I wanted to live under the name of Sanders," she
explained.

"Oh—oh, yes, of course. Winnie the Pooh." He grinned.
"Soulmates, that's what we are." It was about then that he
decided he'd been a bachelor long enough.

In the fall she went to New York to begin the upward grind—understudy, walk-on parts, shoestring-theaters, and roles in outright turkeys. Fraser returned to Boston for awhile, but his work suffered, he had to keep dashing off to see her.

By spring she was beginning to get places; she had talent and everybody enjoys looking at a brown-eyed blonde. His weekly proposals were also beginning to show some real progress, and he thought that a month or two of steady siege might finish the campaign. So he took leave from his job and went down to New York himself. He'd saved up enough money, and was good enough in his work, to afford it; anyway, he was his own boss—consulting engineer, specializing in mathematical analysis.

He got a furnished room in Brooklyn, and filled in his leisure time—as he thought of it—with some special math courses at Columbia. And he had a lot of friends in town, in a curious variety of professions. Next to Judy, he saw most of the physicist Sworsky, who was an entertaining companion though most of his work was too top-secret even to be mentioned. It was a happy period.

There is always a jarring note, to be sure. In this case, it was the fact that Fraser had plenty of competition. He wasn't good-looking himself—a tall gaunt man of twenty-eight, with a dark hatchet face and perpetually-rumpled clothes. But still, Judy saw more of him than of anyone else, and admitted she was seriously considering his proposal and no other.

He called her up once for a date. "Sorry," she answered. "I'd love to, Colin, but I've already promised tonight. Just so you won't worry, it's Matthew Snyder."

"Hm—the industrialist?"

"Uh huh. He asked me in such a way it was hard to refuse. But I don't think you have to be jealous, honey. 'Bye now."

Fraser lit his pipe with a certain smugness. Snyder was several times a millionaire, but he was close to sixty, a widower of notably dull conversation. Judy wasn't—Well, no worries, as she'd said. He dropped over to Sworsky's apartment for an evening of chess and bull-shooting.

IT WAS early in May, when the world was turning green again, that Judy called Fraser up. "Hi," she said breathlessly. "Busy tonight?"

"Well, I was hoping I'd be, if you get what I mean," he said.

"Look, I want to take you out for a change. Just got some unexpected cash and damn, I want to feel rich for one evening."

"Hmmm—" He scowled into the phone. "I dunno—"

"Oh, get off it, Galahad. I'll meet you in the Dixie lobby at seven. Okay?" She blew him a kiss over the wires, and hung up before he could argue further. He sighed and shrugged. Why not, if she wanted to?

They were in a little Hungarian restaurant, with a couple of Tzigani strolling about playing for them alone, it seemed, when he asked for details. "Did you get a bonus, or what?"

"No." She laughed at him over her drink. "I've turned guinea pig."

"I hope you quit that job before we're married!"

"It's a funny deal," she said thoughtfully. "It'd interest you. I've been out a couple of times with this Snyder, you know, and if anything was needed to drive me into your arms, Colin, it's his political lectures."

"Well, bless the Republican Party!" He laid his hand over hers, she didn't withdraw it, but she frowned just a little.

"Colin, you know I want to get somewhere before I marry—see a bit of the world, the theatrical world, before turning hausfrau. Don't be so—Oh, never mind. I like you anyway."

Sipping her drink and setting it down again: "Well, to carry on with the story. I finally gave Comrade Snyder the complete brush-off, and I must say he took it very nicely. But today, this morning, he called asking me to have lunch with him, and I did after he explained. It seems he's got a psychiatrist friend doing research, measuring brain storms or something, and—Do I mean storms? Waves, I guess. Anyway, he wants to measure as many different kinds of people as possible, and Snyder had suggested me. I was supposed to come in for three afternoons running—about two hours each time—and I'd get a hundred dollars per session."

"Hm," said Fraser. "I didn't know psych research was that well-heeled. Who is this mad scientist?"

"His name is Kennedy. Oh, by the way, I'm not supposed to tell anybody; they want to spring it on the world as a surprise or something. But you're different, Colin. I'm excited; I want to talk to somebody about it."

"Sure," he said. "You had a session already?"

"Yes, my first was today. It's a funny place to do research—Kennedy's got a big suite on Fifth Avenue, right up in the classy district. Beautiful office. The name of his outfit is Sentiment, Inc."

"Hm. Why should a research-team take such a name? Well, go on."

"Oh, there isn't much else to tell. Kennedy was very nice. He took me into a laboratory full of all sorts of dials and meters and blinking lights and os—what do you call them? Those things that make wiggly pictures."

"Oscilloscopes. You'll never make a scientist, my dear."

She grinned. "But I know one scientist who'd like to— Never mind! Anyway, he sat me down in a chair and put bands around my wrists and ankles—just like the hot squat—and a big thing like a beauty-parlor hair-drier over my head. Then he fiddled with his dials for awhile, making notes. Then he started saying words at me, and showing me pictures. Some of them were very pretty; some ugly; some funny; some downright horrible... Anyway, that's all there was to it. After a couple of hours he gave me a check for a hundred dollars and told me to come back tomorrow."

"Hm." Fraser rubbed his chin. "Apparently he was measuring the electric rhythms corresponding to pleasure and dislike. I'd no idea anybody'd made an encephalograph that accurate."

"Well," said Judy, "I've told you why we're celebrating. Now come on, the regular orchestra's tuning up. Let's dance."

They had a rather wonderful evening. Afterward Fraser lay awake for a long time, not wanting to lose a state of happiness in sleep. He considered sleep a hideous waste of time: if he lived to be ninety, he'd have spent almost thirty years unconscious.

JUDY was engaged for the next couple of evenings, and Fraser himself was invited to dinner at Sworsky's the night after that. So it wasn't till the end of the week that he called her again.

"Hullo, sweetheart," he said exuberantly. "How's things? I refer to Charles Addams Things, of course."

"Oh—Colin." Her voice was very small, and it trembled.

"Look, I've got two tickets to H. M. S. Pinafore. So put on your own pinafore and meet me."

"Colin—I'm sorry, Colin. I can't."

"Huh?" He noticed how odd she sounded, and a leadenness grew within him. "You aren't sick, are you?"

"Colin, I—I'm going to be married."

"What?"

"Yes. I'm in love now; really in love. I'll be getting married in a couple of months."

"But—but—"

"I didn't want to hurt you." He heard her begin to cry.

"But who—how—"

"It's Matthew," she gulped. "Matthew Snyder."

He sat quiet for a long while, until she asked if he was still on the line. "Yeah," he said tonelessly. "Yeah, I'm still here, after a fashion." Shaking himself: "Look, I've got to see you. I want to talk to you."

"I can't."

"You sure as hell can," he said harshly.

They met at a quiet little bar which had often been their rendezvous. She watched him with frightened eyes while he ordered martinis.

"All right," he said at last. "What's the story?"

"I—" He could barely hear her. "There isn't any story. I suddenly realized I loved Matt. That's all."

"Snyder!" He made it a curse. "Remember what you told me about him before?"

"I felt different then," she whispered. "He's a wonderful man when you get to know him."

And rich. He suppressed the words and the thought. "What's so wonderful specifically?" he asked.

"He—" Briefly, her face was rapt. Fraser had seen her looking at him that way, now and then.

"Go on," he said grimly. "Enumerate Mr. Snyder's good qualities. Make a list. He's courteous, cultured, intelligent, young, handsome, amusing—To hell! Why, Judy?"

"I don't know," she said in a high, almost fearful tone. "I just love him, that's all." She reached over the table and stroked his cheek. "I like you a lot, Colin. Find yourself a nice girl and be happy."

His mouth drew into a narrow line. "There's something funny here," he said. "Is it blackmail?"

"No!" She stood up, spilling her drink, and the flare of temper showed him how overwrought she was. "He just happens to be the man I love. That's enough out of you, good-bye, Mr. Fraser."

He sat watching her go. Presently he took up his drink, gulped it barbarously, and called for another.

CHAPTER TWO

JUAN MARTINEZ had come from Puerto Rico as a boy and made his own way ever since. Fraser had gotten to know him in the army, and they had seen each other from time to time since then. Martinez had gone into the private-eye business and made a good thing of it; Fraser had to get past a very neat-looking receptionist to see him.

"Hi, Colin," said Martinez, shaking hands. He was a small, dark man, with a large nose and beady black eyes that made him resemble a sympathetic mouse. "You look like the very devil."

"I feel that way, too," said Fraser, collapsing into a chair. "You can't go on a three-day drunk without showing it."

"Well, what's the trouble? Cigarette?" Martinez held out a pack. "Girl-friend give you the air?"

"As a matter of fact, yes; that's what I want to see you about."

"This isn't a lonely-hearts club," said Martinez. "And I've told you time and again a private dick isn't a wisecracking superman. Our work is ninety-nine percent routine; and for the other one percent, we call in the police."

"Let me give you the story," said Fraser. He rubbed his eyes wearily as he told it. At the end, he sat staring at the floor.

"Well," said Martinez, "it's too bad and all that. But what the hell, there are other dames. New York has more beautiful women per square inch than any other city except Paris. Latch on to somebody else. Or if you want, I can give you a phone number—"

"You don't understand," said Fraser "I want you to investigate this; I want to know why she did it."

Martinez squinted through a haze of smoke. "Snyder's a rich and powerful man," he said. "Isn't that enough?"

"No," said Fraser, too tired to be angry at the hint. "Judy isn't that kind of a girl. Neither is she the kind to go overboard in a few days, especially when I was there. Sure, that sounds conceited, but dammit, I know she cared for me."

"Okay. You suspect pressure was brought to bear?"

"Yeah. It's hard to imagine what. I called up Judy's family in Maine, and they said they were all right, no worries. Nor do I think anything in her own life would give a blackmailer or an extortionist anything to go on. Still—I want to know."

Martinez drummed the desk-top with nervous fingers. "I'll look into it if you insist," he said, "though it'll cost you a pretty penny. Rich men's lives aren't easy to pry into if they've got something they want to hide. But I don't think we'd find out much; your case seems to be only one of a rash of similar ones in the past year."

"Huh?" Fraser looked sharply up.

"Yeah. I follow all the news; and remember the odd facts. There've been a good dozen cases recently, where beautiful young women suddenly married rich men or became their mistresses. It doesn't all get into the papers, but I've got my contacts. I know. In every instance, there was no obvious reason; in fact, the dames seemed very much in love with daddy."

"And the era of the gold-digger is pretty well gone—" Fraser sat staring out the window. It didn't seem right that the sky should be so full of sunshine.

"Well," said Martinez, "you don't need me. You need a psychologist."

Psychologist!

"By God, Juan, I'm going to give you a job anyway!" Fraser leaped to his feet. "You're going to check into an outfit called Sentiment, Inc."

A WEEK later, Martinez said, "Yeah, we found it easily enough. It's not in the phone-book, but they've got a big suite right in the high-rent district on Fifth. The address is here, in my written report. Nobody in the building knows much about 'em, except that they're a quiet, well-behaved bunch and call themselves research psychologists. They have a staff of four: a secretary-receptionist; a full-time secretary; and a couple of husky boys who may be bodyguards for the boss. That's this Kennedy, Robert Kennedy. My man couldn't get into his office; the girl said he was too busy and never saw anybody except some regular clients. Nor could he date either of the girls, but he did investigate them.

"The receptionist is just a working girl for routine stuff, married, hardly knows or cares what's going on. The steno is unmarried, has a degree in psych, lives alone, and seems to have no friends except her boss. Who's not her lover, by the way."

"Well, how about Kennedy himself?" asked Fraser.

"I've found out a good bit, but it's all legitimate," said Martinez. "He's about fifty years old, a widower, very steady private life. He's a licensed psychiatrist who used to practice in Chicago, where he also did research in collaboration with a physicist named Gavotti, who's since died. Shortly after that happened—

"No, there's no suspicion of foul play; the physicist was an old man and died of a heart attack. Anyway, Kennedy moved to New York. He still practices, officially, but he doesn't take just anybody; claims that his research only leaves him time for a few." Martinez narrowed his eyes. "The only thing you could hold against him is that he occasionally sees a guy named Bryce, who's in a firm that has some dealings with Amtorg."

"The Russian trading corporation? Hm."

"Oh, that's pretty remote guilt by association, Colin. Amtorg does have legitimate business, you know. We buy manganese from them, among other things. And the rest of Kennedy's connections are all strictly blue ribbon. Crème de la crème—business, finance, politics, and one big union-leader who's known to be a conservative. In fact, Kennedy's friends are so powerful you'd have real trouble doing anything against him."

Fraser slumped in his chair. "I suppose my notion was pretty wild," he admitted.

"Well, there is one queer angle. You know these rich guys who've suddenly made out with such highly desirable dames? As far as I could find out, every one of them is a client of Kennedy's."

"Eh?" Fraser jerked erect.

"'S a fact. Also, my man showed the building staff, elevator pilots and so on, pictures of these women, and a couple of 'em were remembered as having come to see Kennedy."

"Shortly before they—fell in love?"

"Well, that I can't be sure of. You know how people are about remembering dates. But it's possible."

Fraser shook his dark head. "It's unbelievable," he said. "I thought Svengali was outworn melodrama."

"I know something about hypnotism, Colin. It won't do anything like what you think happened to those girls."

Fraser got out his pipe and fumbled tobacco into it. "I think," he said, "I'm going to call on Dr. Robert Kennedy myself."

"Take it easy, boy," said Martinez. "You been reading too many weird stories; you'll just get tossed out on your can."

Fraser tried to smile. It was hard—Judy wouldn't answer his calls and letters any more. "Well," he said, "it'll be in a worthy cause."

THE elevator let him out on the nineteenth floor. It held four big suites, with the corridor running between them. He studied the frosted-glass doors. On one side was the Eagle Publishing Company and Frank & Dayles, Brokers. On the other was the Messenger Advertising Service, and Sentiment, Inc. He entered their door and stood in a quiet, oak-paneled reception room. Behind the railing were a couple of desks, a young woman working at each, and two burly men who sat boredly reading magazines.

The pretty girl, obviously the receptionist, looked up as Fraser approached and gave him a professional smile. "Yes, sir?" she asked.

"I'd like to see Dr. Kennedy, please," he said, trying hard to be casual.

"Do you have an appointment, sir?"

"No, but it's urgent."

"I'm sorry, sir; Dr. Kennedy is very busy. He can't see anybody except his regular patients and research subjects."

"Look, take him in this note, will you? Thanks."

Fraser sat uneasily for some minutes, wondering if he'd worded the note correctly. I must see you about Miss Judy Harkness. Important. Well, what the devil else could you say?

The receptionist came out again. "Dr. Kennedy can spare you a few minutes, sir," she said. "Go right on in."

"Thanks." Fraser slouched toward the inner door. The two men lowered their magazines to follow him with watchful eyes.

There was a big, handsomely-furnished office inside, with a door beyond that must lead to the laboratory. Kennedy looked up from some papers and rose, holding out his hand. He was a medium-sized man, rather plump, graying hair brushed thickly back from a broad, heavy face behind rimless glasses. "Yes?" His voice was low and pleasant. "What can I do for you?"

"My name's Fraser." The visitor sat down and accepted a cigarette. Best to act urbanely. "I know Miss Harkness well. I understand you made some encephalographic studies of her."

"Indeed?" Kennedy looked annoyed, and Fraser recalled that Judy had been asked not to tell anyone. "I'm not sure; I would have to consult my records first." He wasn't admitting anything, thought Fraser.

"Look," said the engineer, "there's been a marked change in Miss Harkness recently. I know enough psychology to be certain that such changes don't happen overnight without cause. I wanted to consult you."

"I'm not her psychiatrist," said Kennedy coldly. "Now if you will excuse me, I really have a lot to do—"

"All right," said Fraser. There was no menace in his tones, only a weariness. "If you insist, I'll play it dirty. Such abrupt changes indicate mental instability. But I know she was perfectly sane before. It begins to look as if your experiments may have—injured her mind. If so, I should have to report you for malpractice."

Kennedy flushed. "I am a licensed psychiatrist," he said, "and any other doctor will confirm that Miss Harkness is still in mental health. If you tried to get an investigation started, you would only be wasting your own time and that of the authorities. She herself will testify that no harm was done to her; no compulsion applied; and that you are an infernal busybody with some delusions of your own. Good afternoon."

"Ah," said Fraser, "so she was here."

Kennedy pushed a button. His men entered. "Show this gentleman the way out, please," he said.

Fraser debated whether to put up a fight, decided it was futile, and went out between the two others. When he got to the street, he found he was shaking, and badly in need of a drink.

FRASER asked, "Jim, did you ever read Trilby?"

Sworsky's round, freckled face lifted to regard him. "Years ago," he answered. "What of it?"

"Tell me something. Is it possible—even theoretically possible—to do what Svengali did? Change emotional attitudes, just like that." Fraser snapped his fingers.

"I don't know," said Sworsky. "Nuclear cross-sections are more in my line. But offhand, I should imagine it might be done...sometime in the far future. Thought-habits, associational-patterns, the labeling of this as good and that as bad, seem to be matters of established neural paths. If you could selectively alter the polarization of individual neurones—But it's a pretty remote prospect; we hardly know a thing about the brain today."

He studied his friend sympathetically. "I know it's tough to get jilted," he said, "but don't go off your trolley about it."

"I could stand it if someone else had gotten her in the usual kind of way," said Fraser thinly. "But this—Look, let me tell you all I've found out."

Sworsky shook his head at the end of the story. "That's a mighty wild speculation," he murmured. "I'd forget it if I were you."

"Did you know Kennedy's old partner? Gavotti, at Chicago."

"Sure, I met him a few times. Nice old guy, very unworldly, completely wrapped up in his work. He got interested in neurology from the physics angle toward the end of his life, and contributed a lot to cybernetics. What of it?"

"I don't know," said Fraser; "I just don't know. But do me a favor, will you, Jim? Judy won't see me at all, but she knows you and likes you. Ask her to dinner or something. Insist that she come. Then you and your wife find out—whatever you can. Just exactly how she feels about the whole business. What her attitudes are toward everything."

"The name is Sworsky, not Holmes. But sure, I'll do what I can, if you'll promise to try and get rid of this fixation. You ought to see a head-shrinker yourself, you know."

In vino veritas—sometimes too damn much veritas.

TOWARD the end of the evening, Judy was talking freely, if not quite coherently. "I cared a lot for Colin," she said. "It was pretty wonderful having him around. He's a grand guy. Only Matt—I don't know. Matt hasn't got half of what Colin has; Matt's a single-track mind. I'm afraid I'm just going to be an ornamental convenience to him. Only if you've ever been so you got all dizzy when someone was around, and thought about him all the time he was away—well, that's how he is. Nothing else matters."

"Colin's gotten a funny obsession," said Sworsky cautiously. "He thinks Kennedy hypnotized you for Snyder. I keep telling him it's impossible, but he can't get over the idea."

"Oh, no, no, no," she said with too much fervor. "It's nothing like that. I'll tell you just what happened. We had those two measuring sessions; it was kind of dull but nothing else. And then the third time Kennedy did put me under hypnosis—he called it that, at least. I went to sleep and woke up about an hour later and he sent me home. I felt all good inside, happy, and shlo—slowly I began to see what Matt meant to me.

"I called him up that evening. He said Kennedy's machine did speed up people's minds for a short while, sometimes, so they decided quick-like what they'd've worked out anyway. Kennedy is—I don't know. It's funny how ordinary he seemed at first. But when you get to know him, he's like— God, almost. He's strong and wise and good. He—" Her voice trailed off and she sat looking foolishly at her glass.

"You know," said Sworsky, "perhaps Colin is right after all."

"Don't say that!" She jumped up and slapped his face. "Kennedy's good, I tell you! All you little lice sitting here making sly remarks behind his back, and he's so, much bigger than all of you and—" She broke into tears and stormed out of the apartment.

Sworsky reported the affair to Fraser. "I wonder," he said. "It doesn't seem natural, I'll agree. But what can anybody do? The police?"

"I've tried," said Fraser dully. "They laughed. When I insisted, I damn near got myself jugged. That's no use. The trouble is, none of the people who've been under the machine will testify against Kennedy. He fixes it so they worship him."

"I still think you're crazy. There must be a simpler hypothesis; I refuse to believe your screwy notions without some real evidence. But what are you going to do now?"

"Well," said Fraser with a tautness in his voice, "I've got several thousand dollars saved up, and Juan Martinez will help. Ever hear the fable about the lion? He licked hell out of the bear and the tiger and the rhinoceros, but a little gnat finally drove him nuts. Maybe I can be the gnat." He shook his head. "But I'll have to hurry. The wedding's only six weeks off."

CHAPTER THREE

IT CAN be annoying to be constantly shadowed; to have nasty gossip about you spreading through the places where you work and live; to find your tires slashed; to be accosted by truculent drunks when you stop in for a quick one; to have loud horns blow under your window every night. And it doesn't do much good to call the police; your petty tormentors always fade out of sight.

Fraser was sitting in his room some two weeks later, trying unsuccessfully to concentrate on matrix algebra, when the phone rang. He never picked it up without a fluttering small hope that it might be Judy, and it never was. This time it was a man's voice: "Mr. Fraser?"

"Yeah," he grunted. "Wha'dya want?"

"This is Robert Kennedy. I'd like to talk to you."

Fraser's heart sprang in his ribs, but he held his voice stiff. "Go on, then. Talk."

"I want you to come up to my place. We may be having a long conversation."

"Mmmm—well—" It was more than he had allowed himself to hope for, but he remained curt: "Okay. But a full report of this business, and what I think you're doing, is in the hands of several people. If anything should happen to me—"

"You've been reading too many hard-boileds," said Kennedy. "Nothing will happen. Anyway, I have a pretty good idea who those people are; I can hire detectives of my own, you know."

"I'll come over, then." Fraser hung up and realized, suddenly, that he was sweating.

The night air was cool as he walked down the street. He paused for a moment, feeling the city like a huge impersonal machine around him, grinding and grinding. Human civilization had grown too big, he thought. It was beyond anyone's control; it had taken on a will of its own and was carrying a race which could no longer guide it. Sometimes— reading the papers, or listening to the radio, or just watching the traffic go by like a river of steel—a man could feel horribly helpless.

He took the subway to Kennedy's address, a swank apartment in the lower Fifties. He was admitted by the psychiatrist in person; no one else was around.

"I assume," said Kennedy, "that you don't have some wild idea of pulling a gun on me. That would accomplish nothing except to get you in trouble."

"No," said Fraser, "I'll be good." His eyes wandered about the living room. One wall was covered with books which looked used; there were some quality reproductions, a Capehart, and fine, massive furniture. It was a tasteful layout. He looked a little more closely at three pictures on the mantel: a middle-aged woman and two young men in uniform.

"My wife," said Kennedy, "and my boys. They're all dead. Would you like a drink?"

"No. I came to talk."

"I'm not Satan, you know," said Kennedy. "I like books and music, good wine, good conversation. I'm as human as you are, only I have a purpose."

Fraser sat down and began charging his pipe. "Go ahead," he said. "I'm listening."

Kennedy pulled a chair over to face him. The big smooth countenance behind the rimless glasses held little expression. "Why have you been annoying me?" he asked.

"I?" Fraser lifted his brows.

Kennedy made an impatient gesture. "Let's not chop words. There are no witnesses tonight. I intend to talk freely, and want you to do the same. I know that you've got Martinez sufficiently convinced to help you with this very childish persecution-campaign. What do you hope to get out of it?"

"I want my girl back," said Fraser tonelessly. "I was hoping my nuisance-value—"

KENNEDY winced a bit. "You know, I'm damned sorry about that. It's the one aspect of my work which I hate. I'd like you to believe that I'm not just a scientific procurer. Actually, I have to satisfy the minor desires of my clients, so they'll stay happy and agree to my major wishes. It's the plain truth that those women have been only the minutest fraction of my job."

"Nevertheless, you're a free-wheeling son, doing something like that—"

"Really, now, what's so horrible about it? Those girls are in love—the normal, genuine article. It's not any kind of zombie state, or whatever your overheated imagination has thought up. They're entirely sane, unharmed, and happy. In fact, happiness of that kind is so rare in this world that if I wanted to, I could pose as their benefactor."

"You've got a machine," said Fraser; "it changes the mind. As far as I'm concerned, that's as gross a violation of liberty as throwing somebody into a concentration camp."

"How free do you think anyone is? You're born with a fixed heredity. Environment molds you like clay. Your society teaches you what and how to think. A million tiny factors, all depending on blind, uncontrollable chance, determine the course of your life—including your love-life... Well, we needn't waste any time on philosophy. Go on, ask some questions. I admit I've hurt you—unwittingly, to be sure—but I do want to make amends."

"Your machine, then," said Fraser. "How did you get it? How does it work."

"I was practicing in Chicago," said Kennedy, "and collaborating on the side with Gavotti. How much do you know of cybernetics? I don't mean computers and automata, which are only one aspect of the field; I mean control and communication, in the animal as well as in the machine."

"Well, I've read Wiener's books, and studied Shannon's work, too." Despite himself, Fraser was thawing, just a trifle. "It's exciting stuff. Communications-theory seems to be basic, in biology and psychology as well as in electronics."

"Quite. The future may remember Wiener as the Galileo of neurology. If Gavotti's work ever gets published, he'll be considered the Newton. So far, frankly, I've suppressed it. He died suddenly, just when his machine was completed and he was getting ready to publish his results. Nobody but I knew anything more than rumors; he was inclined to be secretive till he had a fait accompli on hand. I realized what an opportunity had been given me, and took it; I brought the machine here without saying much to anyone."

Kennedy leaned back in his chair. "I imagine it was mostly luck which took Gavotti and me so far," he went on. "We made a long series of improbably good guesses, and thus telescoped a century of work into a decade. If I were religious, I'd be down on my knees, thanking the Lord for putting this thing of the future into my hands."

"Or the devil," said Fraser.

Briefly, anger flitted across Kennedy's face. "I grant you, the machine is a terrible power, but it's harmless to a man if it's used properly—as I have used it. I'm not going to tell you just how it works; to be perfectly honest, I only understand a fraction of its theory and its circuits myself. But look, you know something of encephalography. The various basic rhythms of the brain have been measured. The standard method is already so sensitive that it can detect abnormalities like a developing tumor or a strong emotional disturbance, that will give trouble unless corrected. Half of Gavotti's machine is a still more delicate encephalograph. It can measure and analyze the minute variations in electrical pulses corresponding to the basic emotional states. It won't read thoughts, no; but once calibrated for a given individual, it will tell you if he's happy, sorrowful, angry, disgusted, afraid—any fundamental neuro-glandular condition, or any combination of them."

He paused. "All right," said Fraser. "What else does it do?"

"It does not make monsters," said Kennedy. "Look, the specific emotional reaction to a given stimulus is, in the normal individual, largely a matter of conditioned reflex, instilled by social environment or the accidental associations of his life.

"Anyone in decent health will experience fear in the presence of danger; desire in the presence of a sexual object, and so on. That's basic biology, and the machine can't change that. But most of our evaluations are learned. For instance, to an American the word 'mother' has powerful emotional connotations, while to a Samoan it means nothing very exciting. You had to develop a taste for liquor, tobacco, coffee—in fact most of what you consume. If you're in love with a particular woman, it's a focusing of the general sexual libido on her, brought about by the symbolizing part of your mind: she means something to you. There are cultures without romantic love, you know. And so on. All these specific, conditioned reactions can be changed."

"How?"

KENNEDY thought for a moment "The encephalographic part of the machine measures the exact pulsations in the individual corresponding to the various emotional reactions. It takes me about four hours to determine those with the necessary precision; then I have to make statistical analyses of the data, to winnow out random variations. Thereafter I put the subject in a state of light hypnosis—that's only to increase suggestibility, and make the process faster. As I pronounce the words and names I'm interested in, the machine feeds back the impulses corresponding to the emotions I want: a sharply-focused beam on the brain center concerned.

"For instance, suppose you were an alcoholic and I wanted to cure you. I'd put you in hypnosis and stand there whispering 'wine, whisky, beer, gin,' and so on; meanwhile, the machine would be feeding the impulses corresponding to your reactions of hate, fear, and disgust into your brain. You'd come out unchanged, except that your appetite for alcohol would be gone; you could, in fact, come out hating the stuff so much that you'd join the Prohibition Party—though, in actual practice, it would probably be enough just to give you a mild aversion."

"Mmmm—I see. Maybe." Fraser scowled. "And the—subject—doesn't remember what you've done?"

"Oh, no. It all takes place on the lower subconscious levels. A new set of conditioned neural pathways is opened, you see, and old ones are closed off. The brain does that by itself, through its normal symbolizing mechanism. All that happens is that the given symbol—such as liquor—becomes reflectively associated with the given emotional state, such as dislike."

Kennedy leaned forward with an air of urgency. "The end result is in no way different from ordinary means of persuasion. Propaganda does the same thing by sheer repetition. If you're courting a girl, you try to identify yourself in her mind with the things she desires, by appropriate behavior... I'm sorry; I shouldn't have used that example... The machine is only a direct, fast way of doing this, producing a more stable result."

"It's still—tampering," said Fraser. "How do you know you're not creating side-effects, doing irreparable long-range damage?"

"Oh, for Lord's sake!" exploded Kennedy. "Take your mind off that shelf, will you? I've told you how delicate the whole thing is. A few microwatts of power more or less, a frequency-shift of less than one percent, and it doesn't work at all. There's no effect whatsoever." He cooled off fast, adding reflectively: "On the given subject, that is. It might work on someone else. These pulsations are a highly individual matter; I have to calibrate every case separately."

There was a long period of silence. Then Fraser strained forward and said in an ugly voice:

"All right You've told me how you do it. Now tell me why. What possible reason or excuse, other than your own desire to play God? This thing could be the greatest psychiatric tool in history, and you're using it to—pimp!"

"I told you that was unimportant," said Kennedy quietly. "I'm doing much more. I set up in practice here in New York a couple of years ago. Once I had a few chance people under control—no, I tell you again, I didn't make robots of them. I merely associated myself, in their own minds, with the father-image. That's something I do to everyone who comes under the machine, just as a precaution if nothing else, Kennedy is all-wise, all-powerful; Kennedy can do no wrong. It isn't a conscious realization; to the waking mind, I am only a shrewd adviser and a damn swell fellow. But the subconscious mind knows otherwise. It wouldn't let my subjects act against me; it wouldn't even let them want to.

"Well, you see how it goes. I got those first few people to recommend me to certain selected friends, and these in turn recommended me to others. Not necessarily as a psychiatrist; I have variously been a doctor, a counsellor, or merely a research-man looking for data. But I'm building up a group of the people I want. People who'll back me up, who'll follow my advice—not with any knowledge of being dominated, but because the workings of their own subconscious minds will lead them inevitably to think that my advice is the only sound policy to follow and my requests are things any decent man must grant."

"Yeah," said Fraser. "I get it. Big businessmen. Labor-leaders. Politicians. Military men. And Soviet spies!"

KENNEDY nodded. "I have connections with the Soviets; their agents think I'm on their side. But it isn't treason, though I may help them out from time to time.

"That's why I have to do these services for my important clients, such as getting them the women they want—or, what I actually do more often, influencing their competitors and associates. You see, the subconscious mind knows I am all-powerful, but the conscious mind doesn't. It has to be satisfied by occasional proofs that I am invaluable; otherwise conflicts would set in, my men would become unstable and eventually psychotic, and be of no further use to me.

"Of course," he added, almost pedantically, "my men don't know how I persuade these other people—they only know that I do, somehow, and their regard for their own egos, as well as for me, sets up a bloc which prevents them from reasoning out the fact that they themselves are dominated. They're quite content to accept the results of my help, without inquiring further into the means than the easy rationalization that I have a 'persuasive personality.'

"I don't like what I'm doing, Fraser. But it's got to be done."

"You still haven't said what's got to be done," answered the engineer coldly.

"I've been given something unbelievable," said Kennedy. His voice was very soft now. "If I'd made it public, can you imagine what would have happened? Psychiatrists would use it, yes; but so would criminals, dictators, power-hungry men of all kinds. Even in this country, I don't think libertarian principles could long survive. It would be too simple—

"And yet it would have been cowardly to break the machine and burn Gavotti's notes. Chance has given me the power to be more than a chip in the river—a river that's rapidly approaching a waterfall, war, destruction, tyranny, no matter who the Pyrrhic victor may be. I'm in a position to do something for the causes in which I believe."

"And what are they?" asked Fraser.

Kennedy gestured at the pictures on the mantel. "Both my sons were killed in the last war. My wife died of cancer— a disease which would be licked now if a fraction of the money spent on armaments had been diverted to research. That brought it home to me; but there are hundreds of millions of people in worse cases. And war isn't the only evil—there is poverty, oppression, inequality, want and suffering. It could be changed.

"I'm building up my own lobby, you might say. In a few more years, I hope to be the indispensable adviser of all the men who, between them, really run this country. And yes, I have been in touch with Soviet agents—have even acted as a transmitter of stolen information. The basic problem of spying, you know, is not to get the information in the first place as much as to get it to the homeland. Treason? No. I think not. I'm getting my toehold in world communism. I already have some of its agents; sooner or later, I'll get to the men who really matter. Then communism will no longer be a menace."

He sighed. "It's a hard row to hoe. It'll take my lifetime, at least; but what else have I got to give my life to?"

Fraser sat very quietly. His pipe was cold, he knocked it out and began filling it afresh. The short scratching of his match seemed unnaturally loud. "It's too much," he said. "It's too big a job for one man to tackle. The world will stumble along somehow, but you'll just get things into a worse mess."

"I've got to try," said Kennedy.

"And I still want my girl back."

"I can't do that; I need Snyder too much. But I'll make it up to you somehow." Kennedy sighed. "Lord, if you knew how much I've wanted to tell all this!"

With sudden wariness: "Not that it's to be repeated. In fact, you're to lay off me; call off your dogs. Don't try to tell anyone else what I've told you. You'd never be believed and I already have enough power to suppress the story, if you should get it out somehow. And if you give me any more trouble at all, I'll see to it that you—stop."

"Murder?"

"Or commitment to an asylum. I can arrange that too."

Fraser sighed. He felt oddly unexcited, empty, as if the interview had drained him of his last will to resist. He held the pipe loosely in his fingers, letting it go out.

"Ask me a favor," urged Kennedy. "I'll do it, if it won't harm my own program. I tell you, I want to square things."

"Well—"

"Think about it. Let me know."

"All right." Fraser got up. "I may do that." He went out the door without saying goodnight.

CHAPTER FOUR

HE sat with his feet on the table, chair tilted back and teetering dangerously, hands clasped behind his head, pipe filling the room with blue fog. It was his usual posture for attacking a problem.

And damn it, he thought wearily, this was a question such as he made his living on. An industrial engineer comes into the office. We want this and that—a machine for a very special purpose, let's say. What should we do, Mr. Fraser? Fraser prowls around the plant, reads up on the industry, and then sits down and thinks. The elements of the problem are such-and-such; how can they be combined to yield a solution?

Normally, he uses the mathematical approach, especially in machine design. Most practicing-engineers have a pathetic math background—they use ten pages of elaborate algebra and rusty calculus to figure out something that three vector equations would solve. But you have to get the logical basics straight first, before you can set up your equations.

All right, what is the problem? To get Judy back. That means forcing Kennedy to restore her normal emotional reactions—no, he didn't want her thrust into love of him; he just wanted her as she had been.

What are the elements of the problem? Kennedy acts outside the law, but he has blocked all official channels. He even has connections extending through the Iron Curtain.

Hmmmm—appeal to the FBI? Kennedy couldn't have control over them—yet. However, if Fraser tried to tip off the FBI, they'd act cautiously, if they investigated at all.

They'd have to go slow. And Kennedy would find out in time to do something about it.

Martinez could help no further. Sworsky had closer contact with Washington. He'd been so thoroughly cleared that they'd be inclined to trust whatever he said. But Sworsky doubted the whole story; like many men who'd suffered through irresponsible Congressional charges, he was almost fanatic about having proof before accusing anyone of anything. Moreover, Kennedy knew that Sworsky was Fraser's friend; he'd probably be keeping close tabs on the physicist and ready to block any attempts he might make to help. With the backing of a man like Snyder, Kennedy could hire as many detectives as he wanted.

In fact, whatever the counter-attack, it was necessary to go warily. Kennedy's threat to get rid of Fraser if the engineer kept working against him was not idle mouthing. He could do it—and, being a fanatic, would.

But Kennedy, like the demon of legend, would grant one wish—just to salve his own conscience. Only what should the wish be? Another woman? Or merely to be reconciled, artificially, to an otherwise-intolerable situation?

Judy, Judy, Judy!

Fraser swore at himself. Damn it to hell, this was a problem in logic. No room for emotion. Of course, it might be a problem without a solution. There are plenty of those.

He squinted, trying to visualize the office. He thought of burglary, stealing evidence—silly thought. But let's see, now. What was the layout, exactly? Four suites on one floor of the skyscraper, three of them unimportant offices of unimportant men. And—

Oh, Lord!

Fraser sat for a long while, hardly moving. Then he uncoiled himself and ran, downstairs and into the street and to the nearest pay phone. His own line might be tapped—

"Hello, hello, Juan...? Yes, I know I got you out of bed, and I'm not sorry. This is too bloody important... Okay, okay... Look, I want a complete report on the Messenger Advertising Service... When? Immediately, if not sooner. And I mean complete... That's right, Messenger... Okay, fine. I'll buy you a drink sometime."

"Hello, Jim? Were you asleep too...? Sorry... But look, would you make a list of all the important men you know fairly well? I need it bad... No, don't come over. I think I'd better not see you for a while. Just mail it to me... All right, so I am paranoid..."

JEROME K. FERRIS was a large man, with a sense of his own importance that was even larger. He sat hunched in the chair, his head dwarfed by the aluminum helmet, his breathing shallow. Around him danced and flickered a hundred meters, indicator lights, tubes. There was a low humming in the room, otherwise it was altogether silent, blocked and shielded against the outside world. The fluorescent lights were a muted glow.

Fraser sat watching the greenish trace on the huge oscilloscope screen. It was an intricate set of convolutions, looking more like a plate of spaghetti than anything else. He wondered how many frequencies were involved. Several thousand, at the very least.

"Fraser," repeated Kennedy softly into the ear of the hypnotized man. "Colin Fraser. Colin Fraser." He touched a dial with infinite care. "Colin Fraser. Colin Fraser."

The oscilloscope flickered as he readjusted, a new trace appeared. Kennedy waited for a while, then: "Robert Kennedy. Sentiment, Inc. Robert Kennedy. Sentiment, Inc. Robert Kennedy. Sentiment—"

He turned off the machine, its murmur and glow died away. Facing Fraser with a tight little smile, he said: "All right. Your job is done. Are we even now?"

"As even, as we'll ever get, I suppose," said Fraser.

"I wish you'd trust me," said Kennedy with a hint of wistfulness. "I'd have done the job honestly; you didn't have to watch."

"Well, I was interested," said Fraser.

"Frankly, I still don't see what you stand to gain by the doglike devotion of this Ferris. He's rich, but he's too weak and short-sighted to be a leader. I'd never planned on conditioning him for my purposes."

"I've explained that," said Fraser patiently. "Ferris is a large stockholder in a number of corporations. His influence can swing a lot of business my way."

"Yes, I know. I didn't grant your wish blindly, you realize. I had Ferris studied; he's unable to harm me." Kennedy regarded Fraser with hard eyes. "And just in case you still have foolish notions, please remember that I gave him the father-conditioning with respect to myself. He'll do a lot for you, but not if it's going to hurt me in any way."

"I know when I'm licked," said Fraser bleakly; "I'm getting out of town as soon as I finish those courses I'm signed up for."

Kennedy snapped his fingers. "All right, Ferris, wake up now."

Ferris blinked. "What's been happening?" he asked.

"Nothing much," said Kennedy, unbuckling the electrodes. "I've taken my readings. Thank you very much for the help, sir. I'll see that you get due credit when my research is published."

"Ah—yes. Yes." Ferris puffed himself out. Then he put an arm around Fraser's shoulder. "If you aren't busy," he said, "maybe we could go have lunch."

"Thanks," said Fraser. "I'd like to talk about a few things."

He lingered for a moment after Ferris had left the room. "I imagine this is goodbye for us," he said.

"Well, so long, at least. We'll probably hear from each other again." Kennedy shook Fraser's hand. "No hard feelings? I did go to a lot of trouble for you—wangling your introduction to Ferris when you'd named him, and having one of my men persuade him to come here. And right when I'm so infernally busy, too."

"Sure," said Fraser. "It's all right. I can't pretend to love you for what you've done, but you aren't a bad sort."

"No worse than you," said Kennedy with a short laugh. "You've used the machine for your own ends, now."

"Yeah," said Fraser. "I guess I have."

Sworsky asked, "Why do you insist on calling me from drugstores? And why at my office? I've got a home phone, you know."

"I'm not sure but that our own lines are tapped," said Fraser. "Kennedy's a smart cookie, and don't you forget it. I think he's about ready to dismiss me as a danger, but you're certainly being watched; you're on his list."

"You're getting a persecution-complex. Honest, Colin, I'm worried."

"Well, bear with me for a while. Now, have you had any information on Kennedy since I called last?"

"Hm, no. I did mention to Thomson, as you asked me to, that I'd heard rumors of some revolutionary encephalographic techniques and would be interested in seeing the work. Why did you want me to do that?"

"Thomson," said Fraser, "is one of Kennedy's men. Now look, Jim, before long you're going to be invited to visit Kennedy. He'll give you a spiel about his research and ask to measure your brain waves. I want you to say yes. Then I want to know the exact times of the three appointments he'll give you—the first two, at least."

"Hmmm—if Kennedy's doing what you claim—"

"Jim, it's a necessary risk, but I'm the one who's taking it. You'll be okay, I promise you; though perhaps later you'll read of me being found in the river. You see, I got Kennedy to influence a big stockowner for me. One of the lesser companies in which he has a loud voice is Messenger. I don't suppose Kennedy knows that. I hope not!"

SWORSKY looked as if he'd been sandbagged. He was white, and the hand that poured a drink shook.

"Lord," he muttered. "Lord, Colin, you were right."

Fraser's teeth drew back from his lips. "You went through with it, eh?"

"Yes. I let the son hypnotize me, and afterward I walked off with a dreamy expression, as you told me to. Just three hours ago, he dropped around here in person. He gave me a long rigmarole about the stupidity of military secrecy, and how the Soviet Union stands for peace and justice. I hope I acted impressed; I'm not much of an actor."

"You don't have to be. Just so you didn't overdo it. To one of Kennedy's victims, obeying his advice is so natural that it doesn't call for any awe-struck wonderment."

"And he wanted data from me! Bombardment cross-sections. Critical values. Resonance levels. My Lord, if the Russians found that out through spies it'd save them three years of research. This is an FBI case, all right."

"No, not yet." Fraser laid an urgent hand on Sworsky's arm. "You've stuck by me so far, Jim. Go along a little further."

"What do you want me to do?"

"Why—" Fraser's laugh jarred out. "Give him what he wants, of course."

Kennedy looked up from his desk, scowling. "All right, Fraser," he said. "You've been a damned nuisance, and it's pretty patient of me to see you again. But this is the last time. Wha'd'you want?"

"It's the last time I'll need to see you, perhaps." Fraser didn't sit down. He stood facing Kennedy. "You've had it, friend; straight up."

"What do you mean?" Kennedy's hand moved toward his buzzer.

"Listen before you do anything," said Fraser harshly. "I know you tried to bring Jim Sworsky under the influence. You asked him for top-secret data. A few hours ago, you handed the file he brought you on to Bryce, who's no doubt at the Amtorg offices this minute. That's high treason, Kennedy; they execute people for doing that."

The psychologist slumped back.

"Don't try to have your bully boys get rid of me," said Fraser. "Sworsky is sitting by the phone, waiting to call the FBI. I'm the only guy who can stop him."

"But—" Kennedy's tongue ran around his lips. "But he committed treason himself. He gave me the papers!"

Fraser grinned. "You don't think those were authentic, do you? I doubt if you'll be very popular in the Soviet Union either, once they've tried to build machines using your data."

Kennedy looked down. "How did you do it?" he whispered.

"Remember Ferris? The guy you fixed up for me? He owns a share of your next-door neighbor, the Messenger Advertising Service. I fed him a song and dance about needing an office to do some important work, only my very whereabouts had to be secret. The Messenger people were moved out without anybody's knowing. I installed myself there one night, also a simple little electric oscillator.

"Encephalography...delicate work; involves amplifications up to several million. The apparatus misbehaves if you give it a hard look. Naturally, your lab and the machine were heavily shielded, but even so, a radio emitter next door would be bound to throw you off. My main trouble was in lousing you up just a little bit, not enough to make you suspect anything.

"I only worked at that during your calibrating sessions with Sworsky. I didn't have to be there when you turned the beam on him, because it would be calculated from false data and be so far from his pattern as to have no effect. You told me yourself how precise an adjustment was needed. Sworsky played along, then. Now we've got proof—not that you meddled with human lives, but that you are a spy."

Kennedy sat without moving. His voice was a broken mumble. "I was going to change the world. I had hopes for all humankind. And you, for the sake of one woman—"

"I never trusted anybody with a messiah complex. The world is too big to change single-handed; you'd just have bungled it up worse than it already is. A lot of dictators started out as reformers and ended up as mass-executioners; you'd have done the same."

Fraser leaned over his desk. "I'm willing to make a deal, though," he went on. "Your teeth are pulled; there's no point in turning you in. Sworsky and Martinez and I are willing just to report on Bryce, and let you go, if you'll change back all your subjects. We're going to read your files, and watch and see that you do it. Every one."

Kennedy bit his lip. "And the machine—?"

"I don't know. We'll settle that later. Okay, God, here's the phone number of Judy Harkness. Ask her to come over for a special treatment. At once."

A MONTH later, the papers had a story about a plausible maniac who had talked his way into the Columbia University laboratories, where Gavotti's puzzling machine was being studied, and pulled out a hammer and smashed it into ruin before he could be stopped. Taken to jail, he committed suicide in his cell. The name was Kennedy.

Fraser felt vague regret, but it didn't take him long to forget it; he was too busy making plans for his wedding.

THE END

Duel on Syrtis

Bold and ruthless, he was famed throughout the System as a big-game hunter. From the firedrakes of Mercury to the ice-crawlers of Pluto, he'd slain them all. But his trophy-room lacked one item; and now Riordan swore he'd bag the forbidden game that roamed the red deserts…a Martian!

THE NIGHT WHISPERED THE message. Over the many miles of loneliness it was borne, carried on the wind, rustled by the half-sentient lichens and the dwarfed trees, murmured from one to another of the little creatures that huddled under crags, in caves, by shadowy dunes. In no words, but in a dim pulsing of dread, which echoed through Kreega's brain, the warning ran—

They are hunting again.

Kreega shuddered in a sudden blast of wind. The night was enormous around him, above him, from the iron bitterness of the hills to the wheeling, glittering constellations light-years over his head. He reached out with his trembling perceptions, tuning himself to the brush and the wind and the small burrowing things underfoot, letting the night speak to him.

Alone, alone. There was not another Martian for a hundred miles of emptiness. There were only the tiny animals and the shivering brush and the thin, sad blowing of the wind.

The voiceless scream of dying traveled through the brush, from plant to plant, echoed by the fear-pulses of the animals and the ringingly reflecting cliffs. They were curling, shriveling and blackening as the rocket poured the glowing death down on them, and the withering veins and nerves cried to the stars.

Kreega huddled against a tall gaunt crag. His eyes were like yellow moons in the darkness, cold with terror and hate and a slowly gathering resolution. Grimly, he estimated that the death was being sprayed in a circle some ten miles across. And he was trapped in it, and soon the hunter would come after him.

He looked up to the indifferent glitter of stars, and a shudder went along his body. Then he sat down and began to think.

IT HAD STARTED a few days before, in the private office of the trader Wisby.

"I came to Mars," said Riordan, "to get me an owlie."

Wisby had learned the value of a poker face. He peered across the rim of his glass at the other man, estimating him.

Even in God-forsaken holes like Port Armstrong one had heard of Riordan. Heir to a million-dollar shipping firm, which he himself had pyramided into a System-wide monster, he was equally well known as a big game hunter. From the firedrakes of Mercury to the ice crawlers of Pluto, he'd bagged them all. Except, of course, a Martian. That particular game was forbidden now.

He sprawled in his chair, big and strong and ruthless, still a young man. He dwarfed the unkempt room with his size and the hard-held dynamo strength in him, and his cold green gaze dominated the trader.

"It's illegal, you know," said Wisby. "It's a twenty-year sentence if you're caught at it."

"Bah! The Martian Commissioner is at Ares, halfway round the planet. If we go at it right, who's ever to know?" Riordan gulped at his drink. "I'm well aware that in another year or so they'll have tightened up enough to make it impossible. This is the last chance for any man to get an owlie. That's why I'm here."

Wisby hesitated, looking out the window. Port Armstrong was no more than a dusty huddle of domes, interconnected by tunnels, in a red waste of sand stretching to the near horizon. An Earthman in airsuit and transparent helmet was walking down the street and a couple of Martians were lounging against a wall. Otherwise nothing—a silent, deadly monotony brooding under the shrunken sun. Life on Mars was not especially pleasant for a human.

"You're not falling into this owlie-loving that's corrupted all Earth?" demanded Riordan contemptuously.

"Oh, no," said Wisby. "I keep them in their place around my post. But times are changing. It can't be helped."

"There was a time when they were slaves," said Riordan. "Now those old women on Earth want to give 'em the vote." He snorted.

"Well, times are changing," repeated Wisby mildly. "When the first humans landed on Mars a hundred years ago, Earth had just gone through the Hemispheric Wars. The worst wars man had ever known. They damned near wrecked the old ideas of liberty and equality. People were suspicious and tough—they'd had to be, to survive. They weren't able to—to empathize the Martians, or whatever you call it. Not able to think of them as anything but intelligent animals. And Martians made such useful slaves—they need so little food or heat or oxygen, they can even live fifteen minutes or so without breathing at all. And the wild Martians made fine sport—intelligent game that could get away as often as not, or even manage to kill the hunter."

"I know," said Riordan. "That's why I want to hunt one. It's no fun if the game doesn't have a chance."

"It's different now," went on Wisby. "Earth has been at peace for a long time. The liberals have gotten the upper hand. Naturally, one of their first reforms was to end Martian slavery."

Riordan swore. The forced repatriation of Martians working on his spaceships had cost him plenty. "I haven't time for your philosophizing," he said. "If you can arrange for me to get a Martian, I'll make it worth your while."

"How much worth it?" asked Wisby.

THEY HAGGLED for a while before settling on a figure. Riordan had brought guns and a small rocketboat, but Wisby would have to supply radioactive material, a "hawk," and a rockhound. Then he had to be paid for the risk of legal action, though that was small. The final price came high.

"Now, where do I get my Martian?" inquired Riordan. He gestured at the two in the street. "Catch one of them and release him in the desert?"

It was Wisby's turn to be contemptuous. "One of them? Hah! Town loungers! A city dweller from Earth would give you a better fight."

The Martians didn't look impressive. They stood only some four feet high on skinny, claw-footed legs, and the arms, ending in bony four-fingered hands, were stringy. The chests were broad and deep, but the waists were ridiculously narrow. They were viviparous, warm-blooded, and suckled their young, but gray feathers covered their hides. The round, hook-beaked heads, with huge amber eyes and tufted feather ears, showed the origin of the name "owlie." They wore only pouched belts and carried sheath knives; even the liberals of Earth weren't ready to allow the natives modern tools and weapons. There were too many old grudges.

"The Martians always were good fighters," said Riordan. "They wiped out quite a few Earth settlements in the old days."

"The wild ones," agreed Wisby. "But not these. They're just stupid laborers, as dependent on our civilization as we are. You want a real old timer, and I know where one's to be found."

He spread a map on the desk. "See, here in the Hraefnian Hills, about a hundred miles from here. These Martians live a long time, maybe two centuries, and this fellow Kreega has been around since the first Earthmen came. He led a lot of Martian raids in the early days, but since the general amnesty and peace he's lived all alone up there, in one of the old ruined towers. A real old-time warrior who hates Earthmen's guts. He comes here once in a while with furs and minerals to trade, so I know a little about him." Wisby's eyes gleamed savagely. "You'll be doing us all a favor by shooting the arrogant bastard. He struts around here as if the place belonged to him. And he'll give you a run for your money."

Riordan's massive dark head nodded in satisfaction.

THE MAN had a bird and a rockhound. That was bad. Without them, Kreega could lose himself in the labyrinth of caves and canyons and scrubby thickets—but the hound could follow his scent and the bird could spot him from above.

To make matters worse, the man had landed near Kreega's tower. The weapons were all there—now he was cut off, unarmed and alone save for what feeble help the desert life could give. Unless he could double back to the place somehow—but meanwhile he had to survive.

He sat in a cave, looking down past a tortured wilderness of sand and bush and wind-carved rock, miles in the thin clear air to the glitter of metal where the rocket lay. The man was a tiny speck in the huge barren landscape, a lonely insect crawling under the deep-blue sky. Even by day, the stars glistened in the tenuous atmosphere. Weak pallid sunlight spilled over rocks tawny and ocherous and rust-red, over the low dusty thornbushes and the gnarled little trees and the sand that blew faintly between them. Equatorial Mars!

Lonely or not, the man had a gun that could spang death clear to the horizon, and he had his beasts, and there would be a radio in the rocketboat for calling his fellows. And the glowing death ringed them in, a charmed circle, which Kreega could not cross without bringing a worse death on himself than the rifle would give—

Or was there a worse death than that—to be shot by a monster and have his stuffed hide carried back as a trophy for fools to gape at? The old iron pride of his race rose in Kreega, hard and bitter and unrelenting. He didn't ask much of life these days—solitude in his tower to think the long thoughts of a Martian and create the small exquisite artworks, which he loved; the company of his kind at the Gathering Season, grave ancient ceremony and acrid merriment and the chance to beget and rear sons; an occasional trip to the Earthling settling for the metal goods and the wine, which were the only valuable things they had brought to Mars; a vague dream of raising his folk to a place where they could stand as equals before all the universe. No more. And now they would take even this from him!

He rasped a curse on the human and resumed his patient work, chipping a spearhead for what puny help it could give him. The brush rustled dryly in alarm, tiny hidden animals squeaked their terror, the desert shouted to him of the monster that strode toward his cave. But he didn't have to flee right away.

*　　*　　*

Riordan sprayed the heavy-metal isotope in a ten-mile circle around the old tower. He did that by night, just in case patrol craft might be snooping around. But once he had landed, he was safe—he could always claim to be peacefully exploring, hunting leapers or some such thing.

The radioactive had a half-life of about four days, which meant that it would be unsafe to approach for some three weeks—two at the minimum. That was time enough, when the Martian was boxed in so small an area.

There was no danger that he would try to cross it. The owlies had learned what radioactivity meant, back when they fought the humans. And their vision, extending well into the ultra-violet, made it directly visible to them through its fluorescence—to say nothing of the wholly unhuman extra senses they had. No, Kreega would try to hide, and perhaps to fight, and eventually he'd be cornered.

Still, there was no use taking chances. Riordan set a timer on the boat's radio. If he didn't come back within two weeks to turn it off, it would emit a signal, which Wisby would hear, and he'd be rescued.

He checked his other equipment. He had an airsuit designed for Martian conditions, with a small pump operated by a power-beam from the boat to compress the atmosphere sufficiently for him to breathe it. The same unit recovered enough water from his breath so that the weight of supplies for several days was, in Martian gravity, not too great for him to bear. He had a .45 rifle built to shoot in Martian air that was heavy enough for his purposes. And, of course, compass and binoculars and sleeping bag. Pretty light equipment, but he preferred a minimum anyway.

For ultimate emergencies there was the little tank of suspensine. By turning a valve, he could release it into his air system. The gas didn't exactly induce suspended animation, but it paralyzed efferent nerves and slowed the overall metabolism to a point where a man could live for weeks on one lungful of air. It was useful in surgery, and had saved the life of more than one interplanetary explorer whose oxygen system went awry. But Riordan didn't expect to have to use it. He certainly hoped he wouldn't. It would be tedious to lie fully conscious for days waiting for the automatic signal to call Wisby.

He stepped out of the boat and locked it. No danger that the owlie would break in if he should double back; it would take tordenite to crack that hull.

He whistled to his animals. They were native beasts, long ago domesticated by the Martians and later by man. The rockhound was like a gaunt wolf, but huge-breasted and feathered, a tracker as good as any Terrestrial bloodhound. The "hawk" had less resemblance to its counterpart of Earth: it was a bird of prey, but in the tenuous atmosphere it needed a six-foot wingspread to lift its small body. Riordan was pleased with their training.

The hound bayed, a low quavering note, which would have been muffled almost to inaudibility by the thin air and the man's plastic helmet had the suit not included microphones and amplifiers. It circled, sniffing, while the hawk rose into the alien sky.

Riordan did not look closely at the tower. It was a crumbling stump atop a rusty hill, unhuman and grotesque. Once, perhaps ten thousand years ago, the Martians had had a civilization of sorts, cities and agriculture and a neolithic technology. But according to their own traditions they had achieved a union or symbiosis with the wild life of the planet and had abandoned such mechanical aids as unnecessary. Riordan snorted.

The hound bayed again. The noise seemed to hang eerily in the still, cold air; to shiver from cliff and crag and die reluctantly under the enormous silence. But it was a bugle call, a haughty challenge to a world grown old—stand aside, make way, here comes the conqueror!

The animal suddenly loped forward. He had a scent. Riordan swung into a long, easy low-gravity stride. His eyes gleamed like green ice. The hunt was begun!

BREATH SOBBED in Kreega's lungs, hard and quick and raw. His legs felt weak and heavy, and the thudding of his heart seemed to shake his whole body.

Still he ran, while the frightful clamor rose behind him and the padding of feet grew ever nearer. Leaping, twisting, bounding from crag to crag, sliding down shaly ravines and slipping through clumps of trees. Kreega fled.

The hound was behind him and the hawk soaring overhead. In a day and a night they had driven him to this, running like a crazed leaper with death baying at his heels— he had not imagined a human could move so fast or with such endurance.

The desert fought for him; the plants with their queer blind life that no Earthling would ever understand were on his side. Their thorny branches twisted away as he darted through and then came back to rake the flanks of the hound, slow him—but they could not stop his brutal rush. He ripped past their strengthless clutching fingers and yammered on the trail of the Martian.

The human was toiling a good mile behind, but showed no sign of tiring. Still Kreega ran. He had to reach the cliff edge before the hunter saw him through his rifle sights—had to, had to, and the hound was snarling a yard behind now.

Up the long slope he went. The hawk fluttered, striking at him, seeking to lay beak and talons in his head. He batted at the creature with his spear and dodged around a tree. The tree snaked out a branch from which the hound rebounded, yelling till the rocks rang.

The Martian burst onto the edge of the cliff. It fell sheer to the canyon floor, five hundred feet of iron-streaked rock tumbling into windy depths. Beyond, the lowering sun glared in his eyes. He paused only an instant, etched black against the sky, a perfect shot if the human should come into view, and then he sprang over the edge.

He had hoped the rockbound would go shooting past, but the animal braked itself barely in time. Kreega went down the cliff face, clawing into every tiny crevice, shuddering as the age-worn rock crumbled under his fingers. The hawk swept close, hacking at him and screaming for its master. He couldn't fight it, not with every finger and toe needed to hang against shattering death, but—

He slid along the face of the precipice into a gray-green clump of vines, and his nerves thrilled forth the appeal of the ancient symbiosis. The hawk swooped again and he lay unmoving, rigid as if dead, until it cried in shrill triumph and settled on his shoulder to pluck out his eyes.

Then the vines stirred. They weren't strong, but their thorns sank into the flesh and it couldn't pull loose. Kreega toiled on down into the canyon while the vines pulled the hawk apart.

Riordan loomed hugely against the darkening sky. He fired, once, twice, the bullets humming wickedly close, but as shadows swept up from the depths the Martian was covered.

The man turned up his speech amplifier and his voice rolled and boomed monstrously through the gathering night, thunder such as dry Mars had not heard for millennia: "Score one for you! But it isn't enough! I'll find you!"

The sun slipped below the horizon and night came down like a falling curtain. Through the darkness Kreega heard the man laughing. The old rocks trembled with his laughter.

RIORDAN was tired with the long chase and the niggling insufficiency of his oxygen supply. He wanted a smoke and hot food, and neither was to be had. Oh, well, he'd appreciate the luxuries of life all the more when he got home—with the Martian's skin.

He grinned as he made camp. The little fellow was a worthwhile quarry that was for damn sure. He'd held out for two days now, in a little ten-mile circle of ground, and he'd even killed the hawk. But Riordan was close enough to him now so that the hound could follow his spoor, for Mars had no watercourses to break a trail. So it didn't matter.

He lay watching the splendid night of stars. It would get cold before long, unmercifully cold, but his sleeping bag was a good-enough insulator to keep him warm with the help of solar energy stored during the day by its Gergen cells. Mars was dark at night, its moons of little help—Phobos a hurtling speck, Deimos merely a bright star. Dark and cold and empty. The rockhound had burrowed into the loose sand nearby, but it would raise the alarm if the Martian should come sneaking near the camp. Not that that was likely—he'd have to find shelter somewhere too, if he didn't want to freeze.

The bushes and the trees and the little furtive animals whispered a word he could not hear, chattered and gossiped on the wind about the Martian who kept himself warm with work. But he didn't understand that language, which was no language.

Drowsily, Riordan thought of past hunts. The big game of Earth, lion and tiger and elephant and buffalo and sheep on the high sun-blazing peaks of the Rockies. Rain forests of Venus and the coughing roar of a many-legged swamp monster crashing through the trees to the place where he stood waiting. Primitive throb of drums in a hot wet night, chant of beaters dancing around a fire—scramble along the hellplains of Mercury with a swollen sun licking against his puny insulating suit—the grandeur and desolation of Neptune's liquid-gas swamps and the huge blind thing that screamed and blundered after him—

But this was the loneliest and strangest and perhaps most dangerous hunt of all, and on that account the best. He had no malice toward the Martian; he respected the little being's courage as he respected the bravery of the other animals he had fought. Whatever trophy he brought home from this chase would be well earned.

The fact that his success would have to be treated discreetly didn't matter. He hunted less for the glory of it—though he had to admit he didn't mind the publicity—than for love. His ancestors had fought under one name or another—Viking, Crusader, mercenary, rebel, patriot, whatever was fashionable at the moment. Struggle was in his blood, and in these degenerate days there was little to struggle against save what he hunted.

Well—tomorrow—he drifted off to sleep.

HE WOKE in the short gray dawn, made a quick breakfast, and whistled his hound to heel. His nostrils dilated with excitement, a high keen drunkenness that sang wonderfully within him. Today—maybe today!

They had to take a roundabout way down into the canyon and the hound cast about for an hour before he picked up the scent. Then the deep-voiced cry rose again and they were off—more slowly now, for it was a cruel stony trail.

The sun climbed high as they worked along the ancient riverbed. Its pale chill light washed needle-sharp crags and fantastically painted cliffs, shale and sand and the wreck of geological ages. The low harsh brush crunched under the man's feet, writhing and crackling its impotent protest. Otherwise it was still, a deep and taut and somehow waiting stillness.

The hound shattered the quiet with an eager yelp and plunged forward. Hot scent! Riordan dashed after him, trampling through dense bush, panting and swearing and grinning with excitement.

Suddenly the brush opened underfoot. With a howl of dismay, the hound slid down the sloping wall of the pit it had uncovered. Riordan flung himself forward with tigerish swiftness, flat down on his belly with one hand barely catching the animal's tail. The shock almost pulled him into the hole, too. He wrapped one arm around a bush that clawed at his helmet and pulled the hound back.

Shaking, he peered into the trap. It had been well-made— about twenty feet deep, with walls as straight and narrow as the sand would allow, and skillfully covered with brush. Planted in the bottom were three wicked-looking flint spears. Had he been a shade less quick in his reactions, he would have lost the hound and perhaps himself.

He skinned his teeth in a wolf-grin and looked around. The owlie must have worked all night on it. Then he couldn't be far away—and he'd be very tired—

As if to answer his thoughts, a boulder crashed down from the nearer cliff wall. It was a monster, but a falling object on Mars has less than half the acceleration it does on Earth. Riordan scrambled aside as it boomed onto the place where he had been lying.

"Come on!" he yelled, and plunged toward the cliff.

For an instant a gray form loomed over the edge, hurled a spear at him. Riordan snapped a shot at it, and it vanished. The spear glanced off the tough fabric of his suit and he scrambled up a narrow ledge to the top of the precipice.

The Martian was nowhere in sight, but a faint red trail led into the rugged hill country. *Winged him, by God!* The hound was slower in negotiating the shale-covered trail; his own feet were bleeding when he came up. Riordan cursed him and they set out again.

They followed the trail for a mile or two and then it ended. Riordan looked around the wilderness of trees and needles, which blocked view in any direction. Obviously the owlie had backtracked and climbed up one of those rocks, from which he could take a flying leap to some other point. But which one?

Sweat, which he couldn't wipe off, ran down the man's face and body. He itched intolerably, and his lungs were raw from gasping at his dole of air. But still he laughed in gusty delight. What a chase! What a chase!

KREEGA lay in the shadow of a tall rock and shuddered with weariness. Beyond the shade, the sunlight danced in what to him was a blinding, intolerable dazzle, hot and cruel and life-hungry, hard and bright as the metal of the conquerors.

It had been a mistake to spend priceless hours when he might have been resting working on that trap. It hadn't worked, and he might have known that it wouldn't. And now he was hungry, and thirst was like a wild beast in his mouth and throat, and still they followed him.

They weren't far behind now. All this day they had been dogging him; he had never been more than half an hour ahead. No rest, no rest, a devil's hunt through a tormented wilderness of stone and sand, and now he could only wait for the battle with an iron burden of exhaustion laid on him.

The wound in his side burned. It wasn't deep, but it had cost him blood and pain and the few minutes of catnapping he might have snatched.

For a moment, the warrior Kreega was gone and a lonely, frightened infant sobbed in the desert silence. *Why can't they let me alone?*

A low, dusty-green bush rustled. A sandrunner piped in one of the ravines. They were getting close.

Wearily, Kreega scrambled up on top of the rock and crouched low. He had backtracked to it; they should by rights go past him toward his tower.

He could see it from here, a low yellow ruin worn by the winds of millennia. There had only been time to dart in, snatch a bow and a few arrows and an axe. Pitiful weapons—the arrows could not penetrate the Earthman's suit when there was only a Martian's thin grasp to draw the bow, and even with a steel head the ax was a small and feeble thing. But it was all he had, he and his few little allies of a desert, which fought only to keep its solitude.

Repatriated slaves had told him of the Earthlings' power. Their roaring machines filled the silence of their own deserts, gouged the quiet face of their own moon, shook the planets with a senseless fury of meaningless energy. They were the conquerors, and it never occurred to them that an ancient peace and stillness could be worth preserving.

Well—he fitted an arrow to the string and crouched in the silent, flimmering sunlight, waiting.

The hound came first, yelping and howling. Kreega drew the bow as far as he could. But the human had to come near first—

There he came, running and bounding over the rocks, rifle in hand and restless eyes shining with taut green light, closing in for the death. Kreega swung softly around. The beast was beyond the rock now, the Earthman almost below it.

The bow twanged. With a savage thrill, Kreega saw the arrow go through the hound, saw the creature leap in the air and then roll over and over, howling and biting at the thing in its breast.

Like a gray thunderbolt, the Martian launched himself off the rock, down at the human. If his ax could shatter that helmet—

He struck the man and they went down together. Wildly, the Martian hewed. The ax glanced off the plastic—he hadn't had room for a swing. Riordan roared and lashed out with a fist. Retching, Kreega rolled backward.

Riordan snapped a shot at him. Kreega turned and fled. The man got to one knee, sighting carefully on the gray form that streaked up the nearest slope.

A little sand snake darted up the man's leg and wrapped about his wrist. Its small strength was just enough to pull the gun aside. The bullet screamed past Kreega's ear as he vanished into a cleft.

He felt the thin death-agony of the snake as the man pulled it loose and crushed it underfoot. Somewhat later, he heard a dull boom echoing between the hills. The man had gotten explosives from his boat and blown up the tower.

He had lost ax and bow. Now he was utterly weaponless, without even a place to retire for a last stand. And the hunter would not give up. Even without his animals, he would follow, more slowly but as relentlessly as before.

Kreega collapsed on a shelf of rock. Dry sobbing racked his thin body, and the sunset wind cried with him.

Presently he looked up, across a red and yellow immensity, to the low sun. Long shadows were creeping over the land, peace and stillness for a brief moment before the iron cold of night closed down. Somewhere the soft trill of a sandrunner echoed between low wind-worn cliffs, and the brush began to speak, whispering back and forth in its ancient wordless tongue.

The desert, the planet and its wind and sand under the high cold stars, the clean open land of silence and loneliness and a destiny, which was not man's, spoke to him. The enormous oneness of life on Mars, drawn together against the cruel environment, stirred in his blood. As the sun went down and the stars blossomed forth in awesome frosty glory, Kreega began to think again.

He did not hate his persecutor, but the grimness of Mars was in him. He fought the war of all, which was old and primitive and lost in its own dreams against the alien and the desecrator. It was as ancient and pitiless as life that war, and each battle won or lost meant something even if no one ever heard of it.

You do not fight alone, whispered the desert. *You fight for all Mars, and we are with you.*

Something moved in the darkness, a tiny warm form running across his hand, a little feathered mouse-like thing that burrowed under the sand and lived its small fugitive life and was glad in its own way of living. But it was a part of a world, and Mars has no pity in its voice.

Still, a tenderness was within Kreega's heart, and he whispered gently in the language that was not a language, *You will do this for us! You will do it, little brother?*

RIORDAN was too tired to sleep well. He had lain awake for a long time, thinking, and that is not good for a man alone in the Martian hills.

So now the rockhound was dead too. It didn't matter, the owlie wouldn't escape. But somehow the incident brought home to him the immensity and the age and the loneliness of the desert.

It whispered to him. The brush rustled and something wailed in darkness and the wind blew with a wild mournful sound over faintly starlit cliffs, and it was as if they all somehow had voice, as if the whole world muttered and threatened him in the night. Dimly, he wondered if man would ever subdue Mars, if the human race had not finally run across something bigger than itself.

But that was nonsense. Mars was old and worn-out and barren, dreaming itself into slow death. The tramp of human feet, shouts of men and roar of sky-storming rockets, were waking it, but to a new destiny, to man's. When Ares lifted its hard spires above the hills of Syrtis, where then were the ancient gods of Mars?

It was cold, and the cold deepened as the night wore on. The stars were fire and ice, glittering diamonds in the deep crystal dark. Now and then he could hear a faint snapping borne through the earth as rock or tree split open. The wind laid itself to rest, sound froze to death, there was only the hard clear starlight falling through space to shatter on the ground.

Once something stirred. He woke from a restless sleep and saw a small thing skittering toward him. He groped for the rifle beside his sleeping bag, then laughed harshly. It was only a sandmouse. But it proved that the Martian had no chance of sneaking up on him while he rested.

He didn't laugh again. The sound had echoed too hollowly in his helmet.

With the clear bitter dawn he was up. He wanted to get the hunt over with. He was dirty and unshaven inside the unit, sick of iron rations pushed through the airlock, stiff and sore with exertion. Lacking the hound, which he'd had to shoot, tracking would be slow, but he didn't want to go back to Port Armstrong for another. No, hell take that Martian, he'd have the devil's skin soon!

Breakfast and a little moving made him feel better. He looked with a practiced eye for the Martian's trail. There was sand and brush over everything, even the rocks had a thin coating of their own erosion. The owlie couldn't cover his tracks perfectly—if he tried, it would slow him too much. Riordan fell into a steady jog.

Noon found him on higher ground, rough hills with gaunt needles of rock reaching yards into the sky. He kept going, confident of his own ability to wear down the quarry. He'd run deer to earth back home, day after day until the animal's heart broke and it waited quivering for him to come.

The trail looked clear and fresh now. He tensed with the knowledge that the Martian couldn't be far away.

Too clear! Could this be bait for another trap? He hefted the rifle and proceeded more warily. But no, there wouldn't have been time—

He mounted a high ridge and looked over the grim, fantastic landscape. Near the horizon he saw a blackened strip, the border of his radioactive barrier. The Martian couldn't go further, and if he doubled back Riordan would have an excellent chance of spotting him.

He tuned up his speaker and let his voice roar into the stillness: "Come out, owlie! I'm going to get you, you might as well come out now and be done with it!"

The echoes took it up, flying back and forth between the naked crags, trembling and shivering under the brassy arch of sky. *Come out, come out, come out—*

The Martian seemed to appear from thin air, a gray ghost rising out of the jumbled stones and standing poised not twenty feet away. For an instant, the shock of it was too much; Riordan gaped in disbelief. Kreega waited, quivering ever so faintly as if he were a mirage.

Then the man shouted and lifted his rifle. Still the Martian stood there as if carved in gray stone, and with a shock of disappointment Riordan thought that he had, after all, decided to give himself to an inevitable death.

Well, it had been a good hunt. "So long," whispered Riordan, and squeezed the trigger.

Since the sandmouse had crawled into the barrel, the gun exploded.

RIORDAN heard the roar and saw the barrel peel open like a rotten banana. He wasn't hurt, but as he staggered back from the shock Kreega lunged at him.

The Martian was four feet tall, and skinny and weaponless, but he hit the Earthling like a small tornado. His legs wrapped around the man's waist and his hands got to work on the airhose.

Riordan went down under the impact. He snarled, tigerishly, and fastened his hands on the Martian's narrow throat. Kreega snapped futilely at him with his beak. They rolled over in a cloud of dust. The brush began to chatter excitedly.

Riordan tried to break Kreega's neck—the Martian twisted away, bored in again.

With a shock of horror, the man heard the hiss of escaping air as Kreega's beak and fingers finally worried the airhose loose. An automatic valve clamped shut, but there was no connection with the pump now—

Riordan cursed, and got his hands about the Martian's throat again. Then he simply lay there, squeezing, and not all Kreega's writhing and twistings could break that grip.

Riordan smiled sleepily and held his hands in place. After five minutes or so Kreega was still. Riordan kept right on throttling him for another five minutes, just to make sure. Then he let go and fumbled at his back, trying to reach the pump.

The air in his suit was hot and foul. He couldn't quite reach around to connect the hose to the pump—

Poor design, he thought vaguely. *But then, these airsuits weren't meant for battle armor.*

He looked at the slight, silent form of the Martian. A faint breeze ruffled the gray feathers. What a fighter the little guy had been! He'd be the pride of the trophy room, back on Earth.

Let's see now— He unrolled his sleeping bag and spread it carefully out. He'd never make it to the rocket with what air he had, so it was necessary to let the suspensine into his suit. But he'd have to get inside the bag, lest the nights freeze his blood solid.

He crawled in, fastening the flaps carefully, and opened the valve on the suspensine tank. Lucky he had it—but then, a good hunter thinks of everything. He'd get awfully bored, lying here till Wisby caught the signal in ten days or so and came to find him, but he'd last. It would be an experience to remember. In this dry air, the Martian's skin would keep perfectly well.

He felt the paralysis creep up on him, the waning of heartbeat and lung action. His senses and mind were still alive, and he grew aware that complete relaxation has its unpleasant aspects. Oh, well—he'd won. He'd killed the wiliest game with his own hands.

Presently Kreega sat up. He felt himself gingerly. There seemed to be a rib broken—well that could be fixed. He was still alive. He'd been choked for a good ten minutes, but a Martian can last fifteen without air.

He opened the sleeping bag and got Riordan's keys. Then he limped slowly back to the rocket. A day or two of experimentation taught him how to fly it. He'd go to his kinsmen near Syrtis. Now that they had an Earthly machine, and Earthly weapons to copy—

But there was other business first. He didn't hate Riordan, but Mars is a hard world. He went back and dragged the Earthling into a cave and hid him beyond all possibility of human search parties finding him.

For a while he looked into the man's eyes. Horror stared dumbly back at him. He spoke slowly, in halting English: "For those you killed, and for being a stranger on a world that does not want you, and against the day when Mars is free, I leave you."

Before departing, he got several oxygen tanks from the boat and hooked them into the man's air supply. That was quite a bit of air for one in suspended animation. Enough to keep him alive for a thousand years.

THE END

The Valor of Cappen Varra

"Let little Cappen go," they shouted. "Maybe he can sing the trolls to sleep—"

THE WIND came from the north with sleet on its back. Raw shuddering gusts whipped the sea till the ship lurched and men felt driven spindrift stinging their faces. Beyond the rail there was winter night, a moving blackness where the waves rushed and clamored; straining into the great dark, men sensed only the bitter salt of sea-scud, the nettle of sleet and the lash of wind.

Cappen lost his footing as the ship heaved beneath him, his hands were yanked from the icy rail and he went stumbling to the deck. The bilge water was new coldness on his drenched clothes. He struggled back to his feet, leaning on a rower's bench and wishing miserably that his quaking stomach had more to lose. But he had already chucked his share of stockfish and hardtack, to the laughter of Svearek's men, when the gale started.

Numb fingers groped anxiously for the harp on his back. It still seemed intact in its leather case. He didn't care about the sodden wadmal breeks and tunic that hung around his skin. The sooner they rotted off him, the better. The thought of the silks and linens of Croy was a sigh in him.

Why had he come to Norren?

A gigantic form, vague in the whistling dark, loomed beside him and gave him a steadying hand. He could barely hear the blond giant's bull tones: "Ha, easy there, lad. Methinks the sea horse road is too rough for yer feet."

"Ulp," said Cappen. His slim body huddled on the bench, too miserable to care. The sleet pattered against his shoulders and the spray congealed in his red hair.

Torbek of Norren squinted into the night. It made his leathery face a mesh of wrinkles. "A bitter feast Yolner we hold," he said. "'Twas a madness of the king's, that he would guest with his brother across the water. Now the other ships are blown from us and the fire is drenched out and we lie alone in the Wolf's Throat."

Wind piped shrill in the rigging. Cappen could just see the longboat's single mast reeling against the sky. The ice on the shrouds made it a pale pyramid. Ice everywhere, thick on the rails and benches, sheathing the dragon head and the carved stern-post, the ship rolling and staggering under the great march of waves, men bailing and bailing in the half-frozen bilge to keep her afloat, and too much wind for sail or oars. Yes—a cold feast!

"But then, Svearek has been strange since the troll took his daughter, three years ago," went on Torbek. He shivered in a way the winter had not caused. "Never does he smile, and his once open hand grasps tight about the silver and his men have poor reward and no thanks. Yes, strange—" His small frost-blue eyes shifted to Cappen Varra, and the unspoken thought ran on beneath them: Strange, even, that he likes you, the wandering bard from the south. Strange, that he will have you in his hall when you cannot sing as his men would like.

Cappen did not care to defend himself. He had drifted up toward the northern barbarians with the idea that they would well reward a minstrel who could offer them something more than their own crude chants. It had been a mistake; they didn't care for roundels or sestinas, they yawned at the thought of roses white and red under the moon of Caronne, a moon less fair than my lady's eyes. Nor did a man of Croy have the size and strength to compel their respect; Cappen's light blade flickered swiftly enough so that no one cared to fight him, but he lacked the power of sheer bulk. Svearek alone had enjoyed hearing him sing, but he was niggardly and his brawling thorp was an endless boredom to a man used to the courts of southern princes.

If he had but had the manhood to leave— But he had delayed, because of a lusty peasant wench and a hope that Svearek's coffers would open wider; and now he was dragged along over the Wolf's Throat to a midwinter feast which would have to be celebrated on the sea.

"Had we but fire—" Torbek thrust his hands inside his cloak, trying to warm them a little. The ship rolled till she was almost on her beam ends; Torbek braced himself with practiced feet, but Cappen went into the bilge again.

He sprawled there for a while, his bruised body refusing movement. A weary sailor with a bucket glared at him through dripping hair. His shout was dim under the hoot and skirl of wind: "If ye like it so well down here, then help us bail!"

"'Tis not yet my turn," groaned Cappen, and got slowly up.

The wave which had nearly swamped them had put out the ship's fire and drenched the wood beyond hope of lighting a new one. It was cold fish and sea-sodden hardtack till they saw land again—if they ever did.

As Cappen raised himself on the leeward side, he thought he saw something gleam, far out across the wrathful night. A wavering red spark— He brushed a stiffened hand across his eyes, wondering if the madness of wind and water had struck through into his own skull. A gust of sleet hid it again. But—

He fumbled his way aft between the benches. Huddled figures cursed him wearily as he stepped on them. The ship shook herself, rolled along the edge of a boiling black trough, and slid down into it; for an instant, the white teeth of combers grinned above her rail, and Cappen waited for an end to all things. Then she mounted them again, somehow, and wallowed toward another valley.

King Svearek had the steering oar and was trying to hold the longboat into the wind. He had stood there since sundown, huge and untiring, legs braced and the bucking wood cradled in his arms. More than human he seemed, there under the icicle loom of the stern-post, his gray hair and beard rigid with ice. Beneath the horned helmet, the strong moody face turned right and left, peering into the darkness. Cappen felt smaller than usual when he approached the steersman.

He leaned close to the king, shouting against the blast of winter: "My lord, did I not see firelight?"

"Aye. I spied it an hour ago," grunted the king. "Been trying to steer us a little closer to it."

Cappen nodded, too sick and weary to feel reproved. "What is it?"

"Some island—there are many in this stretch of water—now shut up!"

Cappen crouched down under the rail and waited.

The lonely red gleam seemed nearer when he looked again. Svearek's tones were lifting in a roar that hammered through the gale from end to end of the ship: "Hither! Come hither to me, all men not working!"

Slowly, they groped to him, great shadowy forms in wool and leather, bulking over Cappen like storm-gods. Svearek nodded toward the flickering glow. "One of the islands, somebody must be living there. I cannot bring the ship closer for fear of surf, but one of ye should be able to take the boat thither and fetch us fire and dry wood. Who will go?"

They peered overside, and the uneasy movement that ran among them came from more than the roll and pitch of the deck underfoot.

Beorna the Bold spoke at last, it was hardly to be heard in the noisy dark: "I never knew of men living hereabouts. It must be a lair of trolls."

"Aye, so...aye, they'd but eat the man we sent...out oars, let's away from here though it cost our lives..." The frightened mumble was low under the jeering wind.

Svearek's face drew into a snarl. "Are ye men or puling babes? Hack yer way through them, if they be trolls, but bring me fire!"

"Even a she-troll is stronger than fifty men, my king," cried Torbek. "Well ye know that, when the monster woman broke through our guards three years ago and bore off Hildigund."

"Enough!" It was a scream in Svearek's throat. "I'll have yer craven heads for this, all of ye, if ye gang not to the isle!"

They looked at each other, the big men of Norren, and their shoulders hunched bear-like. It was Beorna who spoke it for them: "No, that ye will not. We are free housecarls, who will fight for a leader—but not for a madman."

Cappen drew back against the rail, trying to make himself small.

"All gods turn their faces from ye!" It was more than weariness and despair which glared in Svearek's eyes, there was something of death in them. "I'll go myself, then!"

"No, my king. That we will not find ourselves in."

"I am the king!"

"And we are yer housecarls, sworn to defend ye—even from yerself. Ye shall not go."

The ship rolled again, so violently that they were all thrown to starboard. Cappen landed on Torbek, who reached up to shove him aside and then closed one huge fist on his tunic.

"Here's our man!"

"Hi!" yelled Cappen.

Torbek hauled him roughly back to his feet. "Ye cannot row or bail yer fair share," he growled, "nor do ye know the rigging or any skill of a sailor—'tis time ye made yerself useful!"

"Aye, aye—let little Cappen go—mayhap he can sing the trolls to sleep—" The laughter was hard and barking, edged with fear, and they all hemmed him in.

"My lord!" bleated the minstrel. "I am your guest—"

Svearek laughed unpleasantly, half crazily. "Sing them a song," he howled. "Make a fine roun—whatever ye call it— to the troll-wife's beauty. And bring us some fire, little man, bring us a flame less hot than the love in yer breast for yer lady!"

Teeth grinned through matted beards. Someone hauled on the rope from which the ship's small boat trailed, dragging it close. "Go, ye scut!" A horny hand sent Cappen stumbling to the rail.

He cried out once again. An ax lifted above his head. Someone handed him his own slim sword, and for a wild moment he thought of fighting. Useless—too many of them. He buckled on the sword and spat at the men. The wind tossed it back in his face, and they raved with laughter.

Over the side! The boat rose to meet him, he landed in a heap on drenched planks and looked up into the shadowy faces of the northmen. There was a sob in his throat as he found the seat and took out the oars.

An awkward pull sent him spinning from the ship, and then the night had swallowed it and he was alone. Numbly, he bent to the task. Unless he wanted to drown, there was no place to go but the island.

He was too weary and ill to be much afraid, and such fear as he had was all of the sea. It could rise over him, gulp him down, the gray horses would gallop over him and the long weeds would wrap him when he rolled dead against some skerry. The soft vales of Caronne and the roses in Croy's gardens seemed like a dream. There was only the roar and boom of the northern sea, hiss of sleet and spindrift, crazed scream of wind, he was alone as man had ever been and he would go down to the sharks alone.

The boat wallowed, but rode the waves better than the longship. He grew dully aware that the storm was pushing him toward the island. It was becoming visible, a deeper blackness harsh against the night.

He could not row much in the restless water, he shipped the oars and waited for the gale to capsize him and fill his mouth with the sea. And when it gurgled in his throat, what would his last thought be? Should he dwell on the lovely image of Ydris in Seilles, she of the long bright hair and the singing voice? But then there had been the tomboy laughter of dark Falkny, he could not neglect her. And there were memories of Elvanna in her castle by the lake, and Sirann of the Hundred Rings, and beauteous Vardry, and hawk-proud Lona, and— No, he could not do justice to any of them in the little time that remained. What a pity it was!

No, wait, that unforgettable night in Nienne, the beauty which had whispered in his ear and drawn him close, the hair which had fallen like a silken tent about his cheeks...ah, that had been the summit of his life, he would go down into darkness with her name on his lips... But hell! What *had* her name been, now?

Cappen Varra, minstrel of Croy, clung to the bench and sighed.

The great hollow voice of surf lifted about him, waves sheeted across the gunwale and the boat danced in madness. Cappen groaned, huddling into the circle of his own arms and shaking with cold. Swiftly, now, the end of all sunlight and laughter, the dark and lonely road which all men must tread. *O Ilwarra of Syr, Aedra in Tholis, could I but kiss you once more—*

Stones grated under the keel. It was a shock like a sword going through him. Cappen looked unbelievingly up. The boat had drifted to land—he was alive!

It was like the sun in his breast. Weariness fell from him, and he leaped overside, not feeling the chill of the shallows. With a grunt, he heaved the boat up on the narrow strand and knotted the painter to a fang-like jut of reef.

Then he looked about him. The island was small, utterly bare, a savage loom of rock rising out of the sea that growled at its feet and streamed off its shoulders. He had come into a little cliff-walled bay, somewhat sheltered from the wind. He was here!

For a moment he stood, running through all he had learned about the trolls which infested these northlands. Hideous and soulless dwellers underground, they knew not old age; a sword could hew them asunder, but before it reached their deep-seated life, their unhuman strength had plucked a man apart. Then they ate him—

Small wonder the northmen feared them. Cappen threw back his head and laughed. He had once done a service for a mighty wizard in the south, and his reward hung about his neck, a small silver amulet. The wizard had told him that no supernatural being could harm anyone who carried a piece of silver.

The northmen said that a troll was powerless against a man who was not afraid; but, of course, only to see one was to feel the heart turn to ice. They did not know the value of silver, it seemed—odd that they shouldn't, but they did not. Because Cappen Varra did, he had no reason to be afraid; therefore he was doubly safe, and it was but a matter of talking the troll into giving him some fire. If indeed there was a troll here, and not some harmless fisherman.

He whistled gaily, wrung some of the water from his cloak and ruddy hair, and started along the beach. In the sleety gloom, he could just see a hewn-out path winding up one of the cliffs and he set his feet on it.

At the top of the path, the wind ripped his whistling from his lips. He hunched his back against it and walked faster, swearing as he stumbled on hidden rocks. The ice-sheathed ground was slippery underfoot, and the cold bit like a knife.

Rounding a crag, he saw redness glow in the face of a steep bluff. A cave mouth, a fire within—he hastened his steps, hungering for warmth, until he stood in the entrance.

"*Who comes?*"

It was a hoarse bass cry that rang and boomed between walls of rock; there was ice and horror in it, for a moment Cappen's heart stumbled. Then he remembered the amulet and strode boldly inside.

"Good evening, mother," he said cheerily.

The cave widened out into a stony hugeness that gaped with tunnels leading further underground. The rough, soot-blackened walls were hung with plundered silks and cloth-of-gold, gone ragged with age and damp; the floor was strewn with stinking rushes, and gnawed bones were heaped in disorder. Cappen saw the skulls of men among them. In the center of the room, a great fire leaped and blazed, throwing billows of heat against him; some of its smoke went up a hole in the roof, the rest stung his eyes to watering and he sneezed.

The troll-wife crouched on the floor, snarling at him. She was quite the most hideous thing Cappen had ever seen: nearly as tall as he, she was twice as broad and thick, and the knotted arms hung down past bowed knees till their clawed fingers brushed the ground. Her head was beast-like, almost split in half by the tusked mouth, the eyes wells of darkness, the nose an ell long; her hairless skin was green and cold, moving on her bones. A tattered shift covered some of her monstrousness, but she was still a nightmare.

"Ho-ho, ho-ho!" Her laughter roared out, hungry and hollow as the surf around the island. Slowly, she shuffled closer. "So my dinner comes walking in to greet me, ho, ho, ho! Welcome, sweet flesh, welcome, good marrow-filled bones, come in and be warmed."

"Why, thank you, good mother." Cappen shucked his cloak and grinning at her through the smoke. He felt his clothes steaming already. "I love you too."

Over her shoulder, he suddenly saw the girl. She was huddled in a corner, wrapped in fear, but the eyes that watched him were as blue as the skies over Caronne. The ragged dress did not hide the gentle curves of her body, nor did the tear-streaked grime spoil the lilt of her face. "Why, 'tis springtime in here," cried Cappen, "and Primavera herself is strewing flowers of love."

"What are you talking about, crazy man?" rumbled the troll-wife. She turned to the girl. "Heap the fire, Hildigund, and set up the roasting spit. Tonight I feast!"

"Truly I see heaven in female form before me," said Cappen.

The troll scratched her misshapen head.

"You must surely be from far away, moonstruck man," she said.

"Aye, from golden Croy am I wandered, drawn over dolorous seas and empty wild lands by the fame of loveliness waiting here; and now that I have seen you, my life is full." Cappen was looking at the girl as he spoke, but he hoped the troll might take it as aimed her way.

"It will be fuller," grinned the monster. "Stuffed with hot coals while yet you live." She glanced back at the girl. "What, are you not working yet, you lazy tub of lard? Set up the spit, I said!"

The girl shuddered back against a heap of wood. "No," she whispered. "I cannot—not...not for a man."

"Can and will, my girl," said the troll, picking up a bone to throw at her. The girl shrieked a little.

"No, no, sweet mother. I would not be so ungallant as to have beauty toil for me." Cappen plucked at the troll's filthy dress. "It is not meet—in two senses. I only came to beg a little fire; yet will I bear away a greater fire within my heart."

"Fire in your guts, you mean! No man ever left me save as picked bones."

Cappen thought he heard a worried note in the animal growl. "Shall we have music for the feast?" he asked mildly. He unslung the case of his harp and took it out.

The troll-wife waved her fists in the air and danced with rage. "Are you mad? I tell you, you are going to be eaten!"

The minstrel plucked a string on his harp. "This wet air has played the devil with her tone," he murmured sadly.

The troll-wife roared wordlessly and lunged at him. Hildigund covered her eyes. Cappen tuned his harp. A foot from his throat, the claws stopped.

"Pray do not excite yourself, mother," said the bard. "I carry silver, you know."

"What is that to me? If you think you have a charm which will turn me, know that there is none. I've no fear of your metal!"

Cappen threw back his head and sang:

"A lovely lady full oft lies. The light that lies within her eyes And lies and lies, in no surprise. All her unkindness can devise To trouble hearts that seek the prize Which is herself, are angel lies—"

"*Aaaarrgh!*" It was like thunder drowning him out. The troll-wife turned and went on all fours and poked up the fire with her nose.

Cappen stepped softly around her and touched the girl. She looked up with a little whimper.

"You are Svearek's only daughter, are you not?" he whispered.

"Aye—" She bowed her head, a strengthless despair weighting it down. "The troll stole me away three winters agone. It has tickled her to have a princess for slave—but soon I will roast on her spit, even as ye, brave man—"

"Ridiculous. So fair a lady is meant for another kind of, um, never mind! Has she treated you very ill?"

"She beats me now and again—and I have been so lonely, naught here at all save the troll-wife and I—" The small work-roughened hands clutched desperately at his waist, and she buried her face against his breast.

"Can ye save us?" she gasped. "I fear 'tis for naught ye ventured yer life, bravest of men. I fear we'll soon both sputter on the coals."

Cappen said nothing. If she wanted to think he had come especially to rescue her, he would not be so ungallant to tell her otherwise.

The troll-wife's mouth gashed in a grin as she walked through the fire to him. "There is a price," she said. "If you cannot tell me three things about myself which are true beyond disproving, not courage nor amulet nor the gods themselves may avail to keep that red head on your shoulders."

Cappen clapped a hand to his sword. "Why, gladly," he said; this was a rule of magic he had learned long ago, that three truths were the needful armor to make any guardian charm work. "Imprimis, yours is the ugliest nose I ever saw poking up a fire. Secundus, I was never in a house I cared less to guest at. Tertius, ever among trolls you are little liked, being one of the worst."

Hildigund moaned with terror as the monster swelled in rage. But there was no movement. Only the leaping flames and the eddying smoke stirred.

Cappen's voice rang out, coldly: "Now the king lies on the sea, frozen and wet, and I am come to fetch a brand for his fire. And I had best also see his daughter home."

The troll shook her head, suddenly chuckling. "No. The brand you may have, just to get you out of this cave, foulness; but the woman is in my thrall until a man sleeps with her—here—for a night. And if he does, I may have him to break my fast in the morning!"

Cappen yawned mightily. "Thank you, mother. Your offer of a bed is most welcome to these tired bones, and I accept gratefully."

"You will die tomorrow!" she raved. The ground shook under the huge weight of her as she stamped. "Because of the three truths, I must let you go tonight; but tomorrow I may do what I will!"

"Forget not my little friend, mother," said Cappen, and touched the cord of the amulet.

"I tell you, silver has no use against me—"

Cappen sprawled on the floor and rippled fingers across his harp. "*A lovely lady full oft lies*—"

The troll-wife turned from him in a rage. Hildigund ladled up some broth, saying nothing, and Cappen ate it with pleasure, though it could have used more seasoning.

After that he indited a sonnet to the princess, who regarded him wide-eyed. The troll came back from a tunnel after he finished, and said curtly: "This way." Cappen took the girl's hand and followed her into a pitchy, reeking dark.

She plucked an arras aside to show a room which surprised him by being hung with tapestries, lit with candles, and furnished with a fine broad featherbed. "Sleep here tonight, if you dare," she growled. "And tomorrow I shall eat you—and you, worthless lazy she-trash, will have the hide flayed off your back!" She barked a laugh and left them.

Hildigund fell weeping on the mattress. Cappen let her cry herself out while he undressed and got between the blankets. Drawing his sword, he laid it carefully in the middle of the bed.

The girl looked at him through jumbled fair locks. "How can ye dare?" she whispered. "One breath of fear, one moment's doubt, and the troll is free to rend ye."

"Exactly." Cappen yawned. "Doubtless she hopes that fear will come to me lying wakeful in the night. Wherefore 'tis but a question of going gently to sleep. O Svearek, Torbek, and Beorna, could you but see how I am resting now!"

"But...the three truths ye gave her...how knew ye...?"

"Oh, those. Well, see you, sweet lady, Primus and Secundus were my own thoughts, and who is to disprove them? Tertius was also clear, since you said there had been no company here in three years—yet are there many trolls in these lands, ergo even they cannot stomach our gentle hostess." Cappen watched her through heavy-lidded eyes.

She flushed deeply, blew out the candles, and he heard her slip off her garment and get in with him. There was a long silence.

Then: "Are ye not—"

"Yes, fair one?" he muttered through his drowsiness.

"Are ye not...well, I am here and ye are here and—"

"Fear not," he said. "I laid my sword between us. Sleep in peace."

"I...would be glad—ye have come to deliver—"

"No, fair lady. No man of gentle breeding could so abuse his power. Goodnight." He leaned over, brushing his lips gently across hers, and lay down again.

"Ye are...I never thought man could be so noble," she whispered.

Cappen mumbled something. As his soul spun into sleep, he chuckled. Those unresting days and nights on the sea had not left him fit for that kind of exercise. But, of course, if she wanted to think he was being magnanimous, it could be useful later—

HE WOKE with a start and looked into the sputtering glare of a torch. Its light wove across the crags and gullies of the troll-wife's face and shimmered wetly off the great tusks in her mouth.

"Good morning, mother," said Cappen politely.

Hildigund thrust back a scream.

"Come and be eaten," said the troll-wife.

"No, thank you," said Cappen, regretfully but firmly. "'Twould be ill for my health. No, I will but trouble you for a firebrand and then the princess and I will be off."

"If you think that stupid bit of silver will protect you, think again," she snapped. "Your three sentences were all that saved you last night. Now I hunger."

"Silver," said Cappen didactically, "is a certain shield against all black magics. So the wizard told me, and he was such a nice white-bearded old man I am sure even his attendant devils never lied. Now please depart, mother, for modesty forbids me to dress before your eyes."

The hideous face thrust close to his. He smiled dreamily and tweaked her nose—hard.

She howled and flung the torch at him. Cappen caught it and stuffed it into her mouth. She choked and ran from the room.

"A new sport—trollbaiting," said the bard gaily into the sudden darkness. "Come, shall we not venture out?"

The girl trembled too much to move. He comforted her, absentmindedly, and dressed in the dark, swearing at the

311

clumsy leggings. When he left, Hildigund put on her clothes and hurried after him.

The troll-wife squatted by the fire and glared at them as they went by. Cappen hefted his sword and looked at her. "I do not love you," he said mildly, and hewed out.

She backed away, shrieking as he slashed at her. In the end, she crouched at the mouth of a tunnel, raging futilely. Cappen pricked her with his blade.

"It is not worth my time to follow you down underground," he said, "but if ever you trouble men again, I will hear of it and come and feed you to my dogs. A piece at a time—a very small piece—do you understand?"

She snarled at him.

"An *extremely* small piece," said Cappen amiably. "Have you heard me?"

Something broke in her. "Yes," she whimpered. He let her go, and she scuttled from him like a rat.

He remembered the firewood and took an armful; on the way, he thoughtfully picked up a few jeweled rings which he didn't think she would be needing and stuck them in his pouch. Then he led the girl outside.

The wind had laid itself, a clear frosty morning glittered on the sea and the longship was a distant sliver against white-capped blueness. The minstrel groaned. "What a distance to row! Oh, well—"

THEY WERE at sea before Hildigund spoke. Awe was in the eyes that watched him. "No man could be so brave," she murmured. "Are ye a god?"

"Not quite," said Cappen. "No, most beautiful one, modesty grips my tongue. 'Twas but that I had the silver and was therefore proof against her sorcery."

"But the silver was no help!" she cried.

Cappen's oar caught a crab. "What?" he yelled.

"No—no—why, she told ye so her own self—"

"I thought she lied. I *know* the silver guards against—"

"But she used no magic! Trolls have but their own strength!"

Cappen sagged in his seat. For a moment he thought he was going to faint. Then only his lack of fear had armored him; and if he had known the truth, that would not have lasted a minute.

He laughed shakily. Another score for his doubts about the overall value of truth!

The longship's oars bit water and approached him. Indignant voices asking why he had been so long on his errand faded when his passenger was seen. And Svearek the king wept as he took his daughter back into his arms.

The hard brown face was still blurred with tears when he looked at the minstrel, but the return of his old self was there too. "What ye have done, Cappen Varra of Croy, is what no other man in the world could have done."

"Aye—aye—" The rough northern voices held adoration as the warriors crowded around the slim red-haired figure.

"Ye shall have her whom ye saved to wife," said Svearek, "and when I die ye shall rule all Norren."

Cappen swayed and clutched the rail.

Three nights later he slipped away from their shore camp and turned his face southward.

THE END

If you've enjoyed this book, you will not want to miss these terrific titles…

ARMCHAIR SCI-FI & HORROR DOUBLE NOVELS, $12.95 each

D-1 **THE GALAXY RAIDERS** by William P. McGivern
       SPACE STATION #1 by Frank Belknap Long

D-2 **THE PROGRAMMED PEOPLE** by Jack Sharkey
       SLAVES OF THE CRYSTAL BRAIN by William Carter Sawtelle

D-3 **YOU'RE ALL ALONE** by Fritz Leiber
       THE LIQUID MAN by Bernard C. Gilford

D-4 **CITADEL OF THE STAR LORDS** by Edmond Hamilton
       VOYAGE TO ETERNITY by Milton Lesser

D-5 **IRON MEN OF VENUS** by Don Wilcox
       THE MAN WITH ABSOLUTE MOTION by Noel Loomis

D-6 **WHO SOWS THE WIND...** by Rog Phillips
       THE PUZZLE PLANET by Robert A. W. Lowndes

D-7 **PLANET OF DREAD** by Murray Leinster
       TWICE UPON A TIME by Charles L. Fontenay

D-8 **THE TERROR OUT OF SPACE** by Dwight V. Swain
       QUEST OF THE GOLDEN APE by Paul W. Fairman & Milton Lesser

D-9 **SECRET OF MARRACOTT DEEP** by Henry Slesar
       PAWN OF THE BLACK FLEET by Mark Clifton.

D-10 **BEYOND THE RINGS OF SATURN** by Robert Moore Williams
        A MAN OBSESSED by Alan E. Nourse

ARMCHAIR SCIENCE FICTION CLASSICS, $12.95 each

C-1 **THE GREEN MAN**
       by Harold M. Sherman

C-2 **A TRACE OF MEMORY**
       By Keith Laumer

C-3 **INTO PLUTONIAN DEPTHS**
       by Stanton A. Coblentz

ARMCHAIR MASTERS OF SCIENCE FICTION SERIES, $16.95 each

M-1 **MASTERS OF SCIENCE FICTION, Vol. One**
       Bryce Walton—"Dark of the Moon" and other tales

M-2 **MASTERS OF SCIENCE FICTION, Vol. Two**
       Jerome Bixby—"One Way Street" and other tales

If you've enjoyed this book, you will not want to miss these terrific titles...

ARMCHAIR SCI-FI & HORROR DOUBLE NOVELS, $12.95 each

D-11   **PERIL OF THE STARMEN** by Kris Neville
            THE STRANGE INVASION by Murray Leinster

D-12   **THE STAR LORD** by Boyd Ellanby
            CAPTIVES OF THE FLAME by Samuel R. Delany

D-13   **MEN OF THE MORNING STAR** by Edmond Hamilton
            PLANET FOR PLUNDER by Hal Clement and Sam Merwin, Jr.

D-14   **ICE CITY OF THE GORGON** by Chester S. Geier and Richard Shaver
            WHEN THE WORLD TOTTERED by Lester del Rey

D-15   **WORLDS WITHOUT END** by Clifford D. Simak
            THE LAVENDER VINE OF DEATH by Don Wilcox

D-16   **SHADOW ON THE MOON** by Joe Gibson
            ARMAGEDDON EARTH by Geoff St. Reynard

D-17   **THE GIRL WHO LOVED DEATH** by Paul W. Fairman
            SLAVE PLANET by Laurence M. Janifer

D-18   **SECOND CHANCE** by J. F. Bone
            MISSION TO A DISTANT STAR by Frank Belknap Long

D-19   **THE SYNDIC** by C. M. Kornbluth
            FLIGHT TO FOREVER by Poul Anderson

D-20   **SOMEWHERE I'LL FIND YOU** by Milton Lesser
            THE TIME ARMADA by Fox B. Holden

ARMCHAIR SCIENCE FICTION CLASSICS, $12.95 each

C-4   **CORPUS EARTHLING**
            by Louis Charbonneau

C-5   **THE TIME DISSOLVER**
            by Jerry Sohl

C-6   **WEST OF THE SUN**
            by Edgar Pangborn

ARMCHAIR SCI-FI & HORROR GEMS SERIES, $12.95 each

G-1   **SCIENCE FICTION GEMS, Vol. One**
            Isaac Asimov and others

G-2   **HORROR GEMS, Vol. One**
            Carl Jacobi and others

If you've enjoyed this book, you will not want to miss these terrific titles...

ARMCHAIR SCI-FI & HORROR DOUBLE NOVELS, $12.95 each

D-71   **THE DEEP END** by Gregory Luce
         TO WATCH BY NIGHT by Robert Moore Williams

D-72   **SWORDSMAN OF LOST TERRA** by Poul Anderson
         PLANET OF GHOSTS by David V. Reed

D-73   **MOON OF BATTLE** by J. J. Allerton
         THE MUTANT WEAPON by Murray Leinster

D-74   **OLD SPACEMEN NEVER DIE!** John Jakes
         RETURN TO EARTH by Bryan Berry

D-75   **THE THING FROM UNDERNEATH** by Milton Lesser
         OPERATION INTERSTELLAR by George O. Smith

D-76   **THE BURNING WORLD** by Algis Budrys
         FOREVER IS TOO LONG by Chester S. Geier

D-77   **THE COSMIC JUNKMAN** by Rog Phillips
         THE ULTIMATE WEAPON by John W. Campbell

D-78   **THE TIES OF EARTH** by James H. Schmitz
         CUE FOR QUIET by Thomas L. Sherred

D-79   **SECRET OF THE MARTIANS** by Paul W. Fairman
         THE VARIABLE MAN by Philip K. Dick

D-80   **THE GREEN GIRL** by Jack Williamson
         THE ROBOT PERIL by Don Wilcox

ARMCHAIR SCIENCE FICTION CLASSICS, $12.95 each

C-25   **THE STAR KINGS**
         by Edmond Hamilton

C-26   **NOT IN SOLITUDE**
         by Kenneth Gantz

C-32   **PROMETHEUS II**
         by S. J. Byrne

ARMCHAIR SCI-FI & HORROR GEMS SERIES, $12.95 each

G-7   **SCIENCE FICTION GEMS, Vol. Four**
       Jack Sharkey and others

G-8   **HORROR GEMS, Vol. Four**
       Seabury Quinn and others

If you've enjoyed this book, you will not want to miss these terrific titles…

ARMCHAIR SCI-FI & HORROR DOUBLE NOVELS, $12.95 each

D-81 **THE LAST PLEA** by Robert Bloch
THE STATUS CIVILIZATION by Robert Sheckley

D-82 **WOMAN FROM ANOTHER PLANET** by Frank Belknap Long
HOMECALLING by Judith Merril

D-83 **WHEN TWO WORLDS MEET** by Robert Moore Williams
THE MAN WHO HAD NO BRAINS by Jeff Sutton

D-84 **THE SPECTRE OF SUICIDE SWAMP** by E. K. Jarvis
IT'S MAGIC, YOU DOPE! by Jack Sharkey

D-85 **THE STARSHIP FROM SIRIUS** by Rog Phillips
FINAL WEAPON by Everett Cole

D-86 **TREASURE ON THUNDER MOON** by Edmond Hamilton
TRAIL OF THE ASTROGAR by Henry Haase

D-87 **THE VENUS ENIGMA** by Joe Gibson
THE WOMAN IN SKIN 13 by Paul W. Fairman

D-88 **THE MAD ROBOT** by William P. McGivern
THE RUNNING MAN by J. Holly Hunter

D-89 **VENGEANCE OF KYVOR** by Randall Garrett
AT THE EARTH'S CORE by Edgar Rice Burroughs

D-90 **DWELLERS OF THE DEEP** by Don Wilcox
NIGHT OF THE LONG KNIVES by Fritz Leiber

ARMCHAIR SCIENCE FICTION CLASSICS, $12.95 each

C-28 **THE MAN FROM TOMORROW**
by Stanton A. Coblentz

C-29 **THE GREEN MAN OF GRAYPEC**
by Festus Pragnell

C-30 **THE SHAVER MYSTERY, Book Four**
by Richard S. Shaver

ARMCHAIR MASTERS OF SCIENCE FICTION SERIES, $16.95 each

MS-7 **MASTERS OF SCIENCE FICTION AND FANTASY, Vol. Seven**
Lester del Rey, "The Band Played On" and other tales

MS-8 **MASTERS OF SCIENCE FICTION, Vol. Eight**
Milton Lesser, "'A' as in Android" and other tales

If you've enjoyed this book, you will not want to miss these terrific titles…

ARMCHAIR SCI-FI & HORROR DOUBLE NOVELS, $12.95 each

D-91 **THE TIME TRAP** by Henry Kuttner
THE LUNAR LICHEN by Hal Clement

D-92 **SARGASSO OF LOST STARSHIPS** by Poul Anderson
THE ICE QUEEN by Don Wilcox

D-93 **THE PRINCE OF SPACE** by Jack Williamson
POWER by Harl Vincent

D-94 **PLANET OF NO RETURN** by Howard Browne
THE ANNIHILATOR COMES by Ed Earl Repp

D-95 **THE SINISTER INVASION** by Edmond Hamilton
OPERATION TERROR by Murray Leinster

D-96 **TRANSIENT** by Ward Moore
THE WORLD-MOVER by George O. Smith

D-97 **FORTY DAYS HAS SEPTEMBER** by Milton Lesser
THE DEVIL'S PLANET by David Wright O'Brien

D-98 **THE CYBERENE** by Rog Phillips
BADGE OF INFAMY by Lester del Rey

D-99 **THE JUSTICE OF MARTIN BRAND** by Raymond A. Palmer
BRING BACK MY BRAIN by Dwight V. Swain

D-100 **WIDE-OPEN PLANET** by L. Sprague de Camp
AND THEN THE TOWN TOOK OFF by Richard Wilson

ARMCHAIR SCIENCE FICTION CLASSICS, $12.95 each

C-31 **THE GOLDEN GUARDSMEN**
by S. J. Byrne

C-32 **ONE AGAINST THE MOON**
by Donald A. Wollheim

C-33 **HIDDEN CITY**
by Chester S. Geier

ARMCHAIR SCI-FI & HORROR GEMS SERIES, $12.95 each

G-9 **SCIENCE FICTION GEMS, Vol. Five**
Clifford D. Simak and others

G-10 **HORROR GEMS, Vol. Five**
E. Hoffman Price and others

If you've enjoyed this book, you will not want to miss these terrific titles…

ARMCHAIR SCI-FI & HORROR DOUBLE NOVELS, $12.95 each

D-101 **THE CONQUEST OF THE PLANETS** by John W. Campbell
THE MAN WHO ANNEXED THE MOON by Bob Olsen

D-102 **WEAPON FROM THE STARS** by Rog Phillips
THE EARTH WAR by Mack Reynolds

D-103 **THE ALIEN INTELLIGENCE** by Jack Williamson
INTO THE FOURTH DIMENSION by Ray Cummings

D-104 **THE CRYSTAL PLANETOIDS** by Stanton A. Coblentz
SURVIVORS FROM 9,000 B. C. by Robert Moore Williams

D-105 **THE TIME PROJECTOR** by David H. Keller, M.D. and David Lasser
STRANGE COMPULSION by Philip Jose Farmer

D-106 **WHOM THE GODS WOULD SLAY** by Paul W. Fairman
MEN IN THE WALLS by William Tenn

D-107 **LOCKED WORLDS** by Edmond Hamilton
THE LAND THAT TIME FORGOT by Edgar Rice Burroughs

D-108 **STAY OUT OF SPACE** by Dwight V. Swain
REBELS OF THE RED PLANET by Charles L. Fontenay

D-109 **THE METAMORPHS** by S. J. Byrne
MICROCOSMIC BUCCANEERS by Harl Vincent

D-110 **YOU CAN'T ESCAPE FROM MARS** by E. K. Jarvis
THE MAN WITH FIVE LIVES by David V. Reed

ARMCHAIR SCIENCE FICTION CLASSICS, $12.95 each

C-34 **30 DAY WONDER**
by Richard Wilson

C-35 **G.O.G. 666**
by John Taine

C-36 **RALPH 124C 41+**
by Hugo Gernsback

ARMCHAIR SCI-FI & HORROR GEMS SERIES, $12.95 each

G-11 **SCIENCE FICTION GEMS, Vol. Six**
Edmond Hamilton and others

G-12 **HORROR GEMS, Vol. Six**
H. P. Lovecraft and others

If you've enjoyed this book, you will not want to miss these terrific titles…

ARMCHAIR SCI-FI & HORROR DOUBLE NOVELS, $12.95 each

D-111 **THE MOON ERA** by Jack Williamson
REVENGE OF THE ROBOTS by Howard Browne

D-112 **SON OF THE BLACK CHALICE** by Milton Lesser
SENTRY OF THE SKY by Evelyn E. Smith

D-113 **OUTPOST ON THE MOON** by Joslyn Maxwell
POTENTIAL ZERO by S. J. Byrne

D-114 **OUTPOST INFINITY** by Raymond F. Jones
THE WHITE INVADERS by Ray Cummings

D-115 **TIME TRAP** by Rog Phillips
THE COSMIC DESTROYER by Alexander Blade

D-116 **THE OTHER SIDE OF THE MOON** by Edmond Hamilton
SECRET INVASION by Walter Kubilius

D-117 **DANGER MOON** by Frederik Pohl
THE HIDDEN UNIVERSE by Ralph Milne Farley

D-118 **THE WAILING ASTEROID** by Murray Leinster
THE WORLD THAT COULDN'T BE by Clifford D. Simak

D-119 **THE WHISPERING GORILLA** by Don Wilcox
RETURN OF THE WHISPERING GORILLA by David V. Reed

D-120 **SPECIAL EFFECT** by J. F. Bone
WARLORD OF KOR by Terry Carr

ARMCHAIR SCIENCE FICTION CLASSICS, $12.95 each

C-37 **THE GREEN MAN RETURNS**
by Harold M. Sherman

C-38 **THE SHAVER MYSTERY, Book Five**
by Richard S, Shaver

C-39 **MARS CHILD**
by Cyril Judd

ARMCHAIR MASTERS OF SCIENCE FICTION SERIES, $16.95 each

MS-9 **MASTERS OF SCIENCE FICTION AND FANTASY, Vol. Nine**
Poul Anderson, "The Star Beast" and other tales

MS-10 **MASTERS OF SCIENCE FICTION, Vol. Ten**
Robert Moore Williams, "Time Tolls for Toro" and other tales

Made in the USA
Middletown, DE
21 January 2023

22634160R00191